DEATH
comes in ✦•••••••••✦
✦•••••••••✦ *through the*
KITCHEN

DEATH

comes in ◆◆◆◆◆◆◆◆◆◆◆◆◆◆
◆◆◆◆◆◆◆◆◆ through the

KITCHEN

Teresa Dovalpage

Published by
Soho Press, Inc.
853 Broadway
New York, NY 10003

Library of Congress Cataloging-in-Publication Data

Dovalpage, Teresa.
Death comes in through the kitchen / Teresa Dovalpage.
Includes recipes.

ISBN 978-1-61695-884-8
eISBN 978-1-61695-885-5

1. Journalists—Fiction. 2. Bloggers—Fiction.
3. Murder—Investigation—Fiction. 4. Food—Blogs—Fiction.
5. Havana (Cuba)—Fiction. I. Title
PQ7392.D69 D43 2018 863'.7—dc23 2017026568

Interior design by Janine Agro

Printed in the United States of America

10 9 8 7 6 5 4 3 2 1

To my journalism mother, la Joan Livingston,
who opened the doors of a new career for me.

PART I

Chapter One

MERINGUE PUFFS

The Cuban customs officer lifted an eyebrow at the bridal gown—a white satin bodice with tulle appliqués, sheer sleeves, and a two-foot train—and took a long, suspicious look at the couple. The woman was a tall blonde in her forties who wore a teal broom skirt, a beige cotton blouse, turquoise-studded cowgirl boots, and a brittle smile. The man, in jeans and a San Diego Padres T-shirt, was a few years younger and a few inches shorter. His hands shook when he opened his passport to the picture page.

"Are you getting married here?" the officer asked.

The woman's pale cheeks tinted with a soft blush.

"Yes," she said, smiling at the wedding dress that was carefully wrapped in a plastic bag.

"To him?" the officer pointed to her companion with a hint of mistrust in his voice. That was unusual, two Americans coming all the way to Havana to get hitched. But both hurried to correct him, almost at the same time:

"No, no!"

"We're just friends."

"*I'm* the one getting married," the woman explained. "To a Cuban."

"I see."

The customs officer reconsidered his initial decision to send the couple over to security. He waved the woman away after taking a cursory look at her passport, which he didn't stamp.

"Welcome to Cuba, Anne."

"Thanks, *compañero*!"

She walked away with her face still flushed. The man, whose passport read Matthew Sullivan, waited nervously while the *compañero* inspected his backpack. The unopened Hugo Boss gift set that contained a watch, a pair of sunglasses, and three red monogrammed boxer shorts made the officer snicker.

"Are they yours?"

"Yes, sir."

When he was finally told to go ahead, Matt let out a sigh of relief and hurried to meet Anne in the waiting room. In a corner, after looking around like conspirators, they exchanged items quickly: Matt cradled the wedding dress in his arms and Anne took the Hugo Boss set.

"Well, that was easy enough," she said.

Matt didn't understand the need to lie, but Anne had insisted, saying that they would have to offer detailed explanations for gender-swapped gifts. He had deferred to her; having traveled to the island seven times, she was the expert on Cuban affairs.

"Why didn't that guy stamp our passports?" Matt asked. "I thought we would have to *ask* him not to do it."

"I guess it's a courtesy to 'good Americans' like us, who come here despite the embargo," Anne answered, shrugging. "For whatever reason, I've never had mine stamped. And I am not asking why."

They picked up their luggage (one big, heavy suitcase for him and two medium-sized ones for her) and went outside the building to the airport parking lot where a small crowd of nationals had been awaiting the arrival of the Aeroméxico flight.

A young, wiry man stepped out of the group. Anne ran to hug him.

"Yony, my love!"

"*Mamita!*"

There was a loud smooching sound. She handed him the Hugo Boss set.

"Cool!"

Matt stood aside, searching the crowd for Yarmila, his Cuban fiancée, but he couldn't find her. He walked back to the airport building, careful not to stumble over the gown's train and ignoring the curious glances that followed him. A security guard stopped him at the door.

"Only people who are traveling today can come in," he said.

"But I was just in there!"

"So? You are out now."

Matt turned around. The crowd had dispersed. Yony and Anne were still kissing, but Yarmila was nowhere to be found.

He made several unsuccessful attempts to call her apartment from a pay phone. The phone rang without response. He asked the security guards if they had seen "a pretty young woman with brown eyes and dark hair." They chuckled and told him they had seen dozens of them. An hour slipped by. By then Matt's hands were shaking so much that the gown's tulle appliqués fluttered like sick doves.

"I bet Yarmila just got tired of waiting," Yony said. "She must be back home now."

It made sense—sort of. The plane had been delayed during

a stopover at Monterrey and arrived at two fifteen instead of one o'clock. But Yarmila could have stayed a little longer, Matt thought. *He* would have waited for her an entire day if necessary.

"If Yarmi is home, why isn't she answering my calls?" he asked, despondent.

"Her phone may be out of order," Yony said. "This is Cuba. Things get broken all the time."

"But . . ."

"Don't sweat it, man," Yony looked around, worried. "Sorry, but we have to go now. We've been here too long and I don't want the cops coming and asking questions. I'll drop you off at her place."

Matt shook his head.

"We agreed to meet at the airport," he said. "That was the plan. You guys can go ahead."

"We aren't leaving you alone!" Anne protested.

"I'll find a taxi later."

"Take it easy, *Yuma*." Yony put a reassuring hand on Matt's shoulder. "Remember: you are in Havana. Here, plans don't always pan out."

Yuma, Yarmila had explained to Matt, was a term that younger Cubans used when referring to Americans. It didn't have the pejorative connotation that Yankee had, like in "Yankees, go home." It was almost affectionate, though it sounded odd to him.

Matt gave up and followed the couple, rolling the big suitcase along the uneven sidewalk and holding the bridal gown protectively against his chest.

Outside the airport premises, a scruffy-looking woman tried to sell them a bunch of withered marigolds. Matt recoiled at the sight of the flowers. Mexicans called them *cempasúchil* and placed them on their deceased relatives' graves on the Day of the Dead.

"It's for the *orishas*," the woman insisted in a husky voice. "They'll make your stay pleasant and safe."

They walked away. Much later, Matt would regret not having made an offering to the *orishas*, whatever they were.

YONY'S CAR WAS AN *almendrón*—a refurbished 1956 Studebaker President sedan, blinding red, with huge hubcaps and a polished chrome bumper. Anne sat in the passenger's seat and began to scratch the young man's neck with her manicured nails. Matt shared the back seat with the dress, his luggage and Anne's. The trunk was filled with a spare tire, assorted tools, and three gas cans.

When they left the airport behind, the city seemed to open up for Matt like a woman or a book. Havana was a fifties postcard swathed in an aura of exhaust fumes; a moving, breathing slide from the past. It wasn't just the old American Fords and Chevys, but also the architecture: pastel stucco exteriors on flaking façades, wrought-iron balconies, and stained glass windows that fractured the sun into flashes of diamonds.

The four-lane Rancho Boyeros Avenue was for the most part empty of vehicles. At the crowded bus stops people scanned the deserted streets with hopeful eyes. The avenue was lined with palm trees and billboards that read LONG LIFE TO FIDEL—a wish fulfilled long ago, as Castro had reached the ripe age of seventy-seven—SOCIALISM OR DEATH, and a collection of laudatory references to Che Guevara. Matt smiled to them as if they were old friends. They had been there the previous year when he'd arrived in Havana. Then, Yarmila had been with him.

When he returned to the airport, she might accompany him

again, he daydreamed. She might even be ready to travel the 2,213 miles that separated Havana from San Diego. Matt knew the exact distance thanks to an interactive map he had sent her as a gift. It was in fact a toy, though a newfangled one: not only did it measure distances between cities but also listed "fun facts" about the places and played regional songs in their original language. He had thought that Yarmila would get a kick out of it.

Matt turned his attention to the dress, caressed the soft fabric and wondered how Yarmila would react when she saw it. Would she be happy, flattered, amused, angry? Ah, the possibilities! Or maybe she was going to dump him in the end and that was why she hadn't been there . . .

He stopped the train of thought and focused on his surroundings. A miniature red car hung from the rearview mirror. It was a replica of the Studebaker, with chrome bumpers and everything. Yony noticed his interest and smiled.

"It looks like the real thing, eh?" he said.

Matt nodded. When they'd first met, he'd thought that the young man's name was Johnny, mispronounced, but Anne explained that he belonged to the "Generation Y," like Yarmila. During the Cold War, many Cuban parents had given their children Russian-inspired names that began with the letter *Y*.

They were now in Centro Habana. Matt saw Revolution Square in the distance, with a giant portrait of Che Guevara in neon silhouette on a wall.

A more modern and subdued vehicle, a Russian Lada, cut them off. Yony stopped barely in time to avoid hitting it.

"*Comemierda!*" he yelled, showing his middle finger to the other driver.

Matt refreshed his mental list of Cuban insults, adding to it the Spanish term for shit-eater.

"I wouldn't be caught dead in that piece of crap," Yony said. "Who drives Ladas anymore?" He was proud of his *almendrón*. With a modified Fiat engine, a Moskvich carburetor, a Canadian transmission, and a number of handmade parts, the Studebaker was a testimony to the ingenuity of the Cuban mechanics.

"Those who can't afford charming oldies like yours, my *amor*," Anne said and pinched his arm.

My *amor*! Matt laughed quietly, thinking that Anne was making a fool out of herself. How could she be in love with that foulmouthed Cuban? How could she date a guy who was at least fifteen years her junior? She was fleshier than her *amor* by around twenty pounds. Next to her, Yony looked skinnier, darker and younger than he actually was.

But the fact that he himself was thirteen years older than Yarmila didn't bother Matt. At all. He imagined her making rice and chicken and enjoying the little gifts he had collected for her over the last two months. Nothing expensive, because she had asked him not to splurge: an apron embroidered with red chilis, a dream catcher, and a San Diego Zoo 2003 calendar. Maybe it was a bit late for that kind of present—it was already March—but he was sure she would love the pictures of the newly born panda bears.

He also brought, in a red velvet box, a pendant made from an iridescent shell that they had found together the year before at El Mégano Beach. Matt had taken the shell to a Tijuana jeweler who mounted it in gold. It now hung from a thin belcher chain.

There was a size-five gold engagement ring in another velvet-lined box.

"I hope Yarmi is okay," Matt said, speaking more to himself than to his companions.

"Of course she is," Anne answered. "Don't worry. Communications aren't Cubans' forte."

"These airport clerks wouldn't talk to us," Yony chimed in. "I was standing in the parking lot for two hours and no one bothered to say a word about the delay. No updates, no news, *nada*."

"You didn't happen to see Yarmila, did you?" Matt asked.

"No, man. If I had seen her, I'd have asked her to wait with me in the car. That chick is a pistol. And a cutie too."

Anne shot Yony a dirty look and the young man blushed, fixing his eyes on the road. Matt ignored the silent exchange. Anne reminded him of his ex-wife—so jealous and possessive at the beginning of their marriage, which hadn't stopped her from discarding him like a pair of old shoes later on.

"Yarmi is a great gal," he said diplomatically.

"She must be an amazing cook too," Anne made an effort to smile. "Every time I read one of her blog posts, I get hungry."

Matt nodded, remembering Yarmila's last entry, which had been about meringue puffs. He visualized a plate full of perfectly baked *merenguitos* and his mouth watered in response.

Merenguitos: clouds of sweetness on the Pinar del Río sky

Hola, my dear readers!

Welcome back to Yarmi Cooks Cuban! Come into my very own kitchen, the virtual space where you can enjoy a taste of sweet and savory, and everything in between, from the heart of Havana.

I have been asked recently for easy-to-make recipes.

"You may not know this, but not everyone has two hours to devote to prep time like you do in Cuba," wrote one snippy reader a few days ago.

In all fairness, she had good reason to be snippy. She wrote that in a comment to my paella recipe, and any paella worth its shrimp *does* take a long time. Woe to the foolish cook who tries to hurry it!

Yes, *queridos*, I am aware of the luxury of time that we enjoy here. So today I am going to present you with the easiest recipe of my culinary repertoire, one that never fails to remind me of my grandmother Hilda.

It was always a special day when Grandma made *merenguitos*, meringue puffs. I ate them greedily, by themselves, but they can also be used to decorate cakes and custards. They are supposed to be "the icing on the cake." For me, they were the cake itself.

The only ingredients you need are egg whites (four for a dozen or so *merenguitos*), a pinch of salt and one cup of sugar. To bake them, use a baking tray or a baking sheet. Such sheets are not available in Cuba, but my boyfriend said he would bring enough baking sheets and parchment to carpet my kitchen when he comes back—which will happen quite soon, by the way.

I will be baking dozens of *merenguitos* for him! I love my boyfriend. Have I ever said that here? I'm sure I have, but just in case . . .

Back to the *merenguitos*.

The most important step is beating the egg whites while gradually adding sugar. Grandma would sit on her rocking chair to prepare them. It was like a ritual. When she put on her apron and took out the yellow and blue bowl, *la merenguera*, we all knew it was meringue time.

She took the rocking chair to the porch. It made a ricki-ra ricki-ra sound that to this day I associate with the sweetness of meringue puffs and my childhood in Pinar del Río. As some of you already know, I am from Pinar—the westernmost province of Cuba—born and raised in a small town called Los Palacios.

I would sit on the floor, next to Grandma. She tasted the mixture from time to time, or asked me to do it—and I happily obliged—then went on beating. The fork made a crystalline sound every time it touched the *merenguera*.

The *merenguera* wasn't a porcelain bowl, though for a moment just now I was tempted to say so, just to make it sound more picturesque. Beautifying the truth, you know. But the un-beautified truth is this: Grandma's bowl was a plastic one, bought in the sixties at the only store in town.

Grandma liked to sing while she cooked and she tailored the music to the food. Mambos were reserved for stews, cha-chas for anything fried (we listened to many a cha-cha back then), and songs of love for desserts. For *merenguitos* she often chose the habanera "Tú," a ballad written in the 1800s by Eduardo Sánchez de Fuentes. She would add sugar to the egg whites every time she began a verse.

While Grandma worked and hummed, I looked at the clouds,

white and fluffy, and imagined they tasted like meringue puffs. I wanted to fly up to the sky and lick them!

Once she'd used all the sugar, the mixture was firm and consistent. Afterward, with a fork, she twirled around tiny portions, carved a cute peak on the top, and placed them on an oiled baking tray. She would bake them for around two hours.

A word about the temperature: we had a rudimentary oven that my dad built himself so there was no way to find out. I'd say that between 200 and 250 degrees Fahrenheit will be right.

When Grandma took the tray out, the *merenguitos* were crispy and brown on the outside but soft and white inside. A little deceiving. But aren't we all like that?

Sometimes, while we waited for the meringue puffs to be ready, Grandma also made *natilla*, egg custard, with the egg yolks because she hated to throw away food. *Natilla* then became the main dessert with the *merenguitos* on top. But egg custard being a more complicated and temperamental dish, I will reserve it for another post.

Try my *merenguitos* and let me know how they turn out.

"Tú"

En Cuba, la isla hermosa del ardiente sol,
bajo su cielo azul,
adorable trigueña,
de todas las flores,
la reina eres tú.

(In Cuba, beautiful island of the blazing sun,
under your blue sky,
lovely brunette,
of all flowers,
you are the queen.)

COMMENTS

Cocinera Cubana said. . .

Hi, Yarmi! Your post brought back so many delightful memories. My aunt used to make *merenguitos* and we are from Pinar del Río too, from the Viñales Valley.

Alberto Pena said. . .

Sounds yummy. You must be as sweet as your grand-ma's *merenguitos*, judging by your profile pic. How can I get to meet you personally, *princesa*? Any chance? I'm single and live in Florida.

Yarmi said. . .

Thanks for commenting, Cocinera. How nice, another *pinareña*! Alberto, you would have to travel to Havana to meet me in person. But I already have an American boyfriend and I don't think he would like that. Ciao!

Chapter Two

UNDER THE SHOWER

When the *almendrón* reached Salvador Allende Avenue, Yony struggled to move the steering wheel, which wasn't being cooperative, to the right. The Studebaker swerved and the smell of burned gasoline filled the car.

"Here is your business, *Yuma*," Yony said, pointing to a house located on the opposite side of the street.

Matt caught a glimpse of a sign that read LA CALDOSA in green neon letters. It wasn't his business, though Yarmila jokingly called him "her capitalist partner." La Caldosa was a *paladar*, a private restaurant that belonged to a friend of Yarmila's. Matt had sent money to his fiancée so she could buy a share of it.

"Do you know the restaurant?" he asked.

"You bet, *Yuma*," Yony answered with a proud smile. "Most of these little *paladares* wouldn't survive without guys like me."

"Why? Do you bring clients to them?"

"Nah, I bring *food* to them."

Matt must have looked perplexed, because Anne hurried to clarify, "Yony is a *bisnero*," she said. "A businessman. He sells beef, chicken, eggs . . . whatever supplies the cooks need."

The word *bisneros* had originally referred to people who bought and sold items in the black market at a time when private business practices were forbidden—all through the seventies, eighties and early nineties. The term was still part of the Cuban vocabulary, even if some small ventures like restaurants and rentals were allowed.

"I also deal with clothes, TV sets, VCRs and everything under the sun," Yony added. "You want something, you tell me and I'll make sure to find it for you."

Matt smiled, thinking of all the things he could buy for Yarmila, like household items and ingredients for the Cuban dishes she wrote about on her blog—the meals that had attracted him to her in the first place.

"I'll stay in touch," he said.

Yony turned the car again, this time running over a cement island—a move that Matt suspected was very much illegal in any country or traffic system—and they drove by the restaurant. Then he made another turn onto Espada Street and stopped in front of a four-story building with peeling walls whose original color was too washed out to tell. It was now gray, with yellow undertones.

Yarmila had been living there for around five months. The first time Matt had visited her, the year before, she was renting a room in Old Havana in a colonial mansion with high ceilings and elaborate moldings on the doors. It was much older than the Espada Street building, but with an aura of faded glory that this one lacked.

Matt picked up his backpack and the roll-on suitcase filled with pots, pans and cutlery for La Caldosa. He had expected to enlist Yony's aid to carry them upstairs but didn't have such luck. The young Cuban didn't volunteer to help, Anne didn't suggest it either and Matt didn't feel comfortable asking. Hadn't he already wasted enough of their time?

Matt offered Yony a twenty-dollar bill. He noticed that the young man had a blue ink tattoo of the Virgin of Charity on his left hand. Though the tattoo was sharp and well done, two small wounds on the back of Yony's hand made the image look as if she had been stabbed in the chest.

"Thanks, *Yuma*," he said, pocketing the money.

Matt managed to get everything out of the car, careful not to ruin the bridal gown.

"Don't slam the door, man," Yony warned him.

"See you guys tomorrow at seven at El Refugio," Anne said.

"Sure."

"Give my regards to Yarmi."

"Have fun!"

The couple drove away.

A mature woman in cutoff jeans and a sleeveless white top came out of the building as Matt stumbled through the door. He put the backpack on the floor and folded the dress over his right arm, inhaling the faint floral notes that the fabric gave off. He had gotten the gown at a Buffalo Exchange store for three hundred dollars—a bargain, the salesgirl assured him, considering that it was a Maggie Sottero. Matt, who had never heard of the brand, took her word for it. He hoped Yarmila didn't mind the fact that the dress wasn't new.

"Are you lost, *compañero*?" the woman asked Matt.

"I'm looking for Yarmila Portal."

"Ah, you are her boyfriend!" The woman got closer to him and patted his back as if she had known him forever. "Welcome! Yarmi told me about you. So nice to finally meet you in person!"

"Are you a friend of hers?" Matt asked, pleasantly surprised.

"More than that. I'm sort of a mother to that girl. Come on, I'll help you."

She grabbed Matt's backpack.

"Oh, you don't have to do that," he protested.

Despite her youthful outfit and bubbly attitude, the woman was over sixty years old and didn't look strong.

"No big deal," she replied. "You have your hands full with the other stuff. I'm used to carrying buckets of water all the way to the fourth floor. By the way, I am Fefita."

"Nice to meet you, Fefita. I'm—"

"Mateo, the journalist! See, I already knew your name. You are famous! Now, follow me. Her apartment is on the third floor."

The woman moved fast. Her short red perm bobbed up and down like the head of a happy hen.

"*Cojones!*" a man's voice thundered from the second floor. "The water pressure is weaker than my grandfather's piss! What the hell is going on?"

"We've been getting just a squirt of water since yesterday," Fefita explained. "I'm afraid we'll have to fix the pump again. Last time it cost three hundred pesos and we had to wait a week for the mechanic to show up. No water for a week, imagine that, Mateo! No baths, no laundry, no toilet flushing . . . It was a horror show."

Matt felt more at ease now—there was something reassuring about the way Cubans talked to total strangers, sharing with them what at times seemed like too much information. He remembered it from the previous year, how Yarmila and other people had trusted him, even if they didn't have any reason to.

They had reached the third floor. Fefita knocked on a door marked with the number six.

"Yarmi, come and greet your *príncipe azul!*" she yelled.

Had she called him "blue prince"? Matt had never heard the term but assumed that it meant Prince Charming. He smoothed over the bridal gown and thought of Yarmila's body filling it.

"Such a beautiful dress," Fefita said, eyeing it with interest. "It looks like a meringue cake. But I didn't know that you guys were getting married. When is the wedding?"

Matt pretended to cough in order to gain time. It could take weeks, or even months, for all he knew about Cuban bureaucracy. But first and foremost, the wedding depended on Yarmila's final answer to his proposal.

He shrugged and said, "Oh, soon."

Fefita knocked on the door again. "Where is this girl? Isn't she expecting you?"

"Yes, of course," Matt mumbled. "I mean, no. Not here."

She looked at the dress, then back at him, and shook her head. They waited a few minutes. Or perhaps only seconds, but they stretched interminably for Matt.

"She may still be at the airport," he said, annoyed. "I should have stayed there. But those two insisted so much that—"

Fefita turned the doorknob and opened the door.

"Yarmila!" she called.

No one answered.

"Let's go in anyway," she said.

They walked into a living room furnished with a rattan sofa, a Soviet-era TV set with tall legs, and a round coffee table. A heavy blue Frigidaire Power Capsule hummed near the door. An old wooden ironing board had been placed in front of the refrigerator, blocking the access to it. The kitchen area was small—filled completely by the cast-iron stove, porcelain washbasin, cracked countertop, garbage can, plastic table and chair.

The apartment was around six hundred square feet. Yarmila had been so excited about moving to her "new" home that Matt had come to think it was an improvement over her previous one, which it wasn't. It reeked of something rotten. He pretended to ignore the smell, but Fefita held her nose in disgust.

"It stinks to high heavens. *Fo!*"

There were two books on the coffee table. Matt looked at the titles: *Seventeen Moments of Spring*, a novel by a Russian author, and *Cocina al Minuto*, a collection of Cuban recipes that Yarmila often quoted on her blog posts.

"What a mess," Fefita said from the kitchen. "How long has this damn chicken been here? *Ay, coño*, look at that bag of sugar. It's full of ants!"

She stabbed the offending items with a two-pronged fork and threw them into the garbage can.

Matt went into the bedroom. There was a bed—neatly made and covered in an olive green bedspread—a dresser, and a computer. An opaque oval mirror hung on the wall. He noticed the oversized bags under his eyes, his limp, thinning blond hair, and his chapped lips. He wondered, like a nervous highschooler, if Yarmila would still like him.

The monotonous sound of a shower was the only noise inside the apartment. Fefita, who had followed Matt, was saying, "Ah, here she is! I don't know how she has enough water pressure to take a shower because I don't, for sure. Hey, girl, hurry up! You have company."

Nobody answered, just the steady and ominous falling of water.

The wedding dress still draped over his arm, Matt approached the bathroom and opened the door. Then he saw Yarmila, lying down in the bathtub under a flow of water, in a soaked yellow dress, with a strangely calmed expression carved on her marble-like face.

Chapter Three

THE SEGURIDAD MAN

There was a brown spot on the wall that at first reminded Matt of a map of Southern California; then it mutated to resemble Fefita's red perm and finally turned into a sketch of Yarmila's lifeless body. The shape-shifting spot graced the left corner of a cell in the Centro Habana police station known as Unidad 13. But the memory of Yarmila's wet corpse was too much for Matt and he started to sob, mourning the loss of his Cuban fiancée and the new life he had hoped to build with her.

When they'd discovered the body, Fefita's cries had attracted other neighbors—Matt recognized the man who had yelled *"cojones"* by his voice; he was now repeating the same word in frightened undertones. A police car had arrived. Two cops had brought him and Fefita to the Unidad and separated them. "Someone" would see him soon, he was told. He had been waiting for an hour in the cell, sitting on a hard cement bench. The other bench, across from him, was covered in dark stains. The floor needed to be swept and it smelled like urine and mold.

Matt recalled the journey that had brought him from his unpretentious but comfortable Chula Vista home to a Cuban jail. He worked for *El Grito de San Diego*, a biweekly, bilingual tabloid that claimed to be all about "border news, culture and entertainment" but, more often than not, devoted the majority of its pages to kidnappings, arsons, killings, and the perennial narco wars in Baja California. The editor and owner, Tijuana-born, San Diego-raised Felipe Estrada, had hired Matt as a copy editor for both the English and the Spanish sections, but the operating budget was so scant and Estrada so persuasive that soon Matt was a feature writer too, despite his initial resistance.

"Don't be a *pendejo*," Estrada insisted. "Lend me a hand here. Don't you see that I need to fluff up the *pinche* paper?"

"*If* I were to write, I'd be a serious journalist, not a hack," Matt replied.

"We can sign your articles as El Gringo Chingón to protect your good name."

But Matt refused to sensationalize the news or to hit the Tijuana streets in search of printable crimes. In truth, he was afraid of messing with the wrong crowd and ending up the subject of a yellow journalism piece himself. Finally, Estrada put him in charge of the kitchen page. Once a week Matt found a chef to interview and write about—not a bad gig, as he often got a free lunch out of it. His favorite places were San Ysidro greasy spoons like El Toro Bravo, "home of the best shrimp tacos," and Miguelina's Burrería at Otay Mesa, which made the meanest *chicharrón* burritos in town.

Despite *El Grito*'s less than pristine reputation, Matt's pieces got around and he soon landed a monthly column in *Foodalicious*, a magazine associated with the Culinary Institute of America. Since the *Foodalicious* editor wasn't interested in taco stands but in "exotic" cuisines, Matt found himself casting his net wider. After meeting with the chef at Andrés, a popular Cuban restaurant in San Diego, Matt began searching the internet for more recipes from the island. And then he discovered *Yarmi Cooks Cuban*, a Havana-based blogspot.

There were few Cuban blogs at that time; some were in Spanish and focused on social issues, written by government opponents. Matt, who had always felt a quiet sympathy for Fidel Castro, avoided them. But he also found the official newspapers boring and too proselytizing. *Yarmi Cooks Cuban* was a breath of fresh air: though she wrote about food, her posts were spiced up with personal touches and stories about her life. Her English, if not perfect, was good enough to be understood. Once they became virtual friends he volunteered to help her, correcting some misspelled words and incorrect prepositions.

They bonded over Cuban dishes, exchanging recipes by email, talking on the phone, and sharing meals when they met in Havana. She had only asked him for one thing—a bottle of extra virgin olive oil—when he visited Cuba the first time. Yet she also used lard freely. Like most Cubans, Yarmila regarded pork in all its permutations as the pinnacle of gastronomic joy.

Matt encouraged her to write a feature for *Foodalicious*. He had pitched the story to the magazine editor, who thought it would be a hit. Yarmila promised him a piece addressed "to the *Yuma* public" if Matt, in turn, would write one for her blog about his Cuban experience. He loved the idea, hoping it marked the beginning of a collaboration that blended love, food and words. But that was something else that wouldn't happen now, he reminded himself, shifting on the hard bench. Another broken dream.

From: yportal@cubarte.cult.cu
To: msullivan@hotmail.com
Sent: Fri, Jan 22, 2003 1:17 pm
Subject: Re: CIA story

My dear, dear Yuma,

I love your letters, even if they come by email—a very impersonal means of communication, in my opinion. But algo es algo, dijo el galgo. *Something is something, said the hound. Don't ask me what the hound has to do with it. Most Cuban sayings make no sense!*

I look forward to writing the story. But I will wait until you come so we can work on it together.

I am thinking of that Mexican dish you told me about, shrimp enchiladas. We could explain the difference between enchilada here and in Mexico. No chiles in Cuba. I bet that my readers (and yours!) will be surprised.

As for that hot "habanero chile" you mentioned, I've never heard of it. We have red and green pimientos, bell peppers, but they are very mild.

Have you already bought your ticket? Let me know so I can wait for you at the airport. Later we either stay in my apartment or rent my friend Isabel's penthouse that is more comfortable than my little place.

Her restaurant is going swell. Isabel is so grateful that you are bringing us all those gadgets. I just don't want you to spend a lot of money. We are used to make do with what we have, and that is that.

Spicy kisses from your Yarmi

A TALL TWENTY-SOMETHING MAN came in. He wore civilian clothes but his buzz cut lent him a military air. He was carrying Matt's passport, which had been taken away along with the rest of his belongings. Was the man a consular officer, a fellow American who had come to Matt's rescue? Matt let that hope glitter in his mind like the iridescent shell that Yarmila had found at El Mégano Beach the year before.

"Hi," Matt said in English.

"*Buenas tardes, compañero,*" the man replied in Spanish. Matt's shell burst to pieces. "I am Pedro."

He didn't add a last name.

"Do you speak Spanish?" Pedro asked.

"Yes."

"Still, we can converse in your native tongue if you favor it."

Pedro's heavily accented English and peculiar word choices blew away Matt's last specks of hope.

"Spanish is fine," he muttered. "We can—converse."

Pedro sat on the other bench and stared silently at him for a couple of minutes. Annoyed, Matt broke the silence to say, "I want to know why I am detained. If I'm going to be interrogated, I request the presence of an embassy officer."

But he was far from feeling as confident as he pretended to be.

What if they hold me hostage and use me as a political pawn? That's what they do in North Korea!

"There is no American embassy in Cuba," Pedro corrected him, adding in a conciliatory tone, "but you are not *detained*. Nobody is going to *interrogate* you, so cool it. You are just a person of interest in this case."

"Am I free to go home?"

"Not so fast, hey, not so fast. You have to wait for Lieutenant

Martínez, who is in charge of the case. I came to ask you a few questions first."

"Who are you?"

"I work for the Ministry of the Interior," Pedro spoke slowly, enunciating each syllable as if he were addressing a kid.

El Ministerio del Interior. La Seguridad. The Department of State Security. Cuba's secret police. By then Matt had read enough Cuban blogs and newspapers to know what Pedro (whose real name was likely a different one) meant.

"I have nothing to do with politics," he blurted out. "Nothing at all!"

"No one has said you are here for political reasons," Pedro replied. "This is a formality, really. We aren't accusing you of anything."

"Oh. Okay. What do you want from me?"

"Tell me how you met Yarmila Portal," the Seguridad man said.

Matt exhaled and started to talk fast. "I am a liberal guy. I'm not your enemy. I *care* about the revolution. I've been rooting for Fidel since I was a college student." That was slightly inflated (fluffed up, as Estrada would say). "I met Yarmila online in February 2002. I was browsing the web and found her blog. I liked it because it wasn't about counterrevolutionary issues."

He needed to impress that on Pedro's mind. He had heard that the secret police considered any American who visited Cuba a potential CIA agent. Anne had cautioned him about talking politics in public places, no matter what his stance was. Anything could be twisted and later used against him, she said. People were paranoid. Even Yarmila had asked him once if he worked "for the intelligence" in his country, a suggestion that made him laugh then. It was no laughing matter now.

"We wrote to each other for months. She invited me to visit her."

He didn't add that he had fantasized about Yarmila and printed the photo she had posted on her profile page—a fresh-faced young woman with dimples in her cheeks and short black hair, in a sexy blue dress that showed her legs. If she had been a homely girl, he would have never traveled all the way to Havana to meet her.

"I came last year around July 26," he went on. "It was the forty-fourth anniversary of the revolutionary triumph."

He remembered the fact from a billboard and threw it in. Pedro smiled knowingly and Matt feared he had said the wrong thing. That was what a good CIA agent might do: try to convince the Cubans that he was a communist or, at the very least, an ally.

Leave politics alone, damn it!

"I spent a couple of weeks here, getting to know her. We liked each other very much. Last month I decided to return and help her with a restaurant that a friend of hers had opened."

He stopped, feeling the weight of his loss heavy upon his shoulders, crushing his spirit. But he wasn't going to cry in front of this cop, or whatever he was. He wasn't going to show any weakness.

"Today, I found her . . ." He cleared his throat. "She was—oh, God, it feels terrible to even say it, but she was already dead when this woman and I . . ."

Pedro looked sympathetic now. He waited until Matt regained his bearings. When he spoke again, he used a casual, friendlier tone, "Your Spanish is very good. Where did you study it?"

"I have a master's in Latin American literature."

"You learned it in college?"

Matt could have said yes, but didn't see the point of lying.

"Not really. I lived in Bolivia and later in Peru."

"When was that?"

"In the seventies."

Pedro frowned.

"Why were you there?"

"My parents were missionaries."

Pedro offered a few comments about American missionaries being envoys of imperialism in underdeveloped countries. Matt let them pass. He didn't consider himself religious, or even spiritual. All the Sunday school classes he had been more or less forced to attend had made him lean toward the atheist side. But he wasn't going to discuss that with a Seguridad guy.

"I understand that you are a journalist," Pedro said, steering the conversation away again. "Have you ever written about Cuba?"

"No, the paper I work for is very Baja-centric."

That was Estrada's favorite word to describe *El Grito*.

"And that means—?"

"We only deal with news about San Diego and Baja California: Mexican issues, border incidents, Latino interest stories . . ."

They made exceptions, of course. Estrada, as the editor and owner, published pretty much whatever he wanted. He had asked Matt to write a special feature about his Cuban experience. "You can be our man in Havana, our foreign correspondent," he told him. "And I'll throw in three hundred bucks for your travel expenses." Matt had promised to think it over. Estrada had wanted a story about the local Chinatown, but Matt had another idea: if Yarmila accepted his proposal, he would write a feature about Cuban weddings, something *bien chingón*. He would have a picture of them together, with Yarmi in her bridal gown, published in *El Grito* for everyone (including his ex-wife) to see. That would show *her*.

"I hope you are telling me the truth," Pedro said. "We wouldn't like to find out that you are the kind who comes here to write lies about our people and the revolution."

"I'm not! I don't know enough to write anything, good or bad, about Cuba."

"How come? You were engaged to a Cuban."

"Yes, but we didn't discuss life here."

"Isn't that strange?"

Matt shrugged. "It is what it is."

He was going to say that they had had more interesting things to talk about, but then it hit him. Yes, it was a bit strange that Yarmila had shared so little with him. She had been eager to learn about *his* country: what people ate there, what clothes they wore, what they thought of their politicians . . . He had found her curiosity normal. Didn't everybody in Cuba want to know what life was like in los Estados Unidos?

"Thanks for your cooperation," Pedro said. "That's all I needed from you. But you don't have to wait here. What were these cops thinking? I'll ask them to move you to a more proper place. These benches are awful, no? Ass-killing."

He left. A few minutes later, a stocky guy in uniform showed up.

"Please, accompany me," he said, more courteously than Matt would have expected.

He obeyed. The guard led him through a brightly lit hall. They met two other cops on the way.

"It's a *Yuma*," he heard one say.

"What the hell is he doing here? Drugs or *putas*?"

"Something worse."

A chill ran through Matt's body. The guard took him to a small office.

"Lieutenant Martínez will be with you soon," he said.

He went away, leaving the door open. Matt sat on a hard chair (an improvement over the bench, though), across from a solid wood desk flanked by two filing cabinets. A framed photo of Fidel Castro presided over the room. There was a Cuban newspaper, *Juventud Rebelde*, on the desk. Matt looked at the date: "Wednesday, March 5, 2003. Year of the glorious anniversaries of Martí and Moncada."

I can't believe I just left home this morning. It feels as if a year has passed.

He hit himself on the forehead. Pedro had forgotten to give him back his passport. Now it was too late to ask for it. But at least he wasn't in a locked cell, like a criminal, anymore. And he wasn't a suspect, but "a person of interest." He just had to meet (briefly, he hoped) with Lieutenant Martínez, whom he imagined disheveled and cigar-smoking, a tropical Columbo of sorts.

nished, in fact. His last meal had been a sip of watery coffee, courtesy of Aero-urs before. He couldn't help it—Yarmila's d once more.

Kike and Marina's *caldosa*

It's about time I devote a post to this nutritive and delicious dish. In case you don't remember, La Caldosa is also the name of a dear friend's restaurant, home of the amazing rice and chicken *a la Isabel*.

Caldosa is a mix of meats and vegetables, boiled together until all the flavors are brought out. Quite simple, though it takes a few hours to gel. Therefore, the first step is making sure that you have the whole morning, or afternoon, to spend in the kitchen.

Fill a *caldero* (the biggest pot you have at home) with water. Boil and add four pounds of pork. Any cut will do, but bones and heads provide a nice consistency. After half an hour, add the chicken: wings, breasts, thighs, and giblets. Again, bones are good.

Simmer for thirty more minutes and a potato, pumpkin, yuca, taro, plantains, cassava . . . Whatever you have—*caldosa* is very accep All the tubers are expected to become soft.

Make sure to add water when it gets too l

In the meantime, take out the pan and fry unless you want to be health conscious and u one chopped garlic, and three bell peppers. Add cumin, oregano, and tomato paste. Let it simmer for a few minutes and pour the mixture into the *caldero*. Boil for another forty minutes, adding salt and pepper to taste.

A common question: when do you know it is ready?

Answer: when the meat and vegetables are so tender that you don't need a knife to cut them.

Caldosa is often served at communal parties, like the anniversary of the Committees for the Defense of the Revolution, on September 28. All the neighbors contribute with something. Even a potato or a couple of onions are appreciated.

I have given you the recipe for a family *caldosa*, but we put as many ingredients as we can in the collective *caldero*.

At the party, people sit around and catch up with their neighbors' lives while they share *caldosa*. There is music, dance, and rum. Don't forget el Havana Club!

Caldosa is one of the few Cuban dishes that has its very own song, composed by Rogelio Díaz Castillo and made popular by El Jilguero de Cienfuegos. I have danced to the *caldosa* rhythm many times!

COMMENTS

Cocinera Cubana said. . .

First time I hear of *caldosa*. When I left Cuba it hadn't been invented yet. It reminds me of *ajíaco*. Or is it the same thing?

Mateo said. . .

That's a new one for me too. Will you make one when I visit next time?

Lucy Adel said. . .

Too much boiling. I'd stick to the *ajíaco*.

Taos Tonya said. . .

Here in New Mexico we will add chile because we put it into everything.

Yarmi said. . .

Cocinera, I'll find out if it is a "modern" dish. You may be right; we have had to become creative in recent years! As for the differences, the *ajíaco* takes less time and each ingredient retains its identity. In the *caldosa*, flavors get so mixed up that you don't know where the plantain ends and where the yuca starts.

Yuma dearest, I will make my very best *caldosa* for you!

Tonya, even in desserts?

Lucy, both are great. Thanks for commenting and *buen apetito*.

Taos Tonya said. . .

Yes, *jita*. Wait until you try my green chile pumpkin pie. *Delicioso*!

Chapter Four

LA CALDOSA

Smells of chicken fried with onions, garlic, and tomato sauce filled the air, mixed with the scent of Alicia Alonso eau de toilette. It was a promising evening at La Caldosa, an evening of foreigners and well-off nationals. Isabel Quintana, the *paladar* proprietress, surveyed the room with a satisfied expression. Four of the five tables were already occupied and they were getting close to the maximum number of patrons allowed. Per state regulations, *paladares* couldn't serve more than twelve clients at a time.

Two gray-haired men shared a table with a couple of Cuban teenagers. The girls spoke Spanish to each other and their companions did the same in German, the linguistic barrier too wide for them to attempt to cross it on either part. There were three women whose chat was thick with the sibilant sounds of the Castillian lisp, and a middle-aged, foreign-looking man dining alone.

In a corner table, a well-dressed Cuban couple proclaimed their status in both behavior and attire. The woman wore a maxi dress with silver appliqués and stylish makeup; the man sported a crisp *guayabera* and ironed jeans. They talked quietly and refrained from excessive gesturing. They had started with a big shrimp salad, the most expensive appetizer on the menu. Isabel figured that they were "dollar-area Cubans," as their less fortunate compatriots called them, and probably worked for a *corporación* like Gaviota or Cubalse. *Corporaciones* were government-owned enterprises that paid their employees in convertible pesos or CUCs, a currency pegged to the American dollar.

Isabel smiled at them, refilled their water glasses and asked if everything was okay. She pampered her dollar-area patrons who, unlike foreign tourists, had the potential to become repeat customers.

"The salad is delicious," the woman said, "but it's getting warm in here."

"Oh, I'm sorry! I will take care of that."

Isabel opened the window and the sounds from the street seeped in—cars honking and slamming on their brakes, motorcycles revving, laughter and shouts from a bus stop. She turned on the stereo and played an Enrique Iglesias CD that a patron had given her in exchange for two free meals. The patron was a Cubalse employee who worked at Quinta y 42 St. Store in Miramar, a convertible-peso supermarket.

Luis, Isabel's husband and the *paladar*'s only waiter, showed up with entrées for the Germans and their friends. Only then did Isabel return to the kitchen—she didn't like to leave the room unattended, afraid of petty theft and eat-and-runs. That night the special was rice and chicken prepared according to her very own and secret recipe. *Arroz con pollo a la Isabel* was moist, colorful, creamy, and a tad spicy. She tasted the chicken, added a teaspoon of saffron to the rice and stirred the simmering *sofrito*, the seasoning base used in most of her dishes.

Taty, the kitchen helper and occasional busboy, was busy

cutting onions—the main entrée was served with an avocado and onion salad. But it wasn't the onion's fault that his eyes swelled with tears as he sliced.

"*Ay*, Isa! I can't believe it still," he said.

She didn't answer.

"I was thinking that this nightmare may still turn out like a soap opera," he went on. "You know how it goes: the pretty girl is found dead at home but in the end, it was her twin sister or someone else who died. And she is alive and having fun in a faraway place!"

Isabel gave him a cold glance. Taty was a young Chinese mulatto whose toned body had the exact combination of muscles and curves to make him attractive to both sexes in a disturbing, feral way.

"Yarmila didn't have any twin sisters," she replied, curtly. "Don't talk nonsense."

"Well, but—"

"Pay attention to what you're doing or you are going to cut a finger off, *comemierda*."

Isabel had found out about Yarmila's death through the grapevine, a few minutes after a police car had stopped in Espada Street and whisked Matt and Fefita away. She had considered not opening the *paladar* that evening, out of respect for her friend's memory, but she had ordered too much food and risked losing it all if a blackout were to happen at night.

"Despite everything, it's going to be a great evening, eh, Isa?" Taty ventured to say after a while. "Have you seen how many people we have?"

"Let's just hope the cops don't show up tonight," Isabel sighed.

He batted his long eyelashes, where too much mascara had been applied.

"Why would they?"

"Because Yarmila was our business partner. As soon as they find out, they will start asking this and that. And I don't have receipts for all the stuff I've bought."

"But she wasn't a partner, legally. Her name isn't on the papers."

"So what? Yours isn't either and everybody knows you work for me. She cooked for us. She was here almost every night. And then, she and Pato—but they'd better not mess with me!" Isabel lifted her breasts in a defiant gesture, the way men grab their crotches to make a point. "I don't take shit from anybody, cop or no cop!"

They continued cooking in silence. After the Enrique Iglesias CD ended, Luis chose an old favorite: Buena Vista Social Club.

"Who could have killed her?" Taty asked, with Compay Segundo singing "Chan Chan" in the background.

Isabel put a saffron-stained index finger to her lips. "Shush! Don't say that word."

"Which one?

"Killed."

"Do you think she offed herself?"

"No, Taty! Why would she? But you never know who is listening to you or how they are going to interpret what you say. And there is *always* someone listening to you. You have to be more careful."

"Okay, okay."

Isabel started slicing a tomato. She longed to have a blender. Yarmila had assured her that her *Yuma* was bringing one, plus other fancy items like a rice cooker and a new set of kitchen knives.

"We can forget that now," she muttered to herself.

Isabel was pear-shaped, in her late forties, with long gray hair tied in a bun. Her legs were wrapped in compression stockings. A starchy white apron covered her polka-dotted dress. Though she moved gingerly, dragging her sandal-clad feet over the tiled floor, Isabel was anything but bashful. A demanding manager, wife and mother, she had been nicknamed La Jefota (Big Boss) by her own husband. She didn't care. She was proud of having kept the *paladar* afloat after many similar ventures that were started at the same time had already failed.

Isabel had turned into an entrepreneur as soon as it became legal to run private restaurants in people's homes. She had been a nurse at the Van Troy Policlinic for twenty years, but quickly figured out that opening a *paladar* made more financial sense than working for the government—even with the heavy tax that had to be paid regardless of the business's income or lack thereof. As a nurse, she had taken home three hundred Cuban pesos a month. Now, she usually got a net profit of two hundred CUCs every month, the equivalent of 2,500 pesos.

She did so well that Luis, an accountant for the Ministry of Transportation, also quit his job and became a waiter at La Caldosa. They hired Taty, who passed as Isabel's nephew, to help in the kitchen and be an occasional busboy. And though it was supposed to be a family business, their success had sparked Yarmila's interest. She couldn't have worked there legally (only relatives were allowed to jointly operate a *paladar*) but she nevertheless became first a cook and later a clandestine capitalist partner.

"How did Pato Macho take it, Isa?" Taty asked. He mixed the onion rings with slices of ripe avocado, sprinkling them with oil, salt and a splash of vinegar.

Isabel added a bay leaf to the *sofrito* and stirred it. She avoided

Taty's expectant gaze. "He is devastated," she said at last. "Furious too. He wants to find out who did it and beat the bastard to a pulp."

"He loved her very much."

"He did, but it's all over. Love will not bring her back. I've told him to get the hell out of Havana."

"Did he go?"

"Nah, he never listens to me. You know how he is."

"Do you think the police will blame him?"

"He is suspect number one, the way things are."

"But Pato didn't mind it," Taty said. "I mean, Yarmila never hid the fact that she had a *Yuma* partner. In any case, the cuckold was that guy, not—"

"Let's leave Pato out of this!"

Isabel stopped stirring the *sofrito* and put a hand on Taty's shoulder. "Do not talk about Pato and her to anyone, hear?" she said firmly. Saliva flew from her mouth. "This is serious business."

"Of course I won't talk!" Taty replied, offended. "I am not a gossip and Pato is like a brother to me."

She turned to her pots again. "I'm sorry, honey," she said. "I am scared and sad. *Ay!* I still remember the last time I saw Yarmi, when I brought her a chicken because she was going to make croquettes for us."

"That was two days ago."

"Yes, just two days. She looked so happy and full of life," Isabel choked on the last word. "She wanted me to go upstairs but I said no, my legs were killing me. I told her to come down and get the damn chicken. I was rude to the poor girl! If I had known that would be the last time we were going to meet—"

The door chime rang.

"Is it someone coming in or someone leaving?" Isabel asked.

Taty stuck his head through the rattan curtain that separated the kitchen from the dining room. "It's Padrino," he said.

A slightly built, short-haired man in his fifties was led by Luis to the only empty table. Padrino wore a white linen shirt, white pants, and a white handkerchief sticking out of his breast pocket. His light brown skin looked darker by contrast. A long Santería necklace of blue beads hung loosely around his neck and a bracelet in the same color encircled his right wrist. He also wore a shorter necklace of three red beads alternating with three black ones.

"A beer and the *arroz con pollo* special, please," he said to Luis, after shaking his hand.

Back in the kitchen, Isabel scooped a generous portion from the chicken and rice pot and made sure it contained only thighs, which Padrino preferred.

When Luis came in to fetch the beer from the refrigerator, Padrino's order was ready.

Ten minutes passed. The solitary foreign diner left, followed by the Spaniards. A young Cuban couple came in, studied the menu, and decided to split an *arroz con pollo*. The Germans ordered more beers and the dollar-area patrons settled on a flan for dessert. Padrino ate slowly, savoring his meal.

Isabel put another batch of chicken in the *sofrito* and began to sauté it. The door chime rang again.

"Yes, this will turn out to be a decent night after all," Isabel started to say. But she cut herself off. There was a cop at the door. Behind him, the red and ice blue lights of a cruiser flashed scandalously. The cop stopped in the threshold as if waiting for someone else to join him.

Luis came into the kitchen, pale and shaky.

"Whatever happens, do not charge Padrino tonight," his wife told him. "I'm afraid that we are going to need the *orishas*' help."

Chapter Five

LIEUTENANT MARTÍNEZ

By looking around the office he was sitting in, Matt could tell that Lieutenant Martínez was the neat, everything-in-its-place-and-a-place-for-everything type. Such a logical person would understand that he didn't deserve to be locked up, he told himself. They had nothing against him, as Pedro had so clearly said.

What good would it do to keep me here? I am not a suspect. Yarmi had been dead for—I don't know, hours, maybe a whole day, when I arrived in Cuba. Yarmi, my love. Did she suffer a lot? How did she die? I didn't see any blood, but the water could have washed it away. I didn't look too closely either. God. Who could have hated Yarmi so much to do that to her? Did she have enemies at work, in the neighborhood, at that Caldosa place? I can't imagine anybody trying to steal from her . . .

He stood up and walked around the office. His legs were weak and numb. He returned to his seat.

It could have been an accident too. Why didn't I think of it before? That makes more sense! A heart attack, a stroke—but she never mentioned any health issues, did she? Pedro was right: I know so little, not only about Cuba but also about Yarmi's life. I only know what she shared with me, and that wasn't an awful lot.

He tried to evoke the lively dark-haired girl who had welcomed him the year before, but instead saw her pale face and closed eyes, the soaked yellow dress. He forced himself to remember the emails they had exchanged, their long, heartfelt phone calls and their love at first sight—or *almost* at first sight. When he arrived in Havana, she had been waiting for him at the airport. It was mid-July, hot and humid. Perspiration and anxiety made his shirt stick to his back as soon as he stepped out of the plane.

He recognized her immediately. The young woman was shorter than he had expected, around five feet tall, when he'd imagined she would be five four at least. Yet that didn't matter because her bright brown eyes, like prisms of light, were much prettier than in the photo, shining with an intensity that surprised him—and scared him a bit. She had an oval Mona Lisa face framed by shoulder-length hair. Her light caramel skin exuded a warm, primal fragrance. He liked everything about her, even her accent, though he couldn't always understand what she said. Yarmila crushed words together, omitted final consonants and often accented the wrong syllables. She wrote better than she talked. Still, she spoke English remarkably well for someone who had never been abroad.

"I know what many words mean because I've seen them used in books," she explained. "The problem is that I haven't heard them so I just take a guess on the pronunciation. Too bad that English doesn't have written accents, like Spanish."

He had hailed an *almendrón* outside the airport—a yellow Chevy Impala—and they had ridden together to the Old Havana building where Yarmila lived. There was a feast waiting for him, she announced. In truth, the meal consisted of a dozen fish croquettes, white rice, black beans, and fried plantains, but Matt pronounced everything "scrumptious."

"That's a new term for me!" Yarmila laughed. "Is it the same as yummy?"

"Even better."

"*Qué* good."

Since the beginning they had communicated in a private kind of Spanglish, a made-up language of love.

At that time Yarmila owned a small computer with a monochrome green monitor. A mountain of cables were piled behind the desk.

"This is where I write my food posts," she said proudly.

Matt surveyed the keyboard with its faded letters and the square mouse with three buttons. It looked ancient to him.

"Maybe I can send you a new computer," he said.

"Why? Mine works fine."

The kitchen had been bigger than the one in the Espada Street apartment and better equipped with a porcelain sink and a freestanding range stove. Yarmila's apartment had been the home's kitchen and pantry area when just one family, the original owners, had occupied the building. Now the former mansion housed twenty-seven people. Yarmila was the only one who lived by herself.

The next-door neighbors had two kids, she told Matt, taking away four croquettes. And at the end of the hall was an elderly couple who subsisted on a meager pension—she set apart a dish for them too.

"Here, we like to help each other."

Matt had been moved by her generosity and fearful, at the same time, that she might expect him to "help" as well, to give her money, to buy stuff for her . . . What if she was really a *jinetera*, a prostitute in disguise? Estrada had warned him: *Cuban girls are smoking hot but they are also trouble. I once had a Cubanita in TJ and she screwed me over royally. She asked for dresses, shoes, perfumes, every* chingada *thing under the sun. Then one day she took a powder. People said she ran off to Miami with someone else. So you be careful, man.* Pónte abusado.

"I'm not rich," Matt had hurried to say, too fast and curtly. "I don't make *mucho dinero*."

As it turned out, he didn't need to be concerned. Yarmila told him that she worked as a translator and researcher (Matt didn't understand what she researched, exactly) for the Institute of Literature and Linguistics. She wasn't working at La Caldosa yet, or at least she hadn't mentioned it. Her Institute salary, though only in Cuban pesos, was enough to cover her needs, she assured him.

"I am a college graduate," she said, pointing to a diploma on the wall.

Yarmila held a *Licenciatura*, the equivalent of a BA, conferred by the School of Foreign Languages of the University of Havana. It was written on parchment, with the Cuban coat of arms on top.

"Many of my former classmates are now working in hotels because they make more money there," she told him. "But I can't get myself to do the same. I didn't study five years to make somebody's bed."

"Good for you."

"Still, it's nice to have extra income, *verdad*? I often cook for other people who want something special, like a birthday cake or a cheese flan."

"Do they pay you well?"

"A few CUCs always help."

Matt had never heard of CUCs before.

"Are they the same as dollars?"

"Sort of. You will need to exchange your dollars to CUCs if you want to buy in tourists' shops."

"And at your day job, are you paid in pesos?"

"I'm paid in CUPs."

Matt kept asking questions about Cuba's double currency, which he found mystifying—he later learned that one CUC was equivalent to twenty-five CUPs, or regular Cuban pesos. Though he was attracted to Yarmila, he didn't dare to make a move yet, and felt awkward being alone with a pretty young woman inside that small room that smelled so strongly of *sofrito*. Yarmila, on the other hand, seemed happy and at ease.

"I didn't used to cook when I lived in Pinar del Río," she said with a smile. "That was my grandma's domain. Thank God I took the time to write down some of her recipes. Once I was on my own in Havana, I found out that I liked to experiment with dishes and twist them around. I also wanted to practice my English and communicate with people abroad, that's how *Yarmi Cooks Cuban* was born. Mom still can't believe that my posts are read in faraway places like San Diego!"

"Oh, they're great. And you must be very good with technology to maintain a blog. They are kind of a new thing, aren't they? I wouldn't even know how to open one."

"Well, this isn't my first. I started one in Spanish, then closed it."

"Why?"

Yarmila seemed suddenly uncomfortable, as if she had said something she shouldn't. She changed the topic of conversation and Matt didn't insist.

They finished eating, the surprise of the night being a flan covered in pink meringue, with the word *bienvenido* on top.

"A special flan for this special *Yuma*," she said, pecking him on the cheek. Her natural, fresh scent settled into his skin.

That had been the extent of their physical contact that evening and for several days afterward. Yarmila flirted with him cautiously and behaved in such a good-girl manner that Matt was ashamed of his initial assumptions. Even when she finally slept with him, the weekend before he left Havana, she had been modest and almost shy in bed.

Contrary to what Estrada had predicted, Yarmila hadn't shown any interest in dresses or shoes, not even when he took her to the tourists' shops. Though she protested, he went ahead and bought a few kitchen utensils, like a good set of carving knives and forks that cost ninety CUCs at the Quinta y 42 St. Store. And meat, oil and imported cheese because they weren't available anywhere else. Matt didn't know how she managed to make all those fancy dishes because the grocery stores were bare.

AN HOUR HAD GONE by, but Matt hadn't even noticed the passage of time. He was still lost in his thoughts when the stocky guard came by.

"Do you want water, *compañero*?" he asked in a friendly tone.

"Yes, please."

He brought a can of condensed milk full of water, which was room temperature, but Matt drank it till the last drop. The can reminded him of a post Yarmila had written about a dessert made with condensed milk. She called it "little mud."

The guard went away and Matt was left alone again in the company of his memories. The next person to come to the door was a young woman. Matt didn't see her face, zooming in on her behind instead. It was a big, round, monumental butt ready to explode inside the tight uniform pants. He stuck his head out of the office to take a better look at her. The woman, who had gotten to the end of the hall, punched a card, turned around and caught him staring. He pretended to be distracted and focused his attention on Castro's photo, which depicted the president as a strong, middle-aged man in green fatigues.

I bet he doesn't look like that anymore. Does he still have a beard? It must be all white now.

His musings were cut short by a female voice. "Good evening, *compañero*."

To his embarrassment, Matt found the woman with the epic behind standing in front of him. She was around twenty-five years old and very tall, with short brown hair and stern gray eyes. Despite her youth, she looked imposing and severe.

"Good . . . good evening," he stammered.

"I'm Lieutenant Martínez."

He gaped at her, too shocked to say a word.

"Are you with me, *compañero*?" she asked.

"Yes," he muttered. "I'm with you."

Lieutenant Martínez's attitude was different from Pedro's. Though she wasn't openly hostile, she acted in a cold, official manner that made Matt feel on edge and insecure. She might have been assigned the role of the bad cop. But she could have also been offended by his ogling her butt.

She proceeded to question him. Matt told her, as he had told the Seguridad agent, how he had met Yarmila, that he was back in Cuba to see her, and how long they had known each other.

"I explained all that to Pedro," he couldn't help but say.

"We work in different departments," Lieutenant Martínez replied. "So you will have to explain everything again to *me*."

After Matt finished his story, he hesitated before asking, "Could you please tell me if Yarmila was—if it was an accident or—?"

"It was a homicide."

Matt looked down and studied Lieutenant Martínez's black

uniform boots. They were old, carefully polished and a size nine at least.

"When was the last time you talked to her?" Martínez asked.

"Yesterday," Matt said. His heart was beating fast and hard.

"Do you remember the time?"

"Early in the morning."

Anne arrived from LA at ten o'clock and he had already called Yarmila by then, but he preferred to omit that fact. He didn't want to get Anne involved.

"How did she sound?"

"Fine, as usual. She was excited. She said she would be waiting for me."

It hadn't occurred to him yet that the four of them could ride together in Yony's car. Anne was the one who suggested it later, when they were already on the plane.

"You didn't have any communication today?"

"I tried to call her from Monterrey between connecting flights, when I found out that we were going to be delayed, but she didn't answer."

"When was that?"

"Around noon."

"Did you call her place of work?"

"No. I called her home."

Martínez asked for the number and wrote it down with a puzzled expression.

"For how long did she have this number?" she asked.

"I don't know. That's the only number I ever had for her."

She made a quick annotation and asked point-blank if he suspected anyone. Matt shook his head mechanically, lost in his private purgatory, until the next question took him by surprise.

"What about Pato Macho?"

"Excuse me?"

"Pato Macho. Was it an issue or were you okay with it?"

Is she talking about a male duck?

"I am not following you, sorry. Did you say 'duck'?"

"Pato Macho is an alias, obviously. His real name is Yosvani Álvarez. Sound familiar?"

"I've never heard that name."

"Are you *sure*?" She stressed the last word.

"I would remember if I had, *señora*."

Matt was translating the respectful term "ma'am" in English, but that was a faux pas. Lieutenant Martínez frowned.

"Call me *compañera*, please," she said. "By the way, how old are you?"

"Thirty-six, *compañera*."

"How old was citizen Yarmila Portal Richards?"

Matt paused before answering. He had all but forgotten Yarmila's second last name. Her maternal grandfather had been from Jamaica—she'd told Matt when he asked about that English-sounding surname.

"Did you hear me?"

"Twenty-four. Or twenty-five. I don't remember."

Shouldn't they know that? Why is she asking me?

"How long were you involved with the deceased?"

The deceased. God.

"Around a year."

"A whole year?"

"Almost a year, if you want to be exact. We met in person last summer. But we had been writing to each other for several months before."

"How much time did you spend together—in person, as you said?"

"Two weeks."

"Are you *sure?*" she repeated.

"Well—more like ten days."

"You didn't see her again afterwards?"

"No. But we talked on the phone. We—"

"So you barely knew her, right? She was more like an acquaintance, wasn't she? Not a *real* girlfriend."

Don't put it like that, bitch.

"That's not accurate, *compañera*," he said as politely as he could.

"How so?"

"We were in contact all the time. We emailed daily. I called her once a week. We communicated on a regular basis. We had a relationship."

"And because you had 'a relationship,' you were planning to marry her and take her to your country afterwards, eh?"

Her tone was neutral but Matt sensed the sarcasm and saw it flicker in her pupils. He knew that Yarmila couldn't have possibly left Cuba with him after their wedding. Once they were married, he would have had to petition her as an immediate relative, a convoluted legal process that could stretch out for months, even a year.

"*Compañero?* Did you understand what I said?"

"Yes, yes. I had invited her to visit me in San Diego first. Then we'd go from there."

While this wasn't a lie, it wasn't the truth either. But he left it at that. Lieutenant Martínez sighed. When their eyes met again, Matt saw a flash of pity in them, instead of the earlier scorn.

"Did you send her money very often?" she asked.

"Every two or three months."

"When was the last time?"

"Let me think. It was . . . around a month ago."

"How much?"

"Five hundred dollars."

"What for?"

"I'm not sure—I believe part of it went to her friend's restaurant."

"Ah! So you do know about the *paladar*."

"She told me she cooked there occasionally."

He was going to add that Yarmila had bought a share, or whatever they called it in Cuba, of La Caldosa, but decided not to bring it up. He thought it might be illegal, not that it mattered now.

"Let's see. You meet this citizen, spend *ten* days with her, don't see her face to face again, send her tons of money," Lieutenant Martínez paused here for effect, "and come back ready to marry her. Is that correct?"

"Yes, *compañera*," Matt let the reference to "tons of money" slip. "That's correct."

It's not worth trying to explain anything to Culo Grande. A few hundred dollars may sound like a million to her. Why bother?

"I must assume at this point that you had no idea she was involved with another man."

With another man. *Con otro hombre*. The Spanish words echoed inside Matt's head and it took him a few seconds to translate and fully understand them. When their meaning sank in, he willed himself to keep quiet and show no emotion. But his shoulders dropped and his heart fell to the level of Lieutenant Martínez's boots.

"She had a lover, a citizen known as Pato Macho," she went on. "They had been together since last October."

It was his turn to ask, "Are you *sure*?" but the irony dissolved in the slight quiver of his voice. He fixed his eyes on the newspaper while she spoke.

"Absolutely. Most of her friends and neighbors knew. It wasn't like they were making a big effort to hide it."

The words hurt him more than Lieutenant Martínez could have imagined. Matt's first wife, a nurse at Scripps Hospital, had divorced him after three years of marriage. Then he found out that she had been having an affair with a doctor for months. Matt had mentioned it to Yarmila, something he would later regret. She asked if the other guy was a Latino. "No, a gringo just like me," Matt answered, but her question had left a bad taste in his mouth. Now he felt it again, in all its bitterness.

"Yarmi never—I do not believe that," he said.

Lieutenant Martínez didn't attempt to convince him. "Is there anything else that you would like to share about citizen Yarmila or your relationship with her? Anything that could help us?"

Right, after the bomb you just dropped.

"Not really."

"It's getting late and you've been here long enough. I'll be back with some papers for you to sign."

She left the office. Matt looked at Castro's photo as if asking him for an explanation.

You know what, compañero? *Yarmi loved me. I loved her. I don't care what that fat-assed broad said. It's a mental game. Now, does she want me to sign papers admitting that I am guilty of something? Guilty of what?*

He remembered a perplexing document called a "certificate of single status" that he had practically forged. Notaría Internacional, the only office where marriage ceremonies between Cubans and foreigners were performed in Havana, required this as part of the documentation necessary for a wedding. None of the attorneys Matt had consulted in San Diego or Tijuana had ever heard of it. In the end, he took his divorce papers to a notary public with a letter he himself had written where he stated, in English and Spanish, that he wasn't married anymore, which made him "single" by default. The notary, who advertised in *El Grito* and was a friend, peppered the page with seals and stamps that made it look awfully official. The letter was in his backpack. He now wondered if the Cuban authorities had deemed it fake.

But it was the closest thing to a certificate of single status that I could come up with! Damn cop. She made it sound as if I were an idiot. Yes, I bought the wedding dress and brought my papers without consulting with Yarmila first . . . I was hoping that we could make it work, despite our age difference and the little time we had spent together. But that doesn't make me a pendejo. *A* pendejo *in Havana—what would Estrada say about all this?*

LIEUTENANT MARTÍNEZ CAME BACK with a form that had the Policía Nacional Revolucionaria stamp on its upper right corner. There were a few handwritten lines about Matt's status as a person of interest in a current investigation, but no mention of Yarmila's death. She asked him to sign it and stapled the form to a photocopy of the first pages of his passport. Then she handed everything to him.

"Thanks for your time and cooperation, *compañero*," she said, without any detectable irony. "Have a good night."

"What about my passport?"

"We are keeping it until you are cleared."

"Cleared of what? Do you guys think that I killed her?"

"Not at all. The citizen had most likely been dead for several hours before you arrived in Cuba. But we may need to talk to you again."

Matt was about to complain, but changed his mind. He was in no position to argue.

"If you want to rent a room in a hotel, this letter," Martínez pointed to the stamped document, "will explain to the manager why you don't have a passport now. Are you carrying any other kind of identification?"

"My driver's license."

"Everything should be fine," she said. "But if there is any problem, tell the hotel manager or the owner of the *casa particular* to contact me."

She wrote a phone number on a piece of paper and gave it to him. Her fingers brushed against his. They were soft, warm—electric.

"Where are you staying?" she asked.

At Yarmi's apartment, he'd thought. But now—"I'm not sure."

"You have to let me know."

He tried to recall the name of the motel where he had stayed during his first visit. It was near a college campus. Was it Colima, like the Mexican city? Colina? Then he flashed back to his last conversation with Yarmila, when she had mentioned that La Caldosa's owner had a *casa particular*—a private home where foreigners could rent rooms, bed-and-breakfast style. Yarmila had assured him that her friend's *casa* was cheaper and more comfortable than a state-owned hotel. He had talked to Isabel on the phone once and hoped that she'd remember him.

"I'll stay with the owner of La Caldosa," he said. "That's a restaurant on Salvador Allende Avenue."

"Yes, the same *paladar* where citizen Yarmila used to work," replied Lieutenant Martínez, and added with a shrug, "I find it a little strange that you want to go there, if you don't mind me saying so. But it's your choice. One of my *compañeros* will take you."

Why strange? Should I ask her? No, I'll keep my mouth shut. The sooner I'm out of here, the better.

They walked together to the lobby, where his belongings had been left in a corner. Martínez stopped to admire the bridal gown. For a few moments she looked like a young, starry-eyed girl hiding behind a uniform. But she soon shifted back to her official pose. She gave Matt his backpack and made a point of taking out his wallet and counting the $2,025 he had brought. She also examined his driver's license and compared the picture to his face.

"You are thinner here," she said.

He had gained twenty pounds in the three years he had been interviewing chefs for *El Grito* and *Foodalicious*.

"It's not recent," he answered.

She looked him up and down and Matt felt self-conscious and shy. Lieutenant Martínez was over six feet tall, her colossal butt the perfect match for her tropical Valkyrie body.

"Don't hesitate to call if you remember something that can help us," she said officiously. "And let me know tomorrow if you are going to stay at—La Caldosa for sure."

He nodded.

"Remember that it's in your best interest. The revolution has thousands of eyes and ears, so you can't hide from us. You can't leave Cuba without your passport anyway."

"I understand."

She gestured for the chubby cop to join them. "Gordo, take the *compañero* to the corner of Salvador Allende Avenue and Espada Street, to a *paladar* called La Caldosa."

Gordo lifted the suitcase with an "uff."

"It has wheels," Matt said.

"Ah, good! Comrade Lieutenant, may I go home afterwards?" Gordo asked. "It's past 8:00 P.M."

"Fine, but bring the cruiser back to the Unidad first."

Lieutenant Martínez escorted them to the police car. After they both got in, Gordo took a last look at his officer's retreating back as she returned to the station.

"*Tremendo mujerón*," he said, which Matt translated mentally as "one heck of a woman."

He nodded in agreement and the cruiser sped away.

Chapter Six

RICE, CHICKEN, *TOCINILLO*

Matt's entrance in La Caldosa caught every patron's eye. It was quite an unusual sight: a foreign-looking guy with a backpack over one shoulder and a wedding dress draped over the other arm, escorted by a fat cop carrying a huge suitcase.

"Like an alien landing on the wrong planet," one of the Cuban girls said.

Her friend giggled. The Germans maintained their blank expressions. Matt hesitated, but the salty aroma of fried chicken encouraged him to take a tentative step inside. Gordo, who seemed to enjoy rolling the suitcase on the floor, left it next to the kitchen after peering through the rattan curtain.

"Here you are, *compañero*," he said. "Good night."

After Gordo left, Matt stood by the door, confused and a little incredulous. Was this supposed to be Yarmila's friend's booming business? He had imagined a different scene—sort of a rustic tavern, homely maybe, but not a cramped, crowded living room. He surveyed the tourists and their companions, the young Cuban couple, and the lonely guy in white.

It was Taty who came to his rescue while Isabel and Luis remained speechless behind the curtain.

"Hi, mister, welcome to La Caldosa, home of the amazing *arroz con pollo a la Isabel*!" he said, with an exaggerated flourish of his hands. "Make yourself at home. Table for one?"

"Yes, please."

Luis finally reacted and led him to a table.

"I'm Yarmila's boyfriend," Matt explained, though the word "boyfriend," *novio*, sounded juvenile and silly. But he couldn't remember the Spanish term for fiancé.

"*Alabao*! You are the *Yuma*!" Isabel came out of the kitchen, wiping her hands on her apron.

"Yes, *señora*. Er, *compañera*. I'm Matt."

"I'm so sorry, Mateo. So sorry!" She hugged him. "What a tragedy!"

"I know how you must be feeling," Luis said. "We are in shock. Terrible, isn't it?"

Matt swallowed hard and nodded. Isabel hugged him. She smelled like grease and spices.

"Thanks for stopping by, Mateo," she said. "We were very concerned about you."

"I didn't know where else to go," Matt admitted. "I was detained for a few hours and I'm still trying to figure out what to do."

Padrino watched him closely. He was chewing a piece of chicken, savoring the crunchiness of it.

"Would you like to try our *arroz con pollo*?" Isabel asked. "You are probably devastated by your loss but—"

"One still needs to eat," Matt replied with a weak, guilty smile.

He dropped his backpack on the floor and looked for a chair where he could put the wedding dress. Isabel took it gently and placed it on top of the suitcase.

"Sit down, Mateo," she said. "Luis, bring him water and a beer. I'll take care of the food."

THE RICH FLAVORS OF the rice and chicken lifted Matt's spirits. He remembered a saying that Yarmila used to quote on her blog: *barriga llena, corazón contento*. Full belly, happy heart. Not really happy, of course, but at the very least at peace, and not starving anymore. Isabel and Luis hovered over him, bringing more salad, more chicken, another beer, touching his shoulders, making him feel welcomed and cared for. Even the guy in white, who had seemed spooky at first with his strange necklaces and bracelet, began to look friendly. He raised a Cristal beer to Matt and said *"a su salud,"* to your health, before drinking directly from the bottle.

When Matt was done with the main dish Isabel insisted he try a black bean soup, *potaje de frijoles negros*, that she had made for herself and Luis, not their patrons. The *potaje* was comfort food at its best: the creaminess of the beans, the tang of orange-marinated pork, and a hint of cumin, as subtle as it should be.

While Matt ate, Isabel kept glancing at the suitcase and the wedding dress.

"I could take your luggage inside," she suggested.

"Please, do," Matt said, relieved. "Give the dress to—somebody. Anyone who wants it. Or sell it, if you can. Whatever."

Isabel avoided his eyes.

"There are some kitchen gadgets and cookware in the suitcase. Everything is for you guys."

"Oh, you don't have to do that!" she protested.

"We can't accept it," Luis said.

"Come on, that's why I brought them. These are things *she* told me you could use."

He wouldn't hear about Isabel and Luis paying for anything.

He also told them to keep the gifts he had brought for Yarmila: the calendar, the apron and the dream catcher.

"Would you like more soup?" Isabel asked.

"That would be great," Matt said, adding with an embarrassed grin, "I normally don't eat that much."

"You need it, dear."

After serving him a second bowl of *frijoles negros* and more avocado and onion salad, Isabel and Luis excused themselves, took the suitcase to the kitchen and opened it with childlike interest. Matt heard their hushed exclamations: "Look at this, incredible . . . and everything is new!" Isabel squealed in delight when she discovered the rice cooker, and Matt hated her for having forgotten Yarmila so quickly. Then he remembered what Lieutenant Martínez had said about a guy nicknamed Pato Macho and took another helping of black beans.

No, that's ridiculous! I don't believe it for a minute. Yarmi couldn't have cheated on me. She'd never said she would follow him to San Diego, but that was natural: she needed time to think it over. She had lived here her whole life. And Matt had liked the fact that she wasn't anxious to leave—it meant she wasn't using him to escape from a bad situation. She was a nice, honest, college-educated girl. *Lieutenant Culo Grande doesn't know what she's talking about.*

Isabel and Luis acted so thankful when they came back that he forgave them for their happiness. They hugged him again and said that his help meant "a million pesos" to them.

"You'll put everything to good use," he said. "I know how hard you guys work. Yarmi was always talking about you."

"Well, I was like a mother to her," Isabel said, retrieving the empty bean dish.

It looked like Yarmi had many "mothers" in Havana. Isabel,

Fefita . . . It was easy for people to like her. Her real mom lived in Pinar del Río, though, and Matt wondered if he should call her and offer his condolences. He hoped that Lieutenant Martínez had already told Yarmila's family of her death. Just in case, he decided to wait a couple of days. *I would hate to be the one breaking the news to them.*

The Germans and their companions left. So did the young Cuban couple. None of them tipped a cent. Luis closed the door and turned off the neon sign. Isabel brought out a perfectly round dessert that, at first, Matt mistook for a flan. She settled it on his table and invited the man in white to come over.

"Hope you don't mind it, Mateo," she said. "This is Padrino, a family friend."

"Nice to meet you, *señor*," Matt said.

He moved his chair and cleared more space for Padrino. The four of them sat together around a dish that reflected the light on its polished golden surface. Matt finally recognized it—it wasn't a flan, but rather *tocinillo del cielo*, Yarmila's favorite dessert.

Better than birthday cake

Tocino del cielo is flan's decadent, slutty cousin.

Tocino means bacon. But *tocino del cielo* (or *tocinillo*, as it is also known) is a misleading term. The reason why a dessert that falls in the same category as flan and egg custard is named after cured pork has always eluded me. The *del cielo* part is easier to understand: it was "from heaven"—where people used to think everything good came from.

When I was a little girl, I always got a *tocinillo* for my birthday. Meringue cake? Forget it. We were given one every year through the ration card, but I was happy to let the party guests have it.

I'll tell you a little secret: though my grandmother Hilda was the kitchen's queen, it was mom who made the best *tocinillo*. Mom had "the touch" for sweets, and this is something you don't learn. Either you have it or you don't. In most dishes, particularly those involving egg yolk, butter and sugar, you need to find *el punto de caramelo*, that specific, indefinable moment when it's perfectly done.

Mom's soups or stews didn't always turn out right, but she got the right *punto* for *tocinillo* and flan. She didn't brag about it, though—and she wasn't just being deferential. She didn't want to embarrass Grandma, who was *la reina*. But she was also afraid that if her talents were recognized she would be asked to cook more often.

That, my friends, didn't sit well with her. Mom was, and is, a liberated woman, a *career* woman, not a housewife. Though born and raised in a rural town, she was rather avant-garde. She managed the local clinic and served as the president of the Cuban

Federation of Women on our block. She was also active with the Committee for the Defense of the Revolution, where she was elected treasurer twice. But housework she didn't enjoy.

Would you like to try her *tocinillo*? Then follow my instructions. But be warned—this isn't an easy recipe.

Start by making the syrup. Boil half a cup of water and a cup of sugar with a few drops of lemon for ten minutes, stirring constantly. (Keep an eye on it all the time, as syrup is one of these unpredictable sweet sauces that gets burned when you least expect it.) Then allow it to cool.

While you are at it, heat half a cup of sugar (again stir, stir!) in a smaller container. Put it aside.

Now, let's start with the *tocinillo* as such. Beat five yolks and two whole eggs together. But do not overbeat! I think mom's success lay in the fact that she didn't beat eggs as if they were going to be used for, let's say, *merenguitos*. Make sure they are well mixed, however.

Add the syrup and a bit of vanilla extract—one teaspoon will suffice. Then strain it, using a colander, pour everything into a pan, and get ready for the most difficult step: the *baño de María*.

Baño de María, which my *Yuma* boyfriend calls "water bath," consists of putting a small pan inside a large one and adding hot water to the larger pan until it reaches halfway up the side of the small one. (Did I confuse you already?)

The small pan, naturally, is where you pour in the strained mixture. Be careful not to burn yourself with the hot water, as I have done so many times. That explains why I am not a fan of *baño de María!*

Bake in the oven for around an hour. Next, turn the *tocinillo* over on a plate and drizzle it with the burned sugar. Refrigerate for three or four hours and enjoy. You deserve it!

COMMENTS

Cocinera Cubana said. . .

Hola, Yarmi! One way of avoiding the water bath hassle is using a pressure cooker. Place the *tocinillo* mold inside and boil for around fifteen minutes.

Maritza said. . .

Yes, this is complicated! Not just the water bath, but everything else. It will take me a whole day, I am afraid. Better to buy it at Versailles, hehe.

Anita said. . .

I'd rather wait until I go to Havana and try your *tocinillo*, dear.

Yarmi said. . .

Cocinera, you are right, the pressure cooker is a possibility, but I am ashamed to say that it scares me to death. A childhood trauma! So here is the story: when I was five years old, a neighbor's pressure cooker exploded and she was left badly disfigured. I do own one, but only use it in emergencies.

Maritza, I bet that if you make your own *tocinillo*, you won't need Versailles at all.

Anita, I will make one just for you when you come.

Besitos, Yarmi

Chapter Seven

THE PENTHOUSE

While Matt ate, Taty stayed back in the kitchen, washing dishes and cleaning things up, though he sometimes popped his head through the curtain. But as soon as Isabel brought out the dessert, he pranced over and grabbed a piece of *tocinillo* with his hand.

"*Niño*, when are you going to learn manners?" Isabel scolded him.

"Ah, mama, don't preach," he answered, playfully licking his fingers and eyeing Matt. "Touching the food improves its flavor."

"Don't say that in front of our clients, *comemierda*!"

"But it is true. Don't you think, mister?"

Matt cocked his head at him. At first he had thought that Taty was a young woman, but the way Isabel called him, *niño*, and his voice, high-pitched but obviously masculine, made him realize his mistake.

Taty gave him a seductive look, then winked. Matt recalled Lieutenant Martínez, the warmth of her skin, the electric feeling of her touch. Was he imagining it? Sex was the last thing on his mind and he had not felt attracted in any way to her or—God forbid—this flamboyant gay guy. But there was something in the air: a lurid, coarse cloud of pheromones floating over their heads. That might just be a Cuban thing, all interactions seemed permeated by subtle, and not so subtle, carnal innuendos. But not all Cubans were like that. Yarmila hadn't acted like the hot-to-trot, sexy Latina that Estrada was sure Matt was chasing. She hadn't acted that way with him, anyway. Maybe with Pato Macho.

Oh, forget it!

Taty returned to the kitchen, walking with an inviting swish-swash of his hips. Isabel gave the party a strained smile.

"Ah, teenagers—what is one going to do with them?"

Her apron was stained with *sofrito*. Matt tried not to stare at the spots. He was ready to ask if her *casa particular* was available, when Isabel said, with a sincere expression of concern, "It's getting late for you to find a hotel, Mateo, and it isn't advisable to go out at night by yourself, at least not in Centro Habana. Things are hairy here."

Matt couldn't help smiling at the phrase. Though he had never heard it, he assumed "hairy," in that context, meant difficult or tough. Yarmila had once promised to teach him Cuban slang.

"I could call my friend Anne and ask if there is an empty room in the house where she is now," he answered. "But as you said, it's late. Originally, I had intended—"

"I know." Isabel said. "I totally understand, my dear. If you want to stay with us, you are very welcome. *Mi casa es su casa*."

"I do not want to impose."

"You are not imposing! Please, consider us as if we were your very own family. We are all friends through—her."

Matt's throat closed. He couldn't disguise his emotion. Isabel put a hand on his shoulder and squeezed. Padrino looked away and so did Luis. Isabel shot them both a warning glance and coughed.

"We have a room," she explained, turning to Matt. "Small but recently painted and renovated, with its own bathroom and everything. Eh, *viejo*?" she prompted her husband. "Tell him."

Despite being called an old man, Luis smiled pleasantly and said, "Yes, it is a penthouse. It has the best views in Havana."

"Quiet too. No street noises."

"And very, very clean."

After extolling the virtues of the room for several minutes, Isabel finally came down to the price. She would charge Matt only fifteen dollars a night, breakfast included.

"And the first night is free," Luis added.

"That's so nice of you," Matt said. "Thanks."

"Don't mention it," Isabel patted his hand. "As I said, we are *familia*."

"So you guys own a *casa particular* and a restaurant?" Matt asked.

"Kind of," Isabel replied, after a brief hesitation. "They are—how would you say? Separate entities. La Caldosa is a legit *paladar*, but I haven't gotten around to the legal stuff for the *casa* yet. It's too darned expensive! I have to pay a fee before I can even register it as a rental for tourists. Then the inspectors show up and ask for money too. I can't afford that now."

"I see."

"So, if someone happens to ask, we'll say you are just staying here as a friend, which you are."

Luis and Padrino had begun to discuss food providers. "The pound of pork costs seven CUCs at the Cuatro Caminos Farmers' Market," Luis was saying. "But I'd rather buy it from a guy that brings it to us for eight."

"I bought a precision scale and always weigh everything here to make sure I'm getting what I'm supposed to get," Isabel said.

"These farmers are the worst kind of thieves. One needs eyes in the back of one's head when dealing with them! But they know better than trying to fool me."

Someone knocked at the door and stepped inside without waiting for a response. The newcomer was a young, tall, dark-haired man in denim shorts and a muscle shirt.

"We are closed, *coño*!" Isabel yelled. "Go away!"

"Come back tomorrow," Luis stuttered, avoiding the young man's gaze.

"Sorry," the man said. His voice was oddly thin for someone his size.

He turned away and left.

"People don't get it." Isabel shrugged. "They don't understand that when the sign is off, it means we aren't serving anyone."

Luis locked the door. Matt registered an expression of shock on Padrino's face.

"Is he a regular client?" Matt asked. "I don't want you guys to lose business because of me."

"We don't know him," Isabel said. "Don't worry."

Luis went to the kitchen and Padrino got busy with the *tocinillo* leftovers. Matt had the impression that La Caldosa's proprietress was hiding something.

ISABEL DIDN'T ACCEPT ANY money for the dinner, not even a tip, but took thirty dollars for the room.

"This is to start," Matt said. "I don't have any idea how long I'll be here. That's up to the Cuban police."

"You can stay as long as you want, dear," Isabel said. "We will take care of you."

Before he could see the penthouse, she insisted he take a tour of the apartment. When they passed by the kitchen, where the contents of the suitcase had been spread over the counter, Matt didn't see the brand-new set of knives or the Cuisinart Elite food processor he had bought at Williams Sonoma. Had Isabel and Luis put them away already or had someone stolen them? Gordo, the other cops, Yarmila's neighbors? In any case, there was plenty of stuff left for the couple: assorted pans and pots, mixing bowls, cookie sheets—all the items that he had lovingly chosen for Yarmila and she hadn't lived to enjoy.

He followed his hosts and pretended to admire the rooms, each of them with their own TV set, as Luis remarked. The biggest one, with a sixty-four-inch screen, was the centerpiece of a bedroom turned into a living room. Isabel pointed to a velvety tapestry that depicted tigers, deer, peacocks, and pink flamingos sunning together at a lakeshore.

"It's made in China," she smiled proudly. "Very elegant, eh?"

"Oh, yes."

"Now Taty will take you to the penthouse while I finish cleaning up here," she said after the grand tour ended. "If you need anything, just come down and knock on our door. Luis and I don't go to bed until well past midnight."

Taty led him outside. A domino table had been set up on the sidewalk and four men played loudly while two others lingered nearby, offering comments, curses and advice. They were all puffing on cigars and the smoke twirled around the tiles, lending the group a ghostly aspect.

Next to La Caldosa was a four-story apartment building. The door opened directly to the stairs.

"It's just a little climb, mister," Taty said encouragingly.

Up they went. The young man carried a flashlight because all the staircase light bulbs had been stolen recently, he explained.

"But the room is very safe. You are going to love it. Everybody loves Isabel's penthouse! It's the best kept secret in Centro Habana."

Taty wiggled his butt in Matt's face all the way to the rooftop.

HAVING NOTHING BUT A three-foot parapet between his body and Salvador Allende Avenue, which stretched forty feet below, was frightening but offered Matt a distinct view of Havana's nocturnal face—a shimmering maze under the stars. The tall, lit-up frames of the hotels told them apart from the smaller, darker and plainer apartment buildings.

To his left, the steeple of the tallest church in the city, Sagrado Corazón de Jesús, glowed against the night sky. To the right he saw El FOCSA Building, where he and Yarmila had once eaten at La Torre restaurant. He tried to find Coppelia, the ice-cream parlor that they had also visited together, but couldn't locate it.

"We call it the Ice Cream Cathedral," Yarmila had told him. "It has the best flavors in the world."

There had been around two hundred people waiting in line under the sun. Matt refused to be part of it, but Yarmila insisted that the oversized queue was part of the experience. "The bigger the better!" she had said enthusiastically. At his request, they had gone up a spiral staircase to the tourist (CUC-only) section, a separate area on the second floor that was built like a flying saucer. In the end, Coppelia came as something of a disappointment. The ice cream's texture reminded him of Häagen-Dazs, but there were only three flavors—chocolate, vanilla and pineapple—and the presentation couldn't even compete with a humble Dairy Queen sundae. He was served a small cup of chocolate ice cream crowned with a dab of whipped cream and a dollop of syrup; there were no sprinkles, maraschino cherries or fudge. But he had truly liked a government owned pizzeria called La Romanita, where she had also taken him . . .

Matt looked up and the shine of the unclouded stars dazed him like an explosion of fireworks. He had never seen such a clear sky, except for on a short visit to Mount Shasta. He stood in quiet awe, enjoying the fragrance of a night-blooming jasmine that grew inside a metal tub. The planter was set against the wall of a boxy, eight-by-eight-foot cement shed built in the middle of the rooftop. Matt also saw what appeared to be strawberries in smaller metal containers scattered around the shed. Strawberries in the heart of Havana! But he couldn't be sure in the semi-darkness, which was only broken by the flashlight.

"Luis grows all sorts of veggies here," Taty said. "The man has a green thumb. If you ever want tomatoes, cucumbers or onions, you don't need to go very far."

There were more tubs, all brimming with huge vegetables. Matt walked around the roof garden, looking for the apartment. Taty opened the door to the shed and turned on a fluorescent lamp inside.

"Come in, mister!" he called.

"Is this the—the penthouse?" Matt asked, torn between irritation and incredulity.

You must be kidding me.

"Yes, of course. Isn't it awesome? Make yourself at home, mister."

"Please, don't call me mister," he blurted out, annoyed. "My name is Matt."

"Yes, I know that." Taty smiled, charmingly bitchy. "I was just trying to be courteous, since you are a *Yuma* and all that jazz. You don't want to be called *compañero*, do you?"

"Just call me Mateo."

"Fine, don Mateo, come and see your boudoir."

Matt considered his options. He could send Taty to *la casa del carajo*, the Cuban equivalent of hell. Or he could put up with the little twerp for a few more minutes and finish the day in peace. Where else could he go at that hour? He groaned and went into the shed. It was furnished with a single bed, a crude pine table, a derelict chair, and a twelve-inch TV set mounted on the wall.

"No remote, sorry," Taty said. "I think a guest left with it. Accidentally, I mean. Because who would want to steal an old Cuban remote?"

The only window didn't have a latch, but there were four metal bars outside. A faded flowery curtain waved in the wind.

"Close the window if you don't want the morning light to wake you up," Taty said, fluffing up the pillows. "Oh, man! See how comfy they are? You are going to sleep like a king."

In contrast with his slender body, the young man's hands were big, with short, strong and knotted fingers—the hands of a stonemason.

Matt examined the place, still in shock. The walls were painted dark blue and the ceiling was Pepto-Bismol pink, a combination that made the space look smaller and claustrophobic. A toilet and a rudimentary shower had been built in a corner, with a white vinyl curtain separating them from the rest of the room. He tried to hide his frustration. The barely three-star Hotel Colina where he had stayed the previous year was a palace compared to this. He wondered why Yarmila had thought they would be better off here than in her own home—a *real* apartment with a *real* bathroom, after all.

"Do you like it?" Taty asked.

"Yes, it's nice."

"Breezy too. But if it gets too hot, turn on the fan."

He pointed to a refurbished General Electric fan.

"I'm off now," he smiled. "Unless you want company, of course."

"I'd rather be alone."

"Okay. Let us know if you need anything. We all go to bed late. Just don't call at five in the morning! Have a great night, mis—er, don Mateo."

Taty giggled and closed the door behind him. Matt dropped his backpack on the floor, flopped down on the bed and stared at the Pepto-Bismol ceiling.

Chin my fucking gao, as Estrada would say.

AFTER A SOAPLESS ROOM temperature shower (room temperature being close to eighty degrees), Matt dried himself with the same clothes he had been wearing all day long. There were no towels or toilet paper in sight. But he tried to keep a brave face.

This isn't the Hyatt, but Isabel didn't expect me to show up tonight. I'll buy some toiletries tomorrow. It's no big deal.

Feeling wired up and exhausted at once, he went outside and paced along the rooftop. It ended abruptly in a section that was missing the parapet. There was another building three feet away and he apprehensively eyed the chasm that separated them. An open door led to a staircase and he saw someone coming up.

Not wanting to be mistaken for a peeping tom, Matt moved in the opposite direction, back toward "the penthouse." The beauty of the night fell heavily on his shoulders, like a lead cape embroidered with his losses. It was a night for lovers, and the word gave him a chill. But he forbade himself to think again about Yarmila or Pato Macho.

It could have turned out worse. I am here, fed and clean, not in a dirty cell at the Unidad.

He bent over to smell the jasmine flowers. The tub garden encircled the shed, surrounding it with containers where garlic, parsley and cilantro grew side by side. There was a small barrel with peppers and fist-sized red fruits he couldn't identify, even after tasting them. They were sweet with a hint of tartness.

Cubans were ingenious, he had to give them that. He could have planted his own garden at home, in the backyard, and had fresh vegetables for over nine months of the year. But why bother when he could buy them at Whole Foods?

Necessity is the mother of invention. How did Cubans say it? *La necesidad hace parir hijos machos.* Necessity makes you bear male children. Yarmi had hated that saying. "It means that boys are more useful than girls!" she'd said once, indignant. She was a feminist, though Matt didn't think they talked a lot about feminism here.

Matt was about to cut a jasmine flower when he touched something squashy and slick. He let out a yelp and retrieved his hand fast.

Good grief. He hoped nobody had heard him. What a *pendejo Yuma.* It had to be a worm, a centipede or some other inoffensive tropical creature that had made its nest there. Oh wait, there were two of them. Three. Four. No, there were five, as long as a man's finger, creeping over the leaves like a stream of black oil. Matt backed off, disgusted, and returned to the room.

He closed the door, turned off the light and got in bed. It welcomed him with a promise of pleasant dreams, or better yet, no dreams at all. But a crazy carrousel danced inside his head, playing snippets of conversations, bringing images back to life. *Did you know Banzer was a brutal dictator? What about Pato Macho? I am so sorry.* Pedro's buzz cut. Lieutenant Martínez's massive behind. Isabel's stained apron. The *arroz con pollo.* Padrino's white clothes.

Taty's smile. *Mister . . . mister.* And floating above them Yarmila, her intense brown eyes, now closed forever. Words from her last email: *Have you bought the ticket already? Let me know so I can wait for you at the airport. Wait for you at the airport—*

A sudden noise roused him. It sounded like the rattle of a metal tub being dragged across the floor.

Is someone outside? Isabel? That little fag?

Then he saw it through the curtain: a tall, muscular figure silhouetted against the sky.

Matt didn't move. He closed his eyes and, like a scared child, willed the apparition away. When he dared to look around again, there were no traces of the stranger. He peered outside. He found only darkness and silence, and the overpowering aroma of the night-blooming jasmine in the air. Just to be safe, he closed the window. It became hot at once, so he turned on the electric fan and went back to bed. This time, sleep came before he even had time to summon it.

PART II

Chapter One

PATO MACHO

Matt woke up disoriented. It took him several minutes to remember where he was—and why he was there. The room was dark and warm. The feeble breeze from the electric fan was no match for Havana's humid heat; the temperature had risen to ninety-one degrees. A thin layer of sweat coated his body and left a salty bitterness on his lips. There was a damp spot where his head had rested all night. He walked barefoot to the "bathroom corner" and took another tepid shower. He put shampoo on the mental list of items he was planning to get that day. The toilet, he soon discovered, wouldn't flush.

Such a penthouse.

DRESSED IN DENIM SHORTS and a gray T-shirt, Matt went outside to breathe in fresh air. A floor below the rooftop, someone had hung a white sheet to dry on a clothesline strung across the balcony. The soft wind made it blow and billow like a miniature sail. He remembered the intruder he had spotted by the window but now, in broad daylight, it looked like a trick played by his sleep-deprived brain. He inspected the shed's surroundings.

The tubs were exactly where they had been the night before. He also poked around the jasmine plant and failed to see the slippery critters that had freaked him out almost as much as the apparition.

He exhaled, relieved. There had been no scary stranger and no mysterious bugs.

He'd been exhausted and spooked. Hey, who could blame him? *But things are okay now, aren't they?* Lieutenant Culo Grande was in charge of the case. She looked like a capable woman. In the meantime, Matt needed to find Yarmila's parents and offer them his condolences. She'd never said anything about Matt meeting them, but still—he had to do the right thing and visit them.

Matt heard a soft thump-thump behind him and turned around instinctively. The metal bat that had been aimed at his head only managed to brush his left shoulder.

"What the hell—?"

He faced a tall man who looked vaguely familiar. He was a young and handsome human specimen, despite being disheveled and crazy-eyed. Matt could have made a run for it. He was closer to the stairs than his attacker was. The guy was too drunk to catch up with him, but he was also stronger and probably faster.

"Your lucky day, *cabrón*," the man said, putting the bat down. He staggered and leaned on the shed's door.

Was he a thief? But Matt had always heard that Havana was a safe place for foreigners.

"What do you want?" he asked.

"It is your lucky day, *cabrón*," the other repeated. "Mine too because I could have killed you and then what? Hear that, *gringo hijo de la gran puta*? I could have killed you, just like you killed her."

"Killed *her*?"

The guy, he recalled in a flash, was the same one who had come into La Caldosa after closing time.

"Yes, Yarmila."

Matt backed away quietly until he reached the parapet.

"You are crazy," was all he could say, in English. All Spanish words had deserted him.

"Don't talk mumbo jumbo to me," the stranger brandished the bat again in an alarming way. "I could just crush your brains, you know?"

The young man's eyes were bloodshot. There were tears in them, ready to roll down his tanned cheeks. He had a gold chain around his neck with a medal of some saint Matt didn't recognize. He spoke again, softly this time.

"I loved her," he said.

A wave of heat washed over Matt. He felt dizzy. He held on to the parapet and looked down to the street. The white sheet was flapping in the wind like a surrender flag.

"I thought you did it because you knew about us," the young man added.

She had a lover, a citizen known as Pato Macho. They had been together since last October.

"Are you—Pato Macho?" Matt asked.

"I am," the man answered with pride, as if there were something particularly honorable in being called a male duck.

"I didn't know about you—you guys, until that cop told me," Matt said.

The blood drained from Pato Macho's face. "They told you," he said flatly.

"How else would I have known?" Matt shrugged and did his best to appear indifferent, if not unafraid.

"So you didn't do it?" Pato Macho insisted, caressing the metal bat. "You didn't kill her?"

"Of course I didn't!"

I can't believe I'm having this conversation with Yarmi's lover.

"You didn't mind it, then?"

"Mind what?"

"Me. Me and her."

Matt inhaled deeply and chose to ignore the question.

"You are a *cabrón con ganas*," Pato Macho snickered. "I told her many times. I was right."

Though he had never heard the expression, Matt sensed he had been called a happy cuckold. "I didn't know a thing, *comemierda*!" he screamed, losing control. "Had I suspected it—"

"Yes, what?"

"I'd have ended our relationship. I wouldn't be here now!"

A noise came from the stairs. Pato Macho's body tensed up. A moment later he jumped to the nearest rooftop, throwing the metal bat away.

"Yarmi liked me best!" he shouted, before disappearing into the other building's stairwell. "I was *el hombre de su vida*, the real man in her life!"

With that he vanished. Matt stood motionless by the jasmine plant. Pato Macho's last words were more painful than the blow to his shoulder, which was gradually turning red under his T-shirt.

He returned to the shed and picked up his backpack from the floor. He started to feel inside, looking for a bottle of aspirin (he was sure he had brought one) when his hand touched a small box. He took it out and opened it. The size-five gold engagement ring shimmered in the red velvet cushion. He threw the box over the parapet. Then he sat on the bed, tortured by images of Pato

Macho and Yarmila together, making love, eating ice cream at Coppelia, laughing. Laughing at him.

"AH, YOU'RE UP ALREADY!" Isabel came in carrying a plastic tray. "Good morning, dear. I brought you a Cuban-style breakfast, *café con leche* and bread with butter. And I didn't spill anything!"

She placed the tray on the pine table.

"Do you know where I could find a phone?" he asked.

"We have one downstairs. You can even make long distance calls."

"It's a local number. I need to get in touch with the detective who questioned me yesterday. She wanted to know for sure where I'd be staying."

Isabel's demeanor changed at once.

"No way!" she yelled. "You can't do that!"

Matt's back stiffened. *What in the world got into her? Is everybody crazy here or what?*

Isabel wheezed and added in a softer tone, "Sorry, but you can't let the police know that I have a *casa particular*. I told you I haven't gotten my license yet."

"I'll tell them that you are letting me stay for free," he said. "Anyway, they probably suspect it. It was a cop who brought me here last night, remember?"

She frowned. "They know everything," she said. "Every single thing that happens, they find out. They even find out *before* it happens. The Committees for the Defense of the Revolution are always watching. Nothing escapes them."

Back at La Caldosa, Isabel handed Matt a cell phone. It was an old and heavy model, with punch buttons, but it did have caller ID. He dialed the number Martínez had given him and the answering machine picked up.

"This is Lieutenant Marlene Martínez from Unidad 13. Leave a message."

He simply said he was staying with La Caldosa's owners, in 902 Salvador Allende Avenue.

"Please, let me know when I can get my passport back," he added.

He didn't want to mention the incident with Pato Macho in front of Isabel. After hanging up, he felt an acute pain in his shoulder. He had almost forgotten it.

"Do you have anything that can help me with this?" he asked, lifting his sleeve. An angry purple bruise had started to spread over his bicep.

"*Ay, pobrecito*! Who did that to you?"

"The cops, when they dragged me out to the police car yesterday." He didn't like to lie, but there was no way of explaining what had happened without sounding silly or worse, a coward and a *cabrón*.

"Bastards! They didn't even respect the fact that you are a foreigner. I don't know what this world is coming to. Let me get you some arnica."

"And a couple of ibuprofens."

"Ibu what?"

"An aspirin will do."

"Ah, yes. Another guest left me a bottle of Bayer aspirins. I'll bring you one." Isabel turned on the big-screen TV, but Matt paid no attention to it. He kept reliving the scene on the rooftop, playing it in his mind and berating himself for his naiveté.

I should have known Martínez was right the minute she told me about Pato Macho. And maybe he had. But he hadn't wanted to admit it to her—or himself. *Yarmi didn't care about me.* That was why she never said that she would marry him or move to San

Diego. That was why she was always distant and a bit cold, even in bed. He'd been blind, just like Anne, who believed that young stud was into her.

But let's take stock here. Things weren't that bad after all. Crazy Pato could have hurt him badly or killed him. Now . . . was Matt going to stay at the "penthouse" like a pendejo, waiting for that dickhead to come back and finish the job? So he could remind Matt again that he, Pato Macho, not this cuckold *Yuma*, was Yarmi's man? *Hell, no.*

Isabel brought him more *café con leche* and two aspirins.

"Are you feeling better?"

He didn't but said yes, wanting her to go away.

I'll ask Anne tonight if I can move in with her.

Matt had met Anne the year before at El Refugio. Yarmila had suggested it, saying that it was a well-established, reputable *paladar*. That evening Anne had been the only other American there, sitting all by herself. She had joined Matt and Yarmi and started chatting in English.

"I've been in Cuba for two weeks," she said. "Total Spanish immersion!"

"My Spanish is still rusty," Matt admitted.

"So is my English," Yarmila chimed in. "But we all can communicate, and that's what matters."

Matt had been proud of his bilingual girlfriend. Anne looked impressed. Yarmila was the first Cuban she had met who spoke English fluently.

"If I didn't know Spanish, my boyfriend and I would have to use sign language," she laughed.

Anne and Matt hit it off, more so after finding out that they both were from California; she lived in West LA and traveled often to San Diego. Back home, they had kept in contact, calling each other to talk about their Cuban crushes and discuss wedding plans. Matt's wedding plans, that is, though Anne had hinted that she might also marry Yony someday.

I need to have a word with her about that. That little prick probably cheats on her too.

Matt felt a wave of resentment against all Cubans. It wasn't fair or logical, but nothing that had happened to him in the last two days was fair or logical. He closed his eyes and ignored the TV—the program was a mind-numbing report about potato crops on the Isle of Youth. Then he heard Taty say, in a sing-songy voice, "Oh, mister—sorry, don Mateo, you're here! Good thing because I was planning to go upstairs and wake you up with a good-morning kiss."

"Hi," Matt sighed.

"How are you doing?"

"Just fine."

"Any plans for today?"

Matt didn't feel like talking. He pretended to be interested in the potato news.

"I know you must be sad and hurting . . . I mean no disrespect." Taty cleared his throat and smiled coyly. "But if you have nothing else to do this evening, would you like to visit Café Arabia? This is my free night here so I work there to make ends meet."

"Is it another *paladar*?" Matt asked. He didn't want to encourage Taty, but there was no need to be rude either.

"No, it's more like a nightclub, a chic one. Don't think of a run-of–the-mill joint. It is a very classy lounge."

Taty leaned closer to Matt, so close he could smell the young man's spicy cologne. His cheeks were rosy. Matt suspected he was wearing powder or foundation, or whatever it was that women put on their faces.

This one must know about Pato Macho too. Why would he ask me to go to a bar a day after my girlfriend's death?

"Thanks, but I'm not the lounge type," he said. "And I've made plans already."

"Where are you going, if you don't mind me asking?"

Pendejo. I do mind.

"I'm meeting some friends at El Refugio."

"El Refugio! Great choice! That's less than five blocks from Café Arabia. Why don't you invite your friends to come?"

He took a card from his pocket, handed it to Matt and flexed his biceps toward him.

"Enjoy an unforgettable evening straight from One Thousand and One Nights, San Lázaro 177. Let us work our magic on you!" the card read.

"Taty, where are you, *coño*?" Isabel yelled from the kitchen. "Come clean the rice, quick! It's full of *gorgojos*."

"*She* is the *gorgoja*," he whispered in Matt's ear. "What a pest!"

Matt remembered a post Yarmila had written about making Cuban-style rice. She mentioned the *gorgojos*—they were weevils, or a similar kind of bug.

"The first show starts at 8:00 P.M.," Taty said. "Think about it, don Mateo. Stop by. Do it for me. See, I get a commission when I bring in new patrons. See you!"

He hurried to the kitchen and began to help Isabel. She was making the night's special—*picadillo*, mincemeat cooked with tomatoes, raisins and olives, served over white rice with fried plantains.

"It should have fried potatoes too, to give it more consistency," Isabel said. "But the *bisneros* haven't brought them in weeks. Let me know if you hear of someone selling potatoes, eh, Taty."

"*Ay*, mama, dream on! The only way to get potatoes in Havana is to place a basket under the TV set and wait for them to drop inside."

"Yep. Every time they start bragging about some super-duper crop, we can forget about it."

Matt turned down the volume and listened to their chat. Taty reminded him of a chef he had once interviewed at a French-Italian fusion restaurant in Hillcrest, a gay guy who had been interested in Matt. The chef let it be known, but didn't attempt to come on to him as aggressively as Taty did.

The documentary had ended. The next program featured schoolchildren in uniform, with red kerchiefs and red berets, singing: *Arriba los pobres del mundo, de pie los esclavos sin pan.* Matt recognized the melody. The kids were singing "The Internationale." *Arise ye workers from your slumbers, arise ye prisoners of want.*

This is surreal. Estrada would want me to write a story for El Grito. Oh, he wouldn't even need to fluff it up. It already had all the elements: pretty Cuban girl, stupid American, handsome native guy, and androgynous temptress. Er, tempter. *Our man in Havana. Our pendejo in Havana.*

"Was Taty bothering you?"

Matt jumped at Isabel's question. She had brought him a glass of orange juice.

"No, not at all." He tasted the juice. It was fresh squeezed, cold and refreshing.

"The kid is trying to figure things out," she said, sitting next to him on the sofa. "His father kicked him out of the house because he is a *mariconcito*, as you can plainly see."

Matt finished the juice and handed Isabel the empty glass, hoping she would return to the kitchen. But she kept on talking, "Last Christmas there was an incident in his neighborhood, a problem with another guy. Taty's father got so mad that he beat him up and told him never to come back because his behavior was bringing shame to the family. That's how people in the countryside are. Barbarians! Thank God that I was here for him." She paused and lifted her breasts. "Taty's mother was a good friend of mine. When she died three years ago, I swore I would take care of her *niño* if he ever needed me. He has no one else in the whole world, except for his godmother, who lives in Las Villas, up in the ass end of the world. So I offered him a job and let him sleep in the apartment when he wants to—I see him as another son. I always wanted several children, but could only have one because of my ovarian problems."

Matt had listened to her speech in respectful silence, but the ovarian revelation made him cringe.

"May I use your bathroom?" he asked.

"Yes, come with me. Let's make sure we have toilet paper, if you are going to need it."

"Thanks."

"Are you?"

"Excuse me?"

"Will you need paper? Let me know so I can give you a roll."

Yarmila had once written about how difficult it was to find paper towels and toilet paper, which were luxury items in Havana. Matt had found it funny at the time.

"Gracias, Isabel," he said. "No paper now, thank you very much."

He slammed the bathroom door in her face.

Cream of cheese: Memories of La Romanita

Today we will *mangiare* a dish that has Italian roots. Very *Italiano*, but with a Cuban twist.

This entrée is called *crema de queso*. Our Cuban "cream of cheese" is basically a soup, but very thick.

The ingredients are easy to find: three tablespoons of butter, the same amount of all-purpose flour, three cups of milk, and five ounces of cheese. Plus salt, cumin, pepper, and nutmeg to taste.

Make a base by mixing butter and flour. Cook for five minutes, or until it looks golden brown. Add the milk and stir. After it thickens, add the cheese and go on stirring. It will soon be totally dissolved into the cream. Sprinkle with salt, pepper, and cumin. Go easy on the cumin!

Serve immediately, topped with shredded cheese. Don't let it get cold. There are some dishes that benefit from a quick nap, but *crema de queso* isn't one of them. If you do need to refrigerate it, add a bit of water or milk before reheating to prevent the soup from becoming too heavy.

When I think of *crema de queso*, the first thing that comes to my mind is La Romanita, a pizzeria located on 11th St., on the corner with 16th St., in El Vedado. I had just moved to Havana and part of my budding romance with the capital was discovering new places to eat every week. I lived at the students' residence and used to take long walks around the neighborhood, sniffing the air until my nose led me to a little restaurant or a well-hidden cafeteria.

These walks were an adventure for a *guajirita* like me, a peasant girl fresh out of Cuba's Cinderella, as Pinar del Río, my province of origin, is derisively called. I got lost a few times. There were no mountains to get myself oriented, only apartment buildings, and at first they all looked alike.

My best friends, Lili and Yusleidys, were also *guajiras*. Havana-born girls were too hoity-toity to hang out with us.

"Wait until they visit our provinces and *then* we will show them," Yusleidys said.

Sadly, that never happened. "Cuba is Havana, and the rest is just countryside," Habaneros would say.

Most restaurants were way over our budget—we did get a small stipend, but it wasn't enough to eat at fancy places. Yet, for La Romanita, we would make sacrifices or ask our families for money. We would pool together our savings and share two pizzas, two creams of cheese, and a flan.

Cheesy kisses to all my readers. *Buona sera* to you!

COMMENTS

Taos Tonya said. . .

I plan to make it tonight. I am having some friends over and we will have a Cuban night. What cheese do you use for the *crema*? Gouda, Asiago?

Yarmi said. . .

Here we only have yellow cheese and white cheese. I use yellow. A Cuban night sounds like fun!

Cubanita in Claremont said. . .

My family is part Italian and I've never heard of that dish.

Maritza said. . .

I am Cuban too. My family left in 1979. I don't remember being able to buy flour at the grocery store. It was sold through the ration card every two or three months. Does your *Yuma* buy it for you? (Wink). My grandma would make a similar dish out of spaghettis, which she boiled and then grinded. She used yellow cheese, whatever kind was available. Here, I would use Gouda.

Yarmi said. . .

The spaghetti base makes sense. I get flour at the grocery store, like everybody else.

Anita said. . .

I haven't heard of *crema de queso* either, at least in California.

Cocinera Cubana said. . .

Juan, Anita, if you go to Miami, visit Marakas Pizza on 42nd Street. They have the best *crema de queso*. Ciao!

Chapter Two

EL REFUGIO

In less than a year El Refugio had gone from chrysalis to butterfly, from humble *paladar* to a star-studded restaurant featured in a Lonely Planet guidebook. When Matt came in, he didn't recognize the polished oak tables, recently varnished but with their Old World charm intact, or the upholstered chairs that lent the room a certain aristocratic air. A bronze and glass chandelier lamp had replaced the cheap, plastic Tiffany knockoff that Anne had made fun of in their first meeting ("courtesy of Walmart—how did it end up in Havana?"). Handcrafted copper sconces, placed over each table, guaranteed that patrons could actually see their entrées. But the most outstanding addition was a wall covered in photos of foreign celebrities (actors, athletes, and singers) posing with the owner or enjoying a meal. Matt hoped that the only thing they had *not* changed was their menu. *Pollo al ajo*, spicy garlic chicken, had been the main attraction of the house, the culinary specialty of the chef and restaurateur, Ricardito Rendón.

Ricardito had also changed. In the most recent pictures he looked more rotund than ever—and he had not been a thin man to start with. Anne, who was a longtime customer of the *paladar*, had told Matt that the owner used to hold a high post in the Cuban Young Communist League as a *dirigente*, a youth leader, during the early nineties. He was later deposed and confined to the "Pajama Plan," which meant he had been sent home with a salary while forbidden to participate in public life again.

"He went from standing at Castro's side during his three-hour speeches to being a social black hole," she explained. "People didn't hear about him for years. Some even thought he had gone to Miami."

Meanwhile, the astute Ricardito bloomed in the relative obscurity of the private sector. After he opened the restaurant, the foreign friends he had made during his tenure as *dirigente* kept him busy, as did the affluent natives, who flocked to the *paladar* out of curiosity to see the former Young Communist leader in his new, humbler incarnation.

"Ricardito doesn't mind it because he laughs all the way to the bank," Anne said. "He did the right thing when he exchanged that old Che Guevara beret for a chef's apron. A man of his time, that's what he is."

The restaurant's fame had spiderwebbed over the city and beyond. It was now labeled "an iconic eatery specializing in New Cuban cuisine."

El Refugio, like most *paladares*, accepted only CUCs.

ANNE WAS SITTING AT the best table, next to a picture window overlooking Malecón Drive. With a sleeveless blue summer dress, oval diamond earrings, and a delicate necklace made of silver discs, she looked like a model taken off the pages of *Condé Nast Traveler*. Matt was relieved that Yony wasn't there yet because the idea of explaining Yarmila's death in Spanish horrified him. But Anne wasn't alone; a young, shapely woman stood next to her.

The woman smiled and kissed Matt on the cheek as if she had known him forever.

"Welcome to El Refugio, Mateo," she said. "Anita was telling me about your wedding plans. I'm thrilled for you! Congratulations!"

She wore a strong carnation scent with high notes of patchouli.

"Just so you know, we offer catering and can also take care of the entire party here," she went on cheerfully. "We do everything, from the wedding cake to the buffet, and provide entertainment if you want. We have a classical pianist, an excellent Buena Vista Social Club-style band, a jazz singer—you name it and we'll find it. We can even open another room, which is normally part of the house, for the reception."

Matt wondered if she was Ricardito's daughter. He knew his wife—a chubby, maternal older lady who was in charge of the desserts.

"Where is Yarmila?" Anne asked.

"She—um—couldn't come," Matt said. He coughed and the young woman took the hint.

"A waiter will be with you shortly," she said. "There is a new wine list and many cool cocktails. Our mixologist's latest creation is the Piñanguini. I will send you guys two on the house."

She left, her round butt high in the air, almost as big as Lieutenant Martínez's. Her conservative, two-piece beige business suit couldn't disguise her curves. Matt followed her with his eyes until she entered the kitchen.

"That's Ricardito's new wife, Leidy," Anne informed him.

"What about his *old* wife?"

"Mercedes? He divorced her. This girl is now his chief executive officer, or something of that sort. Ah, men! They are the same bastards everywhere. No offense to you, my friend."

Anne did not have wrinkles—they were kept at bay by Botox—but her motionless face betrayed a profound sadness that poured through her eyes and spilled over her tight cheeks.

"Yony isn't joining us?" Matt asked.

"He had to go on a business trip. That's what he said, not that I believe it."

"Why? He is a taxi driver," Matt offered, happy to stretch the conversation about Yony's shenanigans for as long as he could. "If he got a last-minute call . . ."

"He is an *illegal* taxi driver," Anne clarified. "He doesn't have a license yet."

She fell silent when the waiter, a young man with a shaved head and pierced ears, placed two cocktails on the table before them. Matt sipped his cautiously. It had a stick of pineapple on top and tasted of orange, marjoram and cinnamon.

"A bit too sweet," Anne said. "Now, enough of Yony and his lame stories. It doesn't matter. I don't care about him *that* much. What's going on with Yarmila?"

Matt took a long, deep breath.

"Why isn't she with you?" Anne insisted. "Did you guys have a fight?"

She had perked up. Her eyes twinkled.

"No," Matt said slowly. "Not really."

"Then? What's up? Just tell me!"

He told her. Everything.

"GOOD LORD," ANNE SAID. "Good merciful lord. Don't they say that Cuba is one of the safest countries in the Caribbean?"

"They say many things that aren't true."

"Poor girl! I was so looking forward to meeting her again. She had promised to cook for all of us, remember?"

Matt didn't but he didn't correct her.

"And the killer is still on the loose, I guess," she went on. "That's so horrible! I wonder if Yony knows. He didn't say anything."

"Cuban papers don't publish this sort of news. Though the grapevine is pretty active."

"Oh, my! I'm in shock." She did look like it. Her face had turned chalky. "So you can't leave now. But why—?"

"They are 'investigating' the case. I was afraid they would consider me a suspect, but I am only a person of interest."

"Big deal. At the very least, you should move out. What if Pato what's-his-name comes back?"

"I thought of going to the Colina Hotel. But without my passport, I'll probably have to get Lieutenant Martínez on board to explain what's going on. Last time I was there, I had the impression that the employees got nervous whenever they dealt with Americans, even under normal circumstances. They seemed afraid of doing or saying the wrong thing."

"Yeah, I've had the same experience in government-owned restaurants. Waiters are not sure if they should call me *señora* or *compañera*, or if it's okay to accept a tip." Anne rolled her eyes. "They can go from nice to nasty in a second. But *casa particular* owners are more flexible and understanding. After all, they are making money off us. I always stay at Villa Tomasa and only have good things to say about it. It's no five-star hotel, but—"

Leidy led a couple to a nearby table. The man was clearly a foreigner: tall, blond and sunburned. The woman, dark and petite, bore a striking resemblance to Yarmila. Both Matt and Anne noticed it, but didn't comment.

"You should come stay at the Villa too," Anne said. "The

owner, Román, is really sweet. The other two guests left this morning so he'll be more than happy to take you in."

"I appreciate it. But I don't want to get you in trouble."

"Why would *I* get in trouble?"

"If the owner asks to see my passport and I have to explain . . ."

"We'll tell him that you had a *problemita*, as Cubans say, at the airport, and your passport was withheld. Which isn't that uncommon, by the way. It happened to me once. He doesn't need to know about Yarmila."

"But the police may show up at his house."

"Well, you'll say they are solving your problem—*resolviendo*, Cuban style."

"Is Yony staying with you?"

"God forbid. Román wouldn't allow it. He's very picky about Cuban guests. Yony and I just go to a motel."

THE DINNER WAS QUIET. Anne hardly touched the *ropa vieja* (shredded beef) served with *moros y cristianos*—black beans cooked together with white rice.

"The white rice represents the Spaniards while the black beans symbolize the dark-skinned Moors that settled on the shores of the Guadalquivir River," read a description of the dish, typed on the menu in English, Spanish and French. "They merged their bloodlines and gave birth to a new race that changed the history of the Iberian Peninsula. Our *moros y cristianos* retain the best of the two ingredients, condensing them in a multicultural dish."

The entrée came with *plátanos verdes a puñetazos*, fried green plantains that took their name from the way the cook hit them, hard with the fist, after they were fried for the first time. Then they took a second dip into the frying pan filled with lard or, in the case of health-conscious chefs, olive oil. Ricardito had used lard.

To break the silence, Matt asked about their host's past. Anne, who liked to play the savvy cosmopolitan, chewed his ear off.

"He was top dog at the Young Communist League, a political farm where they recruit the more committed kids to become Party members. Ricardito created all the organization slogans like *'treinta y uno y palante,'* thirty-one and onward, to celebrate the thirty-first anniversary of the revolution. He organized rallies in support of the government and was Castro's right hand until the day he happened to yell, during a gathering at Revolution Square: *'Él que no salte es gusano,'* he who doesn't jump is a worm and then—"

"Why a worm?"

"That's what the government calls dissidents, worms."

"Oh, yes. So did *not* jumping imply that people were against Castro?"

"It was a silly thing to say, even Ricardito admits it now. Something he came up with in the spur of the moment, to get the masses fired up. Of course, all those old fat Communist Party militants felt that they *had* to jump high to prove their loyalty to the revolution. The incident marked the fall of poor Ricardito, who was sentenced to the 'Pajama Plan' the next week—and he was lucky he didn't end up in jail. Can you imagine Castro jumping up and down, with beard and everything?"

Not only Castro: it was hard to imagine Ricardito himself, who was pushing three hundred pounds, hopping like a kangaroo in the middle of Revolution Square, or anywhere else, for that matter.

"Is that true, Anne?"

"Se non è vero, è ben trovato." She laughed for the first time that night. "It's probably an urban legend, but I like to tell the tale."

She ordered a beer, and then another one. Matt didn't feel like drinking. He had barely tasted the cocktail.

For dessert they chose *natilla*, egg custard, and an éclair to share.

"So yummy," said Anne, enthusiastically savoring the chocolate crust of the éclair. "Whoever has replaced poor Mercedes in the kitchen is every bit as good, if not better."

They were having coffee (Anne's with a shot of whiskey) when Ricardito came to the table, all smiles, and asked how everything was.

"Delicious!" Anne pointed to the empty dessert plate. "This is the best one I've had here."

"Leidy knows just about everyone who is someone on the Havana food scene," Ricardito boasted. "She hired our new baker, a guy that used to work for the Canadian embassy and trained with a Le Cordon Bleu chef."

"The *natilla* was awesome too."

"Ah, Leidy made the *natilla* herself. That girl's got talent, eh! The day we are allowed to have private corporations in Cuba she will be the CEO of El Refugio Inc. because she has capitalist *mendó*."

Anne high-fived Ricardito.

"One has to have *mendó* in beautiful Cuba!" she said, slurring her words just a little.

The bill, with tip included, was seventy-five dollars. Anne insisted on paying it.

"It was my idea to come here."

"Fine—but I didn't remember El Refugio being so expensive before. It looks like Ricardito is catching up with American prices."

"YOU CAN'T GO BACK to that shithole," Anne said after they left the *paladar*. "We are going to Villa Tomasa, period."

"I'm concerned for you. They may want to talk to you too because you met Yarmila once. They know everything."

"They? Who are you talking about?"

"The police. La Seguridad. Both. I'm not sure how their laws work."

"This is ridiculous, Matt. You should tell the cops what happened and why you are moving to another place. They'll understand."

"Or not. This is Planet Mongo."

"That guy attacked you with a metal bat, for God's sake! What if *he* was the one who killed Yarmila?"

Matt hadn't considered it. He had avoided thinking of Pato Macho since the incident.

"Yeah, I may tell Detective Martínez after all." He sighed. "But he didn't look like . . . God, I don't know. I don't even want to—"

"In any case, you are coming with me now. You can send for your things tomorrow."

"All my things are with me." Matt patted his backpack. "I guess I wasn't planning to return to 'the penthouse.'"

"Good. You are getting yourself some *mendó*."

"What the heck is *mendó*?"

"Street-smarts, buddy. Something you and I sorely need if we want to survive in Cuba."

They crossed Malecón Drive, the roadway that stretches for about five miles along the Havana coastline. It was a busy outdoor hangout. There were couples sitting on the wall, families with children, lonely fishermen, older men smoking cigars, and young women in clothes made of lycra. Cops slunk among them while tourists strolled around. The *almendrones* driving under the dim street lights evoked a sense of time warp.

Anne walked unsteadily, tottering in her high heels. Her dress was wrinkled and even her diamond earrings appeared to have lost their shine. Though she tried to hide her tears, Matt saw them. He felt bad for her, and guilty. Shouldn't *he* be the one crying his eyes out? He had just lost his fiancée; the happy life he had created with her in his imagination had been shattered to pieces, and here he was so calm and composed . . . But he remembered that his fiancée had cheated on him with tall, handsome Pato Macho and that his imagined life might have never come to pass at all. The guilty feelings dissolved in the salty breeze that came from the ocean.

"I should have known better," Anne mumbled. "Anybody with a functioning brain would have known that a guy like Yony couldn't be in love with me. But that and then hearing about Yarmila—I'm sorry for her."

"Uh. Me too."

"They use us, Matt. These Cubans . . . they don't care about us. They don't see human beings with feelings, they see dollars. Walking cash. A visa. They are heartless."

"They use each other too," Matt reminded her. "Look at Ricardito and his manager-wife. Do you think she's in love him?"

"It's so dirty. I know it happens everywhere. But here it's more obvious, more in your face."

"Plus we are on the receiving end of it. *Pinches cubanos.*"

"What does that mean?"

"Damn Cubans, in Tijuana slang."

"Well said. Fuckers. And excuse my French."

A car with just one headlight on drove by sluggishly, like a giant iron bug, and covered them in exhaust fumes. They turned onto San Lázaro Street and left behind Malecón Drive.

"It's only a few blocks from here," Anne said. "You're going to like Villa Tomasa. The owner looks like a hippie and the house is relatively modern, with hot water, working showers, and, as they say, 'a color TV.'"

"Do you suppose they still use black and white sets?"

"You bet. I saw one when we visited Yony's sister. She has an old Russian television, huge and boxy. It only gets two channels—of the available three. Ah! All the Villa Tomasa rooms have air conditioning. This is rare here."

"How much does the Cuban hippie charge?"

"Thirty dollars a night, breakfast included. Román makes it himself. He's a great chef."

They passed by a lit-up door, the only bright place in an otherwise dark street. CAFÉ ARABIA read the small, pink neon sign. Music and laughs came from inside. Matt tried to look through the door, but the glass only mirrored back his own face, which wore a bewildered expression.

Anne turned to him. "What are you doing?"

"Is this a bar?"

"Probably a private one. They are called *bares clandestinos*."

"It doesn't seem very clandestine to me."

"They're tolerated, like *almendrón* drivers and other small businesses. Yony and I have been to some."

"Were they any good?"

"They were okay. Cold beer, Havana Club rum, cheap wine. But the mojitos were a rip-off. Way too christened."

They went on walking. Matt remembered the card Taty had given him. "Enjoy an unforgettable evening straight from One Thousand and One Nights."

Chapter Three

SMOKE AND MIRRORS

Villa Tomasa was an unassuming house that wouldn't qualify as a "villa" anywhere else: a plain one-story building with no architectural charm or definite style. But the lawn was cut and well-tended and the front porch newly painted and clean. There was a sign on the door, two blue triangles on a white background—the government-issued logo for the *casas particulares*. Below, another, bigger sign with red letters read: BIENVENIDO A VILLA TOMASA, DONDE SE SENTIRÁ COMO EN SU CASA. (Welcome to Villa Tomasa, where you will feel like at home.)

The door was unlocked. Matt and Anne came into a living room straight out of the fifties, with oil pastels on the walls—marinas and rural scenes—and five porcelain figurines on the mantel of a fireplace that had never been used. Two macramé plant hangers with healthy cacti and a teardrop lamp dangled from the ceiling, over a Rococo-ish coffee table with curved legs and a marble top. There was a Danish credenza in a corner, facing a yellow sectional and a black leather lounge chair. A shiny, flat-screen TV on top of the credenza looked like an anachronism in that setting. The room smacked of kitsch but in the right way, as if the designer had chosen to throw in a splash of tawdriness to make a statement.

A man was sprawled on the lounge chair, his eyes closed and a serene, Zen-like countenance. Anne touched him lightly on the shoulder and he opened his eyes.

"Ah, good evening, Anita." The Zen man noticed Matt. "And this gentleman is—"

"My friend Mateo, who wants to rent a room. He is an American like me, a journalist from California."

"Great. Thanks for bringing him in. Welcome, *señor*."

The man, who introduced himself as Román De La Porte, was dressed in faded blue jeans and a Lacoste shirt. A gold medal with a crucifix hung from his thick pink neck. He was sixty years old, short and red-faced, with blond hair that reached his shoulders. He accepted Anne's explanation about Matt's passport *problemita*.

"You see he has no luggage either," she said, surprising Matt with the added twist to the story. "They kept it too."

"These airport clerks always find a bone to pick with decent-looking foreigners," Román said.

"Hopefully, the issue will be cleared up soon. Matt has notified the higher-ups."

"Good for you, *señor*."

He asked to see the passport photocopy and added Matt's name and date of birth to the ledger.

"This is a formality, since you came with Anita. But just in case—"

His minimum was a three-night stay. Matt handed him ninety dollars.

"Don't you want to see the house first?" Román asked.

"I'm sure it will be fine."

Adjacent to the living room was the dining area, furnished

with a rectangular table that could accommodate eight people, matching chairs, and a china hutch in a corner. They were all old pieces, but had been meticulously restored. Instead of the original leather seats, the chairs were upholstered in velvet, a deep red, the same color as the window shutters. Set in the middle of the wall was a gilded portrait of a white-haired woman dressed in black.

"Nice place," Matt said, impressed. This was by far the most elegant room he had seen in Havana.

"I try to keep it up, which isn't easy," Román answered. "But at least it has no structural problems. Villa Tomasa was built in the early fifties, a 'capitalist' house, as people call them now. They last for a long time. They will still be standing when the last micro-brigade building falls down."

"Are those 'socialist' buildings?" Matt asked.

"Excuse me?"

"The micro—whatever you called them."

Román slapped his knees and laughed. "Ha, that's a good one! The micro-brigades were teams of volunteer construction workers, teachers and bureaucrats who had no training whatsoever as stonemasons or plumbers. All the houses they made fell apart in less than twenty years. *Pura mierda.*"

Anne went to the kitchen to "pour herself a little something." Román showed Matt one of the two available rooms.

"This has its own private bathroom," he said. "There is also a TV. Color, of course. It's small, but you are always welcome to watch the big one in the living room."

The night breeze made an art-deco pendant lamp sway above their heads. It had a brass top and an amber glass shade that bathed everything in golden light. The room was over furnished with a heavy mahogany queen bed covered in a ruffled red gingham bedspread, two nightstands, an armoire, and a faded

Oriental rug. A full-length mirror made the lamp's reflection bounce back.

A Smith-Corona typewriter sat on a roll-top desk next to a collection of *Reader's Digest* magazines from the fifties. The space exuded such a vintage mid-twentieth-century feel that the four Kenner *Star Wars* action figures placed on a wall shelf above the desk seemed utterly out of place. Darth Vader, Han Solo, Princess Leia, and R2-D2 (with a lightsaber) were displayed on a white lace doily that had become yellowish with time.

"Are they popular in Cuba?" Matt asked.

"*Star Wars?*" Román used the Spanish name, *La Guerra de las Galaxias*, Galaxy Wars. "Among some people, yes. I am a fan. I own around sixty figures, if not more."

"Some collection you have. How do you get them here?"

"Former guests send them to me or I buy them in the black market. They are my weakness—one of my weaknesses."

He laughed. A rose-scented air freshener mixed with incense floated around like an invisible cloud. A different, subtler smell emanated from Román's body and clothes, but Matt couldn't identify it.

"You can leave the window open." Román pulled back the window shades. "This is a safe neighborhood."

On the wall, a German cuckoo clock read nine o'clock.

The bathroom contained a small bathtub, a sink, a medicine cabinet, a toilet, and a pink marble bidet bigger than the other pieces.

"It's what is left of the original set," Román explained. "I've kept it because European women love bidets. We do have hot water, though it takes a while to warm up."

Matt looked forward to taking a long shower. A *real* shower, with soap and towels. His injured arm had started to hurt again.

"There are bars of Palmolive, and bottles of shampoo and conditioner." Román pointed to the medicine cabinet. "They are samples, but I have many of them. Now, to the most important room in Villa Tomasa!"

Matt followed him to the pantry area. Anne was still in the kitchen, having an aspirin with a glass of milk. An empty beer bottle sat on the table next to her. Román opened a well-stocked refrigerator.

"If you get hungry at night, come and get whatever you want," he said. "I will also make breakfast for you guys in the morning."

"Román's Spanish omelets are a real treat," Anne chimed in.

Their host smiled. "Thank you, my dear." He turned to Matt again. "Thirty dollars a day is what you pay for *your* use of the room, *señor*. If you decide to bring someone else to spend the night with you, we need to talk about it first, and the price goes up ten dollars."

Fat chance of that.

"No refrigerator privileges for nationals," Román went on. "Sorry about it, but my fellow Cubans have no impulse control. They eat *everything*. They make messes. They steal too. A girl once left in the middle of the night with a whole ham I had just bought."

"No worries. I don't plan to have any guests."

Román didn't seem convinced, but said affably, "That's all, my friend. Hope you enjoy your stay in Villa Tomasa."

"Tomasa is a beautiful name," Matt said.

He was thinking of an enterprising, pretty Tijuana cook who had a restaurant called Tomasita's Kitchen in San Ysidro.

"I named it after my grandmother, Tomasa Suarez De La Porte, the lady in the portrait."

"She looks very distinguished."

"Well, she was. Cuban nobility, you know, from the good old times. This used to be her house and she passed it on to me, God bless her soul. If it weren't for her, I would be eating a cable now."

Comiéndose un cable was a Cuban expression that meant going hungry.

"You have much more than cables to munch on," Matt quipped, thinking of the ham, cheese, eggs, and steaks that filled the refrigerator.

"Thanks to people like you, who keep me in business," Román said. "That's why I love to spoil my guests. You need something, you let me know. Whatever. I am here at your service."

AFTER ASKING ROMÁN FOR five aspirins and downing two right away, Matt took a lengthy, hot and comforting shower. His host's scent had lingered in the room and he finally recognized it.

Isn't pot illegal here? I mean, really illegal, like people go to prison for years if they are caught using? That's what Yarmi told me. She couldn't stand it. But maybe the government tolerated it, as they tolerated clandestine taxi drivers and bars.

He opened the window and let the fresh air in.

IT WAS 10:05 AND Matt wasn't sleepy yet. He didn't want to watch more local television, having had an ample serving of it that afternoon. He didn't want to be alone with his thoughts either. As he smiled at his reflection in the mirror (the amber light favored him, making him look younger and tanned), he had an inspiration. He could visit Café Arabia. With Anne—or better yet, without her.

He got dressed and left the room.

"Anita isn't feeling well," Román told him. "She asked me not to wake her up unless there was an earthquake or a tornado."

His speech had become slower and his eyes were glassy and unfocused. Matt saw four roaches on the table.

"Yes, she needs to rest," he said. "I'm going to sit on the Malecón wall for a while."

"No problem, take your time. I go to bed late."

Doesn't everybody in Havana? I guess it's because none of these people have real jobs.

"I'll be back before midnight. I only want to stretch my legs."

"Sure. Ah, a word of advice: leave your backpack home and don't take anything valuable with you."

"Are people mugged here often, Román?"

"Not every Monday and Thursday. But foreigners stand out, so be careful. Better safe than sorry."

Matt put thirty dollars in his pocket and checked the name and the address on the card that Taty had given him. "San Lázaro 177, Vedado."

Something had changed in the street. The breeze coming from the ocean was charged with stronger aromas. The people Matt encountered, women and men, looked at him with a marked curiosity or a veiled aggression that he had not perceived before. A female voice called to him, *"Oye, chico!"* but he pretended not to hear. A young guy on a bicycle got so close that Matt could smell the man's sweat. He felt eyes upon him. Havana had turned into a different city, more mysterious, seductive—and dangerous.

CAFÉ ARABIA WAS FULL. Matt had to wait ten minutes outside until a "table for one" was ready. Finally, he settled on the cushy chair that the hostess had assigned him and started to cough at once. Smoke was everywhere: hanging over the tables, on the stage like some kind of special effect, and around the patrons' mouths. It billowed in the air, forming a bluish veil that wrapped them in a mist of cigar smoke and alcohol fumes.

Though he had come from a poorly lit street, it still took Matt a few minutes to adjust his eyes to the dark room. Once they did, and after the coughing fit stopped, he noticed that more than half of the customers in the bar were women. There were long-haired, scantily dressed girls with high heels and purple lips that shone under the flickering lights, and heavyset, mature ladies wearing humungous wigs of impossible shades. He wondered if Taty had directed him to a *jinetera* nightclub. His suspicions increased when two women tried to attract his attention, smiling and making subtle and not-so-subtle gestures, one inviting him to her table, the other offering to join him.

Matt ignored them. He didn't want company—that kind of company, anyway. A waitress, pretty and perky, with dark tresses that brushed her butt, came to take his order. She brought a fake candle and showed him a wine and beer list laminated and glued to the table's surface. Matt pointed to a classic mojito—he wasn't particularly fond of them, but they appeared more innocuous than other concoctions with names like "Cuba Libre On Fire" or "Dark and Stormy."

He hadn't come to Café Arabia to get drunk or find women. In truth, he didn't know why he was there. So as not to crawl in bed too early, to escape from memories and self-recrimination, to forget that he had passed, in a matter of hours, from confident American fiancé to cuckold *Yuma* and "person of interest" to the Cuban police. He tried not to think of Yarmila but she was very much with him. This wasn't the kind of place they would have visited together, though. She didn't seem to enjoy the nightlife.

With me, at least.

A show was about to start. A spotlight fell on a small platform at the back of the room. Music began to play and the light cascaded over a woman who had stepped onto the rudimentary stage through a red curtain. Her moves were slinky, feline. Sultry. She blew a kiss to the crowd and it went wild.

"Diva!"

The song was "On the Radio," an oldie from the eighties that Matt hadn't heard in years. The singer, impersonating a young Donna Summer, wore a bikini top that showed her small breasts and a miniskirt that glittered with silver sequins. She looked good but sang badly. Her pitch was too high and the English words were unintelligible, strung together in a haphazard way. She missed the beat several times. After a while, she came down from the stage and started to walk around the tables. She was around five foot eight and her high heels made her tower over the audience.

"Bravo, Donna!"

She blew more kisses and wiggled her butt. Someone yelled, *"Perra! Perra!"*

The crowd erupted. *"Perrísima!"*

Matt had the vague impression that he had seen her before. But the response from the public baffled him.

Are they calling her a bitch?

Based on the approving looks and cheers, he figured that *perra* had a positive connotation, at least in the hazy context of the clandestine bar.

Yes, she reminds me of someone. Yarmi? A Tijuana street vendor?

The singer strutted around, waiting for her fans to place bills under her miniskirt or inside her top. Sometimes she would press her pelvis against their backs. She wrapped herself all over an older woman and kept at it until the woman tipped her. Matt felt repulsed but also, despite himself, shockingly aroused. She sauntered toward him, a grin splashed over her made-up face. He looked for a one-dollar bill, but only found fives and tens in his pocket. Then she stopped at a nearby table and he felt momentarily relieved—and disappointed.

By the time the singer got to his side, Matt was feeling bolder and ready to engage her. He caressed her hard, tight, muscular butt, but didn't dare to meet her eyes. She played with his hair and he blushed like a teenager. He placed the five-dollar bill close to her pelvis, wishing she would go away and at the same time that she'd stay close to him.

"Thanks, mister," the singer purred.

Matt's jaw dropped. He stared at the fake Donna Summer, who had already moved on to the next table, and he finally recognized in the short, dark, knotted fingers that held the microphone the stonemason's hands of Taty.

Waves of embarrassment swept over Matt as he drank what was left of his mojito. He berated himself for having been so blind, so naïve, such an unsophisticated *pendejo*. Café Arabia was a gay bar and all the women present, or most of them at least, were transvestites.

What was I thinking? What kind of an establishment could Taty have invited me to, for crying out loud?

He waited until the song was over. Taty bowed coquettishly and disappeared behind the curtain after a final curtsy. The stage lights went off and the music was turned down. The crowd broke into a round of applause.

"Awesome, *perra!*"

"You are divine!"

Matt requested his bill, which came to seven dollars even. But before he could pay, the performer was back on stage and he was forced to stay. Taty was still wearing his diva attire, but had taken off the shoes. His big feet and strong legs offered a striking contrast with the silky and slinky miniskirt.

"Hi, *queridas*! Thanks for your appreciation, *locas*. You know how much work I put into my shows so every little clap matters.

"Sorry I can't keep my shoes on but they are killing me. It's not easy, I swear, to be standing on my poor *patas* all day long, at the beck and call of my owner, ahem, employer, at La Caldosa.

"When I used to work for the state, I pretended that I was working, my boss pretended he was paying me and everyone was happy. But La Jefota is paying me real money, dollars and CUCs, and she expects me to be her slave.

"That's the problem with capitalism, *loquitas*. You have to plug away! And let me tell you, we are headed in that direction. If we don't go there willingly, they'll drag us. We start with a *paladar* here and a *paladar* there—and in two years you'll be ordering from a McDonald's menu.

"*Ay*, Virgin of Charity! I forgot I am not allowed to make political jokes. My other boss—El Jefe here at Café Arabia, who is terrific, not like La Jefota . . . are you listening to me, Flores?— Flores has told me to be careful. '*Niña*, don't go around opening your big yap or you'll get us in trouble: one thing is to be clandestine and another one is to be against You Know Who.' But we are all for You Know Who!" He winked, stroking an imaginary beard. "Even that handsome *Yuma* over there."

He looked at Matt and everybody's eyes followed Taty's. Giggles spread across the room. Matt wanted to hide under the table.

"Now, talking about *paladares*, McDonald's, and *bares clandestinos* isn't making political jokes, eh," Taty went on. "I'm only using the political economic terms that I learned in my Marxism classes when I was a little pioneer back in Las Villas and the only jokes I knew were Pepito stories. You know, the best economist in today's Cuba is Pepito.

"So the teacher asks his students to define capitalism. 'It's a trashcan filled with glittery things, hamburgers and fast cars,' Pepito says. The teacher is very pleased. 'Excellent, Comrade Pepito. Now define socialism.' 'The same trashcan,' Pepito says, 'but empty.'"

Laugh, applause and cheers erupted. Taty took a bow.

"Diva, you are too much!"

"Tell the story of Pepito and the fisherman!"

"No, Pepito, the *jinetera* and the *almendrón* driver!"

"What about another song?"

As soon as the sketch was over, Matt paid his bill and hurried outside. He inhaled the putrid waft that came from Malecón Drive. He felt dirty and confused, but still hot and bothered. He walked fast toward Villa Tomasa, avoiding other passersby, lost in a memory he thought he had forgotten until Taty's touch had suddenly awakened it.

Chapter Four
THE LIVING LIGHT MISSION

In 1980 Matt was twelve years old, a freckle-faced Ohio transplant living in a remote Peruvian village. His parents were Methodist preachers who had settled in the Ayacucho region to "evangelize the natives." They founded *La Misión Luz Viva*, Living Light Mission, a small church frequented by a dozen people on Sunday mornings and an even smaller group on Wednesday nights. The couple, in their Southern-accented Spanish, urged their neighbors to walk on the path of salvation. They soon found out that the path a number of Ayucuchans had chosen to follow had nothing to do with the Biblical one.

At first, however, the prospects had looked promising. The Catholic Church had lost ground in the area during the seventies while an assortment of Protestant churches flourished, particularly if they were based in El Norte. La Iglesia Americana, as people called these churches regardless of their particular denomination, attracted young Peruvians who favored the ministers' easygoing manners over the priests' guarded standoffishness. The American churches could afford to be generous and distributed scholarships to attend conferences in the United States.

Converts flocked to them. But the political climate was charged. The Shining Path, started as an obscure insurgent guerrilla movement, had gained footing in the Andean highlands. By the end of 1981, the Peruvian government had declared the region an emergency zone.

Matt's classmates talked about the *senderistas*, the rebels, with a mixture of fear and admiration. That February, a Shining Path group had attacked a neighboring town and killed the mayor and five men who were accused of belonging to "the bourgeoisie." Matt knew one of them—a Bostonian painter who had lived there for thirty years and who had never been involved in politics.

"That's Maoism," some said, while others called it *la revolución*.

Whatever it was, Matt's parents were getting nervous. Gringos (nobody called them *Yumas* in Peru) ranked high among the rebels' targets. They were labeled "enemies of the people" and executed summarily when the *senderistas* took over a town. A handful of locals were rumored to be among the *senderistas* or at least to sympathize with them. One was the school teacher, Señor Barreras, who, without openly defending their actions, railed against the injustices that condemned native people to a slow death by poverty and malnutrition. "At least the Shining Path firing squad works fast," he said once.

He didn't mention that, in order to save bullets, the rebels often stoned their prisoners to death. They left their bodies in the plaza for everyone to see. María, who worked as a maid at Matt's house and sometimes attended the services, described the scene in gruesome details.

"When I got to the plaza, the *muertitos* were still there because people were afraid of touching them," she told Matt's mother, crossing herself. "They had lost their eyes and their brains were scattered on the dirt. Some savages, these *senderistas*! I hope they never come here."

Matt started to have nightmares about eyeless and brainless corpses. The day his parents got news from the church headquarters that they would be leaving the mission soon, he slept soundly for the first time in weeks.

María feared the *senderistas*, but her husband Jorge, a silent, short, muscular man who always carried a machete with him, rooted for them. He didn't attend the *Luz Viva* services, though he and his wife lived on the property, and he went out of his way to avoid the Americans. Matt's mother didn't like him and would have asked him to move out if it hadn't been for María. But Matt's father, *el Pastor*, had a soft spot for Jorge.

"We'll eventually win him over," he'd say. "The Lord works in mysterious ways."

In mid-March, a current of dread and mistrust still ran through the town. Matt felt it at school, in the cold shoulder he received from some classmates, and in Señor Barreras's allusions to "the greedy imperialists," which he couldn't always decode. In a vague and not totally conscious way, he knew that he and his parents would always be outsiders—the ones who, if push came to shove, would be stoned by the *senderistas* while most people looked the other way. It wouldn't matter if they didn't know what Maoism was or what *la revolución* stood for. He was relieved the day their plane tickets finally arrived. The family would be traveling to Lima in a few days. From there, they would fly to the States.

His parents emptied the house, giving away tools, chairs and tables to their parishioners. A young couple promised to take care of the mission, meet every Sunday, read the Bible, and hold study groups, but *los pastores* didn't feel optimistic. The deacon didn't plan to send more missionaries any time soon and none of the *Luz Viva* members were interested in attending the Lima-based United Methodist seminary.

"They are more likely to join the *senderistas*," Matt's mother remarked, bitterly.

She and her husband had grown tired and disillusioned. Above all, they were fearful. They wanted a vacation from the Lord's work.

THOUGH HE HAD LIVED in the village for almost a year, Matt had made few local friends. It wasn't that the kids hated him or picked on him. They liked him well enough in the classroom, but there was always a barrier, partly caused by the language—less so as he learned Spanish—but mostly due to his *americano* status. He participated in school events and baseball games yet was seldom invited to other children's homes, except by those whose parents were involved with *Luz Viva*: a grand total of two.

The previous year, while they rehearsed a Nativity play (Señor Barreras had assigned Matt the role of Herod) he got a crush on a girl from his class, a brunette named Esperanza who played a shepherdess. They snuck out together to Cremería Sabor, an ice-cream bar whose main attraction was a soda fountain. But Ayacuchan girls were as old-fashioned as the device itself. Esperanza hadn't allowed him to hold her hand, much less kiss her.

"You can visit my home after asking Papa for permission," she said.

He had been too shy to approach her father, a tall, imposing, mustachioed gentleman who dropped his daughter off at school in a blue Cadillac. By January, Esperanza had an official boyfriend, a local teenager who talked about "beating that gringo to a pulp."

Matt tended to hang out with the Wilsons, the only other

American kids in town. They were the children of an engineer who worked for a lodging company. Blair, the oldest of the Wilson brothers, was the first one to tell Matt about the local prostitutes, *las putas*, and initiated him in the pleasures of voyeurism. The novelty wore off as soon as Matt realized that real women's bodies didn't look quite like those on the glossy *Playboy* pages that Blair treasured. But that didn't prevent him from secretly following María to a hut known as *la casita del baño* whenever she took a bath and his parents weren't around. The *casita*, located in the same compound where the church and the house were built, was connected to the main waterline. The housekeepers' cabin, though only a few feet away, didn't have a water supply.

Matt would tiptoe out of the house after making sure that his parents were busy or gone. While still in the honeymoon period with the mission, before the *senderistas*' attack, they traveled for two or three days at a time, entrusting Matt to María's care. Holding his breath, Matt would find his favorite spot and look hungrily at María as she got naked and poured cans of water over herself. Then he would masturbate quickly, convinced that his actions were sinful and he would be punished for them somehow, someday.

But even at that time, and despite, or maybe because of his parents' lectures about heaven, hell and doctrine, his faith was minimal. He couldn't stand Wesley's sermons. The Methodist rituals put him to sleep. He found the Catholic rites more appealing and colorful, with the bombastic organ and lively choir where some of his classmates sang. He'd have been happy to join the well-dressed people, like Esperanza's family, who attended Sunday Mass at la Iglesia de Santa María de Los Angeles. Though the *senderistas* and Señor Barreras proclaimed that Americans were first-class citizens everywhere—and more so in poor countries like Peru—Matt thought that his parents' religion, with its mechanic recitation of psalms and a barren room without one single image of a *santo*, was very second class.

"Even God would get bored there," he told Blair.

Some Catholic saint days were also public holidays, celebrated with processions and street parties that lasted until dawn. Protestants, Matt complained, didn't have patron saints, much less feast days. That wasn't fair.

It was a saint's day when the unnamable happened to him.

THAT WARM FRIDAY AFTERNOON Señor Barreras had dismissed the class early. It was the feast day of the town's patron saint, San José, and there would be a procession in the evening. Matt's parents were making farewell visits and had ordered him to stay home. He was bored, sitting by the window and munching on the snack that María had prepared for him: sweet caramel cookie sandwiches called *alfajores* and a glass of milk. Then he saw her, dressed in a flimsy muumuu, walking toward *la casita del baño*.

María was a short, plump woman with thick legs. Matt was fascinated by the dark spots of matted hair, *los pelos* that grew wild in her armpits. His mother didn't have *pelos* in hers, he knew that much. Matt wondered if she had hair "down there" but couldn't tell for sure. To see his mother naked would be a mortal sin. To see María, just a venial one.

Matt followed her to *la casita*. When María went inside, he pressed his face against the tiny holes he had opened with a kitchen knife in the lightweight board. It smelled of musk and Castile soap. Usually Matt was careful, looking all over first, but that day he didn't take precautions. His parents would come back late in the evening and Jorge worked until six o'clock. Or so he thought.

Matt felt the hard, cold back of the machete blade against his shoulder. On this warm Havana night, more than twenty years later, the pain from the old blow blended with the fresh one from Pato Macho's bat, merging memory and present in one long, excruciating instant. He stopped on the corner of San Lázaro and Jovellar Streets. He caressed his shoulder and massaged his back, blinking back tears.

It had happened so fast. Jorge's rough hands dragged him to the main house, to the small dark garage, now empty, while he muttered insults—*gringo de mierda*, shitty little American, I am going to teach you—

Matt tried to run away but couldn't. He was paralyzed with fear, afraid that the man would beat him up, or kill him and leave his body there as an example, his eyes out of their sockets. Wouldn't he be justified? Matt had committed a sin against his wife—many times. But Jorge didn't hit him again. He pulled down Matt's pants, unzipped his own, and forced the boy to bend over. He penetrated him furiously and ejaculated inside.

"If you tell anyone, I'll cut your tongue out," were his parting words.

Matt didn't tell a soul. Not Blair, certainly not his parents. He tried to block the pain when he sat at the dinner table that evening. He did his best to behave as usual, but his mother must have noticed something was wrong.

"What is it, dear?" she asked.

"I have a stomachache. May I go to my room?"

"You haven't finished eating."

"I don't feel like it. Please."

She smiled at him. His father caressed his hair. They looked at him, so naïve and lost. So defenseless in this strange world they had dragged him into.

"Okay," she said. "You are excused."

"He doesn't want to leave Ayacucho," he heard his father say, on his way out. "He's made friends here and is doing well at school, but we can't take the risk."

"Kids forget quickly."

HE AVOIDED MARÍA AND Jorge and refused to say goodbye to them. After the green VW Beetle left the village streets behind, Matt said a prayer of thanks to both the Methodist and the Catholic God.

He never talked about what happened, not even during the therapy sessions that he attended as an adult. He hadn't had sexual contact with another man again. He tried to erase the incident from his mind. Why had it returned now, at the most inopportune time?

It's all Taty's fault.

THE PORCH LIGHT WAS on at Villa Tomasa. Román was still sitting in the lounge chair, a joint between his lips and his eyes closed.

"Back so soon, *amigo*?" he asked, elongating the syllables. "The night is young."

It was a quarter to twelve.

Matt suddenly remembered Isabel. It would be inconsiderate to keep her waiting for him and concerned about his whereabouts. She had written La Caldosa's address and phone number on a piece of paper "in case he forgot," and insisted he call her if he ran into any problem.

"Remember, Mateo, we are your family in Cuba," she repeated. "We are here for you."

He dialed her number using an old rotary phone, black and heavy, that he found in the dining room under doña Tomasa's portrait. In a low voice, hoping Román wouldn't hear him, he explained he had decided to stay with a friend and that they would take a trip to "the provinces" very early the following day.

"Sorry for the last-minute notice. I'll call you when I'm back."

Isabel believed him, or pretended to do so.

"Take care, my friend," she said. "I'll be waiting for you."

Don't hold your breath.

He replaced the receiver.

MATT HAD STARTED HAVING vivid dreams shortly after the family returned from Peru. They were always preceded by a buzzing noise and a subtle vibration of his whole body. Most began the same way: he would open his arms, run a few yards and fly up. It was that easy. He found himself floating over the sea, often so close to it that he smelled its salty scent and got splashed by the waves. But all he needed was the desire to rise, and he would soar again. All his senses felt sharpened. The colors were intense and sometimes he could hear snippets of instrumental music, soft and relaxing, nothing like the hair bands he listened to. But there was always a moment when he realized that it was just a dream and became acutely aware of the implausibility of it.

Many years later, he learned that these were called lucid dreams. He took a seminar with a guy who claimed he could teach others how to get in control of them. But Matt was never able to "stage" the scenes as their instructor recommended.

That night at Villa Tomasa, the dream had started as usual. He was happily flying over water. The Pacific? The Caribbean? A small boat floated below. There was someone aboard. Matt descended and discovered it was Yarmila. She was sitting on an olive green bedspread, holding the interactive map that he had bought for her at Toys"R"Us.

He landed by her side.

"This silly thing," she said, pointing to the map, "has lost magnetic north."

The map had turned into a compass.

When Matt woke up, he was lying on his stomach, an unusual posture for him. He rubbed his eyes, walked to the window and stood there, listening to the long, high-pitched song of the crickets for over an hour.

That guy said you could find the answer to most problems in lucid dreams, that whatever you needed to know was available there. Next time I'll make sure to confront Yarmi and ask her why. That might be the only answer I ever get from her.

Fanguito: Little mud

The condensed milk of my childhood came from the Soviet Union. Yes, it is now called Russia, thanks to the perestroika and all that, but I still find it difficult to say that name: it sounds old-fashioned and reeks of the tsars' times. *Bueno*, the condensed milk of the eighties came from the *former* Soviet Union, to be historically and politically correct, and I loved it. But the cans, with red and black cows on the label, were difficult to open. Grandma Hilda joked that they were made out of steel.

One of my indulgences was, and still is, boiled condensed milk, or condensed milk in a *baño de María*. Known as *fanguito*, it's the sweetest dessert you'll ever taste.

The preparation is simple: just boil a closed can of condensed milk for a couple of hours in a big pot. Make sure that the can is totally covered in water all through the boiling process. You may need to add an extra cup or two.

Once you open the can, you'll find out that the milk has turned light brown. That's why people call it *fanguito*, like "a little bit muddy." But the flavor, I assure you, isn't "muddy" at all. An advantage of *fanguito* is that it lasts forever. You don't even have to refrigerate it.

I could eat *fanguito* any day, but my favorite moments to enjoy it are when I am watching movies. My *Yuma* says that, in his country, moviegoers munch on popcorn. I'd rather have condensed milk. By the way, have I told you that I always cry at movies? I cry so much that my girlfriends call me *La Llorona*, the Weeping Woman, and sit far away from me so as not to be embarrassed by my inappropriate bawling. That's why I like *fanguito*: it sweetens everything, even tears.

Enough of my philosophizing! For those of you who are always asking for Nitza Villapol-style recipes, this is a winner. Enjoy.

COMMENTS

Maritza said. . .

You can also make *fanguito* in the pressure cooker and it only takes forty minutes.

Yarmi said. . .

I know, Maritza, but I am afraid of pressure cookers, as you know already.

Cubanita in Claremont said. . .

I remember eating *fanguito* with crackers. My mother made it every week when I attended the school in the fields, back in the eighties.

Taos Tonya said. . .

I eat my condensed milk directly from the can when nobody is looking. Then I get disgusted and barf.

Cocinera Cubana said. . .

Oh, I also cry at movies, particularly when they are about Cuba. I don't remember much because we left when I was five years old, but I still turn into a *Llorona* when I see the Malecón Wall.

Mateo said. . .

It reminds me of *dulce de leche*, a Mexican dessert. But I bet yours is better!

Yarmi said. . .

Yes, Cubanita! *Fanguito* was a popular snack at the *escuelas al campo*. Cocinera, I think you should come and see the Malecón again with your own eyes. You may cry, but these will be tears of joy. Tonya, try cooking it and you will feel less guilty. My Mateo, of course it is better! Because I make it with a secret ingredient: love.

Chapter Five

AGENT PEDRO AND THE CIA

The insistent knocking woke Matt up. He looked at the cuckoo clock. It was ten after eight.

"What is it?" he asked from bed, sounding every bit as annoyed as he was.

"There is a call for you," Román's voice filtered through the door.

Matt got up, wondering who could possibly know that he was at Villa Tomasa when he hadn't told anyone.

"Sorry, but this woman said it was urgent," Román said apologetically, handing him the receiver.

"Hello."

"It's a good thing that you haven't left for the *provinces* yet," Isabel said. "I wouldn't have bothered you but a Seguridad guy showed up here at seven o'clock, demanding to see you. I told him you hadn't come to sleep here and he got mad at me, as if I were hiding you or something."

"Was it Pedro?" Matt asked.

"He didn't say his name."

"What did he want?"

"To talk to you. Right now. He said you must call Unidad 13 as soon as possible."

Matt's hands began to shake. "I'll contact him," he said. "Thanks, Isabel."

He was ready to hang up, but Isabel wasn't done with him yet.

"What did we do to you, Mateo?" she asked in a whiny voice. "We welcomed you with open arms. We treated you as if you were a blood relative! If there was something you didn't like about your room, you could have told me, instead of leaving us like that. I knew you weren't going to any province when you called me last night!"

Matt didn't answer. *Why does she care? I paid her in advance. Jesus. But how does she know where—? Ah, the caller ID!*

"Was it because of Taty?" she insisted. "Please, tell me the truth. If the little shit is causing me to lose clients—"

"This has nothing to do with him."

"But you moved to another *casa particular*."

"It's very difficult for me to stay at a place that reminds me so much of Yarmila," Matt said after a pause.

"I thought we had—"

He slammed down the phone and called Martínez's number. This time she answered right away.

"Yes, Agent Pedro needs to talk to you," she said. "Give me your address and we will pick you up in a minute."

"I can get there by myself," Matt replied, not wanting a police car to appear at Román's door.

"Okay. But don't delay. This is a serious matter."

"I'll take a taxi," he said.

Before he could ask anything else, Martínez had hung up.

GORDO WAS AT THE reception desk and greeted him like an old buddy.

"Back again, eh? Came to see the lieutenant?"

But Martínez was nowhere to be seen. When Gordo announced Matt's presence over the intercom, Pedro came out and ushered him into an unmarked vehicle, a blue Volvo with tinted windows. The Seguridad agent was carrying a black attaché case.

Matt became increasingly hopeful after they left behind Salvador Allende Avenue and sped toward Rancho Boyeros, the road that led to the José Martí International Airport.

"Are you letting me go back to the States now?" he asked, still incredulous.

"No, not yet, *compañero*. We have to clarify a couple of things first. See, it might just be a misunderstanding, but it's a very ugly one."

"A misunderstanding about Yarmila's death?"

"About Yarmila *and you*."

"What do you mean?"

Pedro didn't answer. He drove in silence until they arrived at a gray Soviet-era building with square balconies. It was as weathered as the old ones Matt had seen in La Habana Vieja, but lacked the patina that time had spread over them like golden flakes of an opulent past. Here, the peeling walls were evidence of poor construction and low quality materials, not the passing of years.

The Seguridad man led Matt to a first-floor apartment. Two burly guys in civilian clothes stood at attention, saluted Pedro and ignored Matt.

"Will you explain what this means?" he asked, more irritated than scared. "Why have you brought me here?"

"To have a little talk," Pedro answered at last. "It seems to me that you are the one who has some explaining to do."

THERE WERE ONLY TWO chairs in the room. A video camera was mounted on the wall. Pedro turned it on and ordered Matt to sit down facing it.

"When did you start working for the agency?" he asked.

"What agency?"

"Don't play dumb with me. You know what—CIA."

Matt had heard of the Cuban government's paranoia about American spies, but didn't take it seriously. He knew many tourists, like Anne, who visited the island year after year without being bothered.

"I have never worked for the CIA," he said, shrugging. "I don't think I've ever even met anybody who does."

"And you never tried to get Yarmila Portal to collaborate, eh?"

"To collaborate with whom?"

"With you, with your boss."

"I don't understand," Matt stammered. "You mean my editor at *El Grito*?"

The idea of Yarmila *collaborating* with Estrada was even stranger than him being involved with the CIA.

"Editor *un carajo*," Pedro barked. "I'm talking about the CIA officer who attends to you!"

Attends to me? What kind of movies do these people watch?

"I have no links to the CIA or any other federal agency," Matt repeated. "I told you before: I am *not* an enemy of the revolution."

Yet. But if you keep this up—

Pedro opened his briefcase, took out a printed document and placed it first in front of the camera. Then he showed it to Matt.

Mi amor, he read, his own words, the message he had written in San Diego less than two weeks before. *I would be very happy if you considered doing the little assignment I told you about. You can use old material, modify it a bit, but still make it sound very Cuban and very you.*

"Did you write that?" Pedro asked.

"Why, yes."

He remembered exactly when he had written it, during a break between two features for *El Grito*. He had been excited and confident, so much in love that he wanted to tell everyone about his young, pretty Cuban fiancée. "You look like the cat that ate the canary," the newspaper receptionist had said.

I'm the canary now.

Pedro produced Yarmila's response, another printed page with one of the last emails she had sent to Matt.

"I look forward to the assignment, my beloved *Yuma*," Pedro read aloud. "Not sure if I should try to finish it before you come or wait so we can work on it together. What do you think?"

My beloved Yuma. *Stupid* Yuma *who believed everything she said. Was Pato Macho with her when she wrote that?*

"The subject line reads 'Re: CIA story,'" Pedro pointed out, frowning. "Did you want her to spy on our people and write a report to the CIA?"

Matt broke out in nervous laughter. He had never noticed the identical acronyms before.

"Ah, this is funny? We'll see how much fun you have at Villa Marista!"

Villa Marista was a jail for political prisoners. Matt had read about it on a Cuban website and the description had reminded him of the Hanoi Hilton, with a tropical twist.

"The CIA I was referring to is the Culinary Institute of America," he said.

"Culinary Institute? What the hell is that?"

How could he not know? What kind of intelligence agent is this?

"It's a school where they teach people how to cook."

"Yeah, like in your country people need to be taught how to cook. Are they so dumb that they can't learn it in their own homes?"

"I mean haute cuisine, fancy stuff like—I don't know, rata-touille."

"Huh?"

"A local branch of the Institute runs a magazine called *Foodali-cious*," Matt plowed on. "I had asked Yarmila to write something for it because the summer issue's theme is Caribbean cuisine. I thought she could use a recipe from that cooking book she was always quoting, *Cocina*—"

Pedro tapped his left foot and cut him off. "How could they be called 'CIA'?" he asked.

"The Institute? Well, C, I and A are the first letters of its full name."

"Nah. They couldn't possibly do that. Not legally."

Matt sighed, frustrated. "I told you how Yarmila and I met," he said. "She had a food blog, *Yarmi Cooks Cuban*."

"I know that!"

"So I suggested she take an excerpt and make it into a feature for the magazine. That's all."

"Why would the CIA allow them to do that?"

"Do what?"

"Use their very own name. Why would they let a culinary school or whatever *steal* their name? They have a lot of power."

He sounded angry, as if the idea of someone stealing from the CIA were somehow insulting to him.

"The Institute doesn't use the same name, only the acronym. Acronyms aren't copyright protected."

"Copyright? I don't even know what you are talking about."

God. This is a socialist discussion.

"The acronym 'CIA' also stands for Cleveland Institute of Art," Matt tried to think of other examples that would make sense to Pedro when translated. "It's used for titles as well, like Certified Internal Auditor. It doesn't belong to anybody. It's—just letters."

"You better tell me the truth if you ever want to go back to your country," Pedro said. "This mumbo jumbo about acronyms and copyright isn't helping you. You could spend the rest of your life in a Cuban jail!"

With a gigantic effort Matt managed to remain calm. "Please, read my message in context," he said. "Find the previous ones. Yarmila and I had been discussing Caribbean dishes. I had mentioned the magazine, the full name of the Institute. I told her they were interested in publishing a piece by a Cuban chef."

"I'll see to that," Pedro said. "Our technical department will find out if what you're saying is true."

"Can you pull my messages out? I can show you."

"Pull them out? Out of what?"

"Don't you have internet here?"

Now Pedro was confused and attempting to hide his confusion, which only made it more pronounced. He stood up and so did Matt.

"No, you stay," Pedro said. "You can't go anywhere until this problem is taken care of."

"Since I am officially arrested, I want to see a lawyer," Matt said.

"What for?"

"Because it is my right."

"You have no rights here, *comemierda*! If you turn out to be a CIA agent, you're totally fucked."

Pedro left but his last words, *todo jodido*, kept ringing in Matt's ears. He stared at the camera, a perfect close-up of anger and disconcert.

THE THREE HOURS THAT Matt spent in the room, under the watchful eye of the lens, would stay in his memory as a scene from an absurd movie with no beginning, end or logical storyline. A Kafkaesque plot with a Cuban setting.

Pedro returned and said Matt was allowed to go because the email issue had been clarified. It seemed (*seemed*, he stressed, because it wasn't proven yet) like Matt wasn't actually trying to recruit the late Yarmila Portal to work for the enemy's intelligence. But even so, he was still considered a person of interest and should remain available for further inquiries.

Matt didn't argue. He had made up his mind: the next day, first thing in the morning, he would present himself at the United States Interest Section and ask for help.

Even if they make me pay a fine for coming here without a permit. I don't care. I can't deal with Agent Pedro on my own. I just can't.

They went back to the Unidad. No apologies from Pedro, who at least looked mildly embarrassed. Still, he didn't tell Matt when his passport would be returned.

"Pronto, *compañero*," he said, and shrugged. "Maybe tomorrow."

In the land of mañana, tomorrow never comes.

It was two o'clock. Matt stopped at a nearby *paladar* and ordered the *especial del día*—a dish of white rice, fried plantains and shredded pork. He washed it down with Cerveza Cristal, a locally brewed beer that had a crisp, refreshing taste. It wasn't until he left the restaurant that he saw it was named *El Policía Bueno*, The Good Cop.

ISABEL AND PATO MACHO were waiting for him at Villa Tomasa. Matt touched his shoulder instinctively, though Pato, who was sitting between Anne and Isabel on the yellow sectional, looked harmless and subdued. He hung his head as Matt approached.

Isabel stood up. She wore a long white dress, a cross between a Greek tunic and a housecoat, and a Santería necklace with blue and white beads. She carried a white vinyl purse adorned with saint pins and charms to ward off the evil eye.

"You should have let me know," she clucked, as a way of greeting.

"Let you know what?" Matt asked, preparing himself mentally for another Kafkaesque sketch.

She took him by the arm and led him away from the couch. Her dress smelled like sandalwood incense.

"About Pato," she whispered. "What he did. He's really sorry and has come to say so."

Matt stared at her, incredulous.

Why does she want to get in the middle of this? It's none of her business!

Pato Macho followed them shyly. Under the teardrop lamp, clean and shaven, he wasn't as scary as he had been on the rooftop. He had turned into a scared boy.

"I'm so sorry, *señor*," he stuttered. "I didn't intend to hurt you. I was—eh—drunk."

"That's not the way he usually behaves," Isabel added, with a protective gesture toward the young man.

"Thanks for not ratting me out," Pato Macho blurted out. "I want to apologize."

He was using the respectful Spanish form, *usted*, to address Matt. The day before, threatening him with the metal bat, he had called him *tú*.

"Oh, it's okay," Matt answered, though his arm still hurt.

The two men avoided looking at each other. Isabel elbowed Pato Macho and he spoke again, "I understand that you had nothing to do with what happened to—to her. I hope the cops figure it out too."

"They will," Isabel said. "They know everything."

"I'm not so sure," Matt replied. "That Seguridad officer or whatever he is, Agent Pedro, didn't know shit. It took him hours to check my emails and find out that I wasn't a CIA agent."

He made himself shut up. *Why am I babbling like an idiot?*

"They believe every American is the devil's spawn," Isabel spoke in a soft mumble. "As Padrino says, they don't get that there are *Yumas* and *Yumas*, and that people in your country are all different."

"Padrino is right," Matt said. "Whoever Padrino is."

"You met him the other day at La Caldosa," Isabel reminded him. "You sat together for a while and shared a *tocinillo*."

"Oh, yes, the guy in white. So his name is Padrino?"

"That's what many of us call him—"

Pato Macho, Padrino, Taty—they wear their nicknames like camouflage.

"Because he is our Santería godfather. We believe in the *orishas*, the African gods."

A Cuban godfather. A voodoo don with a gang of spirits instead of hit men.

"I told him about your predicament. After I found out what had happened in the penthouse, I went to him and asked for advice. It was Padrino's idea that we come to see you and that Pato apologize."

Matt shrugged. "It wasn't necessary," he said.

"Padrino can help you." She got closer to him and said in a conspiratorial tone, "He's really, really good."

"Do you think he can do a little—ceremony for me?" Matt asked, trying not to sound sarcastic.

"No, that wasn't my idea. Unless you want him to, of course. A ceremony never hurts, nor does a safety measure. Look at me!"

She pointed to the purse and her necklace. "Today I'm wearing all my weapons to keep the bad spirits away."

They were alone by then. Pato Macho had returned quietly to the sectional and was chatting with Anne again.

"I don't get it, Isabel," Matt said. "How could Padrino help me?"

"He is a detective. He used to work for the *fiana*. That was a long time ago but—"

"What's the *fiana*?"

"The police. He's retired now and, like everyone else, trying to eke out a living, so he went private."

"What can he do for me?"

"Find out who killed Yarmi and convince the police to let you go."

"Does he have that much power?"

"Yes, he does. They respect him. Remember, he was one of them. And he has solved many cases after he retired. For a fee, of course."

Matt wanted to ask if Padrino enlisted the help of the African deities he and Isabel worshipped to solve said cases. But he held his tongue.

Maybe I should see this guy before going to the Interest Section. He'd heard Americans could face fines of thousands of dollars for unauthorized trips to Cuba. The law was seldom enforced, but still.

"I am very much willing to talk to Padrino and, naturally, pay him for his services," he said.

Isabel patted his hand. "Great! He can meet with you tomorrow. I've already made an appointment for 11:00 A.M."

Matt winced. *That was fast.*

"I understand why you prefer to stay here," Isabel sighed, with a wistful look at Román's living room. "You can be sure that Pato will not bother you again, but this is way nicer than anything we can offer you."

She opened her purse and handed him thirty dollars.

"Please, keep it," Matt said.

"You mean it?"

"Yes."

"I appreciate it, Mateo," she said hastily. "I'll pick you up tomorrow and we'll go to Padrino's house."

"Thanks for all your help." *But you are still a snooping bitch.*

Isabel called out to Pato Macho, "Let's go! It's getting late."

They left after exchanging a few more niceties with Matt and Anne. Anne accompanied Pato Macho to the door and kissed him goodbye. "See you soon, *chico*," she said playfully.

"It has been a pleasure, beautiful lady. I hope to see you again."

When they were out of the house, Isabel turned to the young man and hissed, "Can't you stop chasing tail, *coño*? You just don't learn, do you?"

In memory of Nitza Villapol

Hola, my culinary friends! Here we are again, getting ready to prepare another Cuban-to-the-core entrée.

When I say Cuban-to-the-core, you think rice and beans, don't you? And something fried, preferably with *manteca*, because yes, we are lard lovers. We like fried beef, as in *vaca frita*, fried chicken, as in *pollo frito*, and fried fish, as in *pescado frito*.

That may be true, but today we are going to give the frying pan a well-deserved rest. We will be calorie conscious—though not too much, because skinny women aren't popular in Cuba. I want to keep my curves.

We will make grilled steak following a recipe found in Nitza Villapol's cookbook *Cocina al Minuto*. Hey, all you cooks out there: if you haven't yet read *Cooking in Minutes*, go find it at once. It is the Bible of traditional Cuban cuisine and I believe that it has been published abroad and translated into several languages. My grandma treasured her tattered copy, but I am using a more recent version from the nineties, with ingredients that were readily available then.

Let's start with the *adobo*, a seasoning mix made with the juice of one bitter orange, three chopped garlic cloves, and a sliced onion. Set aside a few onion slices for later. Let the *palomilla* (thin cut) steak marinate for two or three hours in the refrigerator.

Melt one tablespoon of butter on the grill (yes, you can use oil, but it won't be the same), season the steak with salt and pepper, and grill it three or four minutes on each side. Then allow the steak to rest for a while—it will be piping hot. Before serving, cover it with raw onions and fresh parsley.

If raw onions horrify you (my *Yuma* boyfriend hates them), just sauté the slices you saved and decorate the steak with them. Serve over white rice.

Easy, isn't it? I loved Nitza. She was every Cuban housewife's best friend because of her creative dishes. She was an inspiration in feast or famine times.

Nitza hosted a TV program also entitled *Cocina al Minuto* and greeted her audience by saying, "Good morning, my TV-watching friends. Here again is *Cooking in Minutes*, with fast and easy-to-make recipes."

She passed away in 1998.

When my time comes, I hope to be remembered as an amazing cook, like dear Nitza. A mojito toast to her sweet soul!

COMMENTS

Cocinera Cubana said. . .

I remember Nitza's show on Sunday mornings. My mother used to watch it when we lived in Cuba when we came back from church. But don't talk about "when your time comes." You are so young, *querida*.

Cubanita in Claremont said. . .

Nitza was like the Julia Child of Cuba, wasn't she? I loved her desserts, particularly the *tocinillo*.

Lucy Adel said. . .

Excuse me, but was steak (or any kind of meat, for that matter) "readily available" during the nineties? That's not what I have heard from my relatives who lived through the so-called Special Period!

Anita said. . .

It's refreshing to know that Cuban women aren't skinny-crazy. Someday I may move there, where my own curves will be more valued than in calorie-obsessed California.

Yarmi said. . .

Lucy, though meat in general wasn't "abundant" in the nineties, people still received some through the ration card. Anita, I heard you are coming soon. Do you plan to stay longer this time? That will be great!

Chapter Six

A CUBAN PRIVATE EYE

The next morning Matt and Anne sat under the teardrop lamp enjoying a cup of strong, sugary coffee. Román was in the kitchen, getting breakfast ready: buttered toast, guava jam and the host's specialty, *revoltillo de jamón y queso*—eggs scrambled with ham and cheese.

"I used to read Yarmi's blog all the time," Anne said. "I loved her recipes and the stories about her family and friends, and all things Cuban. After a while, I felt as if I'd known her forever."

"I guess I *didn't* know her at all," Matt replied. "Ours was a short-lived long-distance relationship."

Long-distance love, morons' love. He'd heard that in Tijuana, walking down Avenida Revolución. Two kids were talking and one had said, *Amor de lejos, amor de pendejos.* He'd thought it was hilarious, then.

"What did she think of the Cuban government, Matt?" Anne asked. "Was she a communist?"

Matt took his time to respond. He thought that Anne was being insensitive, bringing up his dead girlfriend in such a casual manner.

"I don't know," he answered at last. "She never talked politics. Sometimes she would complain about waiting in lines and lack of public transportation, but so does everybody here."

"She must have had an opinion about Castro, Matt. All Cubans do."

"If she did, she didn't share it and I didn't ask. I assumed she was being cautious since people are so afraid of being labeled as worms."

Anne pursed her lips. "Yep, they can be sly about it. Even Yony isn't totally open with me, though I'm sure he wants to leave the country. It's difficult to find out what Cubans really think about politics."

"Or anything else, for that matter." He shrugged and looked at his watch. "Hope Isabel gets here soon."

"Are you seeing her private eye friend today?"

"Yeah, what do I have to lose?"

"Right. You are better off dealing with the Cubans, seeing that you are on their turf. Someone who used to work for the police—you can't beat that! And he is sort of an oracle." She laughed. "Yosvani's mom always consults everything with him."

"Yosvani who?"

"The guy who was here yesterday. I thought that you knew him."

"We—we met briefly."

"Such a sweetheart. And handsome, isn't he? He said his mom wouldn't open the *paladar* until Padrino gave her the green light."

"His mom?"

"Yony believes in Santería too, but he doesn't like to talk about it. I don't know why . . . I find the whole thing fascinating."

Matt wasn't listening to her anymore.

Pato Macho is Isabel's son. Donna Summer is Taty. I am a CIA agent. It can't get more bizarre than this.

Román called them from the kitchen.

"Hey, my friends! Come and jump-start your day with a delicious Cuban breakfast: *revoltillo a la Román*."

ISABEL ARRIVED AT TEN o'clock and began to give Matt instructions right away.

"Put on some sensible shoes because we have to walk a bit," she said officiously. "And bring plenty of cash."

Matt recalled Román's advice. "But it is safe out there?" he asked.

"You are going to be with me so you don't have to worry," Isabel answered. "I'll take care of you."

In San Lázaro Street they boarded a *cocotaxi*, a three-wheeled scooter with two small seats and a yellow egg-shaped cover, to the Sierra Maestra cruise port in Old Havana.

"Now let's take the *lanchita de Regla*," Isabel declared. "It's very cheap. I'll pay for it."

Havana bay was practically empty. There were only two Venezuelan merchant ships moored in the harbor. Matt saw oil stains on the water and caught a whiff of rotten fish while they waited for *la lanchita*, a rudimentary ferryboat which, according to a faded schedule posted at the ticket booth, was already twenty minutes late.

Ten people appeared out of nowhere as soon as the *lanchita* arrived. They were all Cubans. Two of them loaded bicycles on the ferry. The toll taker tried to charge Matt one CUC—he even managed to say the amount in English—but Isabel complained and threatened to call "the administrator."

"Forty cents, national currency!" she yelled. "Twenty for him and twenty for me. That's what it costs and that's what you're getting, *carajo*!"

The toll taker relented. Matt didn't dare to intervene. He followed Isabel on board, feeling embarrassed and cheap. He glanced at her a few times, trying to read her. But her face, stern and with two lines running straight downward from the corners of her mouth, was inscrutable.

Of course, she is doing this for her son. She wants the santero *to find out who killed Yarmi because he is probably a suspect and she is trying to save his ass. She can't care less about me. Nobody does.*

During the short trip, the ferry passed near a monumental statue of Jesus. It was atop a hill, white and glowing under the sun.

"That is El Cristo de La Habana," Isabel said, crossing herself with reverence.

"How does the government allow it?" Matt asked. "It seems strange, such a prominent religious symbol in an atheist country."

"It has been there forever. Batista's wife had it built in 1958, before he was ousted. At first *they* ignored the statue and it began to deteriorate, but now that they are buddies with the Catholic Church, the Pope, the Vatican, and all the saints from the celestial court, they restored it and made it look good and spiffy again. After John Paul II came, they even allowed people to celebrate Christmas again, for the first time in almost thirty years."

"By 'they,' do you mean the government?"

"Yes, *chico*, who else? The powers that be. Every time they go to the bathroom, they change their mind. No wonder everybody is crazy, myself included!"

Matt waited a few seconds before asking, "Are you a Catholic, Isabel?"

"I'm half and half. I believe in Santería and most *santos* have a Catholic counterpart. But I am not fond of priests. I get my advice from a guy's guy, not a skirt-wearing one."

CROSSING THE BAY HAD taken around fifteen minutes. Padrino's home, Isabel informed Matt, wasn't far away.

"It's a nice walk," she said. "You'll get to see the village. Regla is different from Havana, but very cute."

"Cute" wasn't a word Matt would have chosen to describe the small industrial town. It had narrow streets, old houses, and a decidedly un-touristic vibe. He didn't encounter any other foreign-looking person the whole time. There were no stores or *paladares* either. It was hot and humid and the air felt heavier than in Havana. A few minutes into the walk, Matt started to sweat profusely.

They passed by the church of Our Lady of Regla, a square building with white walls, a red tile roof, and a bell tower. Isabel mentioned that *la virgen de Regla* was identified in Cuban Santería with Yemayá, the African goddess of the seas.

"That's what I was telling you about Catholic saints and *orishas*," she said. "The virgin of Regla is the patron saint of Spanish sailors. This chapel was the first thing that greeted them when they approached Havana and the last thing they saw when they left. They asked Santa María de Regla for protection against pirates and storms just as I ask Yemayá for protection against thieves and state inspectors. You may want to ask for her blessing too."

Matt couldn't find a good reason to refuse. He had agreed to seek advice from a *santero* so praying to a mixed-religion deity was very much in line with that.

"I will!" he answered with fake enthusiasm.

"You have a good chance to impress her," Isabel smiled knowingly. "She's into blonds like you."

"Excuse me?"

"Don't blush." She laughed and pinched his arm. "Yemayá, the *orisha*, is a woman. She digs men."

Whatever was left of Matt's Methodist upbringing rebelled against the idea of Virgin Mary "digging" men.

"How can you say that?"

"The *orishas* are very much like us," Isabel explained. "They fight over lovers, get jealous, bear children—they aren't all holy-coly like the virgins and saints."

The church was cool and musty inside, though the air was heavy with the smell of incense and melted wax. Blue reigned supreme. The alcoves on the walls had indigo edges. The window frames were painted bright cobalt. There were plaster statues of saints everywhere and most of them had a splash of blue on their dresses.

Isabel knelt down in front of the altar and lifted her arms.

"My mother Yemayá, cover me with your precious cloak!" she demanded. "I'm here, *virgen santísima*, look at me!"

She crossed herself and kissed her own hand in a dramatic fashion. Matt moved away discreetly. Six women were scattered around, two kneeling on pews and the others standing near a black Madonna. The virgin was enthroned on the main altar and held a mulatto baby Jesus with only one shoe on.

Loud prayers carried over the church.

"Help me, heavenly mother!"

"Dear *negrita*, don't desert me in this time of need . . ."

"Make him come back to me."

Matt sat on a bench and wiped his forehead. He attempted to pray to the blue-clad image but the only words that came to him were from the Our Father. He dutifully recited it.

AFTER LEAVING THE CHURCH, Matt and Isabel ran into an old man who sold pineapple juice from a cart. *Puro y natural*, read the sign nailed to a wood post. *Un peso*. Matt offered two dollars to the vendor. He handed them two cone-shaped brown paper containers filled with a bright yellow liquid. The juice was cold and tangy.

"You didn't need to do that." Isabel scolded him. "Next time, ask me first."

"What are you talking about?"

"You gave that guy two dollars! It said one peso per drink. Twenty American cents would have been more than enough. You have to be more *vivo*, my friend."

Isabel meant street-smart, but because *vivo* also means "alive," Matt thought for a second that she implied he was dead.

Geez, the things you think when you're nervous. And tired.

"Shouldn't we take another *cocotaxi*?" he suggested.

"There are no *cocotaxis* here."

"A taxi or an *almendrón*, then. Anything with wheels."

"This is Regla, Mateo. The only 'things with wheels' you will find are buses that pass every two hours. But we are almost there."

"Almost?"

"*Palante*, man!" She lifted her breasts and looked at him with a mix of pity and contempt. "I have varicose veins but I don't go around whining!"

Matt didn't complain again. They trudged for another half an hour before finding Padrino's place, a dilapidated hut standing on a corner lot. The chain-link fence was modern and stood in marked contrast to the building. It wasn't until they got closer that Matt realized there was also a big house behind a row of trees.

Isabel opened the gate. Two German shepherds came running and growling up to them.

"Ah, come on, Lazarito," Isabel said, petting the biggest and fiercest-looking one. "You know me! Go get your daddy."

A young mulatta in a white dress similar to Isabel's, but tighter and a lot more revealing, came out and yelled at the dogs.

"So sorry, my husband is running behind," she said to Matt, apologetically. "We had an emergency."

"With Padrino?" Isabel asked.

"No, one of his goddaughters. A marital emergency, I should say." She rolled her eyes. "She is with him now, but they will be done soon."

Padrino's wife, who introduced herself as Gabriela, led them past the mango, orange and avocado trees that surrounded the house—a thriving jungle curtain planted there as a protection from prying eyes. There was a vegetable garden where tomatoes, cauliflowers and herbs grew freely. A series of grunts and a not so sweet smell came from a pigpen. A fat sow and three piglets stared at the visitors with mischievous eyes. A dozen hens pecked at the ground, where corn kernels and grains of rice had been scattered. A green VW Beetle was parked under the shade of a big ceiba tree.

The house had a covered porch that ran the length of the building. The main door was open.

"Please, come in," Gabriela said. "And excuse the mess."

Matt didn't see any mess. The living room was wide and bright, with two large picture windows that brought the garden and a flaming red bougainvillea in. The wicker sofa looked old but well preserved, and there were three maple chairs polished by time and use. Gabriela turned on an electric fan.

"Ah, thanks!" Isabel plopped down on a chair and took off her shoes. "I needed it!"

Matt sat on the sofa, across from a statuette of the Virgin of Charity that had fine dark features, like *la Virgen de Regla*. Framed pictures, mostly black and white, covered the wall. A basket full of oranges, bananas and tangerines had been left on the floor. He remembered the pineapple juice vendor's claim: pure and natural. He liked this place, the simplicity of it, way better than Román's kitschy decor or the penthouse's spartan interior.

Gabriela joined them and small talk ensued. The two women tried at first to engage Matt, but he pretended not to understand their rapid-fire Spanish. In truth, he got most of it, except for some obscure colloquialisms like *me tiene obstiná*, that *couldn't* mean, in the context it was used, "I am obstinate." He got the impression it actually meant "I am sick and tired of it." But as the chat went on, he got bored and irritated.

This is surreal. I'm waiting to ask an ex-cop turned santero, *who could also be a police informant, for help. Wouldn't it make more sense to contact the consular officer, or whoever is in charge of the American Interest Section, and find a legal way out of it? I shouldn't have let Isabel con me into coming here.*

Then Gabriela insisted they try what she was cooking—a bright green vegetable soup. She brought them two full cups. Matt eyed their content with suspicion. It looked unappetizing, but tasted surprisingly good.

"I'm also making guava jam," Gabriela said. "But I am not sure I got *el punto* right. Sometimes it turns out too tart."

"Let me see to that," Isabel answered. "If someone in Havana has the *punto* for guava jam, that is me."

Matt excused himself and walked out, despite Gabriela's worried expression and Isabel's disapproving look. Maybe it wasn't good manners in Havana, or Regla, to desert your hostess in the middle of a conversation. But he could blame his linguistic skills, or lack thereof. He was also annoyed at the waste of time. Isabel had made the appointment for eleven o'clock and it was twelve fifteen.

Not that I have anything more constructive to do today, but still—

When Matt passed near the hut, he couldn't help but glance inside. Padrino was sitting on the floor, facing a woman who had her back to the door. She wore a white kerchief wound around her head like a turban. Between the woman and Padrino lay a red tablecloth. A cane had been placed over it. There were three small chunks of coconut on Padrino's side.

The *santero* held them, shook them in his right hand and threw them over the tablecloth. The woman spoke, Padrino nodded, and the procedure was repeated. Matt couldn't hear their voices but the interaction was clear enough. She was asking and Padrino was dispensing answers with the help of the coconut pieces.

The whole thing looked silly to Matt, who wondered if the *santero* used the same approach to solve his cases.

A pig grunted in the pen. Two hens walked by and one pecked at his shoes. Matt refrained from kicking it.

Padrino stood up. His face was contorted and his head bobbed up and down. His body shivered as if he were having a seizure. After the spasms subsided, he started going in circles, leaning on the cane and talking fast while the woman listened and bowed down. Then he stepped over the tablecloth and sent the coconut pieces flying with the tip of his cane.

Matt stared as Padrino changed, in a matter of seconds, from a middle-aged man into a real *viejo*: shaky hands, feeble legs and curved spine. His movements became slow and infirm.

If he is putting on a show, he is the best. Better than Taty as Donna Summer.

Padrino fell down. His head thumped against the floor. Matt expected the woman to run outside asking for help, but she knelt next to the *santero* and began to stroke his forehead until he sat straight, blinked, and looked around.

Matt tiptoed back to the house.

Spirit possession or performance? Or both?

PADRINO MET WITH MATT in a regular office with bookshelves, art posters from the eighties, and a framed diploma issued by the Havana Police Academy. The walls were painted white and the black and white tile floor was spotless. Matt sat on a wooden chair with a wicker seat. Padrino was across from him, behind a mahogany pedestal desk. It had been topped with a piece of glass, but the surface beneath was scratched and stained. All the drawers had crude metal locks that had replaced the original ones. There were pencil sketches and drawings all over the desk. While he talked, Padrino doodled distractedly on a notepad in front of him.

The *santero* looked completely recovered from whatever had happened to him before. He looked composed, healthy and fit. Vestiges of his former self were detectable under the all-white attire and the beaded necklaces. It could have been the buzz cut, the square shoulders, the erect posture, or a vague military rigidity in his demeanor, but Matt sensed the cop's presence inside the *santero*, as if the clothes were just a disguise. That reassured him.

First, they discussed his compensation. Padrino charged fifty dollars for an hour of work, which included consulting his sources—he didn't say if they were earth-bound or supernatural. They could agree on a budget and he would make sure not to go over it.

"I appreciate that," Matt said. "I only have the money I brought because I can't pay you with a credit card, I assume."

"No credit cards, no checks," Padrino answered. "Just cash, amigo. But I will give you a special discount since you came recommended by one of my goddaughters."

"Thanks."

Matt set his budget at six hundred dollars and gave Padrino three hundred to start. Padrino took the bills and placed them inside a drawer without counting them. Then he disclosed what he had already found out about the case, information that was, he added, totally free.

"Yarmila was strangled," he said matter-of-factly. "Nothing was taken from the apartment. There were two hundred dollars in an envelope in plain sight, on her dresser."

"Was she—?" Matt's voice trembled. "Was she raped or—?"

"No, the only sign of violence were the marks on her throat," Padrino said. "It seems like she was left under the shower to erase the killer's fingerprints. He must have gone around cleaning the whole place because there were no other traces of him. Or her. That's all I know, up to now. What about you?"

"What about me?" Matt repeated, confused.

He looked around and noticed a small round table in a corner, with a blue ceramic pitcher and two matching cups on top. A Cuban watercooler, he thought.

"Do you have any suspect in mind?" Padrino asked.

"No, not really. I didn't think Yarmi had enemies. She never mentioned them. I don't see a reason—unless she was two-timing Pato Macho too."

"So you know about that," Padrino said.

Matt struggled to find a face-saving answer. His attention was briefly caught by a framed print that hung above the pitcher. The image looked vaguely familiar but he couldn't identify it.

"Lieutenant Martínez told me," he said slowly, his shoulders dropping. "Then Pato Macho came to the room where I was staying and—"

"Damn kid," Padrino said. "You shouldn't worry about him, though. He's just a big boy."

"A big boy with a temper. And a metal bat."

"That too. Now, even if we have ruled out robbery, I'd still like to know how often you were sending money to Yarmila and how much you gave her altogether."

Matt paused to think it over. "I sent five hundred dollars last year as a Christmas gift, through Western Union. She didn't ask for it," he hurried to add. "It was my idea. In January, a friend of mine came to Cuba and I sent three hundred dollars and a care package with her."

"What was in the care package?"

"Deodorant, soaps, two pairs of shoes. But they were from Payless." He stopped, considering that the name wouldn't mean a thing to a Cuban. "Inexpensive, I mean. Three T-shirts, a denim jacket . . . Nothing valuable."

"Everything is valuable here."

"The most expensive item was an interactive map." Matt smiled sadly at the memory. "A toy, the kind that you can trace a line from one place to another and it tells you the miles and the travel time. I had marked the distance between San Diego and Havana, hoping that it would encourage Yarmila to come with me. I know this sounds silly . . ."

"No, not at all. Did Yarmila like it?"

"Yes, very much. She told me that she took it to her workplace and it was a hit there."

Matt got a whiff of guava mixed with burned sugar. It was pungent and crisp, and made him salivate. The office door was closed, but he could hear Isabel's shrill voice giving Gabriela instructions. She sounded like a backyard hen.

"Did you send her more money?" Padrino asked.

Matt stared at the wall to avoid Padrino's eyes. The print portrayed a young woman with dark hair coming out of a river.

"I wired her another five hundred last month," he said. "She used it to buy a share of La Caldosa. At least that was what she told me."

"That makes thirteen hundred dollars."

Matt sighed. It looked now as if he had been taken for a long, costly ride. But he hadn't seen it like that before. He hadn't even kept a tally.

"Yarmi was my fiancée," he said, as if defending himself from a silent accusation. "She was poor, though she didn't consider herself poor. As I said, she didn't ask for anything. She even told me not to spend a lot on 'stuff.' She wasn't a material girl."

"Did you believe she loved you?" Padrino asked softly.

"Yes. Either Yarmila was an Oscar-worthy actress or I'm the biggest *pendejo* in the world, but I did believe she was sincere. She wasn't interested in money, dollar shops or fancy places. I once invited her to Tropicana and she refused to go."

Padrino listened carefully, with his head cocked toward Matt. "Why?"

"She said it wasn't 'the real Cuba' and she didn't like the way the dancers presented themselves to foreign audiences. She thought it was disrespectful of her country's image or something like that."

"I see."

"Besides, I didn't send her *that* much. For you Cubans a thousand bucks may look like a lot, but it isn't for us."

"Everything is relative," Padrino said.

He looked at Matt with a knowing smile.

"And something else," Matt added. "She wasn't anxious to leave Cuba. She seemed happy enough with her life here so I never had the impression that she was using me to get a visa."

"Were you planning to settle in Havana after you guys got married?"

"Oh, God, no! I don't think I could live here. Yarmi once said she wanted to visit San Diego and hinted that she could travel back and forth."

"That doesn't sound realistic. Unless you are very rich, of course."

A window with metal shutters filtered the sun onto Padrino's desk. Matt watched the light patterns for a few seconds. *Had I been rich, maybe Yarmi wouldn't have cheated on me.*

"I am not," he said at last. "I am a journalist for a small border paper. I couldn't have paid for her trips, or mine, more than once or maybe twice a year."

"Then?"

"I guess she wasn't going to marry me," Matt admitted. "I guess she wasn't my fiancée, after all."

"Was she or wasn't she? Let's make this clear."

Matt took his time to answer again. When he did, his voice cracked.

"I proposed to Yarmila over the phone on February 14. I asked her to be my wife and—she didn't say yes. But she didn't say no either. She told me that it was a serious matter, something to talk over in person."

Suddenly, he recognized the image on the print. It was a representation of the Virgin of Regla, the one he had just seen at the church. It was the only item in the office that gave a clue to Padrino's spiritual role.

"But I went ahead and bought the dress and the ring, and got that stupid certificate of single status that the Notaría Internacional website listed as a requirement just in case she happened to accept my proposal," he went on. "I was too hopeful, wasn't I?"

In the end, she would have rejected me or told me that we'd have to wait. She loved Pato Macho, not me. And I knew it in my heart.

That's the worst part of it, but I won't tell this guy, or anybody else. I suspected the truth and that was why I went for a secondhand dress at Buffalo Exchange instead of a new one from Macy's.

Padrino nodded in silent agreement. "While you were in the apartment, did you notice anything out of place or unusual?" he asked. "I know you were there for the first time, but still."

"Well, let me see . . . I remember a couple of books on the coffee table. There was an old refrigerator that reminded me of my grandparents' times, and an ironing board right in front of it. It was kinda odd, actually, unless she had been planning to iron before she was—"

"Like this?" Padrino showed him his notepad with a crude sketch of the two pieces.

"Yes, exactly," he said. "It would have been impossible to open the refrigerator door unless you moved the ironing board first. Other than that, the place looked neat, though something there stank badly. I don't know what it was. It was then that I discovered the body and—"

He stopped and covered his face with his hands. He saw Yarmila again, rigid in the bathtub. *To think that this would be the last image I'd have of her. After I had expected to find her making merenguitos for me.*

"Is there anything else you want to tell me?" Padrino asked after a short pause.

"I'd like to know why she was cheating on me with . . . that young man," Matt said. "Like, why bother? She could have broken up with me. She didn't have to string me along, did she?"

"That is beyond my skills," Padrino said. "I can, with some luck, discover who killed her. But why she acted the way she did, that's another story. The only person who could give you an answer is now dead."

Matt swallowed hard. It briefly occurred to him to ask Padrino if he wasn't a medium too. Could *santeros* channel spirits or get in touch with them somehow?

No, wait. I don't want him to think of me as a gullible Yuma. *Well, he may be thinking that already. No need to ask such a stupid question and remove all doubt.*

When the interview was over, Padrino wrote down Román's address and phone number and said he would be in touch. He also gave Matt his cell number.

"You can call me anytime," he said.

They shook hands.

"May the *orishas* bless you," Padrino said.

"Thanks," Matt answered. "Ah—do you mind if I ask you a question, Padrino?"

It was the first time he called him by his name, or rather his nickname. The *santero* smiled, amused.

"You can ask all the questions you want, my friend. You are paying me to find the answers."

"It's not about the case."

"Go ahead."

"Are you a Santería practitioner?" Matt asked.

"Yes, I am a *babalawo*."

"That's like a priest?"

Padrino fingered his necklaces. "Close enough."

"Do you use your *babalawo* powers to solve these cases?"

Padrino laughed.

"I ask the *orishas* for guidance in most situations, professional and personal, but they have never told me, 'This guy killed someone, or the money he stole is buried under that tree,'" he laughed louder. "I wish!"

"When you offer spiritual sessions, how much do you charge?"

"Donations only. Some bring me food; others gifts, even animals." Padrino shrugged, then chuckled. "One Christmas Eve, one of my godsons showed up with three piglets. I said to him, 'You're crazy. What am I supposed to do with these oinkers?' And he said, 'Eh, that's up to you. I just want to pay my respect to you and the *orishas*.' That was two years ago. We have been eating pork quite often ever since."

Old Farmer's Broth

Hola and welcome to my kitchen!

I hadn't written in the last few days because I had a cold. *Ay ay ay*, my poor head hurt so much and I couldn't keep a thing in my stomach. And as you know, I love having stuff in this *pancita* of mine!

So I made myself a big batch of what Grandma Hilda called Old Farmer's Broth. It is simple, delicious and *curalotodo*, meaning it can heal everything. I have been having it for the last three days and I am feeling much better, thank you.

People always think *caldo de pollo*, chicken broth, when they come down with a cold, but Grandma Hilda differed. She said that chicken was too heavy for a weak stomach. She made *El Caldo del Guajiro Viejo* instead.

It's easy to prepare. Chop five zucchinis, one pound of green beans, one pound of *quimbombó* (I believe the English name is okra) and a bunch of parsley. While you are chopping, boil five cups of water, then add all the ingredients and bring them to a boil again.

Let it simmer for half an hour. After twenty minutes, you can also add marjoram and cilantro to spice things up a bit. Let it cool for a while and puree everything.

That's it! So green and beautiful you will feel better after looking at it.

My friend Fefita came to see how I was doing. When I told her about the broth, she made a face. As some of you have noticed, Cubans have an aversion to vegetables. "*Fo*," she said.

"*Fo*" means "Arf," my *Yuma* boyfriend told me.

"That must taste like blotter paper," she huffed, without having as much as tasted it. Blotter paper, listen to that! I made her try the *caldo* and she had to admit that it wasn't half as bad as she thought. But still, she brought me a cup of chicken broth.

Have you ever had anything similar to my *caldo*?

COMMENTS

Cocinera Cubana said. . .

Hi Yarmi! Hope you are feeling better. This is almost exactly like Bieler's Broth, only that it has celery instead of okra.

Julia de Tejas said. . .

Be well, amiga. Your broth will be perfect for a cold winter night.

Anita said. . .

I love how you people take care of each other.

Taos Tonya said. . .

Add chile, hita! That will make it even better.

Yarmi said. . .

Thanks, you all! I am back to my usual self and I appreciate your good wishes. Yes, Anita, we love helping each other here. That's part of our *Cubanidad*.

Lucy Adel said. . .

Tonya, I already know that in Taos, wherever that is, you add chile to dessert. Do you put it in your beer too, by any chance?

Folks of all nationalities also take care of their family and friends. That's *not* a Cuban trait, Yarmi. That's universal.

PART III

Chapter One

COMRADE INSTRUCTOR

Marlene Martínez started her workday at six thirty in the morning. She liked to spend some time alone before the phone began to ring and people started to pour in the Unidad. There was a stack of files on her desk. She had meant to shred them all the night before since the information they contained was now stored electronically.

Finally, technology was catching up with the Unidad. A computer had just been assigned to her. When Martínez's boss, Captain Rogelio Ramos, had told her that she was the only person in the building who could use the device, she had beamed. The computer was an old model, with a small screen and an MS-DOS operating system. Marlene wished it had internet access—she had become more familiar with the concept thanks to Yarmila's blog posts—but the service wasn't available inside the police station. Still, "something was something."

"You can dispose of your old papers, *compañera*," Captain Ramos had said. "Now everything will be much easier to organize."

She had stayed until 10:00 P.M. the previous night, transferring all the handwritten information to the computer. She looked forward to reviewing it in its new, improved form. She might see certain things with more clarity now. But when she turned on the computer, the screen blinked annoyingly for several minutes. Martínez tried rebooting. The monitor went blank. She hit the tower case, cursed Captain Ramos, and congratulated herself for not throwing away the paper files.

"So much for technology!"

She opened an old-fashioned but reliable paper folder labeled "Yarmila Portal" and went over her list of suspects. Yosvani Álvarez, aka Pato Macho, had been at the top originally, but she had moved him to the bottom after confirming his alibi: he had spent the morning of the day that Yarmila was killed at El Cincuentenario Bar. Five people had seen him, though there was a period of around an hour, at lunchtime, when he claimed he had gone home. Only his mother could attest to it, which she had of course done.

Pato had broken into tears when Martínez questioned him. Could that have been an act? She didn't think so. She couldn't see him killing Yarmila, or anybody else. More suspicious was his mother, an abrasive woman with a bad temper that she had barely controlled in the detective's presence. Isabel had been defensive of her son, protesting her *niño*'s innocence and badmouthing Yarmila in subtle ways. Marlene concluded that Isabel was the type who made her daughter-in-law's life miserable. And she had no alibi. She said she had been "cooking up a storm at home" all day.

Martínez wrote a question mark next to Isabel's name. The next page was devoted to a couple, Carmela Mendez and Pablo Urquiola. They had caught her attention right away, not only because they were among the few close friends Yarmila had, but also because they used to be members of the Communist Party and had turned into dissidents. That was enough for Marlene to look at them suspiciously.

She reread her notes on them. They lived two blocks away from Yarmila, who visited them often. She had invited them to La Caldosa and paid for their dinner from her own pocket, though Isabel, who provided the information, considered the couple bad for business. "They were her friends, not mine," she had said when Martínez pressed for details. "I only knew they were *gusanos*."

Martínez didn't have to go far to find more information about Carmela and Pablo. La Seguridad already kept a watchful eye and a huge file on them because of their political activities. They wrote for a Miami website that documented human rights violations in Cuba. They listened to Radio Martí and went to the American Interest Section every week to read foreign newspapers and—an unnamed informant assumed—conspire against the revolution. Pablo had once spent three months in prison. They were likely to get an American visa, the Seguridad agent's footnote read, if they ever asked for it. "Difficult to deal with. Obstinate. Won't shut up, especially Carmela," the informer had concluded.

Martínez distrusted them, though she hadn't even met them yet. Couldn't it be possible that these two and citizen Portal had had a disagreement over money? The detective had read that the CIA paid dissidents generously and that all human rights groups were financed by the Americans. Yarmila had been quick to accept Matt's "help" though she obviously didn't love him. Maybe she had tried to get something out of the *gusanos*. Yarmila could have threatened to turn them in, and so they had killed her.

It was a wild assumption, but now that Pato Macho had been discarded, Martínez felt more inclined to consider it. In truth, she disliked the dissidents as much as she was starting to dislike citizen Portal. That was new for her. As a detective, she had always been on the victim's side. But this was no ordinary victim. First, Yarmila did extra work at the *paladar*, a private business that paid her in dollars or CUCs. Why did she do that, when she had been assigned a perfectly good job at the Institute of Literature and Linguistics? Martínez shook her head and scowled at the file.

Don't tell me she cooked for Isabel only in her spare time. I bet she cut her hours short at the Institute to work at La Caldosa.

Then she had cheated on her official boyfriend with Pato Macho. Though Marlene had done her best to conceal it, she had secretly sympathized with Matt. He might be an American, but he seemed like a nice guy. She felt sorry for him, more so after he admitted that he had sent Yarmila a lot of money.

What a sucker. And not bad looking, by the way. More handsome than Pato Macho, who is just a big mama's boy. Martinez would have let Matt go—she didn't consider him a suspect anymore—but it wasn't up to her.

The worst part, in her opinion, was citizen Portal's relationship with the *gusanos*. Fefita, the President of the Committee for the Defense of the Revolution (the same woman who had been with Matt when he found the body, Martínez recalled), hadn't accused her neighbor of any counterrevolutionary activities, but that didn't mean much. The two had been good friends. Marlene had the impression that Fefita had tried to smooth things over. Even so, she had hinted that Yarmila sometimes "kept bad company."

Martínez made a note to call Fefita again. At times like this, she wished she had someone with whom she could discuss things. She could have gone to Jacobo Rodríguez—"Agent Pedro"—but didn't feel comfortable with the idea. The Seguridad guy had put himself in charge of the case, confiscating Matt's passport and searching the crime scene before anybody else, including Martínez, was allowed in. She resented his intrusion and wondered if the secret police didn't trust her. Maybe they thought she wasn't doing her job properly or doubted she could handle a foreigner with enough professionalism.

Martínez had yet another reason to be concerned. At the Unidad, she was used to dealing with petty criminals, drug dealers, *jineteras*, and pimps. This was only the third murder case she'd had. With the other two she had been part of a team, but now she was on her own—except for "Agent Pedro" who hadn't done a thing to be of help to her.

Ah, if she could have called her favorite teacher at the National Revolutionary Police Academy! He had taught research methods and data analysis. Marlene had been his best student. He had recommended her for her first job. But "comrade instructor," as she still called him, was now a believer in Afro-Cuban deities, a dispenser of charms! She had seen him once after he retired, dressed totally in white and wearing a strange necklace.

Marlene couldn't understand how a former detective, someone who was well versed in dialectical materialism, had become a *santero*. But so many people in Cuba believed in Santería. Her own mother kept a glass of water behind the door "to quench the spirits' thirst" and a small saucer full of honey for the *orisha* Oshún. She also had a Virgin of Charity altar hidden in a kitchen corner and she lit candles in front of it.

Marlene snickered. *As if the orishas could materialize and, say, help me solve this case. Come on, Oshún, lend me a hand here. Ha!*

The phone rang, though it wasn't eight o'clock yet. Martínez wanted to ignore it but she finally answered. Her face lit up when she heard the man's voice.

"Comrade Instructor!" she exclaimed. "You won't believe it, but I was thinking of you a moment ago."

"I do believe it, *mija*," he laughed. "It's called telepathy."

She looked down at citizen Portal's file, wondering if she should tell him about the case. Wouldn't that be a breach of code? He wasn't a member of the police force anymore.

"What's up, Comrade Instructor?" she asked.

"I've taken on a case and I heard that you are part of it. Do you have a moment to talk?"

While she listened to him, Marlene's mind flashed back to her mother's altar.

The orisha's helping, huh?

THEY MET LATER THAT day. Martínez didn't like the idea of money being involved—her former teacher had disclosed that he was being paid—but she ended up accepting his offer to work together. After all, she wasn't the one receiving dollars. (Not that she couldn't use them, but she wouldn't have dared.) Besides, what comrade instructor did was his business, and she needed his help as much as he needed hers.

"I've already questioned Yosvani Álvarez and his mother, who was a friend of citizen Portal," she said. "I can give you the recordings if you want. Then we have the *gusanos*."

She talked nonstop about them for around ten minutes.

"Was Yarmila involved with them?" was all comrade instructor asked. "Politically, I mean."

"I don't know for sure, but I don't think so. There is nothing in their Seguridad file about her."

He didn't seem interested in the dissidents. That hurt Marlene's feelings a bit.

"What about Yarmila's family?" he asked.

"I saw her parents when they came to identify her body, but I still have to meet with them again. That wasn't the right moment, you know? The problem is that they live in Pinar del Río."

"I can go," he said.

Marlene exhaled loudly. "I am so relieved to have you here, Comrade Instructor," she said. "Even if you are—even if this is your private business now."

He opened his arms in a gesture that had as much acknowledgment as surrender in it.

"What's a guy going to do? Yep, I've become a *bisnero* all right."

"But not in the bad sense, not like—"

She saw the smile on his face. A smile that became more pronounced when he pointed to the computer. "I see you are all techie now."

"Don't talk to me about that dinosaur!" Martínez huffed. "Can you believe I got it two days ago and it's already broken? *Mierda*! Ah, speaking of computers, citizen Portal must have had one too. Jacobo sent me some of the blog posts she wrote. But they are all in English and I am trying to make sense of them."

Comrade instructor, who had frowned at the mention of the Seguridad agent, said, "I would like to see copies of these posts."

"Of course. But from what I can tell they are rather boring: long, detailed descriptions of fancy food I can't imagine where she found." Marlene felt a hunger pang. "Nothing you can buy through the ration card, for sure. I bet Jacobo has more information, but he isn't sharing it with me. You know how the Seguridad people act, so secretive and stuck up."

"They watch too many movies," comrade instructor said with a sly wink. "But we'll prove to them they ain't so smart."

Chapter Two

FROM EL CINCUENTENARIO TO EL MERCADO

El Cincuentenario Bar smelled like rum and piss. Located on Pocito Street, one block away from Salvador Allende Avenue, the bar had been a neighborhood fixture since 1950. The storefront had been reinforced with metal shutters and a big dumpster was placed against the main entrance every night as an added precaution. A mélange of offensive odors concentrated overnight in the main room. When the bartender, who started his workday at nine thirty in the morning, opened the shutters, the unfortunate passersby crossed the street and held their noses.

Sometimes the occasional cook got inspired to make croquettes, fried in reused lard and served with crackers, but most patrons didn't care for snacks. If they were hungry, there was a private food cart called La Dulcinea a few yards away, across the street, where they could buy Mexican *chicharrones*, refried cracklings, and cheese sandwiches for fifty CUC cents.

At ten o'clock, *los cinco*, the five customary drunks who came by every day, were not interested in anything that wasn't presented to them in liquid form. They weren't smashed yet, but well on their way, having ordered double shots of the cheapest rum, Coronilla.

Their faces, as reflected in the mirror punctuated by fly poop, were red, with jovial jowls and yellow teeth. Their loud voices spilled onto the sidewalk, but their constant requests from the bartender (Hey, *cantinero*!) didn't attract the guy's attention. He was huddled in a corner, reading a *Vanidades* magazine, or rather ogling the models' legs. When the drunks got too annoying, the *cantinero* put the magazine aside and, with a sigh of discontent, proceeded to refill their glasses, making sure to collect his fee first.

One of *los cinco*, feeling exceptionally generous, bought an entire bottle of Coronilla to share with his friends. They began to discuss baseball. Two were Industriales fans while the others rooted for the Santiago de Cuba team. Though curses were exchanged and fists raised, fights among them were unheard of. The five drunks had known one another for years and considered themselves a sort of clan. They would drink, spit on the floor, get up to take a piss, and come back to pat their friends on the back.

It was business as usual at El Cincuentenario.

A young man in blue jeans and a muscle shirt came in. He wasn't a total stranger but a neighborhood kid, and not the kind the regulars were used to seeing there—at least not so early in the day.

"Look who's here," a drunk said. "The grieving boyfriend!"

Pato Macho approached the counter and asked for a double shot. He handed ten Cuban pesos to the *cantinero*, who took them with a sly grin but said nothing. *Los cinco* weren't that discreet, though.

"Coming to drown your sorrows in Coronilla?"

"Did your mama let you come before lunch?"

The young man stared at them until his drink arrived. Then he shrugged and said, "Fuck off."

"Careful there or I will wash your mouth with soap, *bebito*."

Neither the bartender nor the drunks noticed the guy in white who had stopped outside the bar, though his looks were unusual enough to warrant a double take. Men and women dressed in Santería attire were not such an oddity as they had been in the seventies and eighties—after the government had more or less legalized religion by welcoming non-atheists into the Communist Party in the early nineties, more people felt free to make their beliefs known. Still, a guy dressed in full *babalawo* regalia wasn't an everyday sight.

Padrino had positioned himself behind the dumpster. From his vantage point, he was able to watch the scene without being noticed. And he saw how, after a crossfire of insults and laughs at Pato Macho's expense, the latter lost his cool and punched a drunk in the face. The drunk's friends hurried to help him. Two attempted to take on Pato, but they were no match for the athletic younger guy, who kicked one and threw another to the floor. It was only then that the *cantinero* deigned to intervene.

"Eh, *comemierda*, get lost before I call the cops," he told Pato Macho, barely lifting his eyes from the glossy *Vanidades* page that featured an interview with Kate Moss.

But Pato Macho was enraged. So were *los cinco*, who had regrouped and were advancing toward him in a threatening manner. Pato grabbed the Coronilla bottle by the bottom, broke it against the counter and wielded what was left of it.

"*Carajo!*" the bartender barked and lifted the receiver.

Padrino decided to get involved. He came in and took Pato Macho by the arm. While the *cantinero* made a real or fake call asking for the Unidad's support, Padrino managed to drag the young man out of the bar.

"What is this all about, son?" he asked as he walked down

Espada Street with a reluctant Pato by his side. "Don't you know that you are in no position to go looking for trouble right now?"

Pato Macho stopped. They were near La Caldosa. He wiped his forehead and smoothed his shirt.

"Don't tell *la pura* about this," he pleaded.

Padrino nodded in agreement. In the new street lingo, young guys referred to their mothers as "the pure one." "I won't," he said. "But you have to get a hold of yourself. First, you wanted to kill the *Yuma*. Now this. What's up?"

"My nerves are shot," Pato Macho said. "I blew it with the *Yuma*, yes. And I shouldn't have messed with *los cinco*, but I couldn't help myself, Padrino. I'm sorry."

"What did these guys say that pissed you off so much?"

"They started talking about Yarmi."

"Well, son, everybody is talking about Yarmi after what happened to her. You will have to get used to it."

Pato Macho winced. "They said she was a whore and I was a happy *cabrón*."

"*Los cinco* are a bunch of stupid drunks, Pato. Consider the source and don't sweat it."

La Caldosa's window was open. They saw Isabel peeling potatoes at a table.

"You're right, Padrino," the young man muttered. "But you know what's the problem? That they said exactly what I was thinking, and I couldn't take it."

ISABEL OFFERED PADRINO A ritual greeting, crossing her arms over her chest and then leaning, first to the left and then the right, touching shoulders with him.

"*A gua wa o to, Omo Oshún*," he said and proceeded to make the sign of the cross over his goddaughter's head.

"It's nice to see you again," she said.

"I'm working on your friend's case."

"Ah, I knew you would take good care of it."

Though Padrino didn't mention the incident with the drunks, Isabel only needed to take a look at her son to figure it out. Padrino didn't mention that he had started to watch the young man, either. Yes, he had told Matt that Pato Macho was "just a big boy," but the rooftop incident had worried him. If Pato had attacked a stranger with a metal bat, what else could he have done in a fit of rage? Padrino didn't know him *that* well, after all.

Isabel was complaining about her son's behavior. By then, Pato Macho had locked himself in his room.

"He is out of control, Padrino, totally out of control since you know what," she said. "I heard him crying all night long. I wonder if a Santería ceremony may help him. Do you think her spirit is haunting him?"

"Oh, most spirits don't . . ."

Someone knocked at the door.

"That's Yony, one of my providers," she said. "Now, if you would excuse me. But I'd like to talk about this later, please."

Isabel introduced the two men and went to fetch her precision scale from the kitchen. She prided herself on being a good hostess, but business came first. Yony had brought her the five pounds of pork and she wanted to weigh it right away.

Yony already knew who Padrino was. He had seen him eating at La Caldosa and heard about his connections to the police. As a *bisnero*, he would have rather stayed away from him. Yony's activities, though by no means a secret, were very much against the law. He acted as an intermediary between his partners, who worked in CUC-only shops, and the general public. The store clerks would steal the merchandise under their bosses' noses—no big deal, since the bosses were stealing as well. But they wouldn't risk selling; there were too many outsiders who coveted their jobs and could turn them in. They needed people like Yony, who had plenty of connections through his taxi business: Cubans and foreigners with disposable income to buy food, clothes and electronics at half their retail value. The store's prices were so high that Yony and his partners made a profit without squeezing the consumers' pockets too much.

"What are you selling today?" Padrino asked in a friendly manner.

"Just a bit of pork," Yony said, fidgeting with his burlap sack. "Listen, I don't want problems, okay? I can explain this. I am an honest *bisnero*. I'm only—"

"You don't have to explain anything to me," Padrino said. "I don't care about other people's lives. And I have my own business too."

Yony's shoulders relaxed a bit. Isabel came back with the scale and set it on the table.

"Padrino is my godfather, Yony," she said. "You can trust him. You may even gain a client here."

Padrino didn't contradict her. But the *bisnero* still stared at him suspiciously. When the transaction was over, Yony refused to stay for a cup of coffee.

"I have to walk all the way to the Cuatro Caminos Farmers' Market," he said. "I'd better start off before it gets hotter."

"Why do you need to walk?" Isabel asked. "Don't you have an *almendrón*?"

"I had to take it to the mechanic and that's going to cost me an arm and a leg. All these bastards jack up their prices for *almodrivers* like me. They think we are made of money."

"I can give you a ride," Padrino offered. "My old VW Beetle is not as fancy as an *almendrón* but it runs well."

Yony's face lit up. "Thanks, man!"

THEY TALKED CARS FIRST, on the way to Cuatro Caminos. Padrino had learned to take care of the VW by himself.

"I've already figured out most of its tricks and quirks," he said. "It isn't too complicated. Not like these new cars where everything is run by a computer."

"Me, I'm all thumbs." Yony pointed to two small wounds that punctured his Virgin of Charity tattoo. "See, I tried to seal a leak last week and got nailed by a connecting rod or whatever it was. I hate tinkering with cars."

"That's too bad."

Later, Padrino steered the chat to Pato Macho. Yony barely knew Isabel's son, but that didn't stop him from calling him "a mama's boy."

"That's partly her fault too," he said. "You know how mothers are, always overprotecting their kids. Mine is a lot like Isabel. When I visit her, she still fusses over me and calls me 'her baby' in front of everyone. But what am I going to do? I can't disrespect her because chances are she's the only decent woman I'll ever know."

"Yeah, the pure one."

"Right. But she can be a nice pest, particularly with my girlfriends. The Cubans, I mean."

"So you have both Cuban and foreign girls."

Yony spread his arms as much as the small car's interior allowed him to. "I have *dozens* of *Yumas*," he said. "They see me and they can't keep their hands off me . . . I could go to the States tomorrow, if I wanted to."

"Ah, lucky you."

"And my *pura*, she is fine with them. Mom makes rice pudding, even gave a girl a massage—she is a *sobadora* too, a healer. But she doesn't give my Cuban girlfriends the time of day. Isabel is like that, only ten times worse. She is obsessed with that Pato kid."

It didn't take long for the conversation to shift to Yarmila. Yony admitted that he knew, like everybody else, of her affair with Pato Macho.

"But I don't think she took him seriously," he said. "She was too much of a woman for him."

"How did you know her?"

"Her *Yuma* guy is friends with my *Yuma* girl."

"And you? Were you friends with her too?"

Padrino coughed and took his eyes off the road to watch Yony's reaction.

"Not in the way you are thinking!" Yony protested with a forced smile.

"How do you know what I'm thinking?"

"Just in case." He grew somber and looked out the window. "I'm so sorry about this. I picked up her *Yuma* at the airport the other day. *Coño*, we couldn't imagine then that poor Yarmila wasn't there waiting because she had been killed. Life is . . ." He shook his head.

"Did you do business with her?" Padrino asked.

"Well, she didn't need me. Her *Yuma* sent her whatever she wanted. But I would sell her food sometimes. Once, I got an electric fan for her *gusano* friends."

Padrino pricked up his ears. "Who are her *gusano* friends?" he asked, feigning ignorance.

Yony shrugged. "I don't know their names. For one thing, they aren't *my* friends. They like to eat at La Caldosa."

"So you sold her an electric fan and she gave it to them?"

"Yes. People say that *gusanos* get loads of cash from the *Yumas* and maybe they do, but they never buy anything from me."

"She used the money her American boyfriend had sent her to buy stuff for the *gusanos*?" Padrino said, arching an eyebrow. "Isn't that a little strange?"

Yony coughed, then blew his nose. Padrino watched him attentively, wondering if he was just attempting to gain time.

"I thought it was strange too," Yony admitted. "But what was I going to say? A sale is a sale, man."

Padrino waited a few seconds before asking in a casual manner, "When was the last time you saw her?"

Yony scratched his head. "Let me see . . . around two weeks ago. She called me because she wanted to make *caldosa* and needed vegetables and meat. I sold her pumpkins, sweet potatoes, yuca, plantains, and four pounds of pork. I took them to her apartment. She paid me right away. She wasn't like other people who wait until they shit the food to pay for it."

"You didn't hear from her again?"

Another pause. Now Yony cracked his fingers, a habit that always irritated Padrino and put him on guard.

"Yes, a few days later she called me and ordered stuff for *merenguitos*," Yony answered. "She said she had promised her *Yuma* to make some . . . But I got the ingredients Wednesday evening and by that time it was too late. So sad, man." Yony gazed at the streets. "Such a beautiful woman. Death plays no favorites, does it?"

"Do you happen to have any idea of who could have killed her?"

Yony wasn't aware of Padrino's side job as a private detective, but he knew enough about him to realize this talk was an informal interrogation. He thought carefully before answering. "I don't, man," he said. "If I knew, I would tell you. I mean, the murderer is still out there, maybe getting ready to kill somebody else. It's sick. But I know of someone who can help you: Fefita *Comité*."

"Fefita who?"

"She is a neighbor of Yarmi's. People still call her 'Committee Fefita' because she used to be the president of the Committee for the Defense of the Revolution. She resigned after her daughter married a Spaniard and left Cuba . . . I guess she was ashamed. As if marrying a foreigner were a bad thing! Anyway, even if she isn't in charge of watching everyone like she used to be, nobody farts in that building without Fefita knowing it."

"Thanks for the tip, man."

"As I said, I do want to help. Ah, I live in Hamel's Alley number forty-five, in case you need something from me. Food, clothes, gadgets, a TV, whatever." Yony snapped his fingers. "I can find *anything* you want!"

THE CUATRO CAMINOS FARMERS' Market, one of the oldest *agromercados* in Havana, had taken its name from the four streets that converged at its center: Monte, Cristina, Matadero and Manglar. It occupied an entire block. Its two floors housed booths, kiosks and simple wooden boards where the vendors displayed their goods. It had four marble staircases stained by years of use.

The fresh smells of fruits and flowers mixed with the very organic odors of chicken shit and pig poop. Flies surrounded the meat counters where pork ribs and full hams were exposed to bugs, dust and clients' unhygienic touches. Plucked chickens could be seen hanging from strings. Stray dogs were no strangers to the first floor.

And yet, the market wasn't devoid of charm. The high ceilings lent the place a spacious feel. An array of colors made even the humblest booths look festive. The revolutionary red of the tomatoes brought out the greener-than-the-palms shade of the avocadoes and the bright emerald of parsley bunches. Oranges, limes, and lemons were often found in the same stalls, in happy miscellany. Stout country women with stern faces hovered over their garlic, onions, and tubers, and set the prices depending on their customers' ability to pay, which they judged by their clothes and gadgets. A well-dressed young man hooked to a cell phone would be asked to pay two CUCs for four pounds of potatoes while an old, plain-looking house-wife might get the same for twenty Cuban pesos. Bargaining, though, was unheard of.

Padrino stopped his car two blocks past the market. All the spaces around it were already taken by trucks, pickups, and Russian-era cars. He was glad to have a few more minutes to talk to Yony without having to pay attention to the traffic, but the young man wasn't in a talking mood anymore. He responded to Padrino's comments, even the most trivial, with ahems and one-syllable words, not meeting his eye. Padrino couldn't under-stand his change in attitude, especially considering Yony had just offered to do "bisnes" with him.

They walked together to the *agromercado* and were immedi-ately beset by a small crowd of peddlers. They were the ones who couldn't get a government's license to sell inside. Their prices were lower than those set by authorized vendors, but there was always the danger of a cop interrupting the transaction and arresting both parties. Still, many farmers took the risk.

Yony ignored them, hurried in and began to check the chicken stalls. Padrino followed him and pretended to look at the birds too. There were loud roosters and angry hens pecking at their enclosure, at the corn kernels on the floor and at any hands that got too close to them.

"What are you looking for?" Padrino asked Yony.

"A rooster," he answered. "It's for Oshún. I was told to sacrifice a good fat rooster to him."

"A rooster for Oshún?" Padrino frowned. "Who told you to do that?"

"A friend of mine. A guy who knows a lot about Santería."

"I know a lot too," Padrino said. "I can assure you that it isn't advisable to give Oshún a rooster, except in extreme cases. You can offer him cacao butter, cascarilla, rum, even a white dove would be fine, but not a rooster. In a regular ceremony, he won't approve of it."

Yony's expression betrayed his dismay. "Why not?"

"He's very particular about offerings," Padrino explained. "If the bird's blood is on your hands, he'll get *encojonao*, really pissed off. Man, you don't want to have Oshún *encojonao* at you!"

"Huh, thanks for the warning. I may get a dove instead."

Yony walked away fast and disappeared into the crowd. Padrino was left with an unsettling feeling about the *bisnero* and he had the definite intention to find out more about him.

Drunken salad

Hola, mis amigos!

I am so tired that I will make this a short post. Today I went to the farmers' market and that always consumes a lot of time and energy.

The closest one to my house is El Vedado's *agromercado*, located on the corner of 17th and K streets. I actually prefer Cuatro Caminos, the biggest and cheapest of them all. I resorted to El Vedado simply because it is easier to catch a bus that leaves me right at the door.

I bought three mangos, a pineapple, a watermelon and two pounds of rice. I looked like a veritable *burra* carrying all that by myself.

In Pinar del Río, where I am from, the market is never far away. And we grow vegetables and fruits in our own plots so we don't need to go looking for them. Or paying for them.

If someone had told me three years ago that I was going to pay one CUC for five oranges I would have laughed out loud. The problem is that farmers can set their own prices. If they were conscientious, like my parents, they would keep them low so everyone could afford their products, but that isn't the case. Many are in this business just for the money. And you know what? That's wrong.

I also bought a bunch of lilies—at least they were available in pesos. I am a *guajira* at heart—a basic peasant girl. I love veggies and flowers. Roses, not so much, because they are too flashy. My favorites are simple plants like humble marigold, tiny jasmine blossoms, and lilies.

I use flowers to garnish salads and cook them with scrambled eggs. Have you ever tried that? *Huevos revueltos con flores*. I spread lilies over the eggs when they are almost done. They lend the dish a special fragrance, a mix of sweet cloves with hints of vanilla.

Anyway, the main reason why I went to the market is because I wanted to make *ensalada borracha*, drunken salad.

It's very simple. Just slice and mix one pineapple, two mangos, one watermelon, four oranges, one papaya, and whatever other fruit is available. Spread the petals of your favorite flower on top, for extra pizzazz. That's easy enough, *verdad*? But what makes it special is the dressing.

What's the dressing made of, you may ask. Ah, a secret ingredient! Use half a cup of Havana Club *siete años*, our national rum aged for seven years, and combine it with the juice of two oranges and one lime. Pour it over the sliced fruit, chill for an hour and enjoy.

COMMENTS

Cocinera Cubana said. . .

Funny, at home we don't eat a lot of fruit or salads. My friends are often surprised because they assume that Cubans must love veggies, coming from a tropical place. But I don't think it's a tradition, at least not in my family.

Cubanita in Claremont said. . .

Same here, Cocinera. My dad used to say that "that green stuff is just for goats." I tried being a vegetarian for a while and my parents worried to death, thinking I would end up anemic. They kept lobbying for the steak! But I will try the *ensalada borracha*.

By the way, Yarmi, do you eat the flowers when you put them on salads?

Julia de Tejas said. . .
What sold me was "la salsa." May I use Bacardi instead of Havana Club?

Taos Tonya. . .
What about 7 Deadly Zins? That's my favorite wine!

Lucy Adel said. . .
Are the *agromercados* like dollar shops, where everything is sold in CUCs? How can people who are only paid in pesos afford to buy anything there?

Yarmi said. . .
Thanks for all the comments. Sorry it took me a while to respond but I was . . . just like my *ensalada*, a bit *borracha*.

Cubanita and Cocinera, there have been several nationwide campaigns to encourage people to eat more vegetables, particularly after the new agroponics began to yield fruit. But many still snub them.

Yes, of course I eat the flowers. They are delicious!

Sure, Julia, use Bacardi or any kind of rum. Tonya, I've never made it with wine, but I guess it won't hurt. The salad will get *borracha* either way. And so will you!

Lucy, you can pay either in pesos or CUCs. Farmers accept both, though, sadly, they prefer the "convertible" pesos. Too bad.

Chapter Three
HALF-FACED MONA LISA

After Padrino returned home, he resorted to an English-Spanish dictionary to read some of Yarmila's posts. It took him a couple of hours and he was left scratching his head.

Pork and chicken for a caldosa? Really? She must have gotten it from a bisnero. Of course, Matt sent her money, she could certainly afford it. But still. Grilled steak? Maybe her folks sent her food from the countryside, though I doubt it. They often have even less to eat than we do.

He called Martínez and got directions to the home of Yarmila's parents in Pinar del Río. As he was getting ready to leave, Matt phoned him.

"I was wondering if you knew how to get in touch with Yarmi's family," he said. "No matter what happened, I'd still like to meet her folks and offer my condolences."

Padrino hesitated.

"Yarmi was from a town called Los Palacios," Matt went on. "Do you think I should get a taxi and just go there?"

"Not a good idea. The taxi driver will charge you a fortune and you will be wasting your time if you don't have a name or an address. I'll try to find out where they live and let you know."

"Okay."

He sounded disappointed. Padrino hung up.

What if those people don't want to see him?

PADRINO'S VW BEETLE COULDN'T keep up with the tourist buses that he encountered along the way to Pinar del Río. Halfway through the trip, at a booth sloppily built right by the side of the road—an assortment of wooden boards with a sun-bleached thatch roof—Padrino had an unexpected encounter with a gaggle of Matt's compatriots. The bus driver had stopped there, just as Padrino had, to buy something to eat. The booth was manned by a young guy and served only one item: *pan con lechón*, a sandwich with a slice of pork and a dab of mayonnaise and strawberry syrup, a pink concoction that no tourist was brave enough to try. But they all paid their four CUCs for the sandwich without complaint. The vendor, magnanimously, let Padrino and the driver have theirs for twenty pesos.

The tourists, around a dozen, had emerged from a roomy air-conditioned bus designed for fifty people. Padrino listened to them gab about the weather, the hotels where they had stayed, and the best sightings. At first he didn't understand what the "sightings" were. Had these *Yumas* come to Cuba to spy? Were they all secret agents? But they wouldn't be talking about their activities so freely, would they? And the CIA wouldn't recruit so many people over sixty years old, most of them on the porky side. Eventually, catching a word here and another there, Padrino got a clearer idea of who the tourists were and what they had been up to.

"My favorite is the eastern meadowlark."

"So precious! I believe it's endangered."

"For me, the best one was the spotted rail that we found in

Zapata Swamp," a pudgy, round-faced woman said. "But who could have thought, forty years ago, that we would be taking pictures of ourselves at the Bay of Pigs?"

"Remember those Cold War drills? Duck under the table and kiss your ass goodbye?"

The others laughed.

"Now, as for the highlight of my trip, I must say it was the *zunzún*."

"The guide says they eat half their weight several times a day."

"Like somebody we know!"

More laughs.

"Look, there's one on that tree! Snap a picture, quick!"

Padrino examined them, intrigued. Where had these people come from that the sight of a humble hummingbird became the highlight of their day? He also got the impression that they had paid a lot of money for the excursion. For a trip to watch birds. The *santero* stared at the camera-wielding, Birkenstock-wearing men and women, who chewed enthusiastically at their soggy bread with charred pork meat, and he stifled the desire to laugh in their puffy red faces.

AT FIVE O'CLOCK, PADRINO arrived at a remodeled hut that had been plastered over and painted blue. Two brick rooms and a bathroom had been added to the original structure. A zinc roof had replaced the palm leaves that would have once covered it.

Yarmila's parents, Reutilia and Severio, were at first suspicious of him.

"You said you work for the police?" Reutilia asked, looking him up and down. "Are you a detective?"

"A retired lieutenant colonel and a detective, yes, *compañera*," Padrino answered.

"Do you have a badge or something?"

He produced his expired Communist Party card. The couple let him in after a quick look at it.

"I don't know what this world is coming to," Reutilia whispered to her husband.

A print of Fidel Castro and Che Guevara together, from the early sixties, and a picture of a young, unsmiling Yarmila in a black frame were the only wall ornaments in the small living room. Papers and photos blanketed a coffee table. Yarmila's life was spread over it in the form of faded diplomas, tin medals, letters, and yellowish college transcripts.

After a few moments' small talk, the grieving couple started to tell Padrino all about their daughter. Their sadness didn't prevent them from bragging, but who could blame them?

"She was a bright student, the first one in her class." Her mother pointed to a piece of paper with school grades written in blue ink. "Ten points in every subject! When she was in fourth grade, Yarmi was chosen among five hundred kids to go to a Pioneer Camp in Havana."

Reutilia showed Padrino a black and white picture of a solemn little girl wearing a beret.

"She once wrote a long poem to Fidel," Severio said. "She was barely fifteen years old. I wish I had kept it. It was published in our local paper and Yarmi said that it was the best *quinceañera* present that she could get. She hoped someone showed a copy to El Comandante."

"Later she attended the Vladimir Ilich Lenin School, in Havana." Reutilia held a color photo in which a slim teenager stood at attention next to a statue of José Martí, Cuba's national hero. Only half her face was visible; the other half appeared darkened by the statue's shadow. "That was during her induction ceremony. She had just been accepted into the Young Communist League. We were there as well." Reutilia's index finger, leathery and with short, bitten nails, pointed to two unrecognizable figures in the crowd.

"And she went off to college. To the University of Havana! We were so proud of her."

"She was the very first one in our family to get a college degree. Thanks to the revolution."

"Yarmi set an example for her comrades," Reutilia beamed with pride. "Even during the Special Period, when everybody was complaining about the situation, I never heard her say a word against the government. She told the whiners that other people in Latin America were poorer than Cubans. 'Look at Haiti,' she would say. 'Look at these street kids in Brazil. Aren't we better off?'"

Padrino listened to them quietly. Both sounded like hardcore revolutionaries and seemed to believe that Yarmila was too.

"She later found a great job," Reutilia went on.

"We thought that she was going to live in Havana forever, as a model new woman who would give children to our homeland. Instead—"

Severio wiped a tear from his face.

"You guys have to find out who did it!" Reutilia yelled.

"And when you find him, *paredón*! That's what revolutionary justice is for, eh, *compañero*?"

"Even the firing squad would be too good for him!"

"That's what we are trying to do," Padrino said. "I know how sad and angry you must be now, but I do need your help. I have questions; some are difficult ones."

Reutilia stiffened, but she said, "Ask, ask."

Her husband nodded in agreement. "We will do anything to help you find the *cabrón*."

"When was the last time you saw Yarmila?"

"Around two months ago," Reutilia said. "Or was it three months, *viejo*? My head doesn't work right anymore."

"It was early January because I had started planting the first tobacco crop of the year. She spent four days with us."

"Did you notice anything different about her?"

"No, she was her usual spunky self."

"What did she talk about?"

Severio shrugged. "Her new apartment, her friends . . ."

"How much she liked coming back to Los Palacios," Reutilia added. "Nothing out of the ordinary."

Padrino hesitated before asking what they thought of their daughter's fiancé.

"What fiancé?" Severio asked.

"The—the American."

The couple exchanged a puzzled look, then scowled at Padrino as if he had insulted Yarmila's memory.

"What did you say, *compañero*?" Reutilia snapped. "I must have misunderstood!"

"Yarmila was in a relationship with a man named Matt Sullivan," Padrino said.

"What kind of name is that?" Severio barked.

"He was from San Diego."

"San Diego de Los Baños?"

"No, no. San Diego, California."

"California as in the United States?"

"Yes. According to what he said, they were planning to get married."

"Yarmi marrying a Yankee?" Reutilia spat on the cement floor. "What nonsense!"

The term *Yuma* hadn't yet become popular in Pinar del Río,

or at least not under this roof. Here, Americans were still Yankees—the enemy.

"That's not true, *compañero*," Severio said and his jaw clenched. "On my word as a communist, I tell you that Yarmila had no deals whatsoever with Yankees."

"How can you be so sure?" Padrino pressed. "You didn't see her often."

"She would have told us," Reutilia said stubbornly. "She told us everything. We talked on the phone regularly. Yarmi wasn't interested at all in foreigners."

"Much less someone from the evil empire."

"She wouldn't have given a Yankee the time of day!"

Padrino decided to drop the subject. He remembered one of Yarmila's posts about her family. "Are you still working at the clinic, *compañera*?" he asked Reutilia.

Her response surprised him as much as her previous statement about "the Yankee." "What clinic?"

"The one that you manage."

The woman squinted. "I don't manage anything."

"I thought—where do you work?"

"At home. I help Severio with the crops."

"Have you ever had a job, Reutilia? Outside your house, I mean."

"When Yarmi was little I used to clean the classrooms at her school and run errands for the teachers. But a regular job, no."

Padrino was going to insist, but changed his mind. There were other topics more pressing than Reutilia's employment history. "Did you ever meet Pato Macho?" he asked instead.

"Pato who?"

"His real name is Yosvani Álvarez."

"No."

"Did Yarmila have a boyfriend at all?" Padrino refrained from adding "that you knew of."

"She dated some guys, but nothing serious," Reutilia said. "She wasn't planning to *marry* anyone, at least not in the near future."

"Yarmi was very devoted to her work."

"She didn't have much time for men."

Padrino stared at Yarmila's picture. The young woman's expression was unreadable—a half-faced sphinx.

"What about Isabel Quintana?" he asked. "Do you know her?"

Severio nodded. "A woman who has a little restaurant?"

"Yes, a *paladar*. Yarmila cooked for her."

"No, *compañero*." Reutilia retrieved a magazine from the table and showed Padrino the first page, where Yarmila's full name was printed. "She worked at this Institute. The Institute of Literature and—I don't know what else. Look, here is something she wrote for them. She was a writer there."

"She worked as a translator," Padrino said. "But you are right, she was a writer too. Did she ever tell you about *Yarmi Cooks Cuban?*"

They stared at him blankly.

"The food blog," he offered.

Reutilia and Severio didn't know what the word "blog" meant. The whole concept of the internet proved too complicated for them.

"Yarmi liked to cook," Reutilia said. "She was very close to her late grandmother, Hilda, and learned a bunch of recipes from her. Her *sofrito* was the best! Better than her grandma's and ten times better than mine."

"But she wasn't a *cook*." Severio frowned. "She didn't work in a restaurant or anything like that. She was an *intellectual*."

"Now that I think of it, she borrowed my copy of Nitza

Villapol's *Cocina al Minuto* last time she came because she needed it for a work project," Reutilia said. "So she might have written something about food."

Padrino paused before the next question, "Did you ever meet the dissidents she used to hang out with?"

As he had feared, the reference to the *gusanos* aroused a storm of indignation.

"What dissidents?" Severio yelled.

"They were neighbors of hers. An older couple that writes for American papers and—"

"American papers!"

"With all due respect, *compañero*, that's the stupidest and craziest thing I've ever heard," Reutilia said. "Well, that and the Yankee story."

"Please, understand that I am not saying she was *part* of that group, or involved with it. I just said they were acquaintances. I was wondering if you had—"

"Acquaintances, *mierda*! My daughter never hung out with *gusanos*!" Reutilia yelled. "She hated them!"

"It looks like you didn't know Yarmi at all," Severio said gravely.

"I didn't, *compañero*. I am basing my questions on what people who knew her have said."

"Maybe you have been asking the wrong people."

Padrino left shortly after that, fearing he would be unceremoniously thrown out of the remodeled hut if he remained there any longer. It was already dark and he knew he wouldn't be back in Regla until midnight. He was confused and somewhat out of sorts. He found it difficult to reconcile Yarmila's parents' version with Matt's description of his fiancée and the chatty girl he had met a few times at La Caldosa. And yet she was all of those things.

Everything starts with *sofrito*

Sofrito is a magic potion, an amazing gift from the Kitchen Fairy.

A foundation for many dishes like rice and chicken, mince-meat and beans, *sofrito* is an integral part of the Cuban cuisine. You can make enough to last for a week or prepare it fresh for a day's meals, which I'd rather do. But aged *sofrito* isn't bad. It gains in flavor as all the ingredients interact when left in the refrigerator for a few hours. The taste gets more concentrated and potent.

I make *sofrito* as often as I can because it leaves my kitchen smelling like my childhood home. When I'm sautéing the onions in my beloved "cured" *sartén*, the frying pan that mom gave me when I went back to Los Palacios three months ago, I am a teen-ager again. I am listening, all ears, to my grandmother Hilda, who explains in great detail how to keep a man happy forever and ever.

Wait a minute! Grandma wouldn't talk about sex. Is that what you are thinking, *mal pensados*? No way. Old *guajiras*, those shriveled peasant ladies who considered a trip to Havana similar to a visit to Sodom, didn't even mention the names of private parts. It was always "down there" or just a gesture, eyes cast down in a nun-ish way.

"You're becoming a young woman," Grandma told me when I was twelve years old. "You need to get an education. And I am not talking about these silly things they teach you at school."

Grandma Hilda wasn't fond of "uppity girls," as she called the ones who went to college and (gasp!) earned degrees. She'd have been happy if I had just married the *guajiro* next door and had a bunch of kids.

Yep, I was a big disappointment to her.

Her advice for keeping a husband happy consisted of memorizing a collection of recipes handed down from her mother, the only inheritance that she got. My *bisabuela* Fayna was a Canary Islands native. She was a Guanche, the indigenous people that lived there before the Spaniards arrived. I got Fayna's thick black hair and brown eyes, though, unfortunately, I didn't get her height. She was six feet tall and I am what you call "petite."

So instead of showing me how to dress or walk seductively, Grandma Hilda instructed me in the secrets of *sofrito*. I want to share it with my readers today, in case anyone out there is interested in, you know, keeping a husband happy.

Wink, wink.

So here it is.

Start with half a cup of oil or, preferably, lard. My *Yuma* boyfriend will be horrified when he reads this, but real *sofrito*, at least in Pinar del Río, is cooked in lard, easy to get when a pig is slaughtered and less expensive than store-bought cooking oil.

After heating the lard (it can be slightly used: the same one you have fried a steak or a chicken thigh in), add one chopped onion and two garlic cloves, and cook until the onion becomes translucent.

"You should be able to see through it," Grandma explained. "If you can't see the frying pan underneath, keep cooking, but do not let them burn. There is nothing more disgusting than a slice of charred onion!"

Add a sliced bell pepper and sauté it for two or three minutes at the most. At this point, Grandma would use whatever seasoning we had at hand. Obviously, one has to include salt and pepper, but ground cumin, oregano and bay leaves are fine too.

Now come three tomatoes, nicely chopped, and five spoons of canned tomato soup. When we didn't have canned soup, Grandma would put ripe tomatoes in a blender with water and boil the mix with onions and a teaspoon of sugar to make her very own *salsa de tomate*.

After stirring in the tomato sauce, handmade or canned, let everything simmer for a while.

"This is the moment to take out the bay leaves," Grandma would say. "Bay leaves are like cold cream for your face. You put it on, but don't let anyone see you with it."

Toward the end, if we had a bottle of sherry, she would pour a bit, just a *chorrito*, and let it boil for a couple of minutes. Any kind of wine, or even beer, can be used to give the *sofrito* more flavor but don't worry if you don't have it.

Once it is ready, you can use *sofrito* as the base for stews, meats, soups and many other dishes.

"When the belly is full, the heart is happy," Grandma would say. "*Barriga llena, corazón contento*. The secret of a successful marriage lies in what happens at the dining table, not what goes on behind the bedroom door."

Along the same line, one of her favorite sayings was *El amor entra por la cocina*. Does love really come in through the kitchen? Comment and let me know what you think.

Kitchen kisses to you all!

COMMENTS

Taos Tonya said. . .

Here we say that men love sex, food and sports. In that order. *Oye, hita*, but what about cilantro?

Yarmi said. . .

Sports, huh? Here it would be *la pelota*, baseball. As for the cilantro, I never saw my grandma use it in the *sofrito*, so I don't. But I guess it won't hurt. But add it at the end because cilantro burns fast.

Julia de Tejas said. . .

My husband, who is from Mexico and an MD, likes to say, "Death comes in through the kitchen" when he thinks I'm eating too much. Pigging out, *sabes*? I thought that was a real saying and found it shocking. The "love" version sounds better.

Quick question: Would you add *sofrito* to the rice as well?

Yarmi said. . .

Your husband *el doctor* has a twisted sense of humor, Julia. I've never heard the "death" version, I swear. I would add *sofrito* to *moros y cristianos* (white rice and black beans cooked together) and yellow rice, if you are making *arroz con pollo* or a paella. But to white rice alone, definitely not.

Cocinera Cubana said. . .

I use Goya seasoning all the time, but will try your recipe.

Alberto Pena said. . .

With you in the house, love will come in through a barred window! *Linda, mi amor*! I'm so jealous of your boyfriend! I bet he has a happy heart, and a full belly too!

Yarmi said. . .

Uff, Goya! No offense to the painter (it's a joke, I know you are talking about a brand name) but you can't compare homemade *sofrito* to that insipid dust. I tried it once and the food tasted synthetic. Making *sofrito* doesn't take over twenty minutes and you can even prepare it while watching TV.

Chapter Four

THE WOMAN OF MY LIFE

Padrino believed that the crime scene often had all the evidence needed to solve a case. "The walls have eyes and ears," he would say, "but no mouth. You have to figure out what they have seen because they aren't going to tell you."

When he was working on a case he always made sketches, trusting them more than he did photographs. The day after visiting Yarmila's parents, he had gone to her apartment and made drawings of the floor plan and the furniture. He made sure to depict every minor detail, from the ironing board blocking the refrigerator to the knives and forks left on the kitchen counter. Martínez assured him that everything had been kept unchanged, except for Yarmila's computer, which had been seized by Seguridad.

"We also got rid of some rotten food, but there were no fin-gerprints anywhere," she said. "The murderer must have gone around cleaning every damn piece of furniture."

Now, while he listened to the recordings Martínez had given him of Isabel and Pato Macho's interrogations, Padrino took quick notes, but kept peeking at the sketches.

I met Yarmi around a year ago. She told me that she kept a food blog, whatever a blog is, and visited paladares *to get ideas. She didn't have a lot of money, but was so friendly and sweet that I invited her to have lunch on the house a couple of times. She promised to write about La Caldosa and said that her posts were good advertisement because many foreigners read them.*

No, I never saw any of her write-ups. I don't have a computer and all these things are Greek to me.

After she began to cook for us, she also gave me four hundred dollars, which we used to repaint the house and replace the toilet. Yes, compañera, *I am aware that this is illegal. But everybody here does illegal things, no?*

Yes, she was involved with my son. I tried to talk him out of it. I am old-fashioned in that sense—a woman, in my opinion, shouldn't be older than her guy. And then there was the Yuma. *I thought that Yarmi would eventually marry him and move to San Diego, and my poor* nene *would be left heartbroken . . .*

Oh, Pato wouldn't kill a fly, much less his Yarmi! She was the only woman he has ever been in love with. Besides me, of course. But that's another kind of love.

I saw Yarmi for the last time on Tuesday morning. I had brought her a whole chicken to make croquettes. We talked about putting together a special menu and discussed whether Mateo would like a cake or a tocinillo *for dessert. She said she would make merenguitos too.*

No, I didn't go upstairs because my varicose veins were hurting like the devil. I could hardly walk, and she lived on the third floor. Now that you ask, she seemed a little anxious to get back upstairs. But she didn't say that there was someone with her.

What? How could I know? A thief maybe? Her neighbors

had heard about the Yuma *and they probably thought she was rolling in dough. You know how people gossip, particularly that old woman, Fefita.*

I don't think she had any enemies. She was so likable, so kind . . .

Yes, there were some things she did I didn't agree with, like having two men at the same time, but who am I to judge? The truth is I had actually started to see her as a daughter and was dreading meeting that Mateo guy. I knew it was going to be awkward.

I never told her how I felt. I hate to admit it, but sometimes Yarmi scared me. There was something tough about her, an I-take-no-shit attitude, though she didn't flaunt it.

Anyway, I hope you find out who did it because she didn't deserve to die like that. Poor Yarmi! I also hope you don't get on my case for the few little things I've admitted about the paladar *and such.*

———

On Wednesday the fifth I was helping out at La Caldosa from early in the morning. Several people saw me there. My mom wanted me to sharpen all the kitchen knives. She said they were duller than toothpicks. And after lunch, I went to El Cincuentenario Bar. I knew the Yuma *was coming that day and I didn't want to be around if he and Yarmi ate at the* paladar. *I was in the bar when I heard the news—*

Last time I saw her was on Monday the third. I went to the apartment with an old ironing board that I had just repaired for her. She was happy with it but told me not to come again until the Yuma *left.*

On Tuesday . . . uh, I don't remember what I did. Wait, I went to the construction site where I work. I was there at eight in the morning, but there was nothing planned for the day so I just hung out with the guys until four o'clock. And I went home.

Look, compañera, *if you think I had anything to do with what happened to Yarmi, you are wrong. So wrong! I would have killed for* her!

Yarmi was my first woman. Well, not really the first one because I've been sticking my pinga *wherever I could, excuse the language, since I was twelve years old. But she was my first serious relationship. The one I would have married had I had the balls to propose.*

At first I only thought of her as a nice lady. I had never been friends with anyone like Yarmi—a career woman with her own apartment and a salary. A grown-up. I was sure she would say, "What does this little comemierda *want?" if I approached her. I wouldn't have asked her out if she hadn't let me know she was interested.*

And then I was so happy! She was smart and quick, like my mom, but nicer. She could have been the mother of my children, even if she thought I *was a child at times.*

In the end, I can't tell you she was my girlfriend because she didn't see it that way. But to me, she was my true love, the woman of my life. And she was crazy in bed. I learned more with her than with all the girls I had sex with before. She would—

Excuse me! I was trying to cooperate, to tell you everything of importance, as you ordered me to do.

We hooked up after she moved into the Espada Street apartment. She used to live in Old Havana and I only saw her once or twice a month, when she came to the paladar. *Later she started to cook for Mom so we met more often.*

Yes, I think Mom liked her—as a friend. As my girlfriend, not so much. But then she never liked any of my girlfriends. She said I was wasting my time with Yarmi. But time was the only thing that I could spend freely with her. I had so little to offer her: no pesos, no dollars, no CUCs . . .

Yes, Yarmi had told me about the Yuma. *She was already involved with him when we started going out together. But she didn't love him. She made fun of him.*

Marrying the Yuma? No, *compañera Lieutenant. I don't think Yarmi wanted to get married—to him, or me, or anybody else. She was very independent. A loner in a way, so much so that she didn't let me sleep at the apartment, not even once.*

"Everybody in their house, and God in everybody's house," she used to say, though she didn't believe in God.

If you say so—I could be wrong. I never understood her. Some of the stuff she did looked pretty strange to me. But I couldn't ask questions. She would tell me to shut up or ask if I thought I was her husband or her daddy. Then she would laugh. At me.

The strange things were, for example, those—what do you call them? The stuff she wrote and put out there, in the net or the web or whatever it is. Posts, that's right. I didn't read them because they were in English, but she translated one for me and it didn't make any sense. It was all about making grilled steak. I don't remember the last time I ate a steak! Yes, my mom has a paladar, *but she serves mostly pork and chicken. Beef is too expensive.*

There was another post or whatever about a fancy schmancy pizzeria where you can only eat if you pay with CUCs . . . I have never been there, but maybe Yarmi went with her Yuma. *Who knows?*

Sometimes she disappeared for a couple of days and didn't bother to give me an explanation. Or she said she was visiting her folks in Los Palacios. She would come home late, after I had been waiting for hours outside the apartment, because she wouldn't give me a key, and she'd tell me she had been busy at work when I knew that the Institute closes at five. But when I tried to act like a real man and order her around, she would say that our relationship was "for entertainment only."

What? No! I swear, if she had been sleeping with a Cuban, I would have never gone along with it. Who do you think I am, a cabrón? *The* Yuma *was different because he was there first. He wasn't around all the time. And he was a rich foreigner. He could give her nice clothes and take her to real restaurants, while I had to ask my mom for five CUCs if I wanted to invite her for a cup of coffee at the Plaza Carlos III Mall.*

I thought she was with him for the money. Though Yarmi wasn't the kind of woman who would run after dollars or CUCs, like so many others. But again, I had to accept whatever she told me. And she didn't say much, about the Yuma *or anything else. She was pretty tight-lipped.*

She did cook, yes. But not for me. She and my mom would prepare the paladar *meals together, or she fixed some dishes at home and brought them over. Once she made banana bread and our patrons liked it so much that it was gone before I had a chance to try it. She didn't save anything for me, though. She said she wasn't my mama to spoil me.*

This medal I'm wearing? Ah, that's the Virgin of Regla, Yemayá. My mom insisted I wear it to protect myself from harm, the evil eye and whatnot. Yes, I believe in the orishas. *I ask them for things, but they don't always give them to me. I really like Changó because he is the most macho of the gods. I make offerings to him and say his name three times before I leave the house in the morning . . .*

Eh? I don't know who did it! If I knew, I would have kicked the son of a bitch's ass. If I knew, I would be here for a reason because I would have killed him!

Padrino turned off the recorder. People didn't understand what Santería was all about. The *orishas* were forces of nature. Oshún, Changó and Yemayá—those names meant nothing. They couldn't care less how people addressed them. Their personalities were also man-made, like the ceremonial masks worn by tribesmen. That was why people couldn't take the *patakines*, the folktales about them, too literally. The stories were just hidden signals and it was up to individuals to decode them.

Padrino had kept praying to Oshún for guidance about Yarmi. He'd been trying to figure her out even before Matt showed up. *Strange girl, that Yarmila.* Something about her escaped him. Giggly on the surface, but her eyes didn't laugh. They were bright, but too intense and focused, like an old woman's eyes.

Yarmi hadn't believed in the saints; she'd told Padrino so with such a charming smile that he hadn't been able to help but smile back at her.

At first he'd thought she was a daughter of Oshún because she had so many of the *orisha*'s traits. Yarmila swayed when she walked and her hips undulated like the ocean waves. Padrino had assumed she followed Oshún's best-known path, the young woman who drags men after her, wiggling her ass and winking at them.

But Yarmi wasn't that simple. There was a lot more to her than she let on.

After she passed away, he had invoked Oshún every day, begging her for a sign. But the shells were stubbornly mute. Oshún refused to get involved.

I will look for a patakín *and reach out one more time.*

The story that came to Padrino's mind had been passed down to him by his own godfather, an Angolan *babalawo* he had met in Luanda in the eighties. As he recalled the *patakín*, Padrino also remembered the way the old man had pantomimed the baker's change of plans and the *orisha*'s revenge.

"Ah, my Padrino!" he said longingly. "*Aché* for you, wherever you are."

Oshún and the Sneaky Baker

So there was this shrewd woman, a baker who made the best coconut pudding you could dream of. People came from miles and miles away to buy her pastries. The baker was nice to her clients, but never made offerings or cared to please any of the orishas because she was snooty like that.

Ah, but one day she got involved with a handsome stud, a fisherman that all women in the village wanted to sleep with. They flirted with him shamelessly and tried to steal him from her. The baker, being very much into her young lover and wanting to be the woman of his life, decided to ask Oshún for help. If the orisha of love smiled upon her and recognized her as a daughter, she'd have a better chance of keeping the guy all for herself, even if she was a little past her prime.

She knew that Oshún had a weakness for all things sweet—and what is sweeter than coconut pudding? She would use all her tricks to get the goddess's favor! She went to the market and bought the ingredients that she needed, like eggs, sugar, and flour. She didn't have to buy coconuts because she had a big coconut tree in her yard.

On the way home she discovered a duck's nest by the side of the road, half hidden by the shrubs. And there were four big round eggs inside!

Duck eggs are bigger than chicken eggs, but their yolk is thicker and difficult to beat. They are ugly, with brown spots that look like pockmarks. Their taste is stronger and denser too and not suitable for desserts.

So the astute woman kept the chicken eggs for her business and made the coconut pudding with duck eggs. It wasn't, she reasoned, as if Oshún was going to complain about it. Orishas *receive the spirit of offerings, not the material part of them.*

Once the pudding was ready, she brought it to the river and placed it on a piece of wood adorned with marigolds. She said a prayer to the orisha, *beat her chest and asked for her blessing. Then she went home, feeling happy and smug.*

Ha.

Oshún knew the truth. When the baker offered her prayer, it was tainted with guilt, as she knew in her heart that she had cheated the orisha *of a proper offering.*

Oshún turned her face away from the pudding and discarded its spirit.

A few days later, the fisherman went to see a babalawo. *He was falling in love with the baker, he said. He had thought of marrying her, but wouldn't do it without Oshún's approval. Would the woman make a good wife or should he find a younger and better looking one?*

The babalawo *conveyed the man's concern to the* orisha *and waited for an answer. And it came, loud and clear.*

"Stay away from her. She is a fake."

The young man was scared when he heard that. He broke up with the baker and took another wife.

The baker, devastated, drowned herself in the same river where she had made her failed offering to Oshún.

Chapter Five

FEFITA *COMITÉ*

The Committees for the Defense of the Revolution were considered Fidel Castro's ears and eyes. They had been established in 1960, one on every block, as part of a nationwide network in which neighbors watched each other, aware that they all were being watched at the same time. But their role had diminished in the nineties, during the Special Period, when most Cubans were too busy finding food to put on their tables to worry about what others did. Only a few hardcore communists volunteered anymore for the Vigilance and Protection Subcommittee or kept records of the revolutionary commitment of their neighbors. People still belonged to the organization, but skipped the night watches and monthly meetings. Fidel's eyes were going blind; his ears were plugged.

A few years before, Fefita had been the most vigilant eye in that building and on the entire block. People had feared her. But now, she was just an old gossip. Padrino found her outside her apartment, talking to another woman. He heard the words "death" and "a disgrace" as he was going upstairs. He introduced himself as part of the Unidad team working on Yarmila's case.

Once she recovered from the initial shock of seeing a *compañero* dressed as a *santero*, Fefita shook his hand.

"Come in, come in," she said, eagerly. "See you later, Marita."

She led Padrino into her home, whose layout was identical to Yarmila's. It was better furnished, though, with a new TV set and a VCR nestled in a small entertainment center. There were also two mismatched chairs and a maple credenza that was missing a leg. It had been replaced with a pile of fifth and sixth grade textbooks.

"I was just wondering when you guys would call me again," Fefita said, inviting Padrino to sit. "I talked to Lieutenant Martínez the day Yarmi's body was found, but I have a few more things to say."

Padrino produced his small tape recorder and placed it on the credenza.

"Hope you don't mind," he said. "I'm sure that all these things you want to share are important."

"Ah, *compañero*, I don't mind it at all."

She actually looked pleased by the fact that her words were being saved for posterity.

Only the good die young. Yarmi was a good person. Not a saint, but how many saints do you know in these days and times?

Of all the awful things I've seen in my life—and I've seen my fair share of them in sixty-seven years—finding that girl in the bathtub, so rigid and all wet, ranks top of the list. I can't stop having nightmares about it.

We had sort of a mother-daughter relationship, though I had only known her for a few months. She moved into our building last year to be closer to the Institute of Literature and Linguistics. She worked there as a translator. And I bet she was a good one.

Yes, she was also a cook at La Caldosa. Such a waste, a girl with a college degree cooking for a bunch of CUC-earning come-mierdas. But we all do things we aren't proud of, don't we?

Yarmi reminded me of my daughter, Haydecita. They were the same age and even looked a bit alike, with big brown eyes and a pretty oval face. Yarmi knew how lonely I was and sometimes came to keep me company in the evenings. Not every day because she had her own things to do, but at least once a week. That touched my heart. I have neighbors of thirty years who have never bothered to knock on my door and make sure I'm still breathing.

Ay, compañero*! Haydecita lives in Spain. She married a Galician, a guy old enough to be her grandfather, but things didn't work out and now she is on her own in Barcelona. She said Galicia was cold and gray and that she finally understood why her ancestors had crossed the Atlantic to settle in Cuba. She works as a housekeeper now.*

That's what I was telling you about. I am not proud of my daughter's choice. I told Yarmi many times and she would say, "She will come back. Just wait." She gave me hope, unlike all these mean people who said I should be grateful that Haydecita was out of Cuba and able to send me money. As if money were everything!

But it's true that I need it . . . I was a schoolteacher for forty years and got enough medals and awards to fill this apartment. The problem is that my retirement isn't enough for me to make ends meet. I get one hundred eighty pesos monthly. At the Plaza Carlos III Mall, a bottle of cooking oil costs six CUCs. Do you know how much that is in pesos? One hundred fifty-nine! You do the math.

Let's be clear: I am not blaming the revolution. I'm stating a fact. I say it to you and I'd say it to Fidel, if given the opportunity.

Though I'm afraid El Comandante doesn't know what's going on. No disrespect to him, but he is getting on in age, as we all are. Maybe no one has informed him about the disparity between pesos and CUCs.

Sure, back to Yarmi. She was a caring person, which is rare to find today. Once, I told her that I was likely to spend a sad and lonely Christmas, the first one without Haydecita. I didn't think she would remember because we had just met. We weren't close friends yet. But on December 24, at nine in the morning, that girl showed up in my apartment with two pork chops, a dish of arroz congrí, *and a caramelized flan. She woke up at 7:00* A.M. *to make a feast for me.*

Haydecita had sent me money so I could celebrate but I didn't feel like buying anything, much less cooking. If it hadn't been for Yarmi, I would have been depressed and hungry the whole day.

Yarmi was always bringing me stuff. Last thing was a plate of besitos de coco. *She made a bunch of them, so cute and round, all sprinkled with cinnamon. I don't know where she found the coconuts because they are never distributed through the ration card. Perhaps she bought them in the* agromercado.

How could I describe her? She was nice and had manners. Above all, she was bright. She noticed everything, unlike so many people that go around with their heads in the clouds. You talk to them and words pass through their ears and come out their asses. But she listened to people. At least, she listened to me.

I saw her for the last time on Tuesday the fourth, the day of my tai-chi class in Trillo Park. We ran into each other. She was coming into the building with a chicken wrapped in foil as I was leaving for the park. She said she was going to make croquettes and promised to bring me some the next day.

It must have been around ten in the morning. The tai-chi class starts at ten thirty and I usually leave home half an hour before.

I returned at noon. No, I didn't see anybody coming in or out of her apartment. But I don't spend day and night watching my neighbors, no matter what some people say.

Well, her private life—for one thing, Yarmi wasn't promiscuous. She didn't have a line of men outside her doorstep or anything like that. Actually, the only guy who visited her was Pato Macho, and even he wasn't there all the time.

I've known Pato since he was eight years old. He was my student at José Joaquín Palma Elementary School. It took him a long time to learn how to divide and multiply. He was slow and read backwards. I had a few students like that; there was something wrong with their brains' wiring. But he was a good boy, not a troublemaker.

Pato was under his mother's thumb until he fell in love with Yarmi. I think he got himself an older partner because he likes to be told what to do. And he put up with her having another man because he wasn't used to standing up to a woman. Issues, compañero, *issues. We all have our own.*

No, Pato Macho wouldn't have killed Yarmi! I wouldn't put my hands in the fire for anyone, but this kid is the last person I would suspect. He is a sweetheart.

Now, his mother, that's another story. Isabel is so domineering and brazen that I don't understand why her husband has stayed with her all these years. But on second thought, where is Luis going to go that he's worth more? The guy's dumber than a barrel of hair. So is Pato; like father, like son. She is the bisnera *there, the only smart one. No wonder they call her La Jefota.*

So after Pato started going out with Yarmi, Isabel took

that mariconcito, *Taty, under her wing, to have someone to order around . . .*

Yes, the gusanos*! You took the words right out of my mouth because I was just going to bring them up. They were the reason why I wanted to go back to the Unidad and talk to this young detective again. The other day, I couldn't think of what to say when she asked me if I suspected anybody. I was still in shock, you know.*

Yarmi was friends with that couple, Carmela and Pablo. They are counterrevolutionaries. They write for a Miami paper. They criticize the revolution. An American guy visits them. People say he is a spy!

I advised Yarmi not to hang out with the gusanos. *"These two are trouble," I told her. But she had a mind of her own. You couldn't tell her what to do. She always said that Carmela and Pablo were decent people. Misguided, but good at heart.*

Yarmi wasn't a counterrevolutionary, though she didn't participate actively in the Committee for the Defense of the Revolution or the Federation of Cuban Women. She seldom went to meetings and I never saw her do any volunteer work. But that's the norm today: everybody is too busy working for money!

Young people aren't into politics. They have better things to do, Haydecita would tell me when I complained about her lack of commitment. Yarmi was the same way. But I felt that I had no right to criticize her, and even less so when I had resigned as the president of the Committee. I am so sorry now. I should have gotten on her case about that friendship. What if the gusanos *were the ones who killed her? Ay! I will never forgive myself for that! I failed her, and I failed the revolution . . .*

Thank you, compañero. *I'm okay now. Well, not okay, but*

better. I've finally gotten it off my chest. Now it's up to you to do something about it.

As for the Yuma, *I assumed she was using him, as Haydecita had used that old Spaniard to get out of Cuba. It broke my heart, thinking that Yarmi could be left in the same position, alone in a strange country, though she assured me that she had no intention to leave.*

As soon as I saw him, I knew he was Mateo. Yarmi had told me he was a journalist and a nice guy, but kind of simpleminded and washed-out. That was exactly what she said, washed-out. "He doesn't have the spunk that Cubans have," she laughed. But still, she kept him. She always referred to him as her official boyfriend. Then she would say that Pato Macho was just a friend. But who are we kidding here? A friend who comes in at midnight and leaves at three in the morning?

Oh, yes, the Yuma *said that they were getting married. I didn't believe him because Yarmi had never mentioned it. She didn't tell me everything, but I thought this was important enough to share.*

But I didn't have the heart to set him straight. Plus, I had just met him! And then we discovered the body. Ah, the poor guy seemed so out of place, so disoriented in the middle of the turmoil, with that white wedding dress folded over his arm.

The apartment looked as usual. Nothing was out of place . . . at least I didn't notice anything. Except the chicken, fo! There was a very rotten chicken on the kitchen counter, next to a bag of sugar full of ants and some eggs. As if she were getting ready to cook when—but then Yarmi was always cooking, or cleaning, or reading a book. Busy as a bee. Maybe she knew she wouldn't have a lot of time in life to accomplish everything she wanted to do.

Coconut drops: A Jamaican treat

Hola, mis amigos!

Welcome back to Yarmi's Kitchen. It smells so good today (like coconut, sugar and ginger) that I would like to invite you all to hang around here, enjoying a cup of coffee, while I finish a delicious treat: *besitos de coco* for my dear friend Fefita.

In English they are called "coconut drops." But you know how affectionate we are in Cuba, always kissing and hugging each other, so we call them *besitos*, little kisses. They are easy to make. And fun.

You will need one big coconut or two small ones, diced and grated, and one teaspoon of ginger. The other ingredients are a *chorrito* of vanilla—according to my grandma, a *chorrito* could be anything from a teaspoon to half a cup, but in this case, it's a tablespoon—one pound of brown sugar, three and a half cups of water, and a pinch of salt.

This is a Jamaican dish, or perhaps our own version of it. Grandma Hilda used to make it for my grandfather, Abuelo Samuel, who was Jamaican. That accounts for my second last name, Richards, and my initial interest in the English language.

Yes, I am a mutt: my folks came from the Canary Islands, Spain, and Jamaica, which makes me—*Cubana* one hundred percent!

To prepare a batch of *besitos*, start by cracking open the coconut. *Pataplúm*! Grandma would grate it slowly, careful to collect the milk and save it for later. That's a delicacy in itself! If added to rice, coconut milk gives it a creamy texture. Or you can mix it with mango juice to make *mancoco*, a refreshing drink.

Next, bring the water to a boil and throw in the grated coconut. After ten minutes, add the sugar, boil for five more minutes and add everything else. Stir it from time to time so the sugar doesn't stick to the pot. Keep boiling the mix for fifteen more minutes or until it becomes thick and sticky.

With a wooden spoon, take small portions of the paste and place them on an oiled tray. If you want, sprinkle them with cinnamon. Let them cool for ten minutes. And enjoy.

Grandpa Samuel seldom asked for anything, but one of his few requests was that his wife make *besitos de coco* every Sunday. They reminded him of his "other island." He was born in a little town located on the Rio Minho.

"The place was beautiful," he would tell me. "It had green pastures, blue skies, a river where kids used to swim . . . It had everything, except for food and opportunities."

When he was a teenager, Grandpa Samuel traveled to Banes, Oriente, to be a *machetero* in a sugar cane factory owned by the United Fruit Company. A few years later he moved to the other end of the country, Pinar del Río, where he eventually married Grandma Hilda. They grew tobacco and coffee.

Did you know that Pinar del Río produces almost eighty percent of our country's tobacco crop?

Grandpa Samuel passed away when I was ten years old, but I still remember all the stories he told me and the old songs he loved to sing, like one that said: *"My brother did a-tell me that you go mango walk, you go mango walk."*

I repeated the verses after him, even when I didn't have any idea of what the words meant.

I am getting nostalgic . . .

Following Grandma's advice, I have saved the coconut milk and I am going to prepare a glass of *mancoco*. If you want to try it, just mix in a blender, or by hand, a cup of mango juice and half a cup of coconut milk. Add ice cubes and start sipping. *Salud*!

COMMENTS

Julia de Tejas said. . .

You have such an interesting family history, Yarmi. You should research it! The *mancoco* mix sounds great. It reminds me of a Thai dessert: sweet sticky rice soaked in coconut milk and topped with mango slices.

Yarmi said. . .

Julia, what a great suggestion! I will make it next time I have coconut milk available. Yes, I would like to know more about my family, particularly my great-grandmother Fayna, the Guanche, and how she ended up in a remote village in Cuba.

Cocinera Cubana said. . .

I always marvel at how well you write in English. Did you learn it from your grandfather?

Yarmi said. . .

Hola Cocinera.

I learned songs and isolated phrases from him, but he never taught me English, at least not in a formal way. Grandpa Samuel's family was very poor. He didn't have a chance to go to school and could hardly read or write in his native language. But his songs and many of his sayings stayed with me. I found out, after I started the

Licenciatura, my BA studies, that I knew more English than I was aware of.

Taos Tonya said. . .

I wish I were your neighbor too.

Maritza said. . .

Is it true that coconuts are used in Santería to predict the future? Do people offer them to the *orishos*—not sure about the spelling—to get answers about their lives?

Yarmi said. . .

Tonya, you can come and visit anytime! Maritza, these deities are called *orishas*. Santería is actually a syncretism of the belief systems brought in by African slaves and the Catholic dogma that the Spaniards imposed upon them. The slaves combined the saints and their native gods and created sort of composites. Like most oppressed people, they would cling to religion for hope. But few people in Cuba practice Santería anymore. We don't need that. So instead of "offering" a coconut to the *orishas* we put it to a better use: we eat it. *Besitos* to you all.

Chapter Six

THE DISSIDENTS

Though comrade instructor hadn't taken her concerns about the dissidents seriously, Marlene decided to pay them a visit. She knew it was a long shot, and had no proof to even consider them suspects, but still. It wouldn't hurt, she thought. They were avowed *gusanos*, and that, in her opinion, meant that they were up to no good.

Carmela Mendez and Pablo Urquiola had been married for over twenty years. They had shared a deep love for each other and for the revolution, at first, and then a total disillusion with the government. Their feelings for Castro had turned from the fervor of converts to the hatred of apostates. The couple's most prized possessions were a small Centro Habana apartment and a big Cuban flag. The flag had been nailed to a wall next to a Traveling Christ, as people called the Sacred Heart prints. Devout Catholics had had to move them from the living room, where they were initially displayed, to a bedroom, the kitchen, or the darkness of a closet. This had happened during the sixties and the beginning of the seventies. After Pope John Paul II visited Cuba in 1998, the Traveling Christ made a comeback, reemerging shyly in the dining room first and finally reinstated to its original position. It had taken around forty years to make it full circle and the old images showed the wear and tear.

Carmela and Pablo sat under the print and the flag. They were both in their fifties but looked older, with the lines that perfect conviction leaves on believers' faces. Marlene Martínez, sitting across from them, glanced suspiciously at the Traveling Christ, whose fiery eyes glared back at her. They had not been happy to see a uniformed woman at their door. But after Martínez explained she was investigating Yarmila's death, they had agreed to cooperate.

"We liked Yarmi," Pablo said. "We'll help you. Whoever killed her should pay for it."

"I was thinking of her parents this morning," Carmela added. "I can only imagine how devastated they must be."

"Have you met them?" Martínez asked.

"No, they live in Los Palacios. Yarmi would visit them but they never came here, that I know of."

"Was she a close friend of yours?" Martínez asked. "Did she agree with your—work?"

"Yarmila was not an ally," Carmela answered. "I wouldn't say she was with us, but she did sympathize with our work."

Martínez couldn't help but say: "You mean she was a counter-revolutionary, like you?"

"I *was* a revolutionary," Carmela replied, becoming agitated. "I was taking part in the Literacy Campaign when you weren't born yet. I put in more volunteer hours than anyone could count, so don't come and tell me about the revolution! I fought for it and it betrayed me. Do you think I'm afraid of you or your uniform? Ha! Don't kid yourself, *compañerita*. I am now freer than—"

Her husband patted her hand reassuringly. "Calm down, dear," he said. "This isn't about us. The *compañera* just said so."

"That's right," Martínez said. "Let's focus on citizen Yarmila Portal, okay? Did she cooperate with you?"

Had Yarmila been in good terms with the government, behaving like a proper revolutionary, she would have been called a comrade. But she was not, so she was deemed a citizen. Carmela and Pablo, who had been called citizens for over a decade, were well aware of the distinction.

Pablo nodded. "She did more than these people who say, 'Oh, the government is so and so and I hate it,' but don't lift a finger to help us."

Martínez fought against her desire to ask who "these people" were.

"Yarmila would send an email on our behalf when we couldn't find any other way to do it," he went on. "We don't have access to the internet here and it is complicated, and expensive, to use the hotel terminals. The security guards wouldn't let us in unless we pretended to be foreigners, and after a few times, they figured out who we were and stopped us. So Yarmi sent a message for us once or twice, but she also made it clear that it wasn't going to be an everyday thing."

"She probably didn't want to jeopardize her own internet access," Carmela added. "I'm sure her boss at the Institute of Literature and Linguistics read every message that she sent or received."

"What else did she do for you?"

The couple hesitated. While waiting for their answer, Martínez looked around. The apartment was modest at best, with no big TV set or any shiny appliances in sight. The furniture was old. The sofa where she sat had a spring out of place. Maybe these two were being shortchanged by the CIA.

"That was pretty much it," Pablo said at last. "We were friends, but she wouldn't write an article about how *real* life is here, or even translate ours, something she could have easily done because she knew English well."

"She just wanted to play with her silly food blog," Carmela said. "I always thought it was ironic. 'What kind of food do you write about?' I would ask her. 'Soy mince? Mop-tassel steak?' She would laugh."

"The mop-tassel steak is an urban legend," Martínez felt compelled to say. "Have you ever eaten one?"

"No, but I know people who did! What does it matter, anyway? The truth is, she was fishing—" Carmela cut herself off.

"Fishing?" Martínez feigned ignorance. "For what?"

"Don't play dumb with me, *compañerita*! I'm almost old enough to be your mother so don't go and try to put your fingers in my mouth. Yarmila wanted to catch a foreigner and the blog was her hook."

"Carmela!" her husband got red in the face. "How can you—?"

"The naked truth is always better than the best dressed lie," she replied, adding in a softer tone, "but I understand she was solving her problems, like everybody else. I am not blaming her."

There was a pause. Carmela excused herself and went to the kitchen. Soon, the pungent smell of black beans permeated the room. Martínez noticed a buffet and hutch set identical to one she had at home. Hers had been repainted white. The couple's pieces had kept their original brown finish.

"Being a smart girl, Yarmi wanted a better life," Pablo said, almost apologetically. "She did what she thought was right. Because . . . what was here for her? *Nada!* Everything in this country is upside down. When a Cuban national is kicked out of a former 'bourgeois' hotel to make room for a foreigner, when people who were once accused of being traitors come back from Miami showing off their cash and buying things in stores revolutionaries aren't allowed to set foot in, things are bad. Very bad."

"Those were just temporary measures," Martínez mumbled. "There was a reason for austerity, back in the nineties. It isn't like that anymore. You can enter any dollar or CUC shop now."

Carmela came back.

"But Cubans aren't paid in dollars or CUCs!" she exclaimed. "What good does it do?"

Martínez looked at the flag to avoid the couple's eyes. She wanted to ask them if *they* didn't get American money but didn't want to ruin the conversation. "Well, we aren't discussing politics," she hurried to say. "You said you guys were friends with Yarmila. Did you go out together?"

"She didn't have a lot of free time to go out," Carmela said. "We aren't social butterflies either. Because of our reputation as *gusanos*, many people, even relatives, have shunned us. But she did us some favors that we really appreciated. That's why we trusted her. She was a real friend."

"What kind of favors?"

"A couple of months ago she sold me an electric fan at a very good price—twelve dollars. I insisted on paying for it, though she wanted to just give it to us."

An electric fan cost fifty dollars in the store and no less than thirty on the black market.

"Why would she do that?" Martínez asked. "You could have gotten it from the Americans, right?"

"That's what you people think," Carmela replied angrily, "and it is so *not* true. We are paid per article, but not a fortune, and this is our only source of income. The government won't hire us. How are we going to eat? We write for dollars, yes, but we are not 'mercenaries,' as you guys like to call us!"

"Who pays you?" Martínez asked, again unable to contain herself.

"The manager of the website that publishes our articles. Sometimes the papers, if they run our stories. What, are you thinking the CIA? You people are obsessed with that. *Qué comemierdas!* I wouldn't know a CIA agent if I found one in my black beans!"

She was getting excited again. Pablo chimed in. "We are not professional journalists," he admitted. "But people outside of Cuba read what we write. We simply do our job and are compensated for it."

"What do you write about, exactly?" Martínez asked. Except for what she had read in the *expedientes*, she knew little about the details of their work. Not having access to the internet, she had never seen any of the independent journalists' websites.

"Life in Cuba," Carmela answered. "Problems with water, food, human rights issues, political prisoners. Things that happen to us or that we hear about. I may write an article for Cubanet about your visit today."

"Huh, thanks for making me a celebrity." Martínez tried to sound sarcastic. She didn't know what Cubanet was, but she imagined her name read by millions of *Yumas*. In spite of herself, and for a fleeting moment, she relished the idea.

"So, even if she didn't offer to work with us, Yarmi was always interested in our work," Carmela brought the conversation back to the matter at hand. "She asked intelligent questions and didn't try to convince us to give up our ideas. I saw her as a symbol of the younger generation, generous and hardworking. I kept hoping she would become an independent journalist someday."

"Did she tell you she would?"

"Not really. But she left a door open. I mean, she never said never."

Carmela felt relaxed enough to smile. Her husband nodded. The initial tension had diluted. The couple felt happy that someone was listening to them without arguing (too much), someone outside their own circle, even if that "someone" was a cop. A respectful, well-mannered one. Besides, they understood why a young woman like Martínez would still call herself a revolutionary.

As for Marlene, she was also softening toward them. These people didn't look like dangerous criminals or CIA agents. Their home wasn't too different from hers. They might have been *gusanos*, but they were decent ones.

"I understand," she said. "Now tell me, when did you see her for the last time?"

"On Saturday, March first," Carmela said. "My birthday, by the way. We met at La Caldosa for lunch."

"The three of you?"

"No, just me and her. Yarmi took me out to celebrate. She always made these nice little gestures. She told me that her boyfriend was coming on Wednesday and said she'd like for us to meet him. It was okay with me, provided he wasn't one of those Americans who come here for two weeks and try to convince us that we live in paradise."

"Do they?" Martínez asked, shocked.

"Haven't you ever talked to one? They are worse than Seguridad agents."

Martínez shook her head. The only American she had ever talked to was Matt and he hadn't sung the praises of socialism.

"Yarmi assured me that Mateo was cool," Carmela said. "Then we didn't have any more news about her until Wednesday evening, when she was found dead. Poor girl!"

"Do you have any idea who could have killed her?" Martínez asked.

Carmela and Pablo looked at each other and said "no" at the same time.

"Do you know a man nicknamed Pato Macho?"

"That's Isabel's son," Carmela said, shrugging. "Why would he do it? He's just a kid."

"I didn't say he did it. I was just asking about him. How well did you really know Yarmila?"

The couple exchanged another glance. Carmela cleared her throat.

"Sometimes I had the impression that I didn't know her at all," she said. "Yarmila was a closed book."

"Everybody says she was talkative and outgoing," Martínez argued.

"They're right. She talked a lot, but didn't say much, if you know what I'm saying."

Martínez didn't, but Carmela couldn't or wouldn't explain that.

I have heard (from my *Yuma* boyfriend, of course) that there are special machines out there, sophisticated coffeemakers that are plugged in to electricity.

It took me a while to understand how they function until I thought of the electric rice cookers, *las ollas arroceras* that are so popular now. One of my coworkers saved most of her salary for five months to buy one.

"It does all the work," she told me. "No need to check the rice every ten minutes to make sure it isn't burning, no need to add water or salt. *La olla* knows what to do. So smart!"

Call me stubborn, but in cooking matters—*real* cooking matters—this electric stuff doesn't cut it. The rice made in an *olla arrocera* lacks something: flavor, *sandunga*, a bit of salt . . . I find it insipid and dried.

I'd rather put the time and effort into making it the old-fashioned way. I will post my white rice recipe soon.

Now for the coffee.

The best coffee I have tasted in my life is *café carretero*. A *carretero*, literally, is somebody who drives an oxen cart. This traditional way of making coffee involves the use of a *colador*. A *colador* is a rudimentary contraption made of a cloth filter, *la teta* (yes, that means tit), and a wooden or metal base that holds it. Once the filter is put in place, it hangs down, resembling the shape of a breast.

Under the *teta* we place a mug, preferably one made of aluminum, the same one all the time. That's *el jarrito de café*, the little coffee mug. It gets quite dark over the years!

Start by boiling a cup of water. In the meantime, put four teaspoons of coffee inside the cloth filter. Once water starts simmering, pour it over the coffee and let it drain into the mug.

That is *la primera colada*, the first brew, and it is very strong. In many cases, it's the only one we make. But if you don't have a lot of coffee, or if too many visitors happen to arrive at the same time, simply repeat the process. You can make two or three *coladas*.

Some people like to add sugar to the coffee while it's being drained, but I prefer to do it later.

And that, my dear friends, is the true and tried method for making Cuban coffee, *café carretero* style.

Yes, it takes time. We have to boil the water and then pour it over the coffee. (Pretending to roll my eyes here.) Uff! Life in Havana is fast. And in *La Yuma* it is a race, or so I hear. When I find myself lacking in time and patience, I resort to a stove-top espresso maker like the ones you can buy in your country.

I have come to like the espresso maker. *El café* tastes almost like coffee made with the *teta*. Not exactly the same, though. I can't tell you why. Heating the metal may alter the flavor. Or it boils for too long. Whatever the cause is, there is a difference.

I encourage you to try my method. It actually takes less time to boil a cup of water than for the coffee inside a coffee maker to percolate. Trust me on that one.

Before I forget it, do not throw away the coffee grounds! That's a great fertilizer. I have also used it to clean greasy pots—pots where I have fried something with lard.

And that's all for today. I lift my *jarrito de café* and sing to the rhythm of Juan Luis Guerra and his song *"Ojalá que llueva café."*

COMMENTS

Maritza said. . .

My mom doesn't like American coffee. She calls it *agua de borrajas* because it is too watery for her taste.

She used to make her own *coladores* when we moved to New Mexico in the seventies. At that time, it was difficult to find espresso makers so we built the holder with discarded pieces of metal. A clean sock replaced the *teta*. I still remember the aroma of coffee filling our home. It was the smell of Cuba. Thanks for bringing it back.

Cubanita in Claremont said. . .

I am thinking of an old Cuban song, *Ay, Mama Inés, ay, Mama Inés, todos los negros tomamos café.*

I want to dance and have coffee but I am at work! Keep the posts coming!

Julia de Tejas said. . .

I'm going to get me a cup of Café La Llave right now.

Lucy Adel said. . .

I am afraid you are too old-fashioned for life in the States. You should stay in Cuba.

Taos Tonya said. . .

Chinga, Lucy, what a big mouth you have!

Yarmi said. . .

Hola all!

Happy to bring back such nice memories, Maritza. Cubanita, right on! How could I forget *"Ay, Mama Inés,"* by Eliseo Grenet? Julia, I still have to try La Llave. Here, we use Café Pilon. Lucy, I've never said I wanted to leave Cuba, have I?

Sugary kisses from my kitchen.

Chapter Seven

CAFÉ CON LECHE

Marlene Martínez had been longing for coffee all day long. Had Carmela and Pablo offered her a cup she'd have happily accepted it, *gusanos* or not, but they didn't. On her way back, she enhanced the fantasy with fresh milk, conjuring up the image of a big tall mug of *café con leche*, with cream on top. Ah, *la nata*—She loved butterfat. In the eighties, when Marlene was a little girl, she and her brother would run to the kitchen in the mornings, hoping to get there as soon as her mother opened the milk bottle. She was faster and often beat her brother to it. The reward was soft, warm *nata* mixed with sugar.

Now she rarely drank milk. When she did, it was only the dried kind from the dollar shops. Her brother, who had fled Cuba on a raft in 1994, lived in Miami and had all the fresh milk and cream he wanted. He had beaten her to it, in the end.

"Yes, at what price!" she would say to their mother. "I do not envy him."

But she resented him because of his desertion. In her eyes, he had betrayed their homeland. She loved him and hated him. She would have liked to hug him and then slap him hard, until he vomited all the American food he had swallowed in nine years.

Son of a bitch. No offense, Mom!

Marlene was on her way home. It was around ten blocks from the Unidad, over half an hour by foot, but she knew better than to wait for a bus at five o'clock. Her stomach growled and her briefcase, where she kept all the documents related to Yarmila's case, felt heavier in her hand.

Yarmila ate better than most people. Thanks to her Yuma *boyfriend?*

Two men catcalled at her. They were *vagos*, permanently unemployed dudes who hung around Trillo Park hoping that some sort of illicit business would fall on their laps.

"Hey, pretty girl!" one purred.

Marlene stopped and stared them down. She didn't like to be called pretty or complimented in public. She thought that the time-honored Cuban tradition of *piropos*, or flirtatious remarks, ought to be banned. The *vagos* scurried away.

Usually they wouldn't bother her. They respected the uniform, or at the very least were afraid of it. When she wore her civvies, guys felt at liberty to ogle her and make remarks about her behind. Sometimes she wondered if she had joined the police to intimidate men and force them to keep their distance. Her uniform was her armor.

She soon forgot the incident. Her thoughts returned to the glass of milk.

Coño, I am getting obsessed.

Marlene had been reading *Yarmi Cooks Cuban* posts with help from a dictionary and, occasionally, a coworker who knew more English than she did. All these stories about meringue puffs, grilled steak and *caldosa* had made her hungry first, then angry. There would be only rice and beans for supper that evening, and, with any luck, a one-egg omelet. On top of that, she was getting frustrated by the case and the Seguridad's lack of cooperation.

What's Jacobo's problem? Why doesn't he talk to me? What's he trying to hide?

"This is an issue of national security," he had told her. Which was fine with Marlene, but he wasn't playing fair. She'd given him all the information the police had collected and he hadn't reciprocated. Her "new" computer had never been fixed. She didn't have access to Yarmila's blog. Why had it taken him so long to print her emails and posts and send them to her? And he probably hadn't sent all of them.

She was home. Home, for Marlene Martínez, was a long, narrow house in Hospital Street. The door opened directly to the sidewalk but Soledad, her mother, never bothered to lock it, despite Marlene's warnings.

"Why?" Soledad would ask. "There is nothing to steal here and it is hot inside."

When Marlene walked in, the smell of recently toasted coffee, freshly ground, welcomed her. She feared an olfactory hallucination, but saw her mother sitting at the table with the big tall *café con leche* of her dreams in front of her.

"*Mami*, where did you get that?" she yelled.

"Shh!" Soledad stood up, went to the kitchen and came back with another mug. "Don't talk so loud. Walls have ears! I made one for you too. Here, it's still pretty warm."

"But this milk—?"

Marlene took the first sip. She closed her eyes and felt transported to Yarmi's kitchen, as she had imagined it.

"Don't ask and I won't have to tell you." Her mother sighed.

Marlene looked into the old woman's eyes. Soledad had lost her eyelashes and eyebrows during the nineties, when the polyneuritis epidemic broke loose. The hair never came back. Her hands, which always trembled a little, were now wrapped around the glass. In any other moment, Marlene would have refused to share a black-market item. She'd have scolded her mother for dealing with *bisneros*. That would have been the right thing to do. But she didn't feel like doing the right thing.

"You look tired," Soledad said, pointing to the briefcase that Marlene had dropped on the table. "Why are you bringing work home with you, *chica*? You need to rest, to take things easy."

"Yes, I'm tired," Marlene said. She had already finished her *café con leche*.

"Take a bath. We have no running water now, but I filled two buckets this morning, just in case it doesn't come back tonight."

"Thanks."

Marlene picked up the briefcase and walked to her room. The uniform felt heavy on her, more carapace than armor now.

"There is some milk left in the fridge."

No, it was her mother who should drink it. She had a hiatal hernia and was supposed to receive dried milk through the ration card, one pound a month, to soothe her jumpy stomach, but it hadn't been distributed for the last six weeks.

Marlene sat on her bed, the same one she had slept in since her teenage years, and she scattered the content of her briefcase over the bedspread. She divided the documents into three groups: blog posts, emails Yarmila had exchanged with Matt and her blog fans, and transcripts of the interviews with all "persons of interest" in the case.

Something is missing here. Maybe comrade inspector will find it.

Her mother came into the room.

"They don't pay you enough to work overtime," she complained. "Why don't you come with me to Matilda's house? She got two new *Yuma* movies and it's only ten pesos. Neighbors' Night, as she says."

Matilda, a widow who lived next door, owned a VCR and people went to her house in the evenings to watch American movies—for a fee.

"I can't."

"Why not? You don't have a boyfriend. You don't have many friends. You don't have anything else to do. Let's have some fun. God knows you need it."

"I have Duties to fulfill, *Mami*."

Marlene tended to think about work in capital letters.

"Fulfill them at the Unidad, not at home."

She's right. But I can't help it.

"Why have you been so worried recently?" Soledad asked. "What's eating at you, *mija*?"

"It's a case I can't get off my mind," Marlene blurted out. "A young woman who was found dead last week."

"I know, poor thing." Soledad crossed herself, a pre-revolutionary habit that Marlene found annoying. "She worked at La Caldosa, didn't she?"

"Yes."

Everybody in Havana had heard about Yarmila's death. If nothing else, the city was relatively safe, Marlene thought as a small comfort. It wasn't like so many foreign towns where a dead person was a statistic. Here, it was an uncommon occurrence, something that people talked about for months.

"You are trying to find out who killed her?"

Usually, Marlene preferred not to discuss work with her mother. But this wasn't a usual day.

"I'm doing my best," she said. "You haven't heard anything, have you?"

"People say this and that—but I don't pay attention to them."

Even if she knew something, Marlene suspected her mother wouldn't share it with her. Soledad wanted her to leave her current job and get a "normal" one. She wanted her to get married, have children, or, preferably, follow her brother to Miami and bring her along. Her mother, she hated to admit, had turned into a *gusana*.

Marlene stood up and retrieved a cell phone from her pants' pocket. It was the only perk of being a cop, in her mother's opinion. Since they didn't have a landline, Marlene had been issued a personal phone so she could be available at all times.

She dialed a number.

"Listen, Jacobo," she said firmly. "I need to talk to you first thing in the morning. I want to see all the files you have on Yarmila Portal. Either that or I am not handling the case anymore."

She closed the phone.

The problem with these cell phones is that you can't slam them.

"I'll go with you to Matilda's tonight," she said to her mother. "You are right, *Mami*. I *do* need a break."

"Amen," Soledad said.

Lobster *enchilada*

Today I am bringing to the table one of my favorite dishes—full of flavor and easy to prepare.

To avoid misunderstandings, this is different from the Mexican "enchilada," which, I believe, means something with a lot of chile. Correct me if I am wrong, Julia, as you are the expert in Mexican cuisine.

For us, "enchilada" is a kind of stew and we make it with lobster, shrimp or crab.

Lobster is easy to find here. If you live close to the beach, jump in a sailboat, go to the right spot, throw a net and voila! You soon have five or six *langostas* meekly waiting to become supper.

Bueno, it isn't that easy. There is the rather complicated part of cleaning the lobster, cutting away the legs and claws, but I won't get into that here because . . . I never do it myself. I get my lobster from a fisherman who sells just the tails, washed and ready to be cooked.

Like many of our dishes, *langosta enchilada* starts with *sofrito*. Make it the usual way with chopped onions, garlic, bell peppers, tomatoes, tomato sauce and spices, fried in oil or lard. You can add a bit of sugar, but only a teaspoon.

While the *sofrito* is being prepared, cut the lobster tails (four or five will be enough) into three-inch lengths.

Cook them in the *sofrito* for five minutes, or until they turn orange, then add half a cup of white cooking wine, salt and pepper. When the mixture starts to boil, let the lobster simmer for around fifteen minutes.

This is the moment to pour in one cup tomato sauce and a

chorrito of vinegar. Let it cook for ten more minutes—lobster should be tender—and serve over white rice.

I ate lobster *enchilada* for the first time on Varadero Beach when I was eight years old. My parents were *trabajadores de vanguardia*, exceptionally productive workers, and got rewarded with a week's vacation at the Hotel Internacional.

The hotel is right on the beachfront. I haven't been back, but I remember it well: a nice air-conditioned room, a huge swimming pool, and the most beautiful coastline. The water had a hundred shades of blue and the sand was so white and powdery. A few times I caught sight of what people from the area called *el rayo verde*: a green flash that appeared when the sun sank into the ocean. It was magic, I swear.

Has anybody here visited Varadero?

COMMENTS

Julia de Tejas said. . .

Yummy! An enchilada in Mexico is made with tortillas, salsa, cheese, sour cream, and beef or chicken. I love them. But I'll try the Cuban version.

As for Varadero, unfortunately, I haven't been there. Yet.

Yarmi said. . .

Come, then! Funny, I know that by "tortilla" you mean a flat disk made of flour, but for us, a tortilla is an omelet.

Lucy Adel said. . .

I read online that eating lobster was illegal in Cuba. Is that right?

Yarmi said. . .

Alabao! The things that people say . . . No, Lucy, eating lobster is very much within the law. You may gain a few pounds if you eat too much *enchilada* but there is nothing illicit about it.

Anita said. . .

I think that their sale is illegal. That's what my boyfriend, who sells them, would tell me.

Yarmi said. . .

Poor lobsters, they are being slandered! What is illegal is buying and selling food *outside* the official channels, be it government-owned restaurants or *paladares*. But I guess that's the case in most places. There are rigid regulations about handling seafood because it spoils fast. I wish I could invite you all over for a good lobster *enchilada*!

Anita said. . .

Gotcha. I went to Varadero a couple years ago but didn't go to the Hotel Internacional because it was too expensive. I stayed at a *casa particular*. Cheaper, and the owners pampered me.

Cubanita in Claremont said. . .

I've also been there, many years ago, when my family lived in Cuba. I have a vague memory of catching starfish underwater. Can Cubans stay in hotels now? I thought they were reserved for tourists.

Yarmi said. . .

No, Cubanita, that's another misconception. Cubans can stay in hotels. Sometimes tourists are given preference because, you know, we are a poor country and our government needs hard currency. But we aren't turned away if we want to reserve a room.

PART IV

Chapter One
"MY MOJITO IN LA BODEGUITA"

There was no hot water that morning at Villa Tomasa. The gas had been cut off, something that happened once or twice a month. Román managed to make coffee on an electric stove and served ham and cheese sandwiches instead of his signature scrambled eggs. Though Anne and Matt assured him they were fine with the arrangement, their host wouldn't stop apologizing.

"I ordered a hot plate from a *bisnero*, but he hasn't been able to find one," he said. "I am so sorry."

"Don't be," Anne said. "I loved the Cuban mayonnaise that you used this time."

"Well, it isn't the same."

Matt wasn't used to being fussed over like that. He enjoyed the attention and wondered if he should add a big tip for Román before leaving Cuba, or maybe feature Villa Tomasa's breakfasts in *Foodalicious*. His editor might go for it, considering that there would be no wedding story after all.

Matt hadn't heard from Padrino after visiting him on Saturday. That made him nervous. What if the guy was a con artist and

Isabel his sidekick? On the other hand, he hadn't heard from Lieutenant Martínez, or—much to his relief—Agent Pedro.

Anne was talkative and sounded more airy-fairy than usual. After a while, she confided that Yony had apologized and they had patched things up.

"I'll take it for what it is," she said. "A boy toy. It's not taboo anymore. After all, Cher and Madonna paved the way."

Matt nodded, but he found the idea distasteful.

"You can't ask the elm tree for pears, as they say here," Anne added.

"That pretty much sums it up."

"People say that, to become acculturated, you need to be in a relationship with a national. You learn more that way than going to places by yourself or reading travel books."

"It didn't work for me," Matt said slowly. "But hey, to each his own."

"Oh, Matt, I'm sorry!" Anne covered her mouth with her hands. "I wasn't thinking—I didn't mean to—"

He smiled with just a hint of sadness. "That's okay," he said.

But what he really wanted to say was, "Why in the world would you want to become 'acculturated' here?"

AT NOON, ANNE INVITED Matt to have lunch with her and Yony at La Bodeguita del Medio.

"I'm still full," he said.

"Come on! You don't have to eat a lot, it's all about the experience. La Bodeguita is a historic landmark. It was one of Hemingway's favorite restaurants, along with El Floridita. He would say, 'My mojito in La Bodeguita, my daiquiri in El Floridita.'"

"I am not impressed with Cuban mojitos."

"You are becoming a hermit, Matt. And that's not good. Get ready! Then we can hit the eastern beaches in the *almendrón*. You aren't under house arrest!"

"Hope not."

"You need to lighten up. Horrible as all this has been, you might have dodged a bullet with Yarmila."

He considered her last argument and capitulated. "Fine. Let's go see Papa's watering hole."

YONY SHOWED UP AROUND two o'clock. He and Matt waited in the living room for Anne, who was still putting on makeup.

"I thought that only Cuban *mamitas* were late all the time," Yony complained.

"It must be a girl thing," Matt replied. "Universal."

Yony didn't make any reference to Yarmila's death. They kept their topics light—baseball, the weather, the latest American films . . . Yony's behavior was a mix of swagger and immaturity. He spoke loudly and mispronounced many words. Then he peppered Matt with questions about BMWs, Porsches, motorcycles, and race cars.

"I wish I could drive one, man, if only for ten minutes," he said. "That must feel like heaven."

When Anne was finally ready, the three left Villa Tomasa together. Yony had double-parked the Studebaker three blocks away and was getting nervous about it.

"Everybody does it, but with my luck, I'll be the one who gets a fine today," he said.

"Could you offer the cop a *mordida* as drivers do in Tijuana?" Matt asked.

"A bite?"

"I mean a bribe. That's Mexican Spanish."

"It depends. Probably not, unless he asks for it. It could land me in more trouble."

He hurried ahead, leaving Matt and Anne behind.

"Say, Anne, does your—boy toy know what happened to Yarmila?" he asked.

"Yes, I told him. Why? Shouldn't I have?"

"Oh, it's okay. I was just wondering because he didn't say anything about it."

"Cuban guys are not good at expressing their feelings. But he was very sad."

"Did they actually know each other?"

"Yes, don't you remember? We all met at Ricardito's once. He also sold her food and stuff. I think that they were kinda close."

Anne pursed her lips as if she didn't like the idea. Matt had a sick feeling in his stomach. They had reached the *almendrón* and stopped talking. Yony was behind the Studebaker's wheel, his hands tight around it.

LA BODEGUITA DEL MEDIO was packed, mostly with tourists, though a few locals stood out. Matt, Anne and Yony were instructed to wait in the cobblestone street. They stayed there for forty minutes, sweating profusely under the restaurant's yellow and blue sign. Across from them, an elderly black woman dressed in white sat on a wooden stool on the sidewalk. She was posing for pictures, Yony explained.

"If you pay her," he added. "She isn't a real *santera*. But nothing in Old Havana is real, except for the Cathedral. Fake, fake, fake! The City Historian has rebuilt it for foreigners' tastes."

"This doesn't quite suit my taste," Anne replied, fanning herself with a copy of *Juventud Rebelde* that she had bought for fifty cents.

"I mean cheap foreigners, *mamita*, not refined ones like you."

They were finally seated at the back of the restaurant, so close to the next table that Matt could smell the coconut-scented tanning lotion that a Belgian couple had spread over their arms and faces. There was writing on every wall: signatures and messages left by the famous, infamous, and commoners alike. Conversations flowed in English, Spanish, German, and French. The building had a second floor, but it happened to be closed that day. That accounted for the long wait, the busboy told them.

Following the first round of the unavoidable mojitos, Matt dropped Yarmila's name several times and watched Yony's reactions.

"She would have loved this place," he said. "She was fond of nice restaurants, wasn't she?"

Yony shrugged. "I don't think this is such a nice restaurant," he replied. "They have better stuff at La Caldosa. Cheaper too. La Bodeguita is a tourist trap."

Matt agreed with him. The five-CUC-a-piece mojitos were even worse than those at Café Arabia. The lunch as such wasn't bad, but nothing spectacular either. They all ordered what the waiter assured them was the best item on the menu: a combo plate of pulled pork, rice and black beans.

Halfway through the meal, Anne elbowed Yony when she caught him staring at a tall blonde with bouncy implants.

"What's up, *mamita*?"

"Don't do that!"

"Don't do *what*?"

Next, he started picking his teeth.

"Can't you behave, for God's sake?"

"Huh?"

Matt looked the other way.

What a freaking circus. But I'd still like to know how close this guy and Yarmi were.

A local trio began to play. Two old men with guitars and a young one with a pair of maracas sang "*Guajira Guantanamera.*" Matt turned his attention to the pictures that adorned La Bodeguita's walls—Hemingway smoking a cigar, Hemingway shaking Castro's hand, Hemingway and a wrinkled guy. There was also a sign that read *Cargue con su pesao.* Neither Matt nor Anne could translate it.

"*Pesao* is heavy, like in an overweight person," she said. "But does it mean that one should find a fat guy and pick him up?"

Yony clarified it. A *pesao* was also someone without social graces whose presence was a burden for everybody around. "If you bring in a guy like that, or if you become one after drinking too much, then you must go, or take him with you," he said.

"None of us are *pesaos*, if I must say so myself," Anne laughed, finishing off her third mojito. "We are allowed to stay!"

She was the only one having a decent time. Yony looked worried and Matt wasn't in the best of moods either.

I don't trust this boy toy.

Before they left, the waiter encouraged them to leave their marks on the wall. Matt declined, but Anne grabbed Yony's arm and led him to a free spot.

Viva La Bodeguita, she wrote.

Yony drew a heart and scribbled both their names inside. Then he wrote "*Amo a Anita*" (I love Anita) under it.

"Do you really mean it?" she slurred.

"Yes, I do! You are the woman of my life."

They snuck away under the stairs. Matt looked vacantly at Hemingway's pictures. He felt the pulled pork, beans and rice come up to his throat.

FROM LA BODEGUITA, THE lovebirds continued to El Mégano beach. Matt excused himself and took a *cocotaxi* home. Once in his room, he left his wallet on the roll-top desk. There was a sheet of paper in the Smith-Corona, as if waiting for someone to use it. He began to write in a trance, without looking at the keyboard. The shift key for upper case characters didn't work, but he didn't care. What came out was a short, chopped description of his arrival at the José Martí International Airport. He wrote in the third person about the customs officer who hadn't stamped their passports and the flower vendor who had offered them marigolds for the *orishas*.

Who knows? I may turn it into a novel: Trials and Tribulations of a Gringo in Havana.

As he typed away, Matt imagined he was back at *El Grito*. The office was decorated with Mexican cut paper, sombreros, sarapes, and Estrada's dusty collection of posters. They included everything from images of Cinco de Mayo and La Raza celebrations to Vicente Fernández and La India. Matt liked his job, but he had always thought the place was hideous. Now, he admitted with a sigh that he missed it.

ANNE CAME BACK SUNBURNED and tired, her hair matted with seawater and salt. It was the first time that Matt had seen her with no makeup at all. The bags under her eyes were of a deeper blue than usual. Red blotches covered her cheeks and forearms. But she was happy. It had been a great day, she assured him.

"Too bad you didn't come with us. El Mégano isn't fancy, but we had so much fun."

Matt listened quietly. There was no point in telling her that he and Yarmila had spent a whole day at El Mégano the year before.

"I'm planning a one-day trip to Varadero this weekend," Anne added. "Would you like to come along? Yony won't mind it."

"I don't think I should leave the city."

"Here you go again. The cops didn't say you couldn't."

"What if Padrino finds out something? Nah, I'd rather stay."

Anne was silent for a while. When she spoke again, her eyes were soft and dreamy. "I know it sounds absurd," she said, "but I believe that we *do* have a chance."

Matt blinked. For a second, he thought Anne was talking about him and her.

"Yony is really a good kid." She smiled. "He grew up poor, without a male role model. His father left the family when he was two years old and his mother raised him and five more kids by herself. A hard life. On top of that, he's from Oriente."

"What's that?"

"A God-forgotten place in the most eastern region of the country, like a tropical Appalachia. He got out of there on his own and is now doing quite well. A self-made man, you know?"

Though Matt didn't share her enthusiasm, he smiled back and nodded in agreement. Anne wasn't only his compatriot, but the one friend he had in Cuba. He couldn't afford to alienate her by badmouthing her boy toy.

"He does illegal things, but so many normal activities are illegal in this country that everybody ends up being a crook," she went on. "As they say, everything that isn't forbidden is compulsory."

"Yep. I wouldn't like to live here."

"No wonder Yony wants to leave. He finally admitted it. So I am thinking about sending for him someday. Not anytime soon, of course. I still need to get to know him better. But my feeling is that, if we work hard together, he will blossom. He has potential."

Once again Anne reminded Matt of his ex-wife, who had been convinced that if he worked harder (or if she nagged him long enough) he would "blossom," becoming a reporter for the *San*

Diego Journal or another reputable newspaper. She had loathed both *El Grito* and Estrada. Despite his growing distrust of Yony, Matt felt a rush of solidarity with the *bisnero*.

"I wish you guys the best," was all he said.

IT RAINED THAT EVENING. They ended up eating at home. Román improvised dinner: a salad of avocado and onions sprinkled with olive oil and garlic chicken with mashed potatoes. Dessert was *natilla*, creamy custard. And beer, all they could drink, for which their host didn't charge a cent.

"Everything's on the house," he said.

Later, the three of them sat on the sofa and watched *Return of the Jedi* on Román's VCR.

"These are the most awesome movies in the entire galaxy," their host declared, a childlike smile spreading across his ruddy face. "When the next one comes out, will you guys send me a copy? And I'll give you two nights free."

"That's a deal."

THAT NIGHT MATT DREAMED of Yarmila again. He saw a tall building in the distance as he flew through a window and hovered over a crowd that busied itself buying and selling things.

Yarmila was there, flanked by Fefita and Isabel. The three of them were drinking mojitos. When Matt touched ground in front of the women, Yarmila smiled and said, "Girls, I've been wanting to introduce you to my fiancé, Mateo the *Yuma*. And here he is, at last."

"Welcome, Mateo," Fefita shook his hand.

Isabel offered him her drink. "Here, take this. You are part of our family now."

Strangely enough, Yarmila had lost her accent. Isabel and

Fefita spoke perfect English too. That alerted Matt. He realized, with a jolt, that he was dreaming.

"Why did you cheat on me?" he asked Yarmila. "Why did you die on me when I came ready to propose?"

"I didn't die *on you*," she said matter-of-factly. "I was killed, remember?"

"And who killed you?"

She shrugged.

"What about the cheating?" he insisted. "Why did you do that, Yarmi? Why did you string me along if you were really in love with Pato Macho?"

He was almost in tears. Then he remembered that it was all a dream. He was supposed to be in control.

"Ah, stop whining," Yarmila answered in Spanish. "Don't you know by now that Pato is the man of my life?"

Isabel and Fefita cackled. A second before he woke up, Matt understood the dirty little secret of lucid dreams—the fact that you knew you were dreaming didn't actually put you in charge of the dream.

Chapter Two

THE MAGIC OF ONE THOUSAND AND ONE NIGHTS

When Matt got up, at seven o'clock, Román and Anne were still in their rooms. The house was silent; time itself was asleep. He crossed the dining room, tiptoed past doña Tomasa's portrait, and inspected the refrigerator. There were eggs, milk, butter, and a plastic tray with two uncooked pork chops. Matt wasn't the kind who would wake up a host to demand breakfast. He went out for a walk instead.

The city hadn't yet awakened. San Lázaro Avenue was so empty of vehicles that the scarce pedestrians didn't bother to wait for the red light to cross the street. Around the Malecón esplanade, the air was crisp and salty. A lone fisherman sat on the edge of the wall with a makeshift pole. On the horizon, the early rays of the sun broke against the water, creating pale flashes of light.

A couple of blocks later Matt encountered the skeleton of an old building covered in lush vegetation. The shell remained intact, but the interior walls and floors had disintegrated. The balconies opened like eyeless sockets peering into the emptiness inside. Healthy lianas had grown up everywhere. Their green sprouts stood in sharp contrast with the decaying, mold-stricken façade. It looked surreal, like something you'd expect to find in a dystopic movie about a dead civilization.

Matt couldn't figure out how a structure like that had survived so close to the tourist zone. It might have been destroyed by Hurricane Lili, or Isidore, or any of the tropical storms that routinely swept over the island. People had once lived there, people whose dreams had been crushed—like his.

He walked to El Nacional, one of the most expensive hotels in the city, and ventured into a little cafeteria called Film Corner. The formal restaurant, El Comedor de Aguiar, was closed. At that early hour, there weren't any foreign guests around, much less natives. A lethargic waitress dressed in blue jeans and tennis shoes took ten minutes to show up.

"What do you want?" she asked sharply.

Matt ordered a *café con leche* and a *medianoche*, a ham and cheese sandwich. Both were below Villa Tomasa's standards. The bread was hard so he picked at the ham and cheese and ordered a second cup of coffee with milk. The restaurant smelled like stale cigarette smoke and fried dough, which killed his appetite. In a brochure left behind on the table he read that the hotel had counted Johnny Weissmuller, Fred Astaire, and Ava Gardner as guests in its golden days. He also found a copy of *Juventud Rebelde*. The front page was devoted to the upcoming celebration of "the first defeat of imperialism in America." It wasn't until the third paragraph that he realized the story was about the Bay of Pigs invasion.

After breakfast, he lingered in the lobby. The place reeked of bygone opulence—a grandfather clock that didn't work, tarnished brass fixtures, high ceilings with heavy beams, and a long, dusty tiled corridor. There was a Hall of Fame with photos of celebrity guests, past and present. Like the restaurant, it was closed.

The bored, unfriendly faces of the reception clerks made Matt appreciate Román's hospitality even more.

There was an Aeroméxico counter that advertised flights to Tijuana. There was nobody there, but he made a mental note to come back as soon as he had recovered his passport. If it happened before his intended return date on April 1, he could change his ticket there.

Matt returned to Malecón Drive and passed Café Arabia. The sign was turned off and it looked like a regular house. On the next corner he discovered a small shop that advertised *regalos*, gifts. He went in, out of curiosity, and spent the next hour perusing coconut monkeys, T-shirts with the Cuban flag, bottles of Legendario rum, and colorful ceramics. He also sniffed some cigars. Though he had never been a serious smoker, he couldn't help buying a robust Partagás. He enjoyed it on the premises, under the approving smile of the store employee. The old man, dressed in a blue *guayabera* and white pants, asked, "How is it, *señor*?"

"Great!"

Matt wasn't just being polite. He liked it so much that he also got a fruity, tangerine-flavored Romeo y Julieta, and a vanilla-scented Montecristo. He was tempted by a Cohiba, which was supposed to be a favorite of Castro's, but the sixty-dollar price tag discouraged him.

A LIGHT RAIN BEGAN to fall. Matt hurried to Villa Tomasa. Anne wasn't there. She had gone out with Yony, Román told him, and said she would come back late, or not at all. "She seems very much into him," he added with a sneer.

"Ah, women! Then they talk about *us*."

"I feel sorry for Anita," Román said, getting serious. "She is like so many tourists who believe everything these smooth talkers tell them. You should warn her."

"She is old enough to know better."

Matt went back to his room and tried to read a 1957 *Reader's Digest* article about Cardinal Mindszenty, but couldn't concentrate on it. He was still thinking of Yarmila. He went over their conversations, the few days they had spent together, her messages to him, scrutinizing them and looking for hints of deceit. But he found nothing. She always replied to his emails within hours. She seemed to be waiting by the phone every time he called her.

Now, I don't remember seeing a phone at her place. I would have surely noticed one of these big, old-fashioned ones. Would the number still work?

He went to the dining room and dialed Yarmila's number. Absurdly, for a minute, he expected her to answer.

"The Cubacel number you are calling has been disconnected," a recording said.

"What's Cubacel?" Matt asked Román.

"A phone company," his host said. "But only for cell phones."

"Are they very common here?"

"Not really. In most cases, the service has to be paid in CUCs."

"So they are expensive."

"Very. I wouldn't even dream of having one."

Matt went back to his room, mulling it over.

She could have used the money I sent her to get herself a cell phone. No, wait. I started calling this number before we met in person. She'd given it to him in an email a few weeks after they'd started exchanging messages, when he'd told her he was coming down for a visit. She still lived at the Old Havana apartment then. If she wasn't working at La Caldosa yet, where had she found the money to pay for a cell phone?

At 7:00 P.M. Román settled in on the lounge chair to watch *Attack of the Clones* with five carefully rolled joints at hand. Matt turned on the TV in his room. It offered two options—a Venezuelan soap opera where two women screamed at each other and a Cuban documentary showcasing the new housing developments on the Isle of Youth. He remembered the feature Estrada had suggested on Havana's Chinatown. He asked Román for directions.

"That's too far away," he said. "You'll need to take a taxi. But everything is overpriced there. And there are no Chinese left in Chinatown."

"Where are they?"

"They fled Cuba when Fidel took over. They knew exactly what was coming up next."

MATT WALKED BRISKLY FOR the five blocks that separated Villa Tomasa from Café Arabia, avoiding the street holes that had become mud puddles with the rain.

The show was about to start. That night Taty had chosen to impersonate Sara Montiel, a Spanish singer who had been in the news a few months before, when she wedded a Cuban videotape operator forty years her junior. Their May-December romance even merited a mention in *Granma*, the official Communist Party newspaper.

The audience went wild as Taty sang "*Fumando espero*," a tango that had been a hit in the fifties. This time, either because the song was in Spanish or Taty was more familiar with the rhythm, he sounded better. Halfway through the song, he produced a cigarette and started to smoke, walking around the tables and caressing shoulders and arms. He looked feminine and desirable in a high-waisted red pencil skirt and a black top sprinkled with sequins.

Matt listened, enthralled by the illusion that Taty had created. When the singer reached the table, he bent over and said, "I knew you'd be back—mister." He smelled like gardenias, musk and sweat. "I'll be with you soon."

Matt whistled the tango tune. He ordered a shot of rum, a Coke, and chicken wings. The rum arrived promptly, not so the Coke— that never came. The chicken wings, *las alitas*, were a real treat, crispy and wrapped in a piquant sauce that had hints of cumin, red pepper and garlic. He regretted not having brought his remaining cigars to a place where entertainers and patrons smoked with happy abandon. The Romeo y Julieta would have been perfect to accompany the *alitas* and Taty's show.

Five songs and many shouts of *perra* later, the musical part of the show was over. Soft jazz played in the background. Matt ordered more chicken wings and another shot of rum.

As soon as Taty was done walking around the room, collecting compliments and bills, he came over again.

"How are you?" he asked. A mischievous twinkle in his heavily lined eyes contrasted with the formality of the question.

"Fine, all things considered," Matt answered. "And yourself?"

"Happy to see you, *mi santo*."

"Am I your *santo*, honey?" Matt said.

The rum, whirling and running through his veins, gave him the necessary dose of courage to utter the last word. He had never called another man "honey," much less its Spanish equivalent, *cariño*.

"My *santo*, my friend, or whatever you want to be," Taty replied.

Matt didn't know how he was expected to answer. He had always had enough trouble flirting with women.

"Friend will be good—to start," he said.

"And to end? But we do not want this to end, do we?"

The conversation went on, awkward at first and then smooth and easy, stretching like the liana vines Matt had seen that morning over the skeleton of someone's dream. And yet he was self-conscious, nervous, afraid of being found out . . . What would Lieutenant Martínez or Agent Pedro say if they knew where he was, and with whom? But when Taty's fingers closed around his, he didn't doubt it anymore. He saw a beautiful woman with shiny black hair and pouty glossy lips, a pretty girl who smelled of gardenias and sweat. He squeezed Taty's hand in return, ignoring its calloused palm and feeling a delicious pain when Taty's manicured nails drove through his flesh. The music stopped.

"I have to wrap this up," Taty whispered. "Don't go anywhere, okay?"

He got back on stage. It was time for the sketch. Matt hoped that he would keep it short and sweet.

"*Locas*, thanks for being here!" Taty opened his arms. "Thanks for allowing us to embrace you with the magic of one thousand and one nights!"

He blew a kiss at the audience.

"You didn't expect this, did you? Sarita Montiel, the divine one! The first I time I saw Saritísima in *La Violetera*, I fell in love with her. I was ten years old and my mom, bless her soul, had taken me to the matinee at the Alameda movie theater. A place I would return to as a teenager because it had the darkest restrooms and the biggest crowd of hairy, handsome, and very married men looking for—but that is another story.

"That day I came home all happy and giddy and locked myself in my room. I mean, in the room I shared with my brother, a super macho who ate crocodiles alive, and my bitchy older sister. I tried to make myself look like Sarita with red lipstick and my sis's best Sunday dress. I pranced in front of the mirror and started to sing . . .

"*Alabao, loquisimas!* I must have been really inspired because I didn't see it coming. When I least expected it, the door was kicked open and my father appeared in the threshold, his face as red as my lipstick and the veins in his neck bulging with fury.

"'No son of mine is going to grow up a fucking fag!' he yelled, towering above my eighty-pound frame. 'I'll teach you to be a man even if it is the last thing I do on earth!'

"Dad suspected I had 'a little problem,' but he'd never caught me in the act like that. I knew I was in trouble. He had hit me before, many times. He hit my siblings too. I thought he would kill me."

Matt looked around, uncomfortable. Everyone else was engrossed in the story. Some were even smiling. He didn't get it. Did people find *that* funny?

Taty went on, "I was saved by the bell, or rather by my mother, who hurried from the kitchen wielding a carving knife. She got herself between my dad and me. 'Leave the kid alone!' she screamed. 'Don't you see how skinny he is? Don't you dare touch him!'

"'I'd rather see him dead than *maricón*!'

"She grabbed him by the arm and said in a low voice, but loud enough for me to hear, 'So he is a *maricón*, so what? What are you then, when you ask me to insert a rubber bulb in your ass at night, *cochino*?'"

The audience roared.

"Later Mom would try to convince Dad that I was born that way, but he wouldn't hear any of it. I was his biggest disappointment.

"So Pepito's best friend asks him, 'Is it true that seventy-five percent of *maricones* were born that way?' And Pepito replies, 'Sure thing, man.' 'What about the other twenty-five percent?' his friend asks. 'Ah,' Pepito responds, 'those were sucked in.'"

WHEN THE SKETCH WAS over, Taty joined Matt at the table and another performer took his place. It was, or looked like, an older woman with a long blonde mane.

"Who is that supposed to be?" Matt asked.

"Rosita Fornés before the times of cholera." Taty laughed. "She has aged badly, but the bitch was *perrísima* until ten years ago. Nothing like Sarita, but good enough."

Matt watched the impersonator without much interest. When Taty hinted that it was getting late—he didn't say for what—he heartily agreed. They left Café Arabia together and Taty wrapped himself around Matt.

"Where are you staying, my *santo*, now that you left Isabel's penthouse? *Ay*, wasn't the old cow pissed off!"

"Not very far from here."

"In a hotel?"

"No. In another *casa particular*."

"Do you think the *casa*'s owner will let me stay? They don't like Cubans, as a rule."

"I'll make sure you get in," Matt replied.

Taty smiled and squeezed Matt's arm. "You won't regret it."

"Who is Pepito?" Matt asked after a while, to break the silence that was making him edgy. "You mentioned him last time too."

"You have a good memory, my Mateo." Taty smiled. "He's a young boy who says the darndest things."

"Is he a real person?"

"No. But everybody knows a Pepito at school, at work. Cuba is full of them! He's just a twerp, funny and sharp-tongued."

They walked together, arm in arm, to Villa Tomasa. Taty stepped gracefully over the mud puddles and street holes.

Matt hoped and prayed that Román wouldn't notice his companion's big hands and Adam's apple, that he wouldn't get mad, that he wouldn't demand any immediate payment . . . What if he thought that Taty was a *jinetera* and refused to allow him to stay? But Román, stoned and sleepy, listened with a straight face to Matt's incoherent excuses about "bringing a friend in."

"Come on in," he mumbled. "No big deal."

Relieved, Matt hurried to get Taty past the living room, blushing at the thoughts that his urgency might instill in his host's foggy mind. But he reminded himself that Román was seeing him with a beautiful Cuban girl. And what could be more natural than that?

"This is a cool place," Taty looked at the leather sofa and the fake fireplace. "A real *casa particular*, not like 'the penthouse.' I still remember your face when you first saw it!"

Matt closed the door to his room. Under the amber light cast by the art-deco lamp, Taty had recovered some of his most conspicuous masculine traits. There was a five o'clock shadow under the slightly smeared makeup.

"Why are you doing this?" Matt asked.

"Because I like you," Taty said. "Don't think it's about money because I don't want a cent, eh! I've had a crush on you since we met at Isabel's."

"No, that's fine. I meant cross-dressing, if you don't mind me asking. I didn't know it was a common practice here."

"It's more common now than ten years ago. Well, ten years ago I was a little kid living in the rear end of the world so I wouldn't have known any better. I came out when I moved to Havana. As I said tonight, I started early on, but back then no one talked about 'cross-dressing.' People like my dad just called you a *maricón de mierda* if they caught you in drag."

"Oh. I'm sorry."

"That's why I've settled in Havana, where they are more tolerant. And I do it because—*coño*, because I enjoy it. I like seeing myself as a girl. I *am* a girl, deep down. But does this matter now? Why are we wasting time with so much blah-blah-blah?"

His hands started to caress Matt's back, relieving tension and unknotting his fears.

"You're right, *mi santo*," Matt said, yielding to Taty's soothing touch.

AT SEVEN THIRTY TATY woke Matt up singing a Sara Montiel song softly in his ear. They made love once more, and Taty was gone.

Pan de plátano—a banana bread feast at work

One of my favorite snacks is *pan de plátano*, banana bread, which I made last week for my colleagues.

Yes, my colleagues. Some of my dear readers have asked what I do when I am not cooking, or blogging about food. Or eating. As you must know by now, I like to eat!

This is a good time to share with you, my virtual friends, that besides "cooking Cuban," Yarmi also has a regular job, like so many other women in our country.

It has nothing to do with food.

I work at the Institute of Literature and Linguistics. I am one of the youngest researchers here—and I say "here" because I write this post at work, in my office, during lunchtime. My job consists of reading and classifying all the English-language materials that are sent to our offices. I catalogue the books and magazines and send them to the corresponding area of our library, named Biblioteca Fernando Ortiz after a distinguished Cuban ethnographer.

If there is something particularly interesting, I propose it for translation and possible publication. Sometimes I get to do the Spanish version and the articles are published in the Institute's very own newsletter.

The Institute is close to my house so I don't need to take a bus. An advantage if you live in Havana, where distances are long and buses scarce! I can go back and forth in twenty minutes.

Last week, I brought in all the necessary ingredients to prepare *pan de plátano*, a loaf of banana bread. They are easy to find: two cups of flour, one teaspoon of baking soda, a pinch of salt, half a cup of butter, four tablespoons of brown sugar, a beaten egg, and three medium-sized ripe bananas.

Here you can find bananas anywhere: at the farmers' market, from street vendors . . . You can even grow them in your own yard. Butter and eggs are also available. Baking soda is sold at pharmacies. As for brown sugar, everyone gets six pounds a month.

Normally I wouldn't cook at the Institute, of course. Most of us go out for lunch or bring something from home. But I decided to make bread here because of a coworker who just wouldn't stop complaining. She spent a whole morning criticizing the bakery bread because "it tasted like a sponge." (What does a sponge taste like anyway?) I asked why she didn't make bread herself, since she was so picky, and she looked at me as if I had asked why she didn't build a rocket.

"*Tas loca*," she told me.

To prove I wasn't crazy, I set to work at the Institute's underutilized kitchen. The building used to be the home of a bourgeois family and the kitchen area is as big as my apartment. Nobody uses it now, though. The cooktop was cracked on the edges and none of the four burners worked. Luckily, the oven was in perfect shape.

I began by mixing flour, baking soda and salt in one bowl. In another, I combined butter and brown sugar, stirring until they became a creamy paste. I added beaten eggs and mashed bananas, and mixed everything. After pouring the mixture into a pan, I put it in the oven at 390 degrees and baked it for around fifty minutes.

Voila, *pan de plátano* for everyone!

The best part was the aroma of freshly baked bread. The whole Institute smelled so good that a few people who were consulting books at the library came over to ask us for a bite.

"Don't tell me you can't do this at home," I told my bitchy coworker. "*Cuando se quiere, se puede.*"

Yes, when there is a will, there is a way.

Little bread kisses to you all.

COMMENTS

Cocinera Cubana said. . .

It seems simple enough!

Taos Tonya said. . .

Here people used to make bread in *hornos*, outdoor ovens. Some still do.

Maritza said. . .

I don't think it was a Cuban tradition to make bread at home. It was easier to buy it at a *panadería*.

Yarmi said. . .

It *is* easy, Cocinera. Give it a try! Bread is very forgiving so don't worry about making mistakes.

Tonya, I googled the *hornos*. Such interesting structures. I will show them to my parents when I go back to Los Palacios. Maybe they could build one.

Maritza, you can still buy bread at bakeries. I only wanted to show my colleague that we don't need to depend on them all the time. It feels good to be self-sufficient!

I just remembered an old saying from Grandma Hilda: *Las penas con pan son menos*—sorrows hurt less with bread.

Chapter Three
AND LIES KEEP PILING UP

The day after the *café con leche* surprise, Marlene deferred to Duty. Instead of getting herself out of the case as she had threatened to do, she continued working on it. It helped that the Seguridad agent sent her a printed copy of another post through internal mail, saying there were "a few more and some really interesting things" coming soon.

By then the useless computer had been taken away and Marlene wasn't missing it a bit. She had another meeting with comrade instructor, who shared what he'd learned from his visit to Fefita *Comité* and Yarmila's parents.

"I don't see clearly here," he admitted. "For her folks, she was a model communist. For Fefita, she was lukewarm at best. I can see her lying to her parents so as not to hurt their feelings but—"

"I wasn't able to sleep yesterday, thinking of her," Marlene said. "After reading all these posts and meeting her boyfriend, er, boyfriends, I can't help but feel some sort of a connection with Yarmila, though I didn't sympathize much with her when I started working the case." She realized that she had stopped calling her "citizen Portal." "She might have been a counterrevolutionary, but I wish I'd met her."

"You'd have liked her," he said. "Most people did."

"You knew her, didn't you? What was she like?"

She waited with anxious anticipation while her former teacher looked for the right words.

"Very nice," he said finally. "Chatty. Easygoing. But I never talked to her about anything of substance."

"She talked a lot, but didn't say much," Marlene mused.

"That's a good way to put it."

"Carmela, the *gusana*, said it." Marlene looked through her desk. "I have notes from our interview. She befriended them, but wasn't very involved with their activities. Now I am waiting for Jacobo's input. He hasn't bothered to tell me anything yet."

"Why is he keeping that poor *Yuma* in Cuba?"

Marlene smirked. "That poor *Yuma*! Comrade Instructor, your client isn't poor. He is richer than ten of us put together. That being said, I'm all for letting him go. I think Jacobo was so embarrassed about the CIA confusion that he's trying to save face somehow." She chuckled. "Culinary Institute of America—Ha! But unless there is something else going on, he will give him his passport back in a few days. Though with la Seguridad, one never knows."

They discussed the blog posts. He had finished reading them and pointed out some inconsistencies.

"Yarmila wrote that her mother was a manager and a career woman, but she was not," he said. "She is a housewife and not very educated."

"Maybe she was trying to make her folks look good."

"What for? None of her readers knew her family and I suspect they couldn't care less. Then these detailed descriptions of dishes that ordinary people can't afford . . . Even with CUCs, you can't find steak anywhere most of the time."

The truck that delivered food to the police station stopped outside the building. The metallic noise of pots being carried through the hall filled the office. The chow usually consisted of rice and stale Spam.

"You have to read the post about making banana bread from scratch," Marlene said with an annoyed frown. "Where did she get her ideas?"

"And selling lobster *is* illegal. People do it, but it's against the law. She also said that Cubans were allowed to stay in hotels, but she forgot to mention that we can't pay with pesos. How many people can afford to spend eighty CUCs for a night at the Hotel Internacional?"

Marlene nodded. "Reading her blog, you'd think she lived in an alternate universe where everything was easy and nice," she said.

"Unless she was making it up. All of it."

"But as you said, Comrade Instructor, what for?"

LATER THAT DAY MARLENE went to see Fernando Goicochea, the Communist Party Secretary for the Institute of Literature and Linguistics. She walked from the police station to the stone building, fronted by a portico with four marble columns, where Yarmila had worked. The receptionist led her to an office where a middle-aged man with thick eyeglasses, a white *guayabera*, and a Soviet-era Poljot watch sat behind a desk. As they made small talk (Marlene liked to put people at ease before starting an official conversation) she looked outside, curious to see the kitchen where the banana bread had been baked only a few weeks before. Then she caught Fernando eyeing her behind.

Why are all men such pigs? Carajo! *I'm so tired of this!*

"Let's get to the point," she said, cutting him off in the middle of a story about an award that Eusebio Leal, Havana's City Historian, had conferred to the Institute. "When did you see Yarmila Portal for the last time?"

The man's face reddened and he stuttered a bit. "On February twenty-eighth," he said. "It was a Friday."

"That was a while ago. Was she on vacation afterward?"

"Not exactly. She had asked for two weeks off, without pay, starting the next Monday. Her Yankee boyfriend was coming so she wanted to 'spend time' with him. She said it in so many words. But she also spent time with other, younger men. A boy right out of high school!"

FERNANDO HAD AN OBSCENE grin plastered over his face. Marlene felt like smacking him.

"How would you describe her?"

"She—eh—how can I put it nicely?"

"Don't. This is a police case. We don't have time for niceties."

"Fine, then. The truth is that she had ideological problems. I wouldn't say she was a *gusana*, but she leaned that way."

"Explain how."

"In the first place, look at the kind of partner she chose. I am not as rigid as many other *compañeros* in my position tend to be. I do think that *some* Yankees—those who visit Cuba to find out the truth about our country—aren't bad people. The fact that they were born in the monster's entrails doesn't make them evil per se. But still! Aren't there enough good men in Cuba?"

"Besides that, was she a good worker?" Marlene asked. "Did she come every day and fulfill her duties?"

"For the most part, yes." Fernando took off his glasses and

began to clean them, a gesture that Marlene had learned to associate with nervousness. "But she was friends with some disreputable elements, both at the Institute and outside. I mean, we don't have *gusanos* here, but there are a few who criticize everything, who complain for no reason—these were the ones that Yarmila liked to associate with."

"Did she argue with them?"

"Argue? No, no—she *encouraged* them!"

"But Yarmila knew that our economic problems weren't the revolution's fault," Marlene said. "She thought that people should be self-reliant. She even made bread for you guys to prove her point."

Fernando put on his glasses and stared at her. "Made bread for us?" he repeated. "What do you mean by that?"

"I mean what I said. She baked a loaf of banana bread here, at the Institute, for everyone to enjoy."

"Is that some kind of a joke?" Fernando shrugged. "Because, with all due respect, I don't get it."

"I don't joke around when I am working," Marlene replied curtly.

Fernando seemed perplexed. "This must be a misunderstanding," he said. "People aren't allowed to smoke on the premises, much less cook. The building is full of valuable manuscripts and we can't risk a fire."

"It only happened once."

"That's impossible. Where was she supposed to make bread? On a campfire in the backyard?"

"In the kitchen."

"There is no kitchen here."

"Are you *sure*?"

The way Marlene posed this question usually made people

think twice and reconsider their answers. But the Communist Party Secretary didn't show any signs of uncertainty.

"Absolutely, *compañera*. There is a small area with a refrigerator, but we don't have a stove or anything like that."

"What about the original kitchen? The one that the owners used when the Institute was the home of a bourgeois family?"

"This place has never been a private home. It was built in 1947 for La Sociedad Económica de Amigos del País and has been a public building ever since."

Marlene gave up on the subject. "What do you do at the Institute, Comrade Secretary?" she asked.

"I am *investigador titular*, head researcher. I'm also a linguist and a professor at the School of Philology."

"So you teach too."

"Yes, I have a doctorate from Lomonosov University and an honorary doctorate from Sofia University in Bulgaria."

What a pedantic jerk.

"I'd like to see that small kitchen area you mentioned, if you don't mind," Marlene said.

"Indeed, *compañera*. Please, follow me."

He escorted her to the end of a hall where a blue Soviet-era refrigerator (a contemporary of the Poljot watch) made gurgling sounds.

"May I visit Yarmila's office now?" Marlene asked, defeated.

Fernando shook his head. "The deceased citizen didn't have an office," he said. "None of the young researchers do. There are around seventy employees here and many share a workspace."

"Did she have a personal computer?" she asked, thinking of her own fiasco.

"A personal computer, *compañera*?" Fernando rolled his eyes.

"Certainly not! They are assigned by the Minister to *reliable* people. We only have three computers in the building: mine, one that belongs to the library and another for our director."

"Did Yarmila use any of them?"

"Not mine or the director's. As for the one in the library, she'd have needed permission. They are all passcode protected."

"Did you know that she kept a blog? Do you know what a blog is?"

"I do, *compañera*! I consult the internet from time to time."

"Here?"

"We have limited access and our server is very slow. But I know exactly what a blog is and I don't think Yarmila could have kept one. Not at the Institute, in any case."

Marlene was taken aback. She considered arguing but Fernando's tone was conclusive. *Maybe she only worked on it from her home computer. But why lie about such a trivial thing?* She wished she could get access to Yarmila's computer, but Jacobo hadn't allowed her to even see it. *Cabrón.*

They walked to the communal work area. Two young women and a man busied themselves with electric typewriters.

"You may want to interview them," Fernando said. "They knew the deceased citizen better than I did."

"I bet *they* have something nice to say about her," Marlene muttered.

It was then that she realized, for the first time since the investigation had started, that she was totally on Yarmi's side.

LARISA HAD SHORT BLEACHED hair and long acrylic nails painted red. She wore impeccable makeup and a pretty flowing dress with a floral print. Marlene looked at her own nails, short and unpainted.

These 'researchers' take good care of themselves.

Lively and a little impish, Larisa talked a mile a minute, gesturing with both hands.

"*Ay, compañera*, I'm so sorry about Yarmi!" she said. "I can't believe she won't be sitting here with us anymore. She was always so upbeat and fun to be around. Everyone's friend, you know? Even Fernando's. He is talking all tough now, but Yarmi had him wrapped around her little finger. He liked her. He was so jealous of the *Yuma* and that Pato boy!"

"Did you meet them?" Marlene asked.

"I saw Pato a few times when he came looking for her."

"What about the American?"

"The—?" Larisa extended her index and little fingers while holding her middle and ring fingers down with her thumb. "She often mentioned him, but I don't think she would have brought the guy here. She didn't brag about him, as many girls with foreign boyfriends do."

Marlene thought this over. She wouldn't have bragged about an American boyfriend either—not that she had the slightest chance of finding one.

"Did you consider Yarmila a counterrevolutionary?" she asked.

"A counterrevolutionary!" Larisa gasped. "Did the old goat say that? Look, Yarmi wasn't a *gusana*, no way, but she wasn't afraid to complain when she didn't like something. At times she criticized the government and then waited to hear what people answered. But I guess she did that to find out around whom it was safe to talk. She was smart, not like those idiots who open their yap and get in trouble."

By the end of the conversation, Larisa confirmed everything Fernando had said. Marlene was convinced that Yarmila had never used the Institute's computers. Her colleagues had no idea that she kept a food blog. As for the banana bread story, Larisa laughed it off.

"How could she have cooked anything here? With what ingredients? I don't know of anybody who bakes their own bread in Havana. Do you, *compañera*? Tell me so I can go and buy some from them!"

ON HER WAY OUT, Marlene was so distracted that she ended up in the cavernous library instead of the lobby.

Why would Yarmila lie about the banana bread and the Institute's kitchen? Who cared, in any case? What was she trying to do?

Carmela said that Yarmila was "fishing." But she wouldn't have needed to tell such absurd lies to catch a foreigner over the internet. A picture of herself would have sufficed. Who the hell was Yarmila? *I need to find that out before I can even start on who killed her.*

Chapter Four

SEVENTEEN MOMENTS OF SPRING

When Marlene returned to the Unidad, still replaying in her head the conversation she'd had with Larisa, Gordo reported that Comrade Jacobo had been there a few minutes before.

"He left something about that Portal case."

Marlene's eyes lit up. "About time."

"It's hot in here, *cojones*," Gordo complained, handing her the package. "Do you think we can request an electric fan this summer, Comrade Lieutenant?"

"Probably not, Gordo. The Unidad doesn't have the budget for that. And please, don't swear when you are on duty! I'll be in my office, if anybody needs me."

MARLENE TORE OPEN THE sealed manila envelope with the Seguridad agent's signature on the top flap. It contained several pages that, unlike the blog posts she had been reading for the past week, were written in Spanish. There was also a dog-eared book: *Seventeen Moments of Spring*, by Iulián Semiónov. She remembered a television series with the same title. The cover featured two Nazi officers.

A Russian—I mean, a Soviet novel about World War II? Blah.

It had been published by Editorial Arte y Literatura in 1975. The blurb on the back read, "*Seventeen Moments of Spring* (1970), the most famous book by Semiónov, is full of suspense and emotion. Colonel Stirlitz, a Soviet agent who has infiltrated the SS, outsmarts the enemy and contributes to the collapse of Nazi Germany."

Marlene flipped through the book. It was almost five hundred pages.

Does Jacobo think I have time to waste with this crap?

Some passages were marked in red ink. There were handwritten annotations in the margins, all in up-and-down strokes with a slight slant to the right. Intrigued, she sat down and started to read the underlined text.

Page 78

What does being a real agent mean? Putting together information, processing objective data and transmitting it to the center so general conclusions can be drawn and decisions made? Or drawing *your* own conclusions, offering *your* own points of view, proposing *your* calculations? Isaiev believed that he (the agent) should be, above all, objective.

Marlene stopped to read Yarmila's note in the margin:

But what does being "objective" mean? My conclusions are far from objective because I don't have access to the general picture, just a small fraction of it. "The center," on the other hand, has a broader perspective. I should also offer mine, though, for whatever it's worth.

Page 119
We, the detectives, must think with nouns and verbs. "He found." "She said." "He transmitted."

This time, the note was shorter. Marlene read it twice and found herself agreeing with it.

Down with the adjectives! When I use them, they are often based on my perception of reality which can be distorted, or plain wrong. Our reports should focus on facts.

Page 139
During all these years, he had learned to examine his premonitions. He couldn't understand those who asserted that having faith in premonitions was pure nonsense and mysticism. He was able to predict—one or two days before it happened—any important event.

To this Yarmila had commented in a somewhat nervous penmanship:

That's what I call corazonadas, *gut feelings. Yes, they are real. Sometimes, when I am having a conversation with a suspect, I come up with a statement that doesn't make sense to me at that moment, but it turns out to be the right thing to cause a reaction, to prompt him to say what I am hoping for. Recently I have had a sense of foreboding, as if something were about to happen. Not sure if it is good or bad. But it is big, for sure. And it's getting closer. I can almost touch it.*

Marlene nodded sadly. Yarmila's *corazonada* had turned out to be accurate.

Page 403
Sometimes Stirlitz got tired of the hatred he felt for the people he had worked with in the last years. At first, it was a clear, conscious hate—an enemy is an enemy . . .

Yarmila's note read:

An enemy is an enemy, but if you are sleeping with him, literally, you can't help seeing him, and his people, as human beings just like you. The hatred I used to feel for the Yankees has turned into pity. I do not hate my "boyfriend." I pity him, his loneliness, and his absurd, idiotic trust in me.

Marlene put the book down. Had Yarmila believed these characters were real? Did she think she was one of them? An intelligence agent? Was she playing spy with Matt? Did the poor girl have a screw loose?

Marlene looked at the printed documents. They were neatly typed and signed "Agent Katia" with the same slanting handwriting that covered the book's margins.

Report # 16
March 1, 2003

On February 26, Carmela Mendez and Pablo Urquiola went to a meeting with James Cason, head of the American Interest Section in Havana, at his home in Miramar. Selected attendees took part in a workshop about ethics and journalism.

Mendez and Urquiola were not invited to be in the workshop, though they bragged about talking to Cason and his wife, Carmen, who speaks "perfect Spanish."

They received a shortwave radio and a digital camera, which they don't know how to operate. They asked me for help.

They said they would like to see their articles when they go live online on Cubanet.org.

They complained about their old typewriter. I pointed out the fact that other "independent journalists" already have computers. I asked them, "Why the difference?" They didn't say anything but looked upset. They resent having to dictate their articles over the phone or using a hotel internet connection to send them to Miami. They occasionally ask me to "help" with that as well.

I told them that other dissidents had open passes to the Interest Section. Why didn't they? Carmela was furious when she heard that.

They aren't leaders. They are just simpleminded followers and easy to manipulate.

Their next meeting with James Cason will take place, tentatively, early next month. They are planning to attend. I may get invited too since they consider me "a prospective independent journalist."

Operation "Virtual Postcard"
Report # 83
February 17, 2003

The comments have doubled in the last two weeks. Food opens many doors, virtual and physical. Though there are a few exceptions, my readers are still mostly Cubans. Many left when they were very young. Some are anxious to learn more. Others are willing to return.

They are starting to talk about Cuba and the memories they have of their life here—what they ate, what they did, and where they used to live.

They keep coming back to *Yarmi Cooks Cuban* because they are more comfortable reading in English. It makes them feel safer. I am one of them, even if I am here. That was why the first blog in Spanish didn't succeed, in my opinion. It was too Cuban for its purpose. The author was "a foreigner" to them. They simply didn't trust me.

I still need to get more leverage. I plan to share personal stories and have them do the same. Tell them about Havana, our restaurants and beaches, the things they could do here . . . I have already invited some to come.

I will write a fake comment about someone who returned and had a great time. I will also ask M. S. to write a story about his experience in Havana when he goes back to San Diego. I will review it before he publishes it.

Marlene stared at the papers, then looked back at the book and scratched her head.

"*Cojones!*" she said.

An hour later, after calling "Agent Pedro" and having a long talk with him, she dialed Padrino's number. When he answered, she started speaking fast, so eager and excited that words came tumbling out of her mouth:

"You aren't going to believe this, Comrade Instructor! The

deceased citizen, I mean, *compañera* Yarmila, wasn't who we believed she was. No wonder I was feeling so close to her, after all."

"What? Is Yarmila now a *compañera*?" Padrino answered. He remembered the *patakín*: "She was a fake."

"Oh, she always was! She worked for la Seguridad. The blog and her dealings with the *gusanos* were simply ways in which she served the revolution. She used her language skills to do so."

"Wait, *mija*, wait," he said. "Start with the beginning."

"She was part of an operation called 'Virtual Postcard' aimed at bringing back the children and grandchildren of people who left Cuba many years ago," Marlene explained. "She told them what life here is like, though sometimes she fluffed things up a bit. But she did it with good intentions."

There was a brief silence on the other end of the line.

"Fluffed up, huh?" Padrino said finally. He sounded angry now. "You mean all her stories about eating lobster and steak were just written to impress her readers? So they believed that Cuba was a paradise? Her entire blog was full of lies?"

"Well, you have to do what you have to do." Marlene sighed. "But she had more responsibilities. She also informed about the *gusanos'* activities on a regular basis. Because they trusted her, she knew all about their meetings with *Yuma* officials. She had been doing that for two years."

"What about Matt? Was she spying on him too?"

Marlene looked at the papers still scattered on her desk.

"I'm not sure about that part," she said. "I'll find out more because I'm also curious about what she did exactly. But Jacobo said that their 'relationship' wasn't a Seguridad task. In fact, they frowned on it, but she was the kind of agent who liked to do things her way. It seems she thought that, because he was an

American journalist, he could write good things about Cuba. To clean the country's image, you know? Not a bad idea! Anyway, they'll let him go soon."

"And Pato?" Padrino asked. "Was he—helping her clean the country's image too?"

"She told him that their affair was for entertainment only, remember?" Marlene laughed. Then she got serious. "Jacobo says that *compañera* Yarmila Portal will be decorated posthumously in a few days. Now we need to find out who killed her or I will totally lose face!"

Chapter Five

"THE FISH DOESN'T KNOW THAT WATER EXISTS"

When he hung up the phone, Padrino listened to the recordings for the third time, now with a sense of urgency. His desk was covered in the sketches he had made of Yarmila's apartment. He studied them. The first drawing included the coffee table with two books on it, the old Frigidaire, and the ironing board. The stove was there too, surrounded by miniature representations of a knife, a whisk, and the two-pronged fork that Fefita had used to throw the chicken in the garbage can. The second drawing showed the bedroom, the bed, and the door that led to the bathroom. The sketch of the bathroom contained only the bathtub, a toilet, and a simple sink.

He listened to Fefita's words again: "The apartment looked as usual. Nothing was out of place . . . at least I didn't notice anything. Except the chicken, *fo*! There was a very rotten chicken on the kitchen counter, next to a bag of sugar full of ants and some eggs. As if she were getting ready to cook when—but then Yarmi was always cooking, or cleaning, or reading a book. Busy as a bee. Maybe she knew she wouldn't have a lot of time in life to accomplish everything she wanted to do."

Padrino added a triangle to the kitchen counter and labeled it "chicken," drew a square for the sugar, and a few dots to represent the eggs. Then he stopped drawing. He looked at his notes and reviewed Yarmila's posts. He read her *merenguito* recipe:

The only ingredients you need are egg whites (four for a dozen or so merenguitos*), a pinch of salt and one cup of sugar.*

He put the sketches away, took a semiautomatic pistol, the kind Cuban cops carry, from a drawer, went outside and got into his VW Beetle.

HAMEL'S ALLEY WAS A two-block zone located between Aramburu and Hospital streets. Tourist brochures called it "an open air gallery" because it was lined with colorful murals and sculptures made of discarded cash registers, ancient bathtubs, metal ladders, and recycled car parts. It was cubism, baroque and surrealism, all rolled into one, with Afro-Cuban motifs. Everything had been created by Salvador Gonzáles, an artist and a Santería priest himself. Sayings like *El pez no sabe que existe el agua* (The fish doesn't know that water exists) and *Aquel que vende el amor es tan miserable como él que lo compra* (The one who sells love is as miserable as the one who buys it) had been written on the walls. On Sundays neighbors held public rumba parties in the street, but at 6:00 P.M. on a weekday there were only a few people around.

Padrino stopped at the door of a house that also functioned as a clandestine shop. It sold fresh herbs, natural remedies, beaded necklaces and Santería-inspired colognes—*Siete Potencias*, Seven Powers, was their best seller. He made small talk with the owner, a plump woman dressed in white, while keeping an eye on number 45, where Yony lived. The Studebaker was parked outside.

He'd had the intention to go in, but he saw through the window that Yony wasn't alone. A blonde in her forties, obviously a foreigner, kept him company. He decided to wait. A few minutes later, the blonde came out in a huff. Yony went after the woman and tried to stop her, but she barked something in English and went away without looking back.

"Did you see that?" asked the store owner, moving her head reprovingly. "Yony is a *bisnero* and a pretty decent guy, but all these women coming in and out his house, *alabao*! The *Yumas* will be his downfall!"

Shortly afterwards, Yony emerged with a swollen eyelid and walking unsteadily. He wore tattered denim shorts and a T-shirt, and carried a stained paper bag under his left arm. Padrino followed him all the way to La Quinta de los Molinos, the big park and botanical garden located at the end of Salvador Allende Avenue. Once there, Yony disposed of the bag under a tall ceiba. It was a two-hundred-year-old tree considered sacred in Santería, where people often made offerings to the *orishas*.

When Yony left, Padrino quickly inspected the bag. It contained a slaughtered rooster wrapped in newspaper pages. Its small, beady eyes were still open, staring angrily at the world.

He didn't listen to me. I bet Oshún is now encojonao at him.

He returned to Hamel's Alley. He could have detained Yony right away and let Marlene deal with the legality of the issue, but was afraid that the evidence against him wasn't that strong. He couldn't well accuse someone of murder based on a recipe.

I will keep watching him. If he did offer the rooster to Oshún, he must be really scared. He'll sooner or later do something to incriminate himself. They always do.

An hour later Yony came out again. He had changed clothes and now wore cargo pants, a long sleeved shirt, a yellow jacket with huge pockets, and a butterfly bandage over his left eye. He also carried a heavy-looking backpack.

It was seven thirty. There was still enough daylight for Padrino to see Yony's concerned expression. He looked over his shoulder several times before getting into the Studebaker. Padrino hurried to the corner where he had parked the VW Beetle and was soon on the *almendrón's* tail.

Yony drove past El Mégano, Santa María del Mar, Boca Ciega, and Guanabo. These beaches, *las Playas del Este*, though not as clean and attractive as Varadero, had become popular among nationals and low-budget tourists. The Studebaker left behind the last Guanabo houses, Guanabo River, and Los Caballitos amusement park, always following the coastline. The city gave way to an empty landscape punctuated by sparse lights. The next town was Santa Cruz del Norte.

Finally, Yony stopped between Guanabo and Santa Cruz del Norte, outside a dilapidated cabin a few yards away from the ocean. Palm trees, coconut trees and climbing vines grew around it. Without the *almendrón's* lights shining on the front door, Padrino wouldn't have even seen it. A number of rudimentary beach cottages—*cabañitas*—had sprouted all over the area, built by enterprising Cubans who rented them to foreigners.

Padrino parked a block away and walked to the cabin, his footsteps silenced by the sand. As he approached the *cabañita*, he was forced to make a quick retreat and hide behind the trees. Yony and another man came out carrying a boat. It was around twelve feet long, with a built-in engine.

"Come on, *viejo*!" Yony's companion said. He was a younger, lanky guy who resembled the Pink Panther cartoon character. "Just lift the damn thing up!"

Padrino stiffened and his heart began to beat fast.

"That's what I'm trying to do."

"Do it as if you mean it! If that's all the strength you have, I'd hate to see you rowing tonight."

Padrino realized that this was an attempt to leave the country illegally—a crime punished with up to ten years in prison. His take on that was "let them leave if they want to," and he might have just done so in other circumstances. But Yony was the main suspect now and he couldn't afford to lose him. He made a quick call on his cell phone, asking the nearest Unidad for support and giving his location the best he could.

"It's a hut in the middle of nowhere, past Los Caballitos and before the first Santa Cruz lights," he said.

"We know, *compañero*. It's not the first time someone has tried to leave from the same spot. We'll be with you in ten minutes."

But he feared that they wouldn't arrive in time. Yony, still carrying his backpack, and the Pink Panther guy were already onboard. The boat's engine started with a loud cough.

"Stop, stop right there!" Padrino came out of the dark, aiming his gun at them.

Yony turned to him. Pink Panther ducked down. Padrino fired one shot in the air.

"Come back!"

There was no answer. Padrino shot again, aiming closer this time.

"*Pal carajo!*" Pink Panther yelled. He bent as if he were going to retrieve something from the boat's floor. Padrino shot at him.

"Get out of that piece of crap!" he repeated.

Yony hesitated. The engine was still on. But the siren of a police cruiser coming toward them and another shot in the air put an end to the scene. When the two men came off the boat, Padrino saw a stream of blood trickling down Pink Panther's right arm. The guy was shaking and smiling.

What the hell is he laughing at?

Pink Panther didn't seem much older than eighteen.

"Stay there, in front of the house," Padrino ordered. "And don't move!"

When the cruiser stopped by the side of the road, Yony reacted and ran in the opposite direction. Three cops went after him. In the darkness, only broken by the icy blue and red lights, Padrino saw their shadows tackle Yony to the ground, handcuff him and carry him to the car. They came back for Pink Panther, who followed them obediently, a vague smile still on his pale lips.

"Have a doctor see this *pendejo*," Padrino said.

After a brief conversation, the other cops returned to the cruiser. Padrino said he would meet them at the Unidad to file a report. Less than twenty minutes had passed since he'd arrived on the beach.

The report filed by the Unidad 56, where Yony was booked, read:

> On March 18, 2003, the citizen Yony Nogales attempted to leave the country in a makeshift boat. The backpack found in his possession contained five cans of evaporated milk, five cans of Spam, and eight plastic bottles filled with orange juice. There were also twelve hundred dollars distributed in three waterproof envelopes, a compass, a lighter, a pack of Populares cigarettes, and a battery-operated device that resembles a map.

THE JAIL CELL WAS hot. Yony, sweaty and bruised, groaned when Padrino came in and said reprovingly, "You aren't such an honest *bisnero* as you told me you were, my friend."

"I am!" Yony replied. "For the record, I knew you were a cop. I've known it all this time so don't think that you fooled me."

"I am not a cop anymore," Padrino said. "But that's not the issue. Why did you do it, Yony?"

"Because there is no future here! There, I said it. I wanted to get the hell out of this damn country!"

"I thought you had *dozens* of *Yumas* waiting to take you to the States."

"I thought so too," Yony shrugged. "But it just didn't work out. And I am tired, so tired, man!" He stopped and inhaled deeply. "My *bisnes* is shit. No matter how hard I work, I can't do shit with what I make. I sell shit. I buy shit. I am paid in shit!"

"Yes, life is pretty shitty, I won't argue with that. But I wasn't asking why you tried to leave the country. I was thinking of Yarmila Portal. Why did you kill her?"

"I didn't!" Yony treaded hard on the last word. He pounded the cement bench with his fist. "Why are you bringing that up now? As I said, I already have enough shit on me."

"Not really, son," Padrino said quietly. "There is a lot more coming your way."

"Just go to hell, *cabrón*."

A guard who was smoking outside made a move to come in. Padrino held out his hand to stop him and showed Yony the interactive toy.

"Do you recognize it?"

"It's a map, man," Yony muttered. "You wouldn't expect us to cross the Strait of Florida without one."

"Where did you get it?"

Yony stared blankly at the cell wall. "A friend sold it to me," he mumbled.

"Was that friend Yarmila?"

"Eh? No! I sold stuff to her, not the other way around."

"Yarmila's boyfriend sent this to her, Yony. We can prove it. The link is so clear that we can close the case right now."

Yony shrugged. "Which case?"

"Yarmila's, *comemierda*! You killed her and tried to escape to avoid being caught. There is no getting out of this, so do yourself a favor and admit it."

"I don't have anything to admit," Yony said. But his tanned face had turned pale.

"You told me that you never got to deliver the *merenguito* ingredients, remember? But there was a bag of sugar in Yarmila's kitchen the day she died. There were eggs too because she didn't have time to put any of them in the fridge."

"And? Someone else could have sold them to her. Why do you think it was me? I am not the only *bisnero* in Havana."

"But you were the one she dealt with."

Padrino got closer to Yony and reached for his left hand, where the two red circles were still faintly visible, piercing the tattooed image of *La Virgen de la Caridad*. Yony backed off.

"What about this? You didn't get these wounds fixing your *almendrón:* you got them from Yarmila, who stabbed you with her two-pronged fork. It was still in the apartment when we searched it."

"I don't even know what you're talking about."

"But the main piece of evidence against you is that map. You killed Yarmila to steal that piece of crap. *Carajo.* A children's toy, of all things. Why? What was in it that made you turn into a murderous thief?"

"I am an honest *bisnero*," Yony put his hand to his heart for emphasis and looked Padrino in the eye.

"Yes, people say that you're a pretty decent guy," Padrino said, softening. "And lucky too. Let's see: you were making good money. You had a superb *almendrón*. You didn't lack women." As Padrino spoke, counting with his fingers, Yony buried his head in his hands. "Explain to me why a hardworking *bisnero* ended up killing a girl and stealing a toy to boot. I don't get it."

Padrino's avuncular manners soothed Yony. "Will you help me?" he asked.

"No promises."

Yony stared at the Santería necklaces. "You were right about not offering a rooster to Oshún," he said. "I shouldn't have done it."

"Don't bring the *santos* into this. It won't help now."

"He's punishing me, isn't he?"

"Who?"

"Oshún. I'm really fucked. I have the rooster's blood on my hands."

"Only the rooster's blood, son?"

Yony didn't answer.

"You'll be less fucked if you tell me the truth."

"Yarmila was a *chivata*, a government informer," Yony said, his gaze still fixed on Padrino's necklaces. "I was the *comemierda* who trusted her. Everything I told you the day you gave me a ride was true. Except that I did get the eggs and the sugar that she wanted on Monday evening. I saw her at La Caldosa that night and she asked me to bring them to her apartment the next day. 'Just in time to make *merenguitos* for my *Yuma*,' she said.

"I prefer clients to pick up the merchandise at my place, but Yarmi was Yarmi. If she had asked me to deliver the stuff to a Politburo meeting, I'd have probably done it. When I delivered the stuff she was getting ready to iron. She didn't wear lycra pants or short shorts like most girls, but old fashioned dresses and skirts. Despite that, she was always a bit of a flirt. She paid me immediately, eight dollars even, and offered to make coffee for me. In the meantime, she asked what plans my *Yuma* and I had, since she knew Anne was coming too. I said I was going to propose to her and try to convince the old woman to take me out of Cuba.

"'If I don't ask, she can't say yes,' I told her. 'But she may send me packing. Not everybody has it easy like you, *mamita*.'

"Yarmila laughed. I was sure that she was laughing at me. To her, I was a loser. She knew that no rich *Yuma* would ever marry a poor *bisnero* from Oriente. So I felt the need to brag . . . I told her that I had a Plan B if things with Anne didn't work out as expected. My cousin El Pantera and I had built a boat, and we could leave the country anytime. It was ready, waiting for us at a Guanabo house.

"'You built a boat?' she asked.

"She looked at me differently, as if I were less of a loser. Actually, El Pantera had done most of the work. I just gave him money to buy the materials. But she didn't need to know that.

"'Yeah,' I answered. 'It will take us to Key West in a matter of hours.'

"'That's terrific,' she said.

"She smiled. I thought I had finally impressed her. 'You want to come with us?' I asked.

"It was a risky move. And I had sworn not to tell anyone about the boat, but I couldn't help myself. Besides, I didn't have any reason to suspect her. Yarmila bought things from me. She had *gusano* friends and a *Yuma* lover. I assumed she didn't like living in Cuba any more than I did.

"She batted her eyelashes, bit her lower lip, and began to play with her hair. All the things chicks do when they are interested— or pretending to be interested—in a guy. She served coffee in cute demitasse cups instead of regular mugs. When she gave me one, she brushed my hand.

"'I'd have to think about it,' she said.

"'Fine, but think fast,' I said, acting all macho. 'If Anne says no, I'm leaving on my own. In fact, I may just do that. I don't need to land on *La Yuma* with that ugly albatross hanging around my neck.'

"While we were talking, Isabel called out to her from the street. Yarmila invited her to come upstairs, but Isabel yelled something about her varicose veins. I was happy she didn't want to visit because by then I had started getting ideas about Yarmi. I had always liked her and thought that I might have a chance after all.

"'I'll be right back,' she told me.

"She left. I just sat there and looked around. I saw a cell phone, which surprised me because only people with lots of money can afford them. Even with CUCs, buying a line is still a hassle. Then I discovered the interactive map . . . Yes, I knew it was a toy, so what? I never had toys when I was growing up. Never had anything. I began to play with it. I liked it so much that I planned to ask Yarmila to sell it to me or to exchange it for food. But it didn't occur to me to steal that piece of crap. I am not a thief!

"I was busy 'traveling' from Havana to Miami when I heard a strange sound, a beep that made me jump. I couldn't figure out what had made it. It was spooky, man. The second time it happened, I realized that the beeps were coming from the bedroom. I looked out the balcony. Yarmila was still chatting with Isabel.

"I went to the bedroom and the first thing that caught my eye was a computer. A buddy of mine has one and it's always loaded with porn. He charges three CUCs to watch a skin flick. I wondered if Yarmila had porn there too or naked pictures of herself that she had sent to the *Yuma*. The screen showed a landscape with a river and trees. I am not very familiar with these things so I moved the mouse a little and waited to see what happened. The landscape went away and a typed page appeared instead.

"I began to read about a meeting that her *gusano* friends had with a *Yuma*. I didn't get all the details, but realized this was the kind of report that only a *chivato* would write, saying what time these people met, what they talked about and when they were going to get together again. It dawned on me why Yarmila had bought the fan for them, which had seemed weird at first. That's what Seguridad agents do to gain people's trust—give them stuff and act all nice and helpful. And that was also why she had a cell phone and never talked about it: she used it for her *chivatería* business, to keep informing about this and that . . .

"I returned to the living room, peeing my pants out of fear. I had already opened my big fat trap and told Yarmila about the boat, and it's a fact that *chivatos* get extra points when they blow the whistle on rafters. I didn't know what to do next, if I should bolt out of there, go back to Oriente and hide for a few months, or beg her to keep quiet.

"When she came back with a chicken wrapped in tinfoil, I was pretending to read that *Cocina* book as if I had never left the living room. She started to say something about making sugar-baked chicken when the computer made another beeping sound. She walked to the bedroom and saw that the report was still on the screen. Her face told me that was bad news.

"'Have you used my computer?' she asked.

"I told her no, but she didn't believe me. She could see I was scared shitless.

"Her manners changed. Now she was serious, dead serious. I guess she was afraid that I would go around telling everybody what I had seen and blow her cover. I wasn't going to do that, but she must have been scared shitless too. She took her cell phone and started dialing a number.

"I hurried to the door, trying to get out of there before she called *la fiana*. Then she made a mistake, the sort of mistake that bitches make so often. She grabbed my arm and started yelling that I was under arrest.

"I pushed her away. She attacked me with the fork and pricked my hand. Crazy, man! What was that woman thinking? Then she made some kind of karate move to throw me off balance. It didn't work, but she got hold of my arm again and wouldn't let go of me. We fought and somehow—my fingers closed around her throat. She was a skinny thing, nothing like the American horse that Anne is. *Coño*, I don't know why I'm bringing the *Yuma* up now! What I mean is that I only put a little pressure on Yarmila's neck and that was it. She went limp like a rag doll.

"Everything happened too fast. I didn't intend to hurt Yarmila, only to get away from her. But she was like a pit bull. I stood there, calling her name and trying to revive her, but it was too late—she was dead. So I went into damage control. I cleaned every piece of furniture I had touched, the book, the computer, the mouse, the chair I'd sat on, the fork—I've been fingerprinted twice before so I had to be extra careful. I put her body under the shower and left the water running.

"I was crying, man, like a fucking baby. Crying for the awful thing I had just done, a sin against the *orishas*, but also for that beautiful girl I had had a crush on and killed without wanting to.

"I didn't steal any money. I didn't even think of it. I didn't take the phone either. But I did get the map before leaving. Big mistake, I see it now, but at that moment I thought it could be helpful for the trip, just to have an idea about distances and so forth. And I—I just liked that shit. I waited until there was no one around, and snuck out of the building.

"This is the truth, man. You can believe me or not. At this point, I don't care. Oshún didn't accept my offering and now he's really *encojonao* at me."

Dreams of Grandma and *natilla*

Last night I dreamed of Grandma Hilda. Maybe because I have been writing so much about food, she has been on my mind for several days. I don't know if I mentioned it, but my grandma passed away three years ago.

This was a strange dream, and a little scary. We were cooking together, making *natilla*, custard, so close that the tips of our fingers touched over the saucepan. I felt a chill because hers were so cold.

She didn't say a word, just keep stirring milk and cornstarch in the *caldero*.

"What's up, *abuela*?" I asked.

She looked at me sadly and offered me a spoonful of the *natilla* mix. But when I opened my mouth to taste it, I woke up.

I still feel her presence around me. If I didn't have to iron and fulfill my other responsibilities, I would make custard right now. Just in case, you know?

I don't believe in ghosts or anything like that. But when I was in college, a scientist from a university in Kazakhstan visited our class. She talked about some interesting experiments with energy that they were doing in the Soviet Union.

"Energy can't be created or destroyed, only transformed," she said.

She also told us about Kirlian photographs and explained that the human aura was made of energetic patterns. I don't remember a lot more, but it really impressed me.

Could it be Grandma's "energy" that I am feeling?

Do you believe in dreams, dear readers? What can you make out of this?

Bueno, but since this is a blog about food and not ghosts, I will share with you the recipe for the custard that Grandma and I made in my dream.

Natilla is a smooth, rich dessert. So good and creamy that you will want seconds every single time you eat it.

Start by boiling two cups of fresh milk and one can of evaporated milk in a *caldero*, a big saucepan. Add a two-inch lemon peel, one cinnamon stick, and one cup of sugar.

While you wait for the milk to boil (keep an eye on it!), beat five egg yolks. Here, remember that you can use the whites to prepare *merenguitos*.

In a separate bowl, dissolve four tablespoons of cornstarch in half a cup of milk. Make sure to get rid of the lumps.

Mix the eggs with the cornstarch-and-milk blend.

Grandma Hilda used a colander to strain whatever was left of egg whites and the undissolved bits of cornstarch. When I am in a hurry, I tend to skip this step, though.

Go back to the saucepan. Retrieve the cinnamon stick and the lemon peel, and add the mixture of eggs, milk and cornstarch. Let the whole thing simmer, stirring constantly, until it thickens, and add two tablespoons of vanilla extract.

At this stage, if you want, also add raisins. It's so much fun to find them later!

Cook on low heat for around five more minutes. Keep stirring. Pour into individual containers or a big dish and sprinkle with cinnamon powder.

Grandma always refrigerated it immediately, but I also like my *natilla* warm.

If you use the egg whites to make *merenguitos*, you can adorn the custard with them.

Let me know what you think of my *natilla* and that crazy dream.

Kisses to you all!

COMMENTS

Cocinera Cubana said. . .

Ay, your dream was scary! Pray, Yarmi. Ask for protection. I know you aren't a Catholic, but a good prayer never hurt anyone.

Could I use lime peels instead of lemon? Lemon is too strong for my taste.

Cubanita in Claremont said. . .

Oh, Yarmi, you should attend a séance to contact your dead grandma. Do you still have *espiritistas* in Cuba?

I will make the *natilla*. It looks like crème brûlée without the caramel.

Julia de Tejas said. . .

To me, the recipe sounds a lot like like *pastel tres leches*, only with two kinds of milk instead of three. I may use condensed milk instead of sugar.

I don't believe in ghosts either, but I love ghost stories. Particularly if I can listen to them while eating custard in front of the fireplace!

Taos Tonya. . .

Pues, it is *natilla*, Cuban custard, not *pastel tres leches* or crème brûlée or whatever. Stop making it into something it isn't, *pendejas*.

Maritza said. . .

Hey, these are just comments, Tonya. Yarmi, maybe you were hungry, that's all.

Cubanita in Claremont said. . .

Thanks, Yarmi! I made it and the custard tasted just like the one my grandma used to make. Did you find the recipe in Nitza's cooking book?

Cocinera Cubana said. . .

Where are you, Yarmi? You always answer our questions right away. Hope everything is fine with you, *querida*.

Julia de Tejas said. . .

Hi, Yarmi! What's going on? You haven't updated your blog in a while. Is your American boyfriend there now? Well, I am sure you are pretty busy, but don't forget your readers. Take care, my friend.

PART V

Chapter One
THE DEVIL'S WEDDING DAY

In the morning Matt showered for a long time, letting Taty's smell of gardenia and sweat slip away from him and disappear down the drain. For the first time in Cuba, he wished water were hotter. His skin was red and ticklish when he got out of the shower.

When he went to the living room, Anne's suitcases were by the door. Román was counting money and writing in his ledger book. Anne, dressed in a dark blue jumpsuit and brown Uggs, was smoking a joint.

"Are you leaving?" Matt asked, surprised.

"Oh, just going to Varadero for a week. Hopefully, your *problemita* will be solved in the meantime," she whispered. "Any news?"

"Nothing yet."

"You're still welcome to come with me. I'll be all by myself." She paused and added with a wink, "For a while, at least."

"What about Yony?"

"He isn't invited. We had a disagreement. Well, more like a fight. An ugly one."

Despite his own, more pressing concerns, Matt was intrigued, and a bit vindicated. *That's what you get for playing with boy toys*, he wanted to say, but instead asked, "What happened? I thought you guys were doing fine."

"We were," she said. "Until we weren't."

Román came back with the morning coffee. He brought them two small cups and retreated again to the kitchen to prepare breakfast.

"Yesterday Yony invited me to El Refugio," Anne said. "He paid for the meal, which was new. We had *arroz con pollo* and mojitos, plus beer and two glasses of wine. I shouldn't have mixed all that, but he kept ordering more drinks. When we were done, he took me to his house. It's in the strangest, most psychedelic hood I've ever seen with these horrible murals all over . . . Anyway, we made love and it was—oh, I'm ashamed to admit it, but it was truly earthshaking."

At that point, Matt regretted having asked for details.

Women always want to give too much information. Well, some of them.

Then he blushed, remembering his own earthshaking moment the night before, which he wasn't about to share.

Anne brought the joint to her pale lips and inhaled deeply. Then she went on. "When he had me all happy and soft, he dropped the bomb. I mean, he proposed. He had had many women, he said, but I was his one and only, *la mujer de su vida*, as Cubans say."

Cubans say many things that aren't true.

"Remember the day we arrived, when we told the customs officer that *I* was getting married?" Anne smiled sadly. "Perhaps it was a premonition, I told myself. He was *el hombre de mi vida* too! When was the last time I had experienced such passionate lovemaking? Never, that was when. Yes, I could marry him and take him to LA. He could be a security guard at El Mercado.

Or get his very own booth and sell—I don't know, tamales. We would live happily ever after . . . I must have been really drunk to be thinking like that, right?"

Matt gave a polite, noncommittal grunt.

"He assured me that we could bypass the red tape thanks to a friend who worked at the International Notary," she went on. "We could go to his office, like, right then, in his *almendrón*, and come out of the Notaría husband and wife. I—I agreed."

"Jesus, Anne!" Matt said. "After all I've been through, you still—"

"I told you, I was drunk! But when we were getting ready to leave, a rooster crowed. It was a big red bird that had been in the room all the time, watching while we made love. It looked like the devil with its bright beady eyes staring at me."

"The rooster was inside the house?"

"Yes, flying around, not in a cage or anything. Surreal. Maybe they still have cock fights here. Suddenly, I snapped out of it. I had to be crazy to marry that crap-peddling, smooth-talking Cuban redneck! So I told him that I hadn't requested a travel permit from the Department of the Treasury and our marriage wouldn't be valid. It sounded like a decent enough excuse, but he didn't buy it. We began arguing. 'You already said yes!' he yelled. 'You can't play with me like that. I'm a real man, not a *Yuma pendejo*!'

"'You are a *comemierda*!' I replied.

"If nothing else, thanks to him, I have mastered Cuban slang. Then he slapped me."

Matt gasped. "Oh, Anne!"

"Don't pity me. I work out at a Pilates studio four days a week. I'm no shrinking violet. I punched him in the face and got away from him. He tried to follow me, and I gave him a kick in the shin for good measure. Then I left. End of story."

She pretended to laugh but didn't meet Matt's eyes.

"I'm sorry it turned out like this," he said.

"Frankly, it's all for the better. Imagine if I had gone ahead and married him!"

Matt remembered the wedding dress he had brought for Yarmila and his own unanswered proposal. "Yep. Things can always get much worse."

"I'm sure that this voodoo detective will take care of you," Anne said while they had breakfast. "Don't worry too much and have fun. Life's short!"

In truth, Matt was more worried about his attraction to Taty, the night they had spent together, and the pleasure he had experienced when his *pinga*—as Yarmila called his penis, as Taty had also called it—had entered the other man's body. It might just have been a way to release tension, though. Considering how his love for a woman had gotten him in such trouble, it was only natural that he looked for a totally different escape route. But the simplistic explanation didn't satisfy him. Was he gay, *un maricón*, as Cuban men like Pato Macho said disdainfully? If he was, he wanted to find out.

AN HOUR AFTER ANNE had left in a government taxi—she refused to ride in another *almendrón*—Matt got a phone call from Padrino.

"The case is solved," he said. "Lieutenant Martínez will be contacting you soon."

And he hung up.

Matt waited, biting his nails, until two thirty when Martínez summoned him to the police station. He took the first *cocotaxi* that he found in Malecón Drive and didn't even discuss the price in advance. It turned out to be five dollars; he would have gladly paid fifty for the ten-minute trip to the Unidad.

Marlene handed Matt his passport. Her monumental behind was taxing the limits of her olive green uniform. Matt felt like kissing the passport. He briefly wanted to kiss Martínez too.

"Thanks, *compañera*," he said. "So, is—is this it? May I go home now?"

"Yes, of course," she answered, then added with a sly smile, "Next time, try and be more careful when you choose a Cuban girlfriend."

She turned around to leave, but Matt stopped her.

"May I ask, *compañera*—could—you tell me who killed Yarmi?" he stuttered.

Marlene hesitated. The case wasn't technically closed, though, and she didn't feel comfortable sharing the details.

"Sorry, I can't talk about that," she answered, then went back to her office before Matt's pleading eyes changed her mind.

Matt waved down an *almendrón* that took him to El Hotel Nacional. The Aeroméxico employee, a mustachioed young Cuban, charged him three hundred dollars for changing his return flight. He couldn't find one for Tijuana until the following week, so Matt settled for a nonstop flight to Cancun, where he would take another plane to San Diego.

"It leaves in two days," the clerk said.

"Good enough."

From the hotel, Matt went straight to Padrino's house. It had started to thunder when he left El Nacional, but he took the ferryboat and crossed the bay before the rain came down. He had to ask several times for directions—fortunately, most people in Regla knew who the *santero* was, and where to find him. As soon as Matt got to the property, the storm that had been brewing for a couple of hours exploded in gushes of water and crazy whips of gale.

He accepted the cup of coffee that Gabriela brought him.

Padrino was finishing a consultation, but Matt assured her he wasn't in a hurry. He sat on the porch to watch the rain come down. A steady torrent of long-legged ballerinas crashed gracefully on the tiles. The air was charged with the smells of soaked earth, healthy vegetables, rotten fruit, ozone, blue, green, life and death.

"The devil is getting married," people said in the countryside when it rained on a sunny day. It was one of these days—the sun's rays filtered through a veil of raindrops.

The soft voice of Padrino's wife startled him. "Come, *señor*. He's ready to meet with you."

Matt expected to be led to the office where they had had the initial chat, but Gabriela went outside, oblivious to the rain, and walked with him toward the hut.

"The mango lady just left," she said. "I'm sorry she took so much time. It is always the same: she asks for a five-minute consultation and stays over an hour."

The mango lady had lived up to her name and brought a basket of red and yellow fruits. It was placed on the floor, in front of Padrino. Matt felt his mouth water at the sight of it.

"Hi!" he greeted Padrino.

"May the *orishas* bless you."

The *santero* was sitting on a black, red and white rug woven with intricate designs. Two small coconuts lay on it next to a glass jar full of bills and coins—Cuban pesos and CUCs.

Though he was sure that the *santero* knew everything by now, Matt told him about his interview with Martínez and thanked him.

"Whatever role you have had in this, I'm eternally grateful," he said, and meant it. "Do I owe you anything else?"

"No, no. It was easier than I anticipated. I still have to give you fifty dollars back."

"Oh. Please, keep them."

"No, *bisnes* is *bisnes*, as our honest *bisneros* say." He suppressed a laugh. "Well, most *bisneros* aren't honest. But it isn't always their fault."

He opened his wallet, took out three bills and pressed them back into Matt's hands.

Matt hesitated before asking in a low voice, "So—who killed Yarmila?"

"Someone you didn't know," Padrino answered curtly. Like Marlene, he didn't want to talk about the case.

"Did you find out why?"

"We are still working on it. It was one of these crazy Cuban things."

"Most Cuban things are crazy."

"You bet."

Matt studied the rug pattern. He felt cheated. He would have wanted to know more, at least a name or a motive. Padrino noticed, but didn't want to talk about Yarmila's Seguridad activities. They hadn't been made public yet.

"Does it matter now?" Padrino asked in a casual way. "Look, my friend: this is over for you. You will go back to your country and forget even the saint she was named after."

"The saint—?"

"It's an old saying. *Olvidar hasta el santo de su nombre.* It just means you won't even think of Yarmila Portal again."

Matt doubted it.

"It has been a pleasure, *señor*."

Padrino walked to the door, a clear indication that the visit was over. Time was money for both *santeros* and *bisneros*, but Matt was willing to pay for it.

"I would like to know if, by any chance, you—er—your *santos* could help me with a spiritual reading of sorts."

"You mean a consultation?" Padrino stopped and looked at him. Matt couldn't tell if he was confused or amused.

"Isn't that what you do here?"

"It depends. When I perform a reading with the *dilogún*, people find out, in a very general way, if their future holds *iré*, good fortune, or *osorbo*, trouble."

"That will be perfect. May we do it now?"

"I'm afraid not. That kind of ritual is time-consuming and my clients prepare for it a few days in advance. They ask the *santos* for guidance and do specific ceremonies. But," he added quickly, noticing Matt's disappointment, "I could work the coconut for you. This is a simpler divination tool that gives yes or no answers."

"Sure, that will do it. How does it work?"

Padrino took a coconut from the rug and opened it with a pocket knife. He cut four pieces and trimmed them into three-inch bits, leaving the coarse shell on the outside.

"These little pieces of coconut are the *orisha*'s mouthpieces," he explained. "When you ask a question, I throw them and read the results."

"Let's go for it!"

The *santero* smiled at Matt's excitement. "You've never had a spiritual consultation?"

"I once went to a clairvoyant at a psychic fair in Old Town San Diego, but didn't get much out of it. She said that I had been a Viking in a past life."

They both laughed. Padrino returned to the rug and Matt sat down facing him.

"Go ahead," Padrino said.

"Should I ask the questions aloud?"

"No, just take a deep breath and think of what you want to

know. Obi will respond by making the coconut fall in a particular way."

Obi-Wan Kenobi? "Obi who?" he asked suspiciously.

"He's the *orisha* with divination powers."

"Ah. Okay."

"Keep the questions as simple as you can."

Matt breathed in the air that, inside the hut, also carried the
sweet aroma of mangos.

*Has this nightmare ended? No, wait. Will I go on with my life as
usual?*

"Ready," he said.

Padrino threw the coconut chunks in front of him. They scattered on the rug. Two had the white meat up and two showed
their dark, coarse skins.

"This is *ejife*, which means yes, but don't ask more about this
topic," he said. "There will be balance for you. See: two sides of
light, two sides of shadow. That's a positive sign."

"I'll ask a question about a different subject now," Matt proposed, "since I'm advised to drop this one."

"Good idea."

*What was this Taty business all about? Am I going to be attracted
to guys from now on?*

The coconut bits formed a new pattern, with three white sides
and a dark one. Matt assumed that Obi had said yes. He felt
incredulous and a little afraid.

"This is *etawa* and means maybe," Padrino said. "We need to
do a second throwing for clarification. Repeat your question, but
be more precise this time and don't try to cram two into one. Obi
doesn't like that."

"Right. Sorry."

Am I gay?

Matt's eyes followed the coconut chunks as they arranged themselves again in the exact same way.

"The *orisha* doesn't know, or doesn't want to say, what your future holds in that respect," Padrino said. "He can't predict fate all the time, especially when it is tied to many different and contradictory possibilities. Obi is quite cautious about it."

"I understand."

"Anything else?"

"Yes, one more, please."

Will I ever find out who killed Yarmila?

The answer came in four white sides.

"*Alafia,*" Padrino translated. "Yes, and sooner than you expect."

He stood up.

"Thanks so much, Padrino," Matt said. "How can I pay you for this?"

"A donation will do." The *santero* showed him the glass jar.

Matt didn't want to act like an arrogant *Yuma* by dropping in a hundred dollars. He placed two twenties inside.

"Want a mango?" Padrino asked.

"Yes, thanks."

Padrino offered him one and took another for himself. Matt looked out the window. The rain had stopped and he wanted to leave before it started again.

"There is something else I'd like to tell you," Padrino said. "It came to me while I was giving you coconut. If you want to hear it, naturally."

"Of course."

"Everybody has a head *orisha*, a *santo*, or what the Catholics call a guardian angel. Knowing who it is can help you sort stuff out. So I *wouldn't* say you are a son of Obatalá, but I can assure you that you are under his special protection."

Matt wasn't sure he believed that, but nonetheless liked the idea of being under somebody's special protection. He asked with a sheepish grin, "What's Obatalá like?"

"He is the eldest of the *orishas* and the king of them all. His number is eight. He always dresses in white. Half of his roads, or embodiments, are male. The other half are female—"

"Excuse me," Matt cut him off, horrified. "Does it mean that he is gay?"

Padrino smiled. "We don't use these terms here. Embodiments aren't about gender, but manifestation. He can appear as a very young man, a warrior, or an old guy. But he can also be Our Lady of Mercy and she comes as a pretty young girl or a wrinkled crone."

"Which one is mine?" Matt asked, scowling. "The guy or the girl?"

"Both. Obatalá is just one. The *orisha* simply takes different shapes. But you don't need to worry about that. The same thing happens with Changó, the most macho of the *santos*, who has Santa Barbara as his female counterpart. Changó's sons are always getting in trouble because they can't keep their *pingas* in their pants."

"I guess Changó has many devotees."

"He certainly does! As for Obatalá, he is calmer, cooler. His children are quiet and reasonable. Which doesn't mean you can't get into trouble, but you manage to get out of it unscathed, most of the time. You are lucky, after all."

Matt let it sink in. He felt his shoulders relax and exhaled deeply.

I'm lucky.

"Thanks, Padrino," he said.

He bit the mango and his mouth filled with the tarty sweetness of it.

Chapter Two

THE CRACKDOWN

The television was on in the living room, though it was only 8:00 A.M. It was Thursday, March 20. Matt woke up and realized, with a mix of anxiety and relief, that this was his last full day in Havana. He wanted to go to Cathedral Square and buy a few knickknacks, his last souvenirs of a place he wasn't planning to return to anytime soon. Anytime, period. He also planned to say goodbye to Isabel and visit Chinatown, even if there were no Chinese left there.

While having coffee, he found out that the United States had attacked Iraq the day before. He didn't want to think about it. He had already had enough personal conflicts to trouble himself over international ones. But Román was so nervous that he didn't even offer to prepare his signature *revoltillo*.

"What if there is a nuclear war now?" he asked. "Could it happen? Something that destroys the whole Earth?"

"That's very unlikely," Matt said. *You have watched too many Star War movies, buddy.*

"In the news, they are making a big deal out of it," Román insisted. "Like it could be the end of the world or something."

He pointed to the TV. Images of American rockets exploding over Iraq filled the screen. Matt heard Castro's voice repeating the words *imperialists*, *invasion*, and *Yankees*.

"I didn't know that the Cuban government cared so much about American news," he said.

"Oh, they do. Particularly when the news is bad."

Since Román was again glued to the television, Matt decided to finish his breakfast at Casa de la Natilla. House of Custard was an Old Havana café he had read about on the internet, but never visited. It was near Cathedral Square. He strolled leisurely to Obispo Street and ordered a *natilla* and a cup of espresso from the grim-faced waitress. He was the only patron. Sitting outside, under the big blue umbrella, enjoying the breeze that came from the Malecón, Matt felt total peace for the first time since he had touched Cuban soil. It was such a perfect moment that he wished he could keep it in his memory like a bug trapped in amber—the limpid sky with a smoky note to the west, the aroma of vanilla and rum-soaked raisins from the custard, and the taste of black coffee like a dark, liquid amulet slipping down his throat.

A police car zoomed by, breaking the charm. It sped toward Malecón Drive.

"*Tan locos!*" the waitress said.

"Yes, the craziness of it," Matt agreed. "I thought this was a pedestrian-only street."

"Do you speak Spanish?" She smiled at him and winked. "Usually we have no traffic, but today the thing is burning, you know."

Matt replayed the Spanish phrase in his mind. *La cosa está candente.* He had never heard it and ventured to clarify, "What do you mean, burning? Like on fire?"

The waitress winked again in a more pronounced way. "Ah,

you speak Spanish, but you don't speak Cuban! What I mean, *señor*, is that trouble's brewing. And it has just begun."

Matt assumed she was talking about Iraq, but couldn't understand the connection. Did Cubans fear they were going to be attacked next? It didn't make sense to him.

In Cathedral Square he didn't see anything out of the ordinary. There were tourists and vendors, and a band played Buena Vista Social Club songs outside the massive church. He bought two wood-carved rumba dancers, but passed on the Che Guevara T-shirts, key rings and Havana Club bottles that unrelenting peddlers attempted to sell him. He also bought a straw hat. It was getting warm and he put it on immediately.

It was time to return to La Caldosa, say goodbye to Isabel, and thank her. That was, Matt told himself, the proper thing to do. After all, she had put him in contact with Padrino. He might still be waiting for "Agent Pedro" and Lieutenant Martínez to decide his fate if it hadn't been for the *santero's* intervention. He could also have his last Cuban lunch there. It would be like closing a chapter—a short and painful one.

Matt also admitted, if only to himself, that he wanted to see Taty once more. He still needed some sort of closure in that respect as well. And perhaps Isabel, who was so nosy, would know by then who had killed Yarmila. The coconut had said he would find out.

I'm even starting to believe in the orishas *now. Good grief.*

Matt approached a middle-aged, sinewy *cocotaxi* driver and gave him La Caldosa's address.

"Let's go, *señor*."

When they turned onto Reina Street, a police car passed so close that it brushed the *cocotaxi*, wrapping it up in the fetid aura of exhaust fumes.

"Damn it!" Matt said. "Watch out! We don't even have seat-belts!"

"Yes, one needs to be careful today," the driver replied. "I only came to work because I need the money. Food doesn't rain from heaven, as my wife says. But it would have been more sensible to stay home. They are all excited."

He used the word *alborotado*, which could mean excited in a rowdy manner, as in a fraternity party, but also annoyed, disturbed.

"Who is *alborotado*?"

"Everybody, *señor*. Cops, *gusanos*, *chivatos*, everyone! This isn't going to end well."

Another cruiser reached them at a traffic light. Matt locked eyes with the cop seated on the passenger side. The man stared him down. The driver, pale and somber, kept looking straight ahead.

What the hell is going on? People didn't act like this before.

When they arrived at the intersection of Salvador Allende Avenue and Espada Street, Matt gave the driver the five dollars they had agreed on for the ride and two more as a tip.

"*Gracias, señor*. Take care now."

A military truck drove slowly down the center of the street. Matt looked for La Caldosa, but couldn't find it. The bright neon sign that advertised the *paladar* had vanished. He walked around the building, inspecting it.

I could have sworn that it was here.

He turned the corner. The window that looked out upon Espada Street was shut too. He came back to Salvador Allende Avenue and knocked on the door. Nobody answered. He knocked two more times. Finally, Isabel said, in a low and strained voice, "Who is it?"

"It's me, Mateo."

She opened the door a couple of inches.

"Hi!" Matt said, taking off his hat. "How are you doing?"

"What do you want?"

She was curt, bordering on hostile.

"I—I came to say goodbye," he stuttered. "Sorry. I didn't want to inconvenience you."

I'm so dumb. I should have called before. This must be about Pato Macho. He may be here and not over it yet.

He was ready to make a quick, awkward retreat, but Isabel looked around and gestured for him to come in. Once in the dining room, or what had been the dining room, Matt felt disoriented again. The five tables were gone, replaced by a red sofa, two armchairs, and a small ottoman. The big television set had been brought in, and the flamingo tapestry hung on a wall. He was as surprised as the night of his first visit, only in reverse. The *paladar* had mutated into an ordinary Havana living room.

"What happened?" he asked, astonished. "Where is La Caldosa?"

"We closed it."

"Why?"

"People are frightened, and fear isn't good for businesses."

Matt threw his hands up. "For Christ's sake!" he said. "What are you guys afraid of, Isabel? Do you really think we are going to invade Cuba?"

"Invade Cuba?"

"Why is everyone so anxious?"

"Don't you know?"

"Is it about Iraq?"

"*Qué* Iraq *ni* Iraq! There was a crackdown yesterday. Hundreds of people were arrested."

"A crackdown? In Havana?"

"Yes, where else? They are putting everyone they think is a *gusano*, or a *gusano* sympathizer, behind bars. Independent journalists, human rights people, dissidents, even *bisneros*. They jailed that couple who used to come here, Yarmila's friends. And many others." Isabel put a hand over her mouth and added, "I heard this is just the beginning. Go figure!"

"But what does this have to do with your business? Are you a *gusana* too?"

"*Coño*, what a question! Are you stupid or what?" She touched her lips with her index finger. "Shhh! You're going to get us in trouble!"

He remembered the words of the Casa de la Natilla waitress. *La cosa está candente.*

"Please, do tell me, why is everyone so fearful? If you are not against the government—"

"You never know, Mateo. That's the problem. They start with the *gusanos* and go on with the *bisneros,* and the people who buy stuff from the *bisneros,* and the owners of *casas particulares* who don't have a license—in the end, everyone is guilty of something. They know it and we know it. But what they know, and we don't, is *when* they are going to say 'enough' and jail everyone and their sister."

"Who are they?"

"La Seguridad. The government." She touched a spot under her right eye and blinked. "Those who see and hear everything."

"Oh. I get it."

"You probably don't, but that's okay."

Isabel pointed at the closed window. "They are watching," she said. "So I don't want to be rude, but you have to leave now. I don't want them to think that I am opening again or accepting clandestine guests. They really will come for me then!"

"Of course, of course. I understand. I just wanted to say goodbye to you," he blushed before adding, "and Taty if he's here today."

"Taty went to Las Villas with his godmother. I sent Pato there too, and told them both to stay out of harm's way until things cool off. The countryside is safer. There are fewer *chivatos* and fewer Seguridad agents."

"I'm sure that's the right thing to do," Matt said. "Goodbye, Isabel. Thanks for all your help."

He was expecting her to ask about his situation, but she just let out an inaudible "bye" and closed the door behind him.

Matt put on his hat again and crossed Salvador Allende Avenue. He felt rejected, and silly for feeling rejected. He thought of going to Ricardito's, but El Refugio might be closed too. He looked for a state-owned cafeteria and found one at the Plaza Carlos III Mall. A subdued waiter brought him a hamburger with *papitas fritas* (Cuban-style french fries) and a glass of warm orange juice. While sitting by the window, Matt saw two heavy military trucks followed by a camouflaged armored car.

He asked the waiter how he could get to Chinatown. It was nine blocks from Plaza Carlos III. He walked to El Cuchillo de Zanja and saw a green arched entrance but couldn't approach it. A young, stern policeman stopped him.

"Where are you going?" he asked Matt.

There were more cops around. A foreign-looking couple had been pulled aside too, though Cubans circulated without being bothered.

"To Barrio Chino," Matt answered.

"What for?"

"I'm curious to see it. I have read about it."

"Are you a tourist?"

"Yes."

"Where from?"

"London."

Matt didn't know why he had lied. It had been almost an instinctual reaction. He blamed Isabel's paranoia for it. Then he realized that it had worked—the cop's expression softened a bit. But he still wouldn't let him proceed.

"You can't go there now. There is an *operativo* going on."

Though Matt had never heard the term, he assumed it meant a police operation.

"Better that you go back to where you came from," the young cop said firmly.

Matt didn't wait for him to repeat it.

AS SOON AS HE returned to Villa Tomasa, Román pounced on him.

"Do you have your passport? Did they give it back to you?"

"Yes, I have it," Matt said. "Sorry I forgot to tell you about it."

"Let me see it. I need to write down all the numbers and make sure everything looks right. The thing is burning!"

Matt handed him the passport. Román began scribbling frantically in an official-looking book of entries.

"God, I hope they don't come here," he said.

By then, Matt knew better than ask who "they" were.

"You are leaving tomorrow, aren't you?"

"Yes."

Román closed the book. The television was on with more news about Iraq. They went on for a half hour, with no mention of the local crackdown.

THAT EVENING MATT REREAD the instructions that the Aeroméxico clerk had written for him. Though the Havana–Cancun flight didn't depart until noon, passengers were required to be at José Martí

International Airport at eight in the morning. Matt considered showing up an hour later since he didn't have any baggage to check, but didn't dare. What if *they* punished him for being late? *They* could even retain his passport again or call la Seguridad.

Better safe than sorry. I am so close to going home—no need to screw it up. I'll also have to find a taxi. A real one, not a cocotaxi *or an* almendrón, *to make sure I get there on time.*

He wrapped up the rumba dancers and his sombrero in *Juventud Rebelde* pages, and left most of his clothes to Román to make space in his backpack. When he turned it upside down, the shell pendant came out, still in its velvet box. He placed it next to the *Star Wars* action figures and retrieved the page he had typed in the Smith-Corona.

I can't take this. Imagine that another "Agent Pedro" sees it at the airport and thinks it's a report for the CIA!

He tore it up noticing, with a shudder, that he had begun to act like a Cuban.

I've become "acculturated" all right.

He also wrote a note to Anne, asking her to call him when she got back to the States.

She may have already found another boy toy in Varadero.

By dinnertime, Román was in a better mood. He had made *arroz con pollo*. It was different from Isabel's, and better. His secret, he revealed, was adding Spanish chorizo to the dish and garnishing it with corn instead of green peas.

"Every Cuban cook has his own book," he said. "And it isn't always *Cooking in Minutes*."

When Matt asked about a taxi service, Román disclosed that he owned a Moskvtich, a Soviet-era car that ran with a Volkswagen engine, and offered to take him to the airport for ten dollars.

"That will do it, my friend."

Chapter Three

FLOWERS FOR YARMILA

While most cops in Havana were actively taking part in the crack-down, or had been on high alert since the day before, Marlene was home. After solving Yarmila's case, she had asked for sick leave because "migraines were killing her." Captain Ramos had granted it.

"You have been working hard, *compañera*," he said. "You solved this case in less than three weeks. That's remarkable!"

She felt bad about lying, but needed time alone to process what had happened. She still felt connected to Yarmila in a way she couldn't explain. Jacobo had finally given her all the information he had, or so he said, on "Comrade Portal's case."

That morning Marlene stayed in bed until eleven o'clock, long after her mother had brought her a cup of *café con leche*. She protested but Soledad just said, "I like to pamper you, *mijita*. And wait until you see what I'm making for lunch!"

She stretched out and savored the luxury of not having to go anywhere or do anything at all. Then she wondered if anybody had ever pampered Yarmila. It didn't look like she had had a happy life, or any life at all, judging by what Marlene now knew about it. *She spent her final months telling these outrageous lies, spying on her neighbors and hiding her true self.*

Though the case was officially closed, Marlene was still trying to untangle the web of Yarmila's work. Operation Virtual Postcard was straightforward: the blog posts had been designed to lure Americans and Cuban Americans to the island. In one of her reports, Yarmila had written about the importance of bringing hard currency to the country "by any means." Her posts didn't hurt anyone, Marlene thought, even if they were made of outright lies. But was that all? Marlene couldn't help thinking of Matt, his sad eyes when he asked her who had killed his fiancée.

I could have told him, but what good would it have done? Then he'd have wanted to know why, and that wasn't something I was at liberty to tell.

If the blog posts were fluffed up virtual reality, Yarmila's espionage work was more concrete. She had been ordered—or she had volunteered, Marlene wasn't sure how her involvement with the secret police had begun—to befriend dissidents, but without becoming part of their groups. The day before, watching a TV special about the Seguridad's network, Marlene had understood why: the government already had enough people working on that.

Yarmila played the role of a supporting outsider while subtly spreading distrust among the dissidents and their allies. Marlene recalled one of her last reports: "They complained about their old typewriter. I pointed out the fact that other 'independent journalists' already have computers . . . I told them that other dissidents had open passes to the Interest Section. Why didn't they?" She had signed her reports as Agent Katia, a name borrowed from a character in *Seventeen Moments of Spring*.

In the meantime, her job at La Caldosa allowed Yarmila to

keep tabs on Isabel and her clients, as well as the *bisneros* who dealt with them. Most people distrusted those who declared their support of the government, but they were also careful not to get too involved with dissenters so as not to attract unwanted attention from la Seguridad. Yarmila had managed a happy medium, having created for herself a quasi-rebel mask that she wore both in her regular job and at the *paladar*.

She dutifully reported everything that transpired at La Caldosa: how many foreigners ate there, what they said about Cuba, and how other patrons reacted to their comments. Sometimes she would egg them on. She would make a seemingly innocent remark and watch their reactions. She even recorded gestures and silent expressions of discontent.

I don't think that was too difficult. They all trusted her.

She remembered her visit with Pablo and Carmela. How would Yarmila have felt about the crackdown? They were her friends. Or were they? The couple was in prison now.

Personally, I think we've gone too far this time . . . These people weren't criminals. They were only writing about what they saw, just like Yarmila. The difference was that they did it openly and used their real names.

Soledad announced that the mincemeat was ready although she didn't need to, with the spicy aromas coming from the kitchen. Marlene got up and exchanged her pajamas for an old, comfortable robe. It was the first weekday in years that she didn't put on her uniform.

"*Mija*! Come to the table before the *picadillo* gets cold!"

Marlene walked to the dining room dragging her feet. She didn't want to admit it, but the source of the good food embarrassed her. Comrade instructor had insisted on giving her one hundred CUCs.

"You earned it," he had said, pushing the bills into her hands. "I wouldn't have solved this case without your help."

"But I was just doing my job."

"So what? You aren't paid enough for it."

She hadn't argued, not enough, she remembered, ashamed. In truth, she had been glad to get the money. But it still felt wrong.

At first she had wanted to buy exclusively at government stores. "No *bisneros*!" she warned her mother. They had gone to Plaza Carlos III and gotten three pounds of ground beef, two pounds of steak, and a big Spanish chorizo that "smelled like divine glory," as Soledad had said. They had even splurged on a box of all-purpose flour because Marlene had set her mind to make banana bread at home. But they balked at the price of milk—a can of condensed milk went for five CUCs.

"That's ridiculous!" Soledad protested. "Any *bisnero* would sell me three for that amount."

Marlene gave in.

THOUGH THE MEAT WAS tender and well-seasoned, Marlene had trouble chewing the *picadillo*. She felt as guilty as if she were an accomplice in a secret crime. But it wasn't her fault that they didn't get more than a few ounces of meat every month through the ration card, she told herself. She remembered that the Plaza Carlos III butchery had been full of steaks, pork chops, and ribs. All those shelves stocked with cookies, deodorant, toothpaste, Camay soap! She had been tempted by one that smelled like roses but had resolved not to spend the two CUCs it cost. Why wasn't all that sold in Cuban pesos? Regular people like her didn't get any CUCs . . . And why couldn't she buy a pound of lobster legally, eh?

Because lobster was a forbidden meat, Marlene reminded

herself. Despite what "Agent Katia" had written on her bogus blog, their sale was penalized. That brought her thoughts back to Yarmila. Marlene doubted she had made, let alone eaten, most of the dishes she had so diligently described . . .

Dessert was a creamy and fluffy *tocinillo*. Marlene realized that her mother must have also ordered eggs from a *bisnero*. She longed for *merenguitos*, but it would have been silly to sacrifice four or five eggs for such ephemeral delight.

"Aw, *mija*! I wish we could have these feasts more often." Soledad sighed. "I don't even remember the last time we ate that well."

Marlene did remember—when her brother had sent them money from Miami. Soledad used it to buy food, as usual. She hadn't told Marlene, but she had found a Western Union receipt in the trash can. She would have figured it out, anyway. Now she thought that she should write to her brother and thank him. She still didn't approve of what he had done, but—

Life is so short. Look at Yarmila. She couldn't have imagined that she would never make it to thirty years old.

"Don't you think so, *mijita*?" Soledad asked.

Marlene blinked and stared at her. "Sorry, Mom. What did you say?"

"Full belly, happy heart, as the saying goes."

Marlene's belly was full indeed, but her heart wasn't happy. She imagined that Yarmila was also sitting at the table—a spectral, uninvited guest. A cold breeze enfolded her and made her shudder. Soledad noticed too.

"It's getting chilly," she said. "Isn't that strange? It was pretty warm a moment ago."

She stood up and took the empty dishes to the kitchen.

Marlene recalled a sentence from Yarmila's last blog post:

"Energy can't be created or destroyed, only transformed." Was *her* energy there now? Could she hear them?

"Why did you do it, Yarmi?" Marlene whispered. "For the revolution? Was your sacrifice worth it?"

She laughed quietly at herself.

I'd better be careful or I'll end up praying to comrade instructor's orishas.

The temperature in the room seemed to go back to normal. Marlene was clearing the table when a disturbing idea jarred her.

What about me? I am doing the same? Am I another Yarmila, sac- *rificing my life for the cause? Which one? The cause of our shortages?*

"Are you okay?" Soledad asked from the kitchen.

"Sure," Marlene replied as cheerfully as she could.

"You look pale."

"No wonder. My stomach is in shock, after getting so much food at once."

Her mother chuckled. But Marlene wasn't okay.

I wish I had a way of somehow—connecting with her. I could ask *comrade instructor if he knows of some Santería ceremony, but that* *sounds way too crazy. What would he think of me?*

She put the leftover *tocinillo* in the refrigerator. Then she stopped and smiled. She might not be able to "connect" with Yarmila, but she could certainly pay her a visit.

THE COLÓN CEMETERY IS the final home for over one million quiet residents. Founded in 1876 in the heart of El Vedado, it has maintained the neighborhood's elegant and expansive feel with its sprawling layout, tree-lined avenues, and discreet side streets. The necropolis stretches for 140 acres of chapels, mausoleums, graves, urns, and vaults.

Marlene had been in the cemetery just a few times—the first

was when her father died, in 1992, and more recently to accompany Soledad to exhume her parents' remains and bury them in an ossuary. Fifteen years after a burial, or earlier if the space was needed, the bones were usually transferred to the ossuaries, a practice that Marlene considered unsanitary and a bit spooky. *Why not cremate them, eh?* Soledad still came to visit her husband's grave on his death anniversary, but Marlene had always refused to go with her. "That's creepy," she would say emphatically. "My dad isn't there."

She wasn't that sure of her beliefs anymore. When she passed near the seventy-foot high Monument to the Firefighters, she looked up and admired the tall blindfolded angel with wings extended. An old black limousine drove by, covered in floral arrangements and followed by three cars. One was a blue *almendrón*.

The sun was blinding as it reflected off the white headstones. Marlene felt hot and a little dizzy. She looked for Yarmila's grave, trying to get oriented among the many mausoleums, funerary monuments, and larger-than-life sculptures. She had no idea where to go. An older woman carrying a plastic bucket full of flowers approached her.

"I have lilies," she whispered. "Ten for one CUC."

It occurred to Marlene that it wasn't proper to visit someone's grave empty-handed. Hadn't Yarmila written that she loved lilies, that she even cooked and ate them? Maybe *that* part wasn't a lie. Marlene searched her purse, found four twenty-five cent coins and gave them to the woman, who threw in two extra lilies.

"Because you look so sweet," she said.

Marlene, who wasn't used to being called sweet, smiled and asked the vendor if she happened to know where Yarmila Portal was buried. "A young woman who was murdered not long ago," she explained. Her voice quivered when she said "murdered."

"Ah, I know who you are looking for!" the vendor crossed herself. "Poor girl, way too young to be here. Are you a relative of hers?"

"We were friends," Marlene lied.

"Come with me."

Marlene followed her, holding the lilies, which gave out a creamy, spicy fragrance. Her heart was heavy as if she were, in fact, visiting the grave of a lost friend.

The vendor pointed out the marble statue of a woman who had a cross in one arm and a baby in the other. The mausoleum was surrounded by fresh flowers, wreaths, candles, photos, and cards.

"That's La Milagrosa," she said. "Have you heard about her?"

Marlene nodded and looked closely. Yes, she had heard her mother tell her own Milagrosa story many times. When pregnant with Marlene, Soledad had suffered from severe bleeding and was in danger of losing the baby. She had made a special trip to the cemetery to ask for The Miracle Worker's intercession. "And you were born five months later, healthy and cute!" she would conclude with a triumphant smile.

"La Milagrosa and her newborn child died in 1903," the vendor said, noticing Marlene's interest. "When it was time for them to be exhumed and taken to the ossuary, the baby, who had been placed at her feet, was found resting in her arms. Neither of them had decomposed. From that moment on, expecting mothers started to come here asking for a safe delivery. Mothers with sick children come and beg for their recovery too."

A month before, Marlene would have listened to the story with amused disbelief, at best, or with utter contempt. Now, she just listened respectfully. They walked for ten more minutes. Finally, the vendor stopped in front of a small grave that looked recently painted. Instead of a cross, there was a granite vase on top of it with a bouquet of withered roses. The vendor retrieved them, emptied the vase and filled it with water from her bucket.

Many of the neighboring graves were decorated with Cuban flags. Marlene realized that this section of the cemetery was devoted to "homeland heroes," as the TV anchor had called the Seguridad agents that morning. But there was nothing on Yarmila's tomb that indicated she had belonged to the secret police. Only her name was etched, followed by two dates: 1978-2003.

The vendor went away discreetly. Marlene placed the flowers in the vase. Their scent lingered on her hands.

"I believe that you did what you thought was best, Yarmi," she said. "And I am so sorry for what happened—" Though she felt her throat closing, Marlene tried not to cry, for Yarmila's sake. She had been a strong woman. "But see? We caught the *cabrón* who did it. You can rest in peace." Or could she?

A wave of sweet warmth swept over her and dissolved into a cloud of caramel. Marlene closed her eyes and let the smell of *merenguitos* fill her heart and lift the oppressive heaviness from it.

Chapter Four

THE BARACOA WEED

Matt came out of his room at six in the morning, freshly shaved, anticipating a long day of waiting rooms, airport crowds, and insipid food. Román was making breakfast. Besides the unmistakable aroma of Cuban coffee, Matt identified another smell, similar to pot, but stronger and spicier.

Standing in front of the oven, Román held a joint between his lips. He flipped an omelet with the skillfulness of a trained chef.

"Want some?" he asked Matt. He wasn't talking about food.

"No, thanks. It's not legal here, is it?"

"I don't use it all the time," Román explained without answering directly. "Only when I'm nervous, like today. I just heard on the radio an interview with a *chivato*. It looks like the Seguridad had tons of informers infiltrated in human rights groups. Many are coming out now and accusing the people who thought they were their friends."

"So it's in the news," Matt said.

"Finally. Everybody knew, but they didn't admit it until now."

"What are they accusing the human rights groups of, exactly?"

"Man, of being human rights groups!" Román shrugged,

as if stating the obvious. "They call these people mercenaries, pro-Yankees and CIA agents—the usual stuff. I'm scared so I'm cooling off with *la yerba*. Hope you don't mind."

"No problem. But why are you so concerned?"

"Because I have said—things. About the government, the restrictions, the shortages. I've bought stuff on the black market. I am not completely clean, if they want to come after me."

"No offense, but I think that you Cubans are prone to exaggerating," Matt replied. "Think of it this way: even if the authorities wanted to, they wouldn't have the resources to spy on *everyone*. There aren't enough informers to do that."

"It's true, there is a limited number of *chivatos*." Román inhaled from his joint, blew the smoke in the air and watched it disappear. "But we don't know who they are so that makes everybody a suspect. This guy, Manuel David Orrio, posed as an independent journalist. A friend of mine said he wrote critical articles against Fidel, the Committees for the Defense of the Revolution, the Party, and everything under the sun. Guess what? Today he is bragging about how he fooled the *gusanos* and even got the Americans from the Interest Section to confide in him. How many more Orrios are among us?"

He placed the omelet and a buttered toast on a dish.

"In any case," he concluded, "I'm keeping my mouth shut for the time being. Eh, do you want to try *la yerba* or not?"

"If you insist—"

"It will do you good. You look a little out of sorts yourself."

Román took another joint from a kitchen drawer, lit it and passed it to Matt.

"You will be high in the clouds before your plane takes off, man."

La yerba was a potent variety of marijuana, or at least the strongest Matt had ever encountered. He had experimented with pot in college, but it made him feel paranoid instead of relaxed. He had once flushed a baggie down the toilet for fear of being found out. Román assured him that this one was high quality, harvested in the mountains of Baracoa, in Oriente.

"It's good shit," he said, adding virtuously, "not weakened by any of this modern stuff that Habaneros use. Most people don't know better, but I do."

Matt hadn't yet inhaled when he started to cough.

"What do you think?" Román asked.

"Is it—what do you call it, hashish?"

"I call it *yerba*. Weed."

Matt's lungs were filled to the point of explosion. He exhaled painfully.

"Don't ask *la yerba* anything, man, just let it embrace you," Román said.

DURING THE TRIP TO the airport, squeezed inside Román's car, which was smaller than the Studebaker and equipped with harder seats, Matt was aware of a warm tingling in his arms and legs. At first he didn't feel particularly high or euphoric, but as the car sped along Rancho Boyeros Avenue, a soothing sense of satisfaction filled him. His worries receded. He stopped thinking about la Seguridad. The Iraq war could have been happening on another planet, for all he cared. He laughed quietly.

"Feeling good, eh?" Román asked.

"Yes. Oh, yes."

"What did I tell you? It lasts longer than the regular stuff too."

Román parked two blocks away from the main airport building.

"I don't want the guards to mistake me for a clandestine taxi driver," he explained. "But I'll accompany you and make sure you get in."

"Thanks."

A flower vendor intercepted them. Matt realized that it was the same disheveled woman who had offered him marigolds the day he arrived. This time around, the woman had only sunflowers. Just to be safe, Matt bought a bunch for one dollar.

AT THE AIRPORT PARKING lot, the two men shook hands.

"If you ever come back, remember that my home is waiting for you, Mateo," Román said, producing a bunch of cards with the house logo (a Spanish-style building that didn't resemble his place at all) and the slogan *Bienvenido a Villa Tomasa, donde se sentirá como en su casa.*

By then the Baracoa weed had been working its juju because Matt simply said, "I will remember it," and pocketed the cards.

AS SOON AS HE entered the airport lobby, a security guard ordered Matt to get rid of the sunflowers.

"You can't travel with those."

Matt threw them in a trash can, muttering an invented prayer to the corresponding *orisha*. He was pleasantly calmed through the ticket inspection and the *first* passport check. There would be a second one in the waiting room, the customs officer told him.

"Keep all your documents handy until you board the plane," he said.

Two more Americans stood out in the crowd—a blonde girl, long-legged and ponytailed, who, like Matt, carried just a back-pack, and an older, pudgy, sunburned man accompanied by a shapely brunette who was obviously Cuban.

They all waited to have their carry-ons inspected. The line moved slowly. The X-ray scanner was flanked by guards armed with AKMs. More uniformed men patrolled the area. When Matt put his backpack on the conveyor belt, a guard's gun made a menacing turn toward him.

"No suitcase?" he asked.

"No, *señor*."

He should have said "no, *compañero*," but remembered it too late. The guard, fortunately, took it in stride.

"Go ahead and pass through the metal detector."

Matt obeyed, noticing that the other AKMs were also aimed at him, as if they had acquired a life of their own. The guards' faces remained indifferent.

I shouldn't have smoked that shit.

He tried not to look at the guns again. His backpack got momentarily stuck in the conveyor belt, but the guard pulled it out and handed it to him.

Matt entered a well-lit area with a door that led directly to the tarmac. There was a glass window through which he could see the X-ray scanner and the line of people in the other room.

Most of the passengers that waited for the Cancun flight were Mexicans—tanned young men and middle-aged couples. A few were Cubans who lived abroad, easily identified not only by their accent, but because they looked less relaxed than the rest of the crowd. A group of six, who were about to leave the island for the first time, had gathered in a corner. They were the loudest and the most excited.

The room smelled of coffee and fried fish. There were seven rows of seats and a food stand. A queue had already formed around it. A television on the wall showed the same footage that Matt had seen at Villa Tomasa: rockets blowing up over a city that he assumed was Baghdad with Castro's speech in the background, condemning the attack. His voice reverberated.

The colors were vivid and rich, much more than on Román's TV. The images looked three-dimensional.

All of a sudden, a fighter jet came out of the screen and started making low passes over people's heads. It was twelve inches long. It barely missed Matt's right ear before returning to the television. He leaned against a wall. A buzzing sound filled the room.

"We are out of coffee!" the woman at the food stand yelled.

Matt composed himself and chose a seat as far as possible from the TV. His heart was beating fast and his head was spinning. The conversations around him echoed inside his skull.

This is no regular high. Who knows what the hell they grow in Baracoa? Maybe it was laced with something else, something strong and weird.

No use fretting about it now. He made an effort to stay quiet and closed his eyes. But the sounds intensified and became louder and clearer. He followed, unwillingly, a dialogue in Spanish between a couple seated three feet away from him.

"Are you happy to be coming home with me?" asked a male voice with a Texas accent.

"Yes, Papito," a woman replied. "You know how much I love you."

"I'm worried you'll miss your family. You've never been away from them, have you?"

"Oh, I'll miss my mom. We are very close. But she can visit us for Christmas, don't you think, my love?"

"It may take longer. All this has been very expensive: your ticket, the exit visa and everything."

"I know. You have been so generous!" A kissing sound and then, "But let's try, okay? She sees you as a son, Papito. She adores you!"

"The feeling is mutual."

"Speaking of Mom, let me call her quickly before we board the plane."

"Go ahead, darlin'. Give her my regards."

Matt opened his eyes long enough to see the curvy brunette walk away from the middle-aged American. She took a cell phone out of her purse. He caught a few sentences in her rapid-fire Cuban Spanish.

"—leaving in a couple of hours. Make the money last, he's already complaining about how much—will call you as soon as I get there. Yes, *mi amor*, I'll send for you. No need to be jealous of that geezer. What? No, *you* don't go screwing around! Ah, no worries—you're the man of my life."

Matt fought the impulse to warn the unsuspecting Papito, whose solid and stolid back was covered by a sweat-stained *guayabera*. If Yarmila had lived, he would have been in the exact same position, he thought. He thanked the pot from Baracoa that allowed him to observe the scene with amused detachment and to laugh silently at his own lost innocence.

Soon it would all be over. He wouldn't think of Yarmila again. As Padrino had predicted, he would even forget the saint she was named after, though she hadn't been named after any saint. He would go on working for *El Grito de San Diego*, interviewing chefs, and penning features for *Foodalicious*.

But what if he couldn't forget? Ah, then he would write about his Cuban experience. Not a news article, but the semi-autobiographical novel he had started on Román's typewriter. Yarmila, Yony, Pato Macho, Taty and their shared night at Villa Tomasa would inhabit the pages of a dystopic book.

When Matt opened his eyes again, it was a quarter to twelve. An officious woman's voice reminded passengers to keep their passports and tickets with them because they would be checked again before boarding.

Matt's head was throbbing, but at least the sounds had toned down and nothing unusual came out of the TV. They were now broadcasting an interview with a *chivato* who had infiltrated an independent press agency. A presenter announced, "*Compañero* Manuel David Orrio, also known as Agent Miguel, was able to deliver valuable information to the revolution. He outsmarted the mercenaries paid by Yankee imperialism!"

Orrio, a curly haired, smiling guy in a blue shirt, went on to explain that his task hadn't been too difficult.

"They believed everything," he stated. "The more lies I fed them, the more they lapped them up. The hardest part was hiding my real work from my family—Mom nearly disowned me, thinking I had become a *gusano*. Dad wouldn't talk to me, and my poor son was traumatized. They were all so relieved when the truth finally came out!"

Orrio was part of a big Seguridad network. Other agents were interviewed after him but Matt, though interested, couldn't concentrate on the story. He was starving. Luckily, the line in front of the food stand had dwindled down to four people. He ordered a *pan con pasta* that turned out to be two slices of bread with a pinkish spread inside. Though similar in consistency to meringue, the "pasta" tasted like a cross between imitation crab and hot dog.

The gate to the tarmac opened and two guards came in. A plane was outside, so small that Matt doubted it had room for the thirty people who were waiting for it. A Boeing 777 parked nearby dwarfed it even further.

"That's some beast," a young Cuban said, pointing his finger to the Boeing. "*Coño*, it looks like a building!"

"I could live in it."

"Me too! It's larger than my apartment."

The passengers that had been in the adjacent waiting room, European tourists for the most part, began to board the Boeing.

"We're next!" the Cuban yelled and his friends applauded. "Cancun, here we come!"

They improvised a conga, a spontaneous song-and-dance mix.

Nos vamos pa Cancun
a formar el fetecún.
Venimos de La Habana
y nadie nos gana.
Kumbakin kin kin,
kumbakin.

They kept it up until a guard shushed them. "*Compañeros,* behave! This is an airport, not a beer garden! Shut up or nobody will leave today, hear?"

The conga died fast. The Cubans looked embarrassed, like children caught in the act. Even the Mexicans stopped talking. Then, in the total silence that followed the guard's words, Matt heard a name: Yarmila Portal.

He was hallucinating again. He had to be. But Yarmila's face appeared on the TV screen. It pulsated, as if it wanted to break loose and burst into the room. These were her eyes, big, brown and intense; the smile that had won his heart, the pretty button nose . . . That was the very same picture she had once posted on her blog.

"*Compañera* Yarmila Portal Richards is going to posthumously receive the José Martí Medal of Honor for her services to the revolution," said the same presenter who had interviewed Orrio. "Comrade Yarmila, like Agent Miguel and many other silent defenders of our motherland, had infiltrated a counterrevolutionary group and was able to prevent them from causing harm to the revolution. She also served our country, with her pen and her brain, in a number of other ways. She carried on her work in obscurity until a despicable element, paid by Yankee imperialism, cowardly took her life. The killer, citizen Yony Nogales, was apprehended as he tried to flee Cuba and is now awaiting trial. Sergeant Yarmila Portal, also known as Agent Katia, will be promoted posthumously to the rank of Lieutenant of la Seguridad del Estado."

An older couple was shown receiving the medal. The man's face was streaked with tears, while the woman's reflected both satisfaction and proudly suppressed pain.

Yony Nogales. Matt repeated the name and shook his head. That had to be the Baracoa weed's effect. It couldn't be real, could it?

A security guard asked the passengers for the Cancun flight to line up by the door.

"Passports and tickets in hand!" he commanded.

Matt joined the queue behind the Texan and his girlfriend. His hands trembled when he took out the passport and opened it to the first page.

The guard took his own sweet time inspecting the documents. Matt looked back at the television, but the Seguridad ceremonies had given way to images of the Iraq bombing again.

His gaze wandered to the glass window. He gasped. There, his face pressed against the glass, was Taty, in the black sequined top he had worn to impersonate Sarita Montiel. Matt felt guilty for not noticing earlier. Had the poor guy come all the way from Las Villas, or wherever he was, only to say goodbye to him?

But how in the world did he know—?

He let a group of Mexicans go ahead. He wanted to talk to

Taty. But the young man wasn't alone. Next to him were Isabel and Luis, smiling and waving. Matt waved back, cautiously, and discovered Padrino, all in white, behind them.

"*Con permiso, señor.*"

A couple walked in front of Matt. By then more people had gathered in the window, their faces elongated, their eyes shinier and bigger than they should have been. Pato Macho was among them, and that seemed highly improbable. Why would *he* want to say goodbye to him? And even more improbable, Matt realized with a chill, was Yarmila's presence, her right arm around her lover's shoulders. Yes, Yarmila, wearing the wedding dress he had bought for her at Buffalo Exchange, was right there, winking wickedly at him.

"Aren't you boarding too?" the guard asked.

Matt was the only passenger left in the waiting room.

"Yes, I—"

"Let me see your passport. Are you okay?"

Matt looked back at the window. It was now empty. His head thumped as if the entire crowd had taken residence inside.

"Just a little dizzy."

"Too much Cuban sun, eh? Do you need help?"

"No! No, thanks."

"Go ahead and hurry up."

Matt steadied himself and, without looking back, left the waiting room and began to walk briskly toward the pocket-sized Aeroméxico plane.